"As deeply enthralling as a dream, the world of Ambar lures you in with its rich mythology and fiercely tender romance. A story exquisitely told, with magic on every page."
—AUSMA ZEHANAT KHAN,
author of *The Bloodprint*

"A thrilling start to an exciting new series set in a fresh, magical new world . . .
I couldn't put it down!"
—S. A. CHAKRABORTY,
author of *The City of Brass* and *The Kingdom of Copper*

"*Hunted by the Sky* plunges readers into an original and imaginative world that is both beautifully brutal and brutally beautiful. Tanaz Bhathena's writing crackles with visceral detail and pointed metaphor, creating an immersive reading experience. Readers are certain to fall for Gul and Cavas as they find their own value in a world that tries hard to devalue them. A fresh and intelligent fantasy."
—MEGAN BANNEN,
author of *The Bird and the Blade*

"With *Hunted by the Sky*, Tanaz Bhathena pens a story that is as fierce as it is tender. Her girls are beautifully complicated. Her world is lush, intricate, and unique. This book not only left me breathless, it made my heart soar."
—KRISTEN CICCARELLI,
internationally bestselling author of *The Last Namsara*

"A mythical tale of love, sisterhood, vengeance, and hope, *Hunted by the Sky* is an epic adventure you don't want to miss."
—TASHA SURI,
author of *Empire of Sand*

"Filled with magic, prophecy, and ancient goddesses, *Hunted by the Sky* is an engrossing novel that will keep the reader up long past bedtime. Tanaz Bhathena's fantasy is perfect for fans of thoughtful world-building and fantastical mirrors to our own reality. A whirlwind of heartfelt storytelling."
—JODI MEADOWS,
New York Times–bestselling coauthor of *My Plain Jane* and author of the Fallen Isles Trilogy

"Captivating . . . Steeped in medieval Indian magic, *Hunted by the Sky* is a breathtaking adventure of a book that draws you in from page one."
—SUKANYA VENKATRAGHAVAN,
editor of *Magical Women* and author of *Dark Things*

"*Hunted by the Sky* offers YA fantasy readers something deliciously fresh while giving us everything we love: a richly imagined landscape, fascinating magic, and a tenacious young heroine pitted against impossible odds."
—ELLY BLAKE,
New York Times–bestselling author of the Frostblood Saga

"A dazzling, rich story with a complex heroine, intricate magic, and bone-sharp prose, *Hunted by the Sky* is the fantasy novel I've been waiting for all year."
—SWATI TEERDHALA,
author of the Tiger at Midnight series

RISING LIKE A STORM

TANAZ BHATHENA

Farrar Straus Giroux
New York

Farrar Straus Giroux Books for Young Readers
An imprint of Macmillan Publishing Group, LLC
120 Broadway, New York, NY 10271
fiercereads.com

Our books may be purchased in bulk for promotional, educational, or business use. Please
contact your local bookseller or the Macmillan Corporate and Premium Sales Department
at (800) 221-7945 ext. 5442 or by email at MacmillanSpecialMarkets@macmillan.com.

Library of Congress Cataloging-in-Publication Data

Names: Bhathena, Tanaz, author.
Title: Rising like a storm / Tanaz Bhathena.
Description: First edition. | New York: Farrar Straus Giroux Books for Young Readers, 2021. |
    Series: [The wrath of Ambar ; book 2] | Audience: Ages 12–18. | Audience: Grades 10–12. |
    Summary: "Gul and Cavas must unite their magical forces—and hold on to their growing
    romance—to save their kingdom from tyranny" —Provided by publisher.
Identifiers: LCCN 2020024589 | ISBN 9780374313111 (hardcover)
Subjects: CYAC: Fantasy. | Magic—Fiction. | Love—Fiction.
Classification: LCC PZ7.1.B5324 Ris 2021 | DDC [Fic]—dc23
LC record available at https://lccn.loc.gov/2020024589

First edition, 2021
Book design by Michelle Gengaro-Kokmen
Printed in the United States of America

ISBN 978-0-374-31311-1 (hardcover)
1   3   5   7   9   10   8   6   4   2

We acknowledge the support of the Canada Council for the Arts.

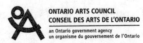

To Dad—for teaching me that losing a battle doesn't mean that you've lost the war.

AMBAR

N
W E
S

YELLOW
SEA

SAFID

SALT PLAINS

BRIMLANDS

THE

AMIRGARH

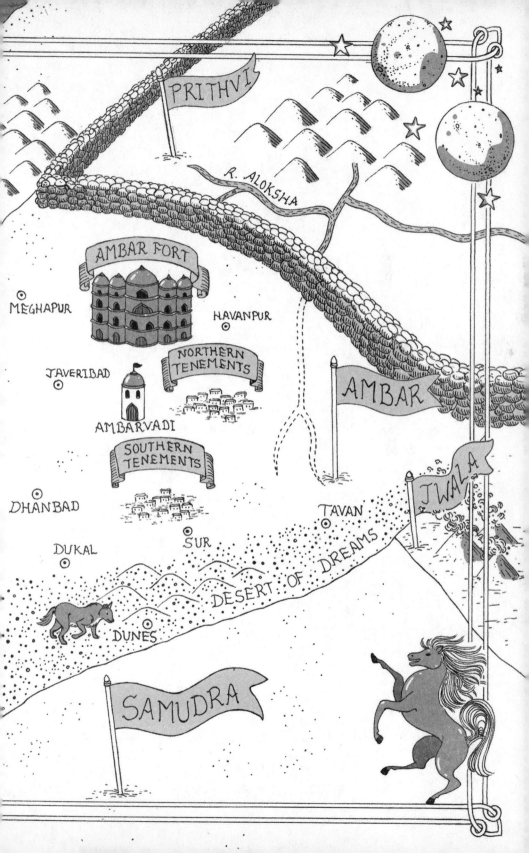

THE LEGION OF THE DEAD

Somewhere in the Desert of Dreams
20th day of the Month of Song
3 months into Queen Shayla's reign

1

GUL

When the bounty hunter finds me, I'm squatting behind the partially broken wall of an outdoor restroom in Tavan, bare from the waist down, my skin prickling in the cold light of a yellow half moon. I hear him first—his breaths heavy and ragged—before I catch him peering at me from behind the wall, his gaunt face coated with a layer of shimmering Dream Dust. His spell nicks the tip of my earlobe, leaving behind a cut that could have severed my whole ear had I not rolled out of the way, my bladder growing taut and painful, every urge to urinate gone.

A grunt, followed by another spell in the dark. Debris strewn across the wet floor sticks to my palms as I crawl over it: the broken shards of a tile, grit, gravel, and goddess knows what else. My heart beats out a scattered rhythm as the restroom glows again with red light, more tiles clattering to the ground. I hold in a breath, not daring to make a sound.

If only I could get to my daggers.

Right now, they're sheathed in my belt, which hangs on the wall—two seaglass blades shaped like the curling horns of a shadowlynx—in full view of anyone taking aim from the outside. The star-shaped birthmark on my right arm grows warm. My magic, as always, senses the danger I'm in. I know I could fight the bounty hunter magically, without my daggers. I also know that, by doing so, I could potentially rupture an organ or injure myself in some other stupid way, making it easier for him to take me to Queen Shayla and claim the five thousand swarnas she has offered for my capture.

"Is someone there?" I say under my breath.

I'm not looking for an *alive* someone; certainly, I'm not hoping to draw the attention of the bounty hunter. But a living specter or two might be lingering nearby. Each chained to our world by a single, desperate wish, living specters are spirits of the dead that remain invisible to magi and non-magi. Though everyone can hear and feel the presence of the specters, only half magi like Cavas can see them. Over the past twenty years, Tavan's specters have protected its boundary, circling the golden bars the Pashu king Subodh magically erected to protect the city. The combined powers of the bars and the specters keep the city not only invisible but also unbreachable by outsiders.

So how did a bounty hunter show up here? I wonder. *Are the specters fading?*

Specters *could* fade, disappearing for good from the living world once their most desperate wish was fulfilled. Without spectral magic, the golden bars can vanish, creating gaps in Tavan's boundary like holes in an aging tapestry.

Esther, the only other half magus in Tavan, warned me about this possibility many times over the past three months. "Our specters won't hold on forever," she said. "Yes, it's true that most have remained behind to protect the city because I asked them to. But spectral magic isn't something I control. It is solely guided by the spirit's own will. Many of these specters were marked women and girls from Tavan, who were tortured to death. They simply wished for King Lohar to die. Now that he's gone, few will be willing to stay behind."

My breath rushes out—a sound that makes the bounty hunter

mutter. His looming shadow sways erratically against the bathroom floor. I wonder if he's feeling dizzy, a common aftereffect of the Dream Dust. Inhaling too much of the Dust can make you question what you see with your own eyes—a solid advantage in my favor right now. But I don't dare look up to confirm this. The bounty hunter is still armed. I can't predict how the Dust will affect his aim.

I'm not sure about my own aim, either. I haven't practiced death magic once in these three months, though I've carried my dagger belt everywhere like a shackle binding my hips.

If you'd listened to Esther, you wouldn't be in this state right now, my conscience chides. Heat shoots up my right arm, my fingertips glowing a dull orange. If we were still talking, Cavas would have likely told me about the specters' fading. But Cavas has barely spoken to or looked at me since our fight last month, ignoring every attempt I've made at reconciliation.

A rock clatters outside, followed by a man's enraged shout.

I crane my neck up, risking a peek through the hole in the bathroom wall. Instead of the bounty hunter, I see only the night sky—as starry and cloudless as the sky goddess's eyes in my dreams.

Are you there, Goddess? I think. *Can you hear me?*

But the goddess remains silent, the way she has ever since we arrived in Tavan.

A breath brushes my injured ear, sending burning pinpricks over my skin. A childish giggle, followed by a familiar singsongy voice: "Wallowing in self-pity again? Shame. What if the Legion saw their Star Warrior now?"

"Whosssit?" the bounty hunter shouts from somewhere beyond the wall, his words slurring together. "Ssssat you, marked witch?"

"Indu," I whisper, ignoring him. Indu is a living specter, who died as a young girl. She helped me and Cavas several times in the past, leading us to Tavan after we fled Ambar Fort. Relief floods my aching limbs. "Indu, can you raise an alarm?"

"I already have, silly girl," the specter says. "I did it the moment this man and his troop slipped in."

His troop? "There are more?" I demand, horrified.

"What do you think?" Indu snorts. "They're not as Dust-addled as this one, either. Are you going to fight him now, or do you want me to hand your daggers to you?"

Good point. I can't hide in this musty bathroom forever.

Heart in throat, I rise in a leap, expecting to be shot at any moment. Luck favors me—the bounty hunter shoots but lops off only a few strands of my braid. I unsheathe my daggers, tightening my slippery hands around a pair of familiar hilts. Magic pours through me in a rush, the seaglass blades expelling a burst of green fire.

My first two spells miss their target, but my third one shapes itself into an arrow that impales the bounty hunter's left eye and flies out the back of his turbaned skull in a cloud of blood, cloth, and bone fragments.

"Thank the goddess," Indu says. "You're not completely out of touch."

Yes, I think, relief mingling with nausea. My magic, so unpredictable since I was a girl, did exactly what I wanted it to today.

"You said there were more bounty hunters. Where are they?" I ask Indu, ignoring the shivers running down my limbs.

"At the southern boundary—next to the reservoir. Esther, Kali, and the boy are holding them off for now while Raja Subodh checks on the other city borders. Hurry, Star Warrior!"

The boy. There is only one boy in Tavan right now, and that's Cavas, his face flashing before me in various imagined stages of death.

No, I think as I race southward. Cavas may hate me right now—certainly, he can't stand the sight of me—but I am not going to let him die tonight. Or any other night on my watch.

Screams and jets of red light announce the battle happening near the reservoir, now a dark rectangle of water in the distance. I see Kali first, dressed in her sleep tunic, shooting spells with her daggers, barely

5

holding off three bounty hunters. Behind them, another masked figure laughs as Cavas struggles to dodge his spells behind a rusty, old metal shield. Next to Cavas, over a dozen other figures struggle against more bounty hunters—stick-wielding Tavani women from the Legion of the Star Warrior, the army Esther trained herself and named in my honor. I scan them now, doing a rough body count—fifty women from the Legion against a little over twenty bounty hunters. The numbers are clearly on our side.

But the magic isn't. The women of Tavan were drained of their magic by King Lohar's troops years ago.

As if sensing my approach, Cavas spins around, his brown eyes widening.

"Get out of here!" he shouts as my spell hits the bounty hunter making a grab for his shoulder.

The spell is effective: Almost instantly, the bounty hunter lets go. But my anger has always acted like a jambiya when it comes to death magic—double-edged and deadly. My focused green spellfire blooms red, setting fire to the bounty hunter's hand and Cavas's arm, forcing them both to the ground to douse the flames.

Queen's curses.

"Cavas!" I shout. "Cavas, are you hurt?"

"Gul, watch out!" Kali yells a second before a jet of red light takes off another chunk of my hair. There is no time to check on Cavas to see if he's okay. There is no time to think about anything except the three spells heading my way, nothing except *protect, protect, protect.*

My shield explodes in a glow of orange light, rebounding the bounty hunters' spells and nearly throwing me flat on my back. Sweat breaks out over my chest and ribs. My bladder is aching again, and my lungs no longer feel like they can process air.

There are simply too many bounty hunters.

So? Attack them first, fool. Amira's voice echoes in my head—a memory from an old training session in Javeribad. Amira, who is now imprisoned at Ambar Fort with Juhi and probably being tortured because she tried to save me.

I raise my daggers high. My spell elongates, shapes itself into two green talwars, their blades killing one bounty hunter and forcing the other two back.

My head pounds and my nostrils prick with the scent of blood—my own. Using death magic again after so long has left me shaking at the knees and soon enough the bounty hunters will see it, too.

I think I'm about to collapse when a roar thunders behind me.

Subodh!

The Pashu king lunges forward, a giant golden mace held in his front paws, his teeth bared in a snarl. The sight of his furious, leonine face unnerves the remaining bounty hunters, though most still stand their ground, their attention now split between me and Subodh. Soon enough, it's clear who the bigger threat is. Subodh's reptilian tail swats off spells like flies; his spiked mace rings eerily in the air right before cracking over a bounty hunter's head.

"Legion, to me!" a woman commands. I make out Esther's tall form raising a lathi and rallying the two other women in blue. "Charge!" Esther shouts.

Subodh's entering the fray seems to have simultaneously revived the Legion's confidence and unnerved the enemy. The surviving bounty hunters flee toward the boundary—through the too-wide gap between the golden bars that I see only now. Subodh follows to the edge, raising his mace over his head. For a moment, I think he's going to send a killing spell their way, but he simply aims the weapon at the sand from which another golden bar rises, up, up, and up, disappearing into the night sky.

"Indu," Subodh commands between pants, his rumbling voice vibrating in the silence.

"The barrier is now protected, Pashuraj," Indu replies.

The new golden bar does not flicker or move. It continues holding firm, no new bodies slipping in.

Subodh turns to me, his large tongue lolling to the side, his great yellow eyes reflecting the moon.

"Nice to see you finally make an appearance, Star Warrior," he says.

2
GUL

I stiffen at Subodh's pronouncement, feeling every eye turn to take me in. My gaze meets Sami's, the only woman from the Legion, apart from Esther, who actively tried to befriend me when we first arrived in Tavan. She gives me a small smile now, but Sami is also the type who would try to cheer up someone during an earthquake.

Behind the Pashu king, Esther is kneeling next to Cavas, stripping away his charred sleeve to check on his heavily blistered arm. I hold my breath. From here, the damage doesn't look *too* bad.

Right?

He will be all right, child. Subodh's voice purrs in my head. *Then again, he wouldn't have been hurt if you'd been practicing your magic, would he?*

I clench my teeth. While I may be the only human in this camp capable of telepathically communicating with animals, whispering is a magic that the Pashu, a race of part-human, part-animal beings, invented. Unlike Subodh, I have not yet learned a way to protect my mind against external penetration, and I'm sure I will never have the mastery over it that he does, slipping in and out of minds so easily that his

9

thoughts might as well have been my own. Subodh's magic isn't the only thing making me uneasy today. It's also what he said—the truth that I've been avoiding this whole time.

Shortly after we arrived in Tavan, Esther asked me to start training with the Legion of the Star Warrior—"In case any specters fade and there's a breach in the boundary," she explained.

Training with the Legion wasn't an issue for me—not much, anyway, apart from being the worst combatant during every practice battle. But Esther insisted that I use magic during practice to prepare the Legion for the forthcoming war with Queen Shayla. And this I absolutely refused to do.

"If I lose control of my magic again the way I did at Ambar Fort, I could seriously injure or, worse, kill someone!" I argued with Esther each time.

Even Cavas, who was with me on that awful day, doesn't understand my reluctance to use my magic.

"What happened to the girl who wanted revenge so badly?" he asked me a month ago. "The Scorpion killed your parents, not Raja Lohar. She even framed you for his murder. She's put a bounty on our heads because she's scared of you! Wouldn't she laugh if she found out you were running scared of yourself?"

Cavas may have his own powers as a half magus, but he hasn't felt death magic's eerie song in his blood. He does not know what it feels like to kill someone with magic—especially when your magic controls you instead of the other way around. Yes, Shayla did murder King Lohar. But *I* killed two of his three sons shortly afterward. *I* called on the sky goddess for help at Ambar Fort, allowing her to fuel my power and my rage. Because of that, because of what I did, Cavas's father is now dead, Amira and Juhi languish in prison, and Amar, the true heir to the throne, has been forced into exile. Because of me, our kingdom suffers a worse ruler on its throne.

"What happened to the boy who wanted nothing to do with magic in the first place?" I taunted back. "You think I don't know the real reason you're angry with me, Cavas? You think I don't hear the specters talking? I know you want to avenge your father's death. If so, *do it.* Go find Shayla's minion in Ambarvadi and kill her yourself! You don't need me. Not unless *you're* the one who's running scared."

We haven't spoken since. And based on the way Cavas avoids my gaze now, I doubt we ever will.

Out loud I ask Subodh: "Why didn't any of you come find me? You know I could have helped."

I brace myself for a scathing reply: *Would you have helped?* Or *We didn't really trust you to come help us.*

The real response—Kali's—makes my heartbeat quicken: "Cavas asked us not to."

My friend's formerly long hair, shorn completely to infiltrate Ambar Fort, is slowly growing back in short spikes. Her pretty face is pinched with exhaustion. "He said that as the Star Warrior, you need to be protected," Kali says. "He also said you suffer enough while you sleep."

I say nothing. I haven't had a single night free of bad dreams since we've arrived in Tavan. In fact, I'm pretty sure I wake everyone on my floor with my screams—though no one has ever mentioned it.

Except for Cavas.

As if sensing my thoughts, Cavas locks eyes with me. We study each other openly for the first time since our fight last month. I note the new hollows in his cheeks, the shadows circling his dark-brown eyes. I try to pinpoint the emotions I see there. Is he still angry that I didn't use magic for so long? Relieved that I finally did?

I'm gathering the courage to talk to him when another voice says:

"Well, it's not a party when she's awake, either. Not only does *she* suffer, but she makes the rest of us suffer, too."

3

GUL

I whip my head around to face the speaker, a girl in her early twenties wearing the Legion's practice uniform. Her short blue tunic and matching trousers look fresh and unsoiled, despite our fight with the bounty hunters. Rodabeh, I think her name is—Roda, for short—her forehead tattooed like Esther's and Sami's with the Legion's black-and-silver stars.

Does she wear her uniform to bed? I wonder peevishly.

Now, with the imminent danger of the bounty hunters abated, I once more grow aware of my own state: my long sleep tunic stained with filth, my bare legs prickling in the cold desert air. My leggings, I recall, are still hanging on a hook in the restroom.

What a mess I must look.

Judging by her smirk right now, Roda must have the same thought. At lathi practice, she is the first to roll her eyes when my posture is corrected, the first to laugh when I'm knocked out during a spar. Deep down, I can't blame her for it. Roda, like many others in the Legion, was expecting the fabled Star Warrior. The girl who would lead to a tyrant king's downfall. A leader of women.

12

Instead, they got me.

"That was uncalled for, Roda," Esther says now. "Gul was here when we needed her. Without her, we wouldn't have been able to hold off the bounty hunters."

"Well, it's *because* of her that we're in such bad shape," Roda points out. "Because she sits like a straw dummy during our practice sessions, refusing to do magic."

"Roda!" Sami exclaims. "How could you—"

"That's enough," Subodh cuts in. "Savak-putri Gulnaz and Xerxes-putra Cavas, I'm glad to see you *both* here now—*together*. As you should be if we are to have any hope of winning the forthcoming war."

White fog rises in the air overhead; Indu's forlorn voice singing from within:

> *The sky has fallen, a star will rise*
> *Ambar changed by a king's demise*
> *A girl with a mark, a boy with her soul*
> *Their fates intertwined, two halves of a whole*
> *Usurpers have come, usurpers will go*
> *The true king waits for justice to flow.*

It's the new prophecy—the one the living specters began reciting several weeks ago, hinting that Amar was still alive. I do my best to ignore the couplet that has bothered me since the time I first heard the prophecy:

> *A girl with a mark, a boy with her soul*
> *Their fates intertwined, two halves of a whole.*

Subodh, who I'm sure understands what the lines mean, has refused to explain them to me, though I've asked him several times.

"They don't matter unless you use your powers to train the Legion, Star Warrior," he always says, his great face shuttered of expression.

Cavas once admitted that the Pashu king didn't tell him anything about the prophecy, either. "Subodh knew you would come to me," he said, raising an eyebrow. "He said that I needed to persuade you to train with magic first. That's the only way either of us will get answers."

I note the frown on Cavas's face now as he stares up at the foggy specter.

Subodh is watching Indu as well. "Good timing," he says, and I wonder if he asked the specter to sing that particular prophecy now. Not only can Subodh whisper to animals, but as a Pashu, he can also do other magic that most humans cannot—which includes seeing living specters.

I study him carefully—his thick brown mane sticking out in every direction, the long scar marring his face, from the corner of one great yellow eye, across the bridge of his flat nose, disappearing into the fur sprouting from his right jaw. Many in Ambar call Subodh a lion simply by looking at his face and ignoring the rest of him. But Subodh is a rajsingha—part lion and part human—and for many years, he ruled the Pashu kingdom of Aman in the northeast of the continent. Subodh alternates between walking on all fours and walking the way humans do—on his hind paws—though I suspect he finds the latter more boring. His reptilian tail—gifted by the gods after he lost his real one in an ancient war—swishes behind him, green scales tipped with sharp horns. I'm not sure how old Subodh is, but age has done nothing to affect his strength or his magic, the glow of which now outlines his form.

"As you know, Rani Sarayu has been tracking the movements of the new queen of Ambar with her birds," Subodh says, his voice, as always, sounding to me like thunder before a storm.

I frown, puzzled by the sudden shift in topic. Sarayu is a simurgh—part human, part eagle, part peacock—and the current queen of the Pashu, her information network comprising every single bird on the continent. She has also supplied Tavan with food over the past twenty years. I glance at the darkened reservoir, half expecting Queen Sarayu to rise from it the way I once saw, her magnificent wings nearly spanning the water from end to end.

"Earlier today, we received a letter from the new rani, along with our usual food supply." Subodh holds up a scroll, its opened wax seal embossed with Shayla's new emblem. An atashban—the deadly magical crossbow used by the Sky Warriors—crossed over with a trident. I stare at the scroll, glowing white at the edges with magic.

"Shayla sent you this?" I ask.

"She did. Knew exactly which bird to pick, too," Subodh says calmly. "As of last week, Rani Shayla closed the last of the labor camps that Lohar established and released their prisoners. She has offered to do the same for Tavan—provided that we give up the fugitive Star Warrior and her two companions."

"For goddess's sake!" Esther scoffs. "She *had* to close the labor camps if she had any hope of gaining the public's favor. Raja Lohar is dead, and Gul is widely regarded as his murderer. There's no point in keeping the labor camps open, is there?"

"Has . . ." The question sticks in my throat. I'm still remembering the way Shayla tried to drain my magic that day, her spell like a hundred blades skewering my insides. I release a breath. "Has she gained the public's favor?"

"She did gain favor—when she announced her plans for the labor camps three months ago," Subodh says. "But soon after, she brought in new tariffs and land tithes across the kingdom. Ambar's coffers were depleted thanks to two wars and Lohar's obsession with finding the Star Warrior. Rani Shayla has worsened matters by announcing higher payouts to the Sky Warriors and by giving them better living accommodations in the city. Realistically, she knows she doesn't have a choice there, either. To draw power to herself, she needs to keep her forces loyal.

"The people of Ambar will have to make up for the deficit through the tithes, and for the first time in years, they have begun protesting them. When she was a Sky Warrior, people despised Shayla for her cruelty. As queen, many don't trust her claim to the throne. They complained about her in secret before. Now they do so more and more openly. Last week, someone painted *Maro Kabzedar Rani* in blood across the Ministry of Truth's doors."

Die Usurper Queen. Though I've thought the same thing many times myself, a shock goes through me upon hearing the news.

"I didn't know people were so angry," I say. "I thought she'd have engineered a better claim to the throne by now, having some royal blood in her."

According to Shayla, Lohar was the real usurper, the one who took the throne by killing Queen Megha, the monarch before him. Shayla claimed to be Megha's illegitimate daughter, kept away from her mother and the throne by a selfish father.

"Royal blood doesn't always translate into likability," Kali says, shrugging. "People would still prefer Raja Amar on the throne. If we can find him."

I frown, mulling over the scroll's contents. "I could give myself up—" I begin.

"No!" Cavas, Subodh, Esther, and Kali interrupt as one.

"But—"

"If you're giving yourself up, then so am I," Cavas says in a hard voice. "The bounty is on both of our heads, remember?"

"She is not going to let any of us go free, Gul," Esther says before I can respond. "Especially not Raja Subodh. Also, the Legion isn't so cowardly that we won't fight for you."

No, the Legion does not lack courage. But tonight, from what little I saw, it's clear that the women of Tavan aren't ready to face bounty hunters, let alone Sky Warriors in magical combat.

"Which brings me to you and Cavas," Subodh says. "If you join powers, we will be capable of taking on the Sky Warriors as well."

Cavas's frown deepens into a scowl. I wonder if he's remembering the time I tapped into his magic in Chand Mahal, turning us both invisible; or when he held my magic back inside the king's palace, preventing me from killing Amar in a fit of rage.

My jaw grows taut. Each time Cavas and I have joined powers, we have done so out of desperation. And almost every time afterward, we have fought. Cavas was never really comfortable with his powers, and I always despised how easily he could curb mine.

Their fates intertwined, two halves of a whole.

"This has something to do with the new prophecy," I state, attempting to prod Subodh again. "I don't know why you won't tell me about it."

"Are you ready to use magic while training with the Legion?" the Pashu king asks.

"Why does that matter?" I ask, my voice rising. "I just *burned* Cavas; I could have killed him! Do you really trust me not to kill someone else?"

The question gives everyone pause. Roda stares at me, saying nothing, while Esther and the other women from the Legion evade my gaze. Even Subodh and Kali are silent. Then:

"You wouldn't have killed me," Cavas says quietly. "You have good aim. I don't know why you doubt yourself so much."

Heat suffuses my face. I frown, irritated by how quickly my body reacts to his words—especially to any hint of praise.

"Interesting," Subodh says. "Neither of you has spoken to the other this past month, yet the first person Cavas tried to protect tonight was you, and the first person you tried to save was Cavas. You are terrified of hurting Cavas—and he implicitly trusts you not to hurt him. Over and over, despite your hurdles, you are drawn together, only cementing what the prophecy has foretold."

This time, both Cavas and I direct scowls at Subodh.

"Raja Subodh." It's Esther who speaks, moonlight catching the silver stars tattooed across her forehead. "Prophecies can be vague and open to multiple interpretations. I, too, am puzzled over this one. Perhaps you *should* tell Gul and Cavas more about what it really means. It might help them make a more informed decision about whether or not they wish to join powers."

Something flickers in Subodh's great yellow eyes: Sadness? Resignation? Despair? Perhaps a mix of the three.

"In the prophecy, which the sky goddess revealed to the living specters, she calls you and Cavas *two halves of a whole*," Subodh says finally. "Now, in most interpretations, this would indicate a romantic connection. In your case and Cavas's, it is different. Your connection is more than one of mates—it is one of *complements*. You haven't heard of the term, have you?"

"No," I say. I try to recall every scroll I've read, every bit of education I received before being forced to drop out of school at age nine. Cavas, Kali, and Esther look equally befuddled.

"The term first appeared centuries ago," Subodh says. "It was when the gods and the great animal spirits walked this earth. No humans and few Pashu existed. During this time, two young goddesses were drawn to each other—the first with glowing skin as dark as midnight, the second whose complexion resembled a desert at moonrise. First as friends and then as lovers, they shared their hearts and bodies and magic for many years; so attuned were they to each other that many called them two halves of a whole.

"Yet not all was perfect in their relationship. The second goddess enjoyed flirtation and was popular among the other gods. She and the first goddess often fought over this. One day, after a stormy tiff, the two lovers broke off their relationship, and the second goddess rashly agreed to bind with someone else. The second goddess's suitor—the god of thunder—had a temper as fiery as the storms he created. He knew that his mate-to-be did not really love him, and in a fit of rage, he killed the first goddess. In despair, the second goddess poured every bit of her magic into her lost lover's body. But it was too late. Neel could not be revived in her original form."

"Wait—Neel?" I interrupt. "Do you mean the *moon goddess*, Neel?"

"The very same," Subodh says. "Though I thought you may have recognized this story sooner."

"I did recognize it but got confused," Cavas admits. "Legend always says that Neel's skin was blue and Sunheri's was golden—exactly the color of the two moons."

The Pashu king makes a purring sound in his throat, one that I've come to associate with skepticism or dismissal.

"Legends shape themselves to suit a storyteller's convenience," Subodh tells us. "Casual embellishment aside, most other facts of this story hold true. The first goddess was Neel, the second goddess, Sunheri."

As he speaks, everyone looks up at the yellow moon—lonely and wan in the night sky without her glowing blue companion.

"Sunheri couldn't revive Neel as a deity. But her magic did work—somewhat. Shortly after Neel died, a moon appeared in the night sky, blue like the glow emitted by the young goddess's skin when she was alive. You all know the rest of the story, I presume."

Everyone nods. The sky goddess took pity on Sunheri, who gave up her life as a goddess to turn into a moon herself, appearing alone each night, waxing and waning, turning full and swarna-bright only once during the night of the moon festival—the one night when Neel appears in the sky.

"Complements are capable of more than love," Subodh continues. "They can pour their own untapped magic into each other, amplifying each other's powers to do things they normally couldn't accomplish alone."

Like turning invisible. The fine hairs at the back of my neck rise. "So Cavas and I . . . we're like living amplifiers for each other?"

"Not exactly. Amplifiers are substances that can be used by any magus to enhance their powers—be it seaglass, mammoth tusk, sangemarmar, or firestone. These are used while forging magical weapons. There are other, more dangerous options—illicit enhancers that can be consumed directly and cause hallucinations. Complements, however, are not weapons or objects to be wielded at will. A complement is, essentially, your other half. You need to have an emotional connection to join powers. Your complement can also diffuse your powers—which can lead to problems if you don't trust them."

"Why Gul? Why me?" Cavas interrupts. "What makes *us* so special? Surely other people out there could be living amplifiers to each other. Others who could act as replacements for either one of us."

Replacements? My cheeks grow hot. What in Svapnalok does Cavas mean? Does he want us to be with other people?

"*Complements*, not amplifiers, Xerxes-putra Cavas," the Pashu king chides. "You both are more than mere objects. Though your question is valid. Why *Gul*? Why *you*? Why the both of you *together*? Could you find other complements if you left each other? Perhaps. I cannot say. Finding a replacement might be akin to finding a single red rose in a field of pink ones. I haven't read about or heard of anything resembling complements in Svapnalok since Sunheri and Neel. Indeed, I thought the very idea might have been confined to the gods until I found out about you two turning invisible at Ambar Fort."

"The sky goddess made the prophecy about Gul being the Star Warrior," Kali says after a pause. "Does she have something to do with this as well?"

"She doesn't," I answer almost immediately. "She told me she didn't."

In the first proper vision I had of the sky goddess at Ambar Fort, she promised that she didn't send Cavas my way—that I found him on my own.

"Then I can only assume there is other magic at work here," Subodh says, lifting his great head to stare at the moon again. "The gods don't often meddle with human affairs, but Ambar is in danger of being fragmented in ways that are worse than anyone could have imagined. Perhaps the magic that links Cavas and Gul as complements was initiated by another god. Balance must be restored. Wherever injustice goes, justice must follow."

The last line, spoken nearly word for word by the sky goddess in my vision, sends chills down my spine.

"You're better off handing me in to Shayla," I tell them after a pause. "No, listen to me—she may have put a bounty on both Cavas and me, but *I'm* the one Shayla really wants. You don't need to keep me safe."

"Do you really trust Rani Shayla to keep her word?" Subodh asks pointedly.

I open my mouth and then shut it. I remember the young serving girl, her pleas ringing in King Lohar's chambers before Shayla's dagger slit her neck.

"You're asking me to lead a rebellion," I say with a sigh. "But no rebellion is successful with only fifty warriors. Maybe some people are unhappy in Ambar, but that doesn't mean much. People will complain about the tithes first, but eventually they'll pay. They'll give up their coin the way they gave up their marked girls to Raja Lohar."

"You underestimate the wrath of the Ambari citizens, Savak-putri Gulnaz," Subodh says. "Over these past three months, more and more have been rising to speak out against the taxes. Including the zamindars."

"The zamindars are only bothered because their treasuries are affected," I say, rolling my eyes.

"I didn't say their motives were altruistic. But zamindars rising up against Rani Shayla *does* work in our favor."

True. Ambar's wealthy landowners are certainly a powerful force. But then—

"Shayla will probably brand them traitors and execute them," I say in a dull voice.

"She has done that," Subodh admits. "The last zamindar who complained was executed by the Sky Warriors without a trial. He was from a village called Dukal. Zamindar Moolchand, I think his name was."

"She had *Zamindar Moolchand* killed?" I had never liked Dukal's lech of a landowner, but I didn't expect him to die like this. "But he was so *careful*. He never got on the wrong side of the law if he could help it."

"It doesn't take much to get on the kabzedar rani's wrong side. She'll make a mistake at some point. And we need to be prepared for that."

When Subodh says *we*, I know he means *me*. I am the one who needs preparation. Not a Pashu king who has fought in wars since before I was born. Not Kali, who escaped from a labor camp and was an adjutant at the Sisterhood. Certainly not Esther, who has been training women in combat for the past twenty years. Even Cavas has shown more inclination to fight this war than I have.

What if I fail again? Or worse—what if I succeed and leave Ambar in a worse state than before?

You must be a leader when all hope is lost. The sky goddess's words, spoken in a dream, sting like a newly sharpened blade.

"I am not going to force you to fight," Subodh tells me. "If you wish, you and Cavas can leave with Rani Sarayu for Aman. From there, you both can sail away to the lands that lie west of the continent. You would be free."

"I don't think I will ever be free, Raja Subodh," Cavas says wearily. "Ambar is where I was born, the only home I've ever known. As terrible as things are right now, that's what it will always be for me. My nightmares won't leave me alone in some foreign land."

"What are you trying to say?" the Pashu king asks.

"I'm saying that I don't want to give up on Ambar yet."

Guilt pools like tar in my belly. I can tell that Cavas means what he says. That, regardless of his own motives, he really doesn't want to give up on our kingdom.

Unlike Cavas, though, I have never been selfless. I seriously consider the Pashu king's offer, weighing its pros and cons. Pros: I can leave Ambar right away. I won't have to deal with any of this. Shayla will forget about me eventually, absorbed by other problems in the kingdom. Cons: The Legion will likely fight a losing battle against the Sky Warriors. Juhi and Amira will be stuck in captivity. Worst of all, Cavas will still be here, and I'll feel like a piece of mammoth turd.

Out loud I say: "I don't think I could give up on Ambar, either." I look into Subodh's fiery yellow eyes. "I'm the one who made a mess of everything by infiltrating Ambar Fort. If I left, I . . . I wouldn't be able to live with myself."

Someone coughs in the distance—Kali, alternating her gaze between me and Cavas, an all-too-understanding look on her face.

A hand rests on my shoulder, squeezes gently.

"Are you ready to train with the Legion with magic?" Esther asks.

I unclench my teeth. "I'll try. But if someone gets hurt, then I won't—"

"No one will get hurt," Esther cuts in. "I *promise*. I've been talking to Kali. We'll take precautions."

"We absolutely will," Kali asserts. "Like we did at the Sisterhood. That was more dangerous, with so many magi novices under one roof!"

"And you and Cavas will need to begin training with me as well to learn how to use your powers as complements," Subodh says. "How about after breakfast tomorrow, at the temple? You both will have plenty of time for lathi practice or boundary patrol later."

"I'm fine with that arrangement—if Gul is," Cavas says.

I say nothing. My nerves, stretched thin by everything that has happened tonight, feel brittle, breakable. I do want to help the Legion. I know I *will* have to use death magic at some point if we are to have any hope at surviving the forthcoming war with Shayla.

So why does it feel like others are making my decision for me? Why do I feel trapped?

When I look up again, Cavas is watching me, a furrow between his brows.

"Gul?" he asks softly. "Are you all right?"

I want to say *I'm not sure.* That I need more time to think about this. But it's been so long since Cavas has looked at me with anything other than anger. And everyone else, with the exception of a bored Roda, looks so hopeful.

"I'm fine with it," I force out the words. "The arrangement, that is."

It's not like we have any more time to spare. The attack tonight made that obvious.

"Now, if you don't mind," I say, no longer able to ignore the blade-like feeling in my belly, "I really have to use the bathroom."

4

CAVAS

The night does not end when the bounty hunters are evicted from Tavan.

My eyes have barely flickered shut when Gul starts screaming in the room at the end of the hall, caught once more in the sort of nightmares that leave me numb, unable to make a sound.

Not Gul, though. She yells out spells, as if casting them in the dark; she calls for people who live and die in her dreams—her parents, Juhi, Amira, me.

Always me, despite our frosty silences with each other over this past month.

Every night I've heard her scream and stayed put. I've bitten the inside of my cheek raw. I could pretend that I don't know what Gul is seeing or reliving. But I do know. We were together, after all, in Raj Mahal the day Papa died.

Not died, but killed, I correct myself. *My father was killed.*

Murdered by Captain Alizeh, a Sky Warrior so devoted to the Scorpion that she did everything she could to help place the latter on Ambar's throne. Based on the weekly reports we receive from Queen Sarayu's birds, I know that Alizeh has been promoted to general. She continues doing the Scorpion's dirty work: making threats, raiding villages, leaving behind piles of burned bodies and severed heads as reminders of the punishment meted out to anyone dissenting against the new land tithes—magi or non-magi.

Our regrets are scars we live with, day in and day out, Papa had told me. *If you don't go to help Gul today, you are going to be filled with the same sort of regret.*

For weeks after my father was killed, my greatest regret was going back to Ambar Fort to save Gul. Though, deep down, I was relieved Gul didn't die, initially it was easier to blame her and simply ignore the truth— that Alizeh had been aiming to kill me, not Papa.

It was my fault that Papa was killed. All mine.

In my nightmares, I am forced to accept this. In my nightmares, I remain trapped inside Ambar Fort, chasing the waxing yellow moon painted on the inside of the wall bordering the two palaces, searching for a way out. Instead of people, the fort is populated with living specters: servants who'd worked and died for previous monarchs, princes and princesses lurking behind the many windows of Rani Mahal, their skin gray, their embellished silver clothes marred with dark streaks of blood.

Don't you want to find the man who died for you, boy? they ask me. *Don't you want to see your father?*

The worst ones can change their appearances to look like Papa and immolate right before my eyes, painfully exacting in their mimicry of his voice. Some nights, I find it easier not to sleep whatsoever, anxiety a set of claws hooked under my skin.

I find respite only when I relive the incident at Raj Mahal in a different way. When, in the light of day, I imagine Alizeh's death spell missing its target, sinking into the Sky Warrior holding me in place instead of Papa. Most times, though, I picture myself with a spear, impaling Alizeh with it before she raises her atashban.

"Cavas, no!" Gul screams from her room. "Run! Get away from here!"

A lone shvetpanchhi perches on my windowsill and begins whistling, the way it often does a couple of hours before dawn. I watch the moonlight reflect off the large, carnivorous bird's white feathers, no longer intimidated by its presence or its bulbous red gaze. I may not be a whisperer like Gul and Subodh, but this particular bird has done nothing to harm me. Perhaps it prefers rats to scrawny human boys.

My left arm, burned to blisters by Gul's spell, is pasted over with one of Esther's herbal remedies and thickly bandaged. I can feel the diluted blood bat venom in the salve working; my arm no longer aches as much. By tomorrow, it will be a mess of scars but fully functional otherwise, Esther promised.

"Rest that arm as much as possible," she advised me. "You'll need to be alert when you begin training tomorrow."

Great advice, of course. Yet, when it comes to Gul, I've often found myself ignoring any advice—good or bad. I wasn't lying tonight when I told Subodh that I didn't want to give up on Ambar. But I also have never been able to give up on one other person, despite everything we've put each other through.

And so, tonight, instead of lying still, or tossing and turning in a bed that has always felt too big and too soft, I find myself racing barefoot down the dusty hallway to Gul's room and cracking open her door.

She's thrashing, well into the throes of a new nightmare now, sweat matting long strands of her hair to her forehead.

"Amira!" she shouts. "Juhi! Don't hurt them—*no*!"

"Shhhhh." I catch hold of her wrists, feeling her too-hot skin, the rapid pulse of her blood against my thumbs. "It's okay, Gul. It's okay."

Her head snaps back, a vein green and taut along the side of her smooth throat, bare save for the necklace she never takes off—three silver beads on a worn black cord, now nestled in the sweaty hollow formed by her clavicles. Eventually, though, her limbs grow lax. Her cries soften.

Though her pulse still races, her body has recognized my touch and readily—perhaps *too* readily—accepts its comfort.

"Amira and Juhi are strong," I tell her, ignoring the flush creeping up my face. "They've been through worse than this."

Juhi endured a brutal marriage to King Lohar and an escape from Ambar Fort. Amira survived the atrocities of a labor camp itself. Together, with Kali, they formed the Sisterhood of the Golden Lotus and banded with other lost girls and women, training in combat and death magic to defend themselves. Juhi's ability to scry the future guided them through the years and brought them to Gul when her parents died.

Eventually, Juhi and Gul found me—Juhi having known my father during her time as Lohar's queen—and did their best to coax me into helping Gul infiltrate the palace complex.

A girl with a mark, a boy with her soul. The new prophecy has always made me uneasy—and Subodh's explanation tonight about complements did little to curb that feeling. The others may have chosen to ignore it, but I saw the indecision on Gul's face. I feel it now in the tremors that rack her limbs, her lids flickering open, her pale-gold eyes slowly focusing on mine.

"Cavas?" she whispers, surprised.

My heart skips a beat, but I say nothing in response. I force my expression into one of nonchalance and examine the shadows darkening her eye sockets, the sweat coating her bronze skin. Under my gaze, her trembling limbs slowly grow still.

Reluctantly, I release her hands. Before I can move off the bed, though, Gul reaches out to grip my arm—so quick that for an instant I think she's a meddling specter.

"Wait. Stay a bit," she says.

I sit next to her on the bed, struggling to find a topic of conversation.

"Who was it today?" I ask finally, not seeing any point in diplomacy.

"Papa again. Then Ma. Amira, Juhi . . ." Her voice trails off. She doesn't mention my name and I don't acknowledge that I heard her call for me.

"You . . ." She hesitates, the tip of her tongue flicking out to moisten her chapped lips. "Are *you* all right, Cavas?"

I'm about to answer when I hear her voice in my head, clear and resonant: *He blames you, Gul. He still holds you responsible for his father's death.*

"What did you say?" I blurt out.

She frowns. "I asked if you're all right."

"No, after that. You said something." *Without moving your mouth.*

"I didn't say anything."

"Must be one of the specters," I murmur. Some, like Indu, are fond of playing pranks. But Indu is supposed to be on patrol duty now, having taken over the faded specter's place at the southern boundary. She can't possibly come here without putting everyone at risk again—and I know she wouldn't do that.

"Cavas?" Gul says, sitting up. "Is something the matter?"

"Nothing."

This close, I can see fine brown lines surrounding her pupils, the dark rims of her gold irises. Those pretty, far-too-perceptive eyes narrow at me and I know she isn't going to let go of the matter easily.

To distract her, I say, "Hold on. There's an eyelash on your face."

I touch her cheekbone with a finger, brushing aside the errant hair.

Which lands on her jaw.

I curse, and her lips twitch with a suppressed smile. Yet, even after the eyelash is gone, I don't move away. My thumb lingers, tracing the velvety curve of her lower lip. A jolt goes down my arm and I drop my hand, ignoring the slight hitch of her breath. When I set out to distract Gul, I hadn't intended to distract myself, too.

"It smells nice in here," I say, hoping to draw attention away from my burning face. "Like flowers."

It's true. Beneath the odors of dust and stale air, I can smell something light, familiar, and fragrant. Jasmine, maybe?

"Must be the h-ha—hair oil I use," Gul says, a yawn breaking her reply. "It's made of chameli flowers. One of Esther's concoctions."

So it *is* jasmine. The tension in Gul's shoulders finally eases, and I suppress a sigh of relief.

I'm about to respond when a shadowy form catches my eye—the pale gray figure of a young female specter hovering over Gul, sniffing her hair.

Gul stiffens, sensing her presence. Living specters may be invisible to magi, but they can still touch them if they wish. They can make themselves heard the way this young girl does, a giggle bursting from her lips when Gul looks up at her without seeing her.

"Is . . . is that a living specter?" she asks.

"It is . . . was," I reply as the specter whooshes out the open window, leaving a cool rush of air in her wake. "A younger one, I think. But she's gone now."

"I must have given her quite a show with all that screaming."

"I doubt it. Most of them are only curious. You *are* the girl from the prophecy, you know," I say, smiling.

Gul doesn't smile back. Two furrows indent the space between her brows. I wonder what she's thinking when I hear her voice in my head again: *I should have died the day the Sky Warriors first came for me. The day Shayla murdered my father and mother.*

I wrench my hand away from hers. The loss of contact leaves me bereft, reminds me of being singed by a stove. Perhaps Gul, too, must have sensed something similar, because the color has drained from her face, her skin turning ashen.

"Cavas, what happened?"

"Shubhraat, Gul."

I don't wait for her to wish me a good night in return.

5

CAVAS

The first thing I do after leaving Gul's room is head to the western part of Tavan, toward the big city temple. I normally spend my mornings patrolling the city's boundary with Esther to look for any faded specters. After our patrols, I slip into the temple to talk to my mother. The place is always devoid of worshippers and I don't know if anyone prays here anymore. As suspected, it is empty at this early hour as well. I pull out an old green swarna from my pocket and rub it between my thumb and forefinger, watching the coin glow.

"Ma?" I whisper. "Are you there? I . . . I need to talk."

Unlike Latif and Indu, specters who like to show off their invisibility by appearing one body part at a time, my mother materializes without dramatics, her long gray hair flowing as she steps out from behind one of the temple's thick, engraved pillars. To my surprise, she holds up a sprig of delicate purple flowers—the sort that begin budding on tulsi bushes during the Month of Flowers and bloom only during the Month of Song.

"What's this for?" I ask.

"Does a mother need an excuse to give her son a present?" she asks lightly, though her gray eyes are full of concern.

I marvel at the tiny flowers, taking in their strong, clove-like fragrance, before tucking the sprig into my pocket. "Thank you, Ma."

"It was my pleasure." She pauses. "But you didn't call me here for chitchat, did you, son? Not with the way you ran out of Gul's room."

I've had three months to accustom myself to it, but some days, it's still strange to hear Ma call me her son, to see bits and pieces of me reflected in her: in the slight tilt of her head as she watches me, the cut of her jaw, the bump tipping her nose, which is smaller than mine.

"You saw what happened?" I ask.

"I saw you go there and comfort her. But then something else happened, didn't it?"

I take a deep breath. "It's probably nothing."

"*Cavas* . . ." Her voice inflects: a warning to not evade the question. "What is it? Was it another specter?"

"It wasn't," I say truthfully.

Moonlight pours in through the temple from all sides, outlining her spectral form, turning her gray face silver. Right now, I can almost pretend that she's still alive, her expression more forbidding than the ones carved onto the stone figures of the gods in the temple's sanctum.

Ma continues to frown. "I know you won't let me see you then, but if it was someone from your spectral dreams, you need to tell me, son."

"No, Ma, it wasn't." I emphatically shake my head. "Besides, I don't need you in my spectral dreams." It's bad enough that *I* see specters turning into Papa; the least I can do is spare Ma the pain of seeing him die.

"I wasn't able to protect you when you were young." Ma's voice is low, bitter. "It seems fitting that you'd keep me away now, too, doesn't it?"

"That wasn't your fault. You and Papa did your best to keep me safe."

By now I've understood and accepted Ma's reasons for wanting to remain a secret when I was a boy. If I'd seen Ma back then, I would have asked Papa a hundred questions. I would have eventually figured out that

I wasn't Papa's son and that the man who sired me was a magus who lived in the Sky Warrior barracks.

"You are so much like your Papa," Ma says sadly. "He would also pretend things were perfectly fine when they weren't."

A flush rises up my neck. I wonder if this is true. If I'm really like Papa or the man whose blood I share—though I don't know who he was. I have my suspicions, of course. General Tahmasp, the former commander of the Sky Warriors, appears in my mind again the way he has several times in the past.

"So why did you call me, then?" Ma asks, distracting me from my thoughts. "Is it Gul?"

"Yes. She . . . she keeps having nightmares," I say. "It sounds awful, but we've been fighting for so long that I spent a lot of time pretending I didn't know about them. Tonight I couldn't help myself. I had to go see if she was all right. I was sitting next to her, holding her hand when . . . I . . . I thought I heard her voice in my head. She was blaming herself for Papa's death."

There's a long silence.

"I know it's crazy—being able to hear voices like that," I say.

"Why would you say such a thing?"

"No one should have access to another person's thoughts! Well, apart from living specters—but you can't help it. I don't want to know what's in Gul's head!"

"You also blamed her for Xerxes's death," Ma says, her tone cool. "Why does it bother you if she does the same?"

I take a deep breath, feeling the telltale prick of blood curling up my ears. *Don't lose it, Cavas.* Ma isn't as patient with my anger as Papa was. She has the tendency to leave me midsentence, refusing to respond until I calm down.

"That's not the point," I say. "Besides, I don't blame her for it anymore."

"Perhaps not. But you took out your anger in other ways, didn't you? You gave her a hard time for not using her magic during training."

33

"I wasn't angry about that; I was frustrated. And I wasn't the only one. Without Gul doing magic, there's no way we can win this war!"

"You mean, there's no way you can take your revenge the way you want to," Ma retorts.

I grimace. It's near impossible to hide your thoughts from a living specter—especially if she also happens to be your mother. Ice travels down my spine when Ma's hand briefly cups my cheek. Spectral touches can be cold to the point of discomfort. Not that I would ever tell Ma this.

"Your father loved you, Cavas," she says, her voice hard. "He sacrificed himself willingly to save you. But all you want to do is throw that away!"

"How could he love me if I wasn't really his son?" The thought, always held back from being voiced when Papa was alive, spills out. "How could he love me when giving birth to me killed you?"

"He didn't love you at first," Ma admits. "He wasn't even willing to look at you. That first month after you were born, Ruhani Kaki took you to her little hut and kept you with her while Xerxes grieved for me. She still went to him each week, though, hoping to persuade him to take you back."

Curiosity pokes out a head, breaching the grief clouding my chest.

"Then one day, something strange happened," Ma continues. "You put your hand on his knee and smiled at him. That's when something changed. He picked you up and began playing with you. At the end of the day, when Ruhani Kaki wanted to leave, he said he would keep you for the night. But I knew—and so did Ruhani Kaki—that he wasn't going to let you go."

My throat closes for a brief moment. "Ma. Who was my real father?"

My mother stiffens. Her hand drops to the side. "Why does that matter?"

"It was General Tahmasp, wasn't it?" I prod. "That's why he was nicer to me than he was to the other stable boys. Ma, wait! Please don't go."

In desperation, I reach out to grab her wrist and feel its icy touch go right to my pounding head.

"What is it you want to hear, Cavas?" Ma says, her voice low, dangerous. "That the man who sired you raped me to do so? That your papa, who always held his head high, was forced to lower it when everyone in the tenements called me a whore? Tell me, son: Is the general the sort of man you would call your *real* father?"

"N-no! Of c-course n-not!" I stutter, letting go of her hand. I don't know what makes me feel worse—Ma's anger or her pain. "I . . . I'm sorry I asked, Ma. It was stupid of me. Why does it matter how I came into the world?" I lie.

General Tahmasp was dead now, I remind myself. *What was the point of verifying a truth that will only hurt Ma all over again?*

My mother's fury burning bright in her eyes deflates as suddenly as it arose. "My son, my son. I'm the one who's sorry. It *does* matter to you— the way it would to any child. I don't blame you for wanting to know. Yes, it's true. The magic in your blood comes from the man who sired you. But this"—she presses a hand over my heart—"*this* was shaped by the man who raised you. You think the way Xerxes would; you even scowl like him when you're mad. Your nightmares aren't about General Tahmasp dying, they're about your papa. It's why you're so desperate to avenge him, isn't it?"

"Yes," I whisper. *It's my fault that Papa died.* Mine, *not Gul's.*

"By Javer, stop that!" Ma snaps. "It's not your fault, either, son. Your father *chose* to come to that palace with you. He *chose* to throw himself in the way of that atashban. If anyone was responsible for Xerxes's death, it was Xerxes himself. I'm glad he isn't a living specter, Cavas. It's not restful, this life. I wander endlessly, sleeplessly. Stuck to the living world when I'd rather be released of its clutches."

"Why are you still here, then?" Pain twists my insides into a knot. As much as I don't want to lose my mother, I still don't know why she hasn't faded like so many other specters.

"I want to see you safe. But you aren't," Ma says simply. "You haven't been for a long time. Now listen carefully. Don't discount the threat you are in right now under Rani Shayla's rule. But also, don't underestimate your own power. You are more than what you've believed to be. The living world calls you half magus, but you are *also* half non-magus. My blood gives you powers that magi do not have, powers that have made you a seer."

"Ma, there are other seers out there. And I'm sure the Scorpion is using them to the best of her advantage."

"Yes, but *those* seers don't have the Star Warrior as their complement."

I bite my lip. I was wondering when Ma would bring up my bond with Gul.

"In fact, maybe that explains how you accessed her thoughts," Ma says thoughtfully. "I don't understand the magic behind it; I doubt most people do. But anyone can sense that more than lust connects the two of you at this point. Don't look so shocked, young man. I know what you're thinking when you look at her."

Saints.

"Have you told Raja Subodh about this?" Ma asks, ignoring my embarrassment.

"Not yet. You're the first. I . . . I thought I was going mad, honestly."

"It's not bad to be afraid of something you don't understand," my mother says gently. "But it doesn't mean you are going crazy. It's dangerous to think that way. Fear of the unknown can make people do terrible things. Many years ago, some magi grew afraid of us. They first accused us of taking away their jobs and later said we were stealing their powers.

"But things are changing now. Magi, too, saw cruelty under Raja Lohar's reign; they lost siblings, children, and mates. They don't trust the new queen, either. To them, Gul will always be important—even if Rani Shayla has declared her a traitor. As for non-magi, they are looking to the Star Warrior as well. But they will also look to *you*. They will see themselves in you—and will fight for you when the time comes."

My already taut nerves begin fraying. Revenge is one thing, but—

"I'm not a leader, Ma. Who is going to listen to me?"

"You won't know until you begin. Talk to Gul. To Raja Subodh. Tell them about what happened tonight."

Ma's body begins disappearing the way Latif's does, bit by bit, until only her face remains for a brief moment. "The Sky Warriors are close. Too close . . ."

Her last word is a hiss, the sound hovering in the space where she once stood. Moments later, a throat clears.

I spin around, facing Gul, whose gaze darts from my face to the pillar behind me. "What happened tonight? What is it you aren't telling me?"

I note the rosy tint to her brown cheeks and wonder if she overheard my conversation with Ma. "How long have you been standing there?"

"Not long. Why? Were you waiting for someone else?"

For a brief moment, there's no sign of the girl who screamed her fears into the dark. Gul's gold eyes sparkle the way they did the first time I saw her at the moon festival. Right before we kissed. My gaze, traitorous thing, instantly skips to her mouth, to her slightly fuller upper lip. I force it back to her eyes.

"Only thinking," I say.

She clears her throat. "I want to thank you. For coming to my room tonight. It helped, seeing you. Felt like I wasn't alone."

Guilt floods my face with heat. Behind Gul, dawn is breaking, the sky a pale lavender. Soon enough, the others will wake and it'll be time for breakfast.

Tell her. My conscience sounds a lot like Ma. *Tell her you could hear her voice in your head.*

"You don't need to thank me," I say instead. "I acted like an ass for the past month. I'm sorry for that. I didn't have any right to pressure you into using magic. No one does. You were right when you said I wanted revenge for Papa's death. I still do. But that doesn't mean I have the right to transfer my burden onto you."

"I thought burdens lessen when they're shared," she says, a hint of humor entering her voice.

"Mocking me with my own words, are you?" I give her a sheepish grin. "I suppose I deserve it. But you don't have to do this, Gul."

She sighs. "You don't need to lie to me, Cavas. You only began talking to me tonight because you hope I'll use my magic during training. Despite your words, I know you're still hoping I won't take you up on your offer."

My protest balls up in my throat. She's right. I am lying. Not only do I want Gul to fight with magic, I want her to amplify my own when I take aim at General Alizeh and sink a spear into her chest.

"Besides, I no longer have a choice, do I?" Her voice hardens, a note of bitterness creeping in. "Who knows how long the specters will hold the boundary safe? Doesn't matter, does it, if I end up killing someone in the process."

"You won't kill anyone!" I protest. "Maybe you injured me a little last night, but my arm is healing nicely. I'll be fine in a couple of days."

She says nothing, her forehead furrowed, her gaze steadily holding mine. Once again, I find myself studying her smooth brown skin, the perfect pink of her lips. I wonder again about what happened in her bedroom—how I ended up hearing her voice.

Before I can say anything, though, Gul begins speaking again:

"Subodh tells me that Shayla's ascent to the throne is the worst thing possible for Ambar. Maybe that's true. But Shayla isn't stupid. She closed the labor camps for a reason. She needs the support of the citizens to legitimize her rule."

"You're putting too much weight on a single grand gesture," I point out. "It'll take more than shutting labor camps for Ambaris to side with a usurper."

"And you think they'll side with *me* instead?" she scoffs. "Non-magi will never trust a magus leader. As for magi—they looked the other way when their own girls were being kidnapped and drained of magic. Some of them also helped the Sky Warriors. *They* won't join any rebellion."

38

"Maybe *some* people won't join the rebellion. But what about the rest? No, wait, hear me out. Raja Subodh says that Ambar's coffers are empty, right? And that the Scorpion has begun taxing magi and killing off anyone who complains. Don't you think it will affect the people? Make them angry?"

"Maybe, but most people will simply pay the tithes out of fear."

"They might. But there's a limit to how much people will tolerate. Raja Subodh gets new reports every week about what's happening in the kingdom. More and more people are questioning how a mere Sky Warrior took over the throne a week after a legitimate heir was crowned. Ambaris are slow to anger, but they do get angry, Gul. Everyone has a tipping point. That's what led to the non-magi rebellion during Rani Megha's rule."

"Are you telling me they're angry now?"

"I'm telling you that it's in the nature of a scorpion to sting. It can't help itself."

"You're saying Shayla will make a mistake," Gul says wryly. "Isn't that too much to hope for?"

"Probably. But what have we got to lose?"

She remains quiet for a long moment. Then: "So we begin training today."

"I guess so." A little bit of the weight that has been crushing my ribs ever since Papa died lifts.

"I'm not taking responsibility for your getting blown up during a session."

She's only half joking. Her hands shake slightly as she reaches to move a strand of hair sticking to her cheek. It falls back into place. I struggle to keep my own hands in check.

"You won't blow me up, Gul. I'm your complement, remember? Any sign of trouble and I'll rein you in."

I expect her to raise an eyebrow or stab back with a witty retort. But she doesn't even smile.

"How can you be sure that I won't lose control of my magic again? The sky goddess . . . I asked her for help that day in Raj Mahal, Cavas. And she gave it. She let go of her hold on my power and I completely lost control. What's worse . . . I liked it. I *liked* destroying everything." A visible tremor goes through her. "I know it sounds disgusting."

"It doesn't," I say quietly. "I get it. Maybe I wouldn't have before, but now I do. When Papa died, I wanted to destroy the whole world. There are days when I still do."

When I imagine filling up bottles upon bottles with madira and fire-stone powder, planting them in the Sky Warriors' barracks. When I think of the innumerable ways I can carve the smile off General Alizeh's face.

I am worse than you, I want to tell Gul. *You don't hide your violence the way I do.*

But, coward that I am, I say nothing. Instead, I press my palms to Gul's trembling ones, exactly the way people do while making an oath.

"You won't lose control as long as I'm with you," I tell her. "I promise."

6

GUL

For breakfast, Cavas and I head back to the housing area, which lies east of the temple. Various small shacks populate the land along with two tall buildings linked by a compound.

Once a vibrant city built for travelers, Tavan was one of the few places in Ambar that stood up to King Lohar during the Great War, protesting his hunt for the Star Warrior—a girl with a star-shaped birthmark prophesied to bring an end to his reign. In retaliation, Lohar invaded Tavan, killed its governor, and turned the city into a labor camp for marked girls.

It was not until the Battle of the Desert, and the invasion of the Pashu kingdom of Aman, that things changed for Tavan. But the city's relative freedom came at a price. King Lohar unleashed his maha-atashbans—giant versions of the Sky Warriors' deadly crossbows—which nearly decimated the Pashu forces and destroyed Tavan. He also shot a spell, shackling Subodh to the city, unable to break free. The Pashu king and the Tavani women survived only because of the shimmering golden bars

I now see in the distance and thousands of living specters, who had risen as one, turning the city and its inhabitants invisible.

As long as I can see the bars, I am safe, I remind myself. It's only when I *can't* see them that I need to start worrying.

Over twenty years have passed, but Tavan still holds traces of the labor camp, its old libraries and havelis lying in ruins, depictions of red atashbans marking many of the houses like wounds. The building where Cavas, Kali, and I are now housed once formed the barracks of the guards, though it, too, is designed like a haveli. Remains of old paintings still embellish its cusped-arch doorways, and an enormous, latticed balcony overhangs the courtyard below.

Wooden posts jut from the earth outside, broken black chains hanging off them. Girls like me were chained here once. Made sport of by the guards for the birthmarks on their skins.

Called Freed Land by the Tavani women, the compound is both a reminder of the past and a testament to the future. Over the past two decades, this patch of land has been allowed to run wild. Broom-shaped honeyweed bushes grow from the base of the posts, with tiny clusters of starry blue flowers. Dew clings to clumps of the wild desert grass, which brushes my bare ankles as I walk, sidestepping a thhor plant's prickly green limbs.

Across the compound is another building, which functioned as solitary confinement of the most dangerous prisoners. Now it's a mess hall and activities center. Women have begun practicing with lathis on the roof overhead, their shadows dancing with the rising sun. The air fills with sounds of clacking bamboo. A cry rings out, and I wonder if someone has broken a bone. The Legion are experts at spinning lathis, but accidents do happen, and I'm sweating at the thought of facing them at practice today.

As Cavas and I approach the mess hall, a figure steps out of it.

Esther is dressed for practice in a short blue tunic and billowing blue trousers. Silver-and-black stars etch the dark-brown skin of her forehead, along with a tiny gold star carefully marked above her chin. Her real birthmark—the one that got her imprisoned in Tavan years ago—is a mole in the shape of a shooting star on her left cheek. She now smiles as she looks down at me.

"Ready for your first training session with Raja Subodh?" she asks us.

Before either Cavas or I can answer, a voice rises overhead in a taunt, cold fog chilling my skin: "We'll be lucky if they both come out of it in one piece."

"Ignore her, please," Esther says, rolling her eyes. "My older sister has developed a habit of mocking people ever since she turned into a specter."

"Wait—Indu is your sister?" Cavas asks, surprised.

Sorrow flickers across Esther's features. "She was my twin," she explains, seeing the confusion on my face. "Older by a few minutes. She died trying to save me from being tortured. She only wants to see me safe now. That's why she's still here. Hanging on."

Queen's curses.

I never knew, could have never guessed, that Indu was Esther's sister. For a brief moment, I can imagine another figure, gray and spectral, forming beside Esther, the faded half of a whole. But then I blink and the image vanishes. Only Esther remains, her shoulders drooped with exhaustion, her pain so palpable that I feel myself breathing it in.

"I'm sorry," I say. "I didn't know."

"No need to be sorry. I don't talk about it much."

"What about Latif?" I ask, recalling the other specter I know best, having brought Cavas and me together initially, then helping us reach Tavan, along with Indu, after chaos erupted at Ambar Fort. "Is he still here?"

"He is," Esther says. "In fact, he brought me this today; he found it near the southern boundary, where our battle took place last night."

She holds up a broken arrowhead, its gold point glistening in the sunlight. Small firestones glint at the center of the arrowhead, forming a perfect triangle.

"This is no ordinary arrowhead. This is—"

"—the tip of a Sky Warrior's atashban," I finish, my heart sinking.

"Did you find a Sky War—" Cavas begins sharply.

"No," Esther reassures. "But more living specters faded this morning—this time at the northern boundary. I was with Raja Subodh this morning, checking on them. Three specters faded right before my eyes. As of now, Indu and Latif are scouring the border for any other infiltrations."

I feel the blood drain from my face. Cavas is no better, his complexion turning ashen.

"There's no need to panic yet," Esther says, forcing a smile. "But I'm glad you'll begin training with us, Gul. *Properly* training with us. I have to go now. I'll see you later at patrol, Cavas."

"Yes, Esther Didi."

I feel Cavas's eyes on me as we enter the mess hall, grateful he can't see the mess of knots my stomach is in.

In the desert, food is meager and rationed closely, our meal today consisting of a whole peeled orange and a few dried dates. Normally, like Cavas, I would inhale whatever is placed before me. Today, every bite feels like a chore. While in the past I was mostly ignored by the Legion, this morning they watch me the way a flock of hungry shvetpanchhi would eye a lone rat—ready to pounce at any sign of weakness.

"So it's true?" I hear someone say in a voice clearly meant to carry. "She *can* do death magic?"

"She can." After last night, Roda's sarcastic tone is instantly identifiable. "Though I'm not sure she'll live up to the promise she made Raja Subodh and Esther Didi."

I swallow the last bit of orange, the juice like acid in my throat.

Yes, I can do magic, I want to tell these women. *I can also kill people. I've done it before, without mercy.*

The crown prince of Ambar and his brother might have been blots on the human race, but I haven't forgotten how I lost control over my magic that day, how I relished losing control. Had it not been for Cavas,

I might have killed Prince Amar as well—completing Shayla's dirty work for her.

I force myself to finish the last bite of date—though, by now, my appetite is completely gone.

"Are you okay?" Cavas asks.

"I have to use the restroom," I lie, rising to my feet, not daring to meet any gazes directed my way.

The living specters are fading. Tavan's boundary may be full of new holes by now. Though Esther didn't say it, I know that Latif's finding the tip of the atashban has changed everything. The bounty hunters from last night might have very well been a test—sent by the Sky Warriors to see how weak we truly are.

I step out into the courtyard, where Agni is nibbling on some grass, her red coat gleaming, her mane brushed to a fiery glow. Sensing my presence, the mare lifts her head, almost knocking me over in an attempt to nuzzle me.

What are you doing here? I ask her, whispering through the bond we formed a little more than two years ago. *Why aren't you at the reservoir?*

The reservoir is where I normally find Agni lounging during the day, when she isn't chasing living specters around the temple. Animals can also see living specters—when the spirits bother revealing themselves, Agni told me.

Some of the specters kept spooking Ajib, Agni says. *I got tired of them as well. Indu is the worst of the lot.*

A pang goes through me at the mention of Ajib, the only one of Juhi's stallions who survived the dust storm on our way here. On a normal day, I would sympathize with Agni about the specters, but right now, I think of what Esther revealed to me earlier today about Indu being her sister. I recall one of the visions I saw in a dust dream three months earlier—a young gray-faced girl with pigtails and a ripped tunic leading me through Tavan's front gates. I wonder now if that had been Indu as well.

Does Dream Dust allow us to see living specters?

"Wouldn't you like to know," a voice speaks right in my ear before blowing in it.

Indu cackles when I move back with a start, nearly falling. I scowl. I forgot that specters could read minds if they so choose.

"Esther said you were scouring the city for Sky Warriors," I say, changing the subject. "Did you find any?"

"If I did, I wouldn't be playing pranks on the likes of you, would I, Star Warrior?" Indu retorts.

Agni nudges my shoulder—*Don't you have training or something?* she asks. I force myself to turn back in the direction of the city temple, its sandstone walls weathered with time, ancient magic thrumming under the surface of the rock.

Inside the temple, the Pashu king is on all fours between two overhanging bells in front of the sanctum, studying the stone faces of the gods. Once Cavas arrives, we settle cross-legged on the ground behind Subodh, who finally turns around, getting straight to the point:

"Have either of you meditated before?"

"I haven't," I say. "I know Kali and Amira meditated in the past to restore their drained magic."

"I've seen people meditate in the tenements," Cavas says. "Papa told me stories about non-magi gaining magical powers by praying to the gods. Not that I saw anything happen on my watch. There was nothing going on there except a lot of deep breathing," he adds wryly.

"Breathing deeply is, indeed, a form of meditation," Subodh says. "Though you need to understand that it takes enormous willpower and years, if not decades, of dedication to obtain magic if you aren't born with any—or to regain magic once it's lost. The sort of meditation we'll practice today is different and wouldn't be possible if you both didn't have preexisting magic. Ritual chants will not be enough here. Neither will the wakeful slumber of an ascetic. This is meditation that's used in battle—that turns your whole body into a weapon. The Pashu have used it in wars for centuries. Humans have used it, as well, to great effect."

Meditation? In *battle*?

Amid the seething mass of nerves in my belly, I feel other emotions stirring. Excitement. Intrigue.

"Humans place a lot of stock in the power of magic," Subodh continues. "But magic in the hands of an untrained mind can be dangerous. To master your magic in battle, you will need to master your mind first. And that's where meditation comes into play."

Use your mind, princess.

Amira's words echo in my head, and for the first time, ever since I came here, I feel the tension dissipate from my shoulders. I've done this before. With the exception of whispering, every type of magic I've performed has been by using my mind, mostly by focusing on memories that have made me feel safe.

"Stand, please," Subodh instructs. "You aren't going to use any weapons today, but I want you to face each other, your legs braced slightly apart."

Cavas and I do so after a moment of awkwardness.

"Now, for this first exercise, I simply want you to listen to the sounds of your body," Subodh says. "To your breaths, your sighs, to the blood flowing through your veins. What we're looking for is called sthirta—or a state of stillness."

So that's what it's called, I think, relieved to finally put a word to the calm that comes over me when I whisper to animals or raise a magical shield, or when I find the perfect memory to cast death magic.

"Normally, when people meditate, they close their eyes. You, on the other hand, will need to keep your eyes open during battle. It may be difficult at first, but still much easier once you concentrate on the power flowing through your veins—yes, you too, Xerxes-putra Cavas."

Cavas's chest rises and falls in a sharp intake of air. "I . . . I've never done it before. Accessed my magic, that is. It's always been Gul who has drawn on my power."

"That's not true," I tell him. "You stopped me from casting a death spell against Rajku—*Raja*—Amar. You held back my power with your own."

"And you will be able to do so again," Subodh says. "The point of meditation is ultimately for you both to telepathically communicate with each other."

"Telepathically? You mean like whispering?" I ask, surprised. "I thought humans couldn't whisper to each other!"

"They can't. What complements do isn't exactly whispering, either," Subodh says. "For one, whispering can be done only within a certain distance. As a whisperer, you can feel an animal's pain, but you cannot share their powers. From what the Pashu have heard about the goddesses Sunheri and Neel, we know they shared powers in a battle between the gods and the great animal spirits centuries ago. Stories suggest that the two goddesses also could read each other's minds from great distances. Now, I don't know how that power will work in humans, but it can be safe to assume that it might be the same."

I think I hear Cavas gasp, but I can't be too sure. My mind is spinning from everything Subodh has suggested—the implications of the sort of power to which Cavas and I have access. Though the question is—

Do I really want that? Do I really want Cavas in my head, reading my innermost thoughts about him?

If my face were a piece of coal, it would spontaneously combust by now.

Cavas, on the other hand, simply frowns, as if mulling over something. His mouth opens and then snaps shut as Subodh begins speaking again.

"Before you begin meditating, think of the god or goddess you trust the most. Or if you don't believe in the gods, think of magic itself, the overwhelming heat of it limning your hands. Often, your first choice will be your best one. Focus on that as you breathe. When you reach a state of sthirta, try to communicate with each other. Without speaking out loud."

The sky goddess is the first to come to my mind, of course. Despite my apprehensions and what happened at Raj Mahal, she's the one I focus on. I breathe in and out. In. Out. It takes a while, but eventually my breaths form a rhythm of sorts, merging in an unending circle.

A memory takes shape. I am a child of five or six, sitting in my mother's kitchen, waiting impatiently for her to finish rolling hot jaggery, ghee, and sesame into perfect, spherical laddoos. I have learned that Ma will eventually let me have them—sometimes two or three at a time—if I don't act on impulse and grab for them while they're still cooling.

Today, I force myself to exercise the same sort of patience that I did with the laddoos. My heartbeat quickens, then steadies. Warmth gathers in my solar plexus, filling my whole body. It takes a moment to realize that I haven't blinked once so far—and that, for some reason, it hasn't bothered my vision.

Everything slows.

Cavas's eyes flicker at half their normal speed, a ripple feathering his clenched jaw. His body emits a white glow; when I glance down, I realize mine is doing the same.

Cavas, I call out to him the way I'd whisper to Agni or any other animal. My voice sounds strange, lower than normal in my head. *Can you hear me?*

I wait for a response, but all I can hear is the sound of his breaths, filling the silence in a rush of air. My ribs expand, grow taut. *Cavas?* I reach out again.

You need to open your mind to him, daughter. The sky goddess's voice is warm, the way it was in my dream. Next to Cavas's struggling form, I see her begin to take shape: the spinning chakra on her right forefinger, her skin reflecting the colors of the morning sky. *As complements,* both *of your minds possess strong barriers. You need to lower yours if you want him to reach you.*

You're here, I think, startled. *I thought you . . . you . . .*

You thought I abandoned you, she says gently.

You never answered when I called. All these months, when I was so confused, when I'd wondered if I was doing the right thing by holding back my magic.

I wanted you to make the decision on your own. The gods meddle with many things, but we do not meddle with your free will. That you are here of your own volition is a powerful first step. The rest will become easier with practice.

Late though it is, her advice calms my nerves. I focus on Cavas again, trying to open my mind to his thoughts. It's hard, much harder than whispering or summoning death magic. Sweat pours down my forehead and back, a spike of pain bridging my nose and curving around the top of my spine. The scent of copper floods my nostrils, a dull thud pounding my head. Then I hear it. A voice.

Gul? Cavas sounds faint, strained. *Can you hear me?*

I think I answer him, but I can't be sure. Spots have burst before my eyes, turning the world a brilliant, blinding white.

When I open my eyes again, I'm lying on the floor, the discordant sound of voices slowly filtering back in. A pair of faces stare at me from above: a boy and rajsingha, twin parts worry and astonishment marking their faces. I grow aware of several more things: I'm sweating like I've run five miles in the desert sun; there's a terrible ache in my temples; and both of my nostrils are bleeding.

"I failed, didn't I?" I try to joke.

"No," Subodh says, his rumbling voice softer than I'd heard it before. "You were alarmingly successful. Both of you."

"You began glowing really quickly," Cavas says as he helps me sit up and hands me a clean cloth to hold against my nose. His eyes blink rapidly. Normal again. "I mean, I was shocked at how fast you did it. I had a tough time—lots of stops and starts before my skin began glowing.

Then everything sort of . . . slowed down." Cavas frowns. "I know this sounds strange—"

"It doesn't," Subodh says. Of the three of us, the rajsingha is the only one who looks unperturbed. "Go on."

"There was a voice . . ." Cavas says. "I think it was the sky goddess. I couldn't see her, but I think she was standing next to me. I heard her tell Gul to open her mind to me."

"Is that what happened, Gul?" Subodh asks me.

"Yes." I hesitate before adding, "I heard you, too—eventually. You called me by my name. And then I fainted."

"Don't worry; it's a part of the process," Subodh says. "And you were out for only a few seconds, Gul. Some minds are simply more receptive than others. Your mind is strong, child, but it's also stubborn."

"No surprises there," I mutter, drawing a reluctant laugh from Cavas. "Maybe Cavas can share some tips on how he read *my* mind."

"Good luck with that. I don't know how it happened the first ti—I mean today."

On another day, I might have missed it. But I've known Cavas long enough by now to register the slight hitch in his breath when he lies, the rapid flutter of his lashes as he evades my gaze.

"No," I say slowly. "When you said 'the first time,' you didn't mean today. You mean you've done this before. Right?"

There's a sharpness in my tone that makes Cavas wince. Subodh remains quiet, his eyes shifting between the two of us.

"Only once." Cavas clears his throat. "I, uh. I heard your thoughts. Last night—when I came to see you in your room. You were blaming yourself for my father's death."

Every part of my body grows numb for a split second. "So that's why you left so suddenly. Because you heard my thoughts."

"Yes." There's a worried look on his face. "I . . . I wanted to tell you this morning at the temple. But I didn't know how."

How about with: 'Gul, I think I can read your mind and it's freaking me out'?

I bite my tongue. Cavas isn't used to having magic. I know—understand completely—how difficult and scary it must be to realize that he's a complement to a girl whose death magic destroyed everything in her path. *So why am I angry? Why do I feel hurt that Cavas doesn't yet trust me?*

You don't trust him, either. At least, with your mind, a familiar voice rumbles in my head.

Subodh's pale eyes reflect my flushed face, strands of hair sticking to my cheeks.

You can reach my mind by whispering, I retort.

It took the Pashu centuries to develop our skills with whisper magic. You are but human.

"You both can have that conversation out loud, you know," Cavas says, sounding annoyed. "I mean, I know you're talking about me."

"I was only thinking about how you were able to read Gul's mind before," Subodh lies smoothly. "I believe you did so when she was especially vulnerable, such as after a nightmare."

"I thought meditation was supposed to strengthen our minds, not weaken them!" I say tightly.

"Strength and weakness aren't separate from each other, Star Warrior. Those who are strong now have been weak in the past," he says, looking somewhere at the pillars over my head. "Power always claims a price."

Of course it does. It did with my mother, who begged the sky goddess for another daughter and then died to save me. It does with Juhi, who collapses nearly every time she makes a prophecy. The reminder makes me deflate, my anger departing nearly as quickly as it had arrived.

"Let's stop training for today," Subodh says, and I think I hear sympathy in his voice. "I will see you again tomorrow. Perhaps things will be better then."

Cavas and I step out of the temple, and we walk awhile in silence.

"You're still angry with me, aren't you?" he asks when we reach the reservoir. I spot Ajib and Agni nearby, nibbling on grass, their glossy tails flicking in the heat. Sensing my presence, Agni looks up and nickers.

Later, I whisper, sending a calming thought her way.

I turn to study Cavas's watchful face again and sigh. "Let's move out of the sun for a bit." Taking refuge in the shade of a nearby dhulvriksh, I finally say what's on my mind:

"I *was* angry with you before. I'm not anymore. But I do worry at times that you don't trust me. After our conversation yesterday, I thought . . . I mean, it's not like I don't have my own trust issues," I admit. "There's this part of me that's constantly afraid of losing my magic. That hates the thought of being weak or helpless in any way. It's why I reacted so badly, though you did the right thing by holding me back from killing Amar at Ambar Fort. I guess it's why it was so difficult for me to open my mind to you this morning. The sky goddess knew, of course. She outright told me that my pride and my unwillingness to ask for help would lead to my downfall."

"Nice to know the Star Warrior is as human as the rest of us."

I turn around, ready to snap, when I notice the amusement dancing in his brown eyes.

"But you're wrong to think that I don't trust you," Cavas says.

My heart skips a beat when he takes my hands in his, exactly the way he did at the temple earlier today.

"This is new to me," he continues. "And last night, you looked so vulnerable. I wanted to protect you. Silly, right?" A laugh follows, as soft as a breath. "A boy with little power of his own trying to protect the most powerful magus Ambar has seen in a generation."

"I'm not the most powerful magus Ambar has seen in a generation. I'm *not*!" I insist when he scoffs. "I've always needed help from others!"

"Leaders don't work alone, Gul."

I say nothing for a long moment. "Let's promise that we'll be honest with each other from now on. No matter what."

"Fine." His eyes take on a sudden, wicked gleam. "Answer this then: Are you thinking of kissing me, right now?"

"What?" I blink, startled by the question. "No!"

Liar.

"I thought we were going to be honest with each other."

"Do *you* think of kissing *me*?" I challenge in response.

"Every single day." There's no hint of humor now, nothing except stark honesty in that dark-brown gaze.

My heart kicks hard under my ribs. Without saying a word, I pull away from him and begin walking back toward the barracks. He doesn't follow, but I can feel him watching me from under the tree.

Then, from a few feet away, I call out:

"Every hour, every minute, every second!"

Cavas's face splits into a grin a second before I spin around and run, the hot desert air fanning my face, his triumphant whoop ringing in my ears.

7
GUL

Since Subodh's training session took up most of the morning, I arrange to train with the Legion after lunch.

With magic. With magic.

The reminder thrums in my blood as I climb the stairs to the roof of the activities building, my seaglass daggers strapped securely to my hips. A group of women is already busy with lathi exercises, their long bamboo staffs spinning so quickly that it makes me dizzy to look at them.

"Shubhdivas, Gul ji!" It's Sami, sweat patching the armpits of her blue tunic, her deep-brown skin aglow. "Ready for practice?"

I swallow against my rising panic and wish her a good day in return. Sami's use of the honorific after my name always makes me feel awkward, but she never listens when I ask her to simply call me Gul.

"What are we planning today?" Sami asks, eyeing my daggers eagerly. "Should we—"

"I think we should have the Star Warrior warm up a bit before we begin," a voice cuts in.

It's Falak, Esther's second-in-command, who normally leads these practice sessions. Older than Sami—in her midforties—Falak always dresses for battle, a brown leather cuirass tied around her sleeveless blue tunic and matching arm braces. A ridged white scar stretches from her right cheek down her neck and ends somewhere below the Zaalian amulet tied around her bare right arm. She narrows her eyes at me now and I wonder if she's assessing the numerous ways she can crack her lathi over my head.

"Lathi practice will be good for her," Falak addresses Sami, though she continues to watch me. "Will loosen up any stiff muscles. Put away those daggers for a bit, Star Warrior. They might hinder you during exercises."

Strangely, my first instinct is to say *no*, the thought of being separated from my daggers instantly making me uneasy. But Falak is right. I'm not yet proficient enough in lathi that I can handle any extra weight on my body. So, reluctantly, I undo the belt that holds my magical weapons and put them where she instructs me to.

Staff in hand, I take my place at the back. The roof, though large, has enough room for only ten women to do exercises at one time. After the exercises, duels will take place, one after another, allowing for maximum fighting room.

I begin the warm-up exercise with the opening stance Esther taught me on the first day of practice: left foot forward, gripping the lathi from its center with both hands, my left hand always above the right. The exercise, when performed slowly, appears fairly simple. Bring the lathi down, raise it back over your right shoulder, bring it forward, and shift stances from left foot to right foot.

With added speed, the movement shifts from elegant to deadly, showcasing the fast, characteristic spins that make lathi a martial art to be reckoned with. Speed, as expected, is not my friend. Any attempts to move faster and I will simply trip over my own feet or—worse—send my lathi spinning in an arc into the air before it lands somewhere in the courtyard below.

"Watch your stance, Star Warrior!" Falak calls out shortly into the session. "Move your feet along with your lathi and it will spin more easi—by Zaal! Be careful, girl!" she shouts as my feet cross over in a dangerous move, nearly making me fall over.

Spinning the lathi is no joke, but after so many weeks of training, I certainly am.

Three months in and I still haven't got the hang of the most basic exercise, still don't have the speed or the accuracy of the other women, who spin their sticks in every direction Falak instructs them to, moving from one stance to another so quickly that I can barely see what they're doing.

By the time we take a break, my body feels like an oven. My heart pumps at twice its usual speed and my clothes stick to me like an unwanted layer of skin. I look enviously at Sami, who walks over to me, not seeming the least bit winded.

"Are you all right, Gul ji?" she asks quietly.

I'm going to collapse doesn't seem like the right answer, so I simply nod.

"You practiced Yudhnatam before, didn't you?"

"I did."

The martial art of Yudhnatam was my earliest exposure to combat at the Sisterhood of the Golden Lotus. The Sisters, however, had quickly discovered that a small and agile body did not necessarily translate to good combat skills. *Useless*, Amira had called me on more than a hundred occasions.

"Well, lathi is similar," Sami tells me now. "It requires breath control and balance. It needs agility—"

"Neither of which I have," I cut in. "Look, Sami, I was never good at Yudhnatam. I won't be any good at lathi, either."

"But you're good at magic," Sami whispers. "Don't deny it! I saw what you were capable of yesterday."

Yes, I think, dread pooling in my belly. *But you didn't see everything.*

"Time for dueling," Falak shouts after the last batch of women finish their exercises. "Rohini will partner with Nav. We'll watch them spar and try to look for ways they can improve their technique."

We step aside as two women enter a circle drawn on the ground with red chalk, their lathis held before them in a defensive position, leaping at each other barely a second after Falak's sharp whistle.

The duelers are of unequal height, Nav taller and more muscular than Rohini. But, somehow, both are evenly matched, their sticks slicing the air, crashing so hard at times that I wonder if they'll break. Unlike the lathis used by Ambar's thanedars and other law enforcement officials, these are simple weapons, unenhanced by magical amplifiers. I can't help thinking that in an actual magical battle, they will not last. A thanedar or Sky Warrior could easily shoot a spell that would not only kill these women but also turn their lathis into piles of wood chips.

Are you going to tell them that? The voice in my head sounds a lot like Esther's. *Are you going to help them before it's too late?*

Before I can speak up, though, cheers rise from the circle. Nav, who has ducked Rohini's swing, hits the other's right shoulder blade. Hard.

"Are you trying to break my bones?" Rohini shouts.

"My point," Nav shouts back, grinning.

"Yes, well done, Nav," Falak says. "What went wrong, Rohini?"

"I left my right flank undefended," Rohini mutters. "She tired me out."

"She did," Falak agrees. "To avoid that, you need to attack more than you defend. Get your jabs in first."

After dismissing them, Falak looks toward me. "Very well, Star Warrior. Let's see what you are made of. And please—feel free to use magic this time. We'll make sure your opponent uses a magically reinforced shield to deflect spells."

"Wait," I begin, a stone forming in my throat. I force myself to swallow. "Where's Kali? Shouldn't she be here, too?"

Falak frowns. "She should, but Kali joined Esther today to help check on the boundary. The shield should work fine. It has mammoth tusk chips in it."

"You don't understand," I say. "A shield may not be enough if—"

"We're not so inept at fighting, Star Warrior," Falak cuts in impatiently. "We've been doing it for years! Come now. We haven't got all day."

I grit my teeth, ignoring the snickering in the back.

"Falak Didi," I begin again, but Falak has already blocked her ears to my protests.

"In the ring, Star Warrior!" she commands before holding up a hand to stop Sami from following. "Not you. You go too easy on her, Sami. I think it's time she dueled with someone else. How about Roda?"

Roda rises to her feet, pale-skinned and brown-haired, her black-and-silver tattoos forming a starry crown over delicately arched eyebrows. She saunters over, whistling, spinning the lathi expertly with one hand.

"Are you sure, Falak Didi?" Roda asks, narrowing her hazel eyes at me. "We might not have a Star Warrior once I'm done with her."

Laughter follows her comment.

"That's enough," Falak says, frowning. "This is a *practice*, mind you, so you'll focus only on hitting your opponent's shoulders and sides. You do not aim for the head or the legs—*do you hear me?* Now pick up your shield."

Roda smirks, sliding the polished wooden shield over her left arm. "Yes, Falak Didi."

"Wait, you want your daggers, don't you, Star Warrior?" Falak asks.

I'm tempted to say *yes*. Roda chews on her lower lip, her smirk gone, her gaze shifting between me and the daggers. A couple of well-placed spells and she'd be bouncing around the roof like a frightened rabbit.

If *my magic cooperates and does exactly what I want it to.*

The last thought turns my blood to ice. Annoying as Roda is, I don't want to be responsible for her untimely death.

"The lathi will be fine," I tell Falak.

"Are you sure? These lathis aren't amplified with magic enhancers."

"That doesn't matter. Magic simply requires a weapon to channel it. Any weapon will do," I bluff.

And I'm not planning to do magic, in any case.

Falak frowns. "Fine. Now listen, Star Warrior, keep an eye on your footwork and keep moving. Because in an actual fight, someone *will* try to break your legs or skull. Now, are you both ready? Good—begin!"

Barely a second goes by before Roda brings her lathi down over my left shoulder with a hard spin. I raise my own weapon and block it—seconds before another hit comes my way. Sweat beads on my forehead, slides down my neck. The silence around us turns to whispers, then to instructions and catcalls, mostly directed at me:

"From the right, Star Warrior!"

"Watch those feet, Star Warrior!"

"Don't kill Roda with your nonexistent death magic, please!"

Laughter erupts when I stumble at the last comment. Roda's lathi catches me in the torso instead of the shins, where she'd originally aimed, making my eyes water.

"Gul ji, are you all right?" Sami cries out. "Roda, that was a foul move! She aimed for her legs, Falak Didi!"

"I'm fine," I mutter—not that anyone's listening. Maybe I should simply get knocked out again and save myself further humiliation.

"I noticed that!" Falak says, her tone sharp. "Watch yourself, Roda. Or you'll be banned from practice for a week."

Roda raises a brow. "If anyone should be banned from practice, it should be this so-called Star Warrior. She acts like she's *so* good, like she's better than the rest of us because she can do some magic. But the way she fights . . . Zaal's beard, we'd be better off renaming ourselves the Legion of the Dead."

More laughs follow Roda's comments. Though Falak's frown deepens, she says nothing.

My face burns. *Is that what they feel? That I think I'm too good for them?*

I recall the sky goddess's words, spoken to me once in a dream: *Cast your pride aside, for it can lead to your downfall.* I glance heavenward, momentarily tempted to call on the goddess for help now.

Roda's lathi lashes out again. Instinctively, I raise my staff to block it, the blow rattling all the way to my bones. Eyes narrowing, Roda attempts another hit. Then another. And another.

For long moments we dance around each other, lathis clacking, until I miraculously land a blow on Roda's shoulder, making her wince.

Someone shouts in the background, but I'm not sure what they say because in that instant, Roda's lathi slaps my right ear. Stars burst before my eyes, and I am suddenly pinned to the floor, skull pounding, the tip of an unforgiving staff pressed right against my throat. I curse myself for not listening to Falak and leaving my seaglass daggers behind.

Stop, stop, stop. I can't gasp the words out loud; I can barely breathe. Falak's and Sami's voices blur in my ears. Red begins flooding my vision like a sky at sunset.

They want your magic, Gul, a voice in my head purrs. *So why don't you give it to them?*

I raise my right arm, green light scorching my open palm and blasting back Roda and her shield several feet. Screams echo in my ears. My head pounds, worse than it ever has before, and all I want to do is sleep. But I force myself to blink and sit up, my eyes adjusting to the scene around me. With the pressure on my throat now gone, my previous rage turns to horror.

I'm surrounded by sawdust, my palms indented with a straight line of burns. For a wonder, my nose isn't bleeding. A small group of women stands next to a figure on the ground. Roda, her magically reinforced shield lying splintered beside her.

No. *Nonono.*

A hand grips my shoulder. ". . . okay?" Sami's voice breaks through.

"I'm fine," I say hoarsely. My ribs squeeze, as if held tight by invisible ropes. "Roda . . . is she—"

"She'll be all right," another voice says. Falak, who's also crouched next to Sami, a curious look on her scarred face. "You only knocked her out."

"She's not hurt, is she?" I ask, trying to rise to my feet. "I didn't ki . . ." My voice trails off, choking on itself.

"Sit!" Falak says sternly. "We want to make sure you aren't dizzy."

"I'm not!"

But Sami's hands hold me in place while Falak asks me several questions: *What's your full name? Where are we? What day is today? How many fingers am I holding up?*

"Savak-putri Gulnaz. Tavan. Twenty-first day of Song, three," I answer rapidly. Seconds later, someone from the other end of the roof terrace cries out:

"Roda's awake!"

"May I see her, please?" I beg.

"I don't see why not," Falak says, and Sami helps me to my feet.

I make my way over to the other side. One of the women is sitting next to Roda, asking the same questions Falak asked me. Roda's face is chalky, but her eyes appear clear, and she answers everything correctly. Finally, Roda looks up at me.

"Here to finish me off?" she says.

"I'm so sorry! I didn't mean . . ." My voice trails off when I see Roda's grin. "What's so funny?"

"She's only joking, Gul ji," Sami says with a laugh of her own. "Roda has taken worse blows before."

"Though never with magic," Roda admits. "That was more brutal than I expected."

"It's not funny." My hard tone makes every smile slip. "It's not funny when I injure someone so badly they can't walk for weeks on end. It won't be funny when my magic kills someone—when I lose complete control over it the way I did now."

I take a deep breath. "I won't do it. I won't use magic on you in practice battles!"

"You can't be serious!" Roda cries out, her voice hoarse. "Magic is exactly what we'll be facing out there!" She points to the distant golden bars gleaming in the light of the afternoon sun. "You *not* practicing with magic will only be more dangerous!"

"Roda's right," Falak says, her voice firm but not unkind. "We *need* you to use your magic, Star Warrior. We need to know what it's like out there and learn how to protect ourselves. We don't have any magic of our own, remember?"

I swallow, suddenly feeling very small. Yes, Falak's right. The women of Tavan don't have their magic anymore. But I can also, very easily, kill them.

Why doesn't anyone understand that?

"You really don't have any magic left?" I ask, changing the topic. "I mean, Kali was also at a labor camp. She got her magic back with meditation."

"Yes, she told me." Sami looks oddly ashamed. "We've tried, Gul ji. Raja Subodh taught us to meditate himself. But it didn't work for everyone. Sometimes, a few sparks shot from my fingers. But they weren't enough to shape into a proper spell."

"Frankly, none of us stuck it out the way we should have," Falak says. "It's frustrating to sit still and concentrate on communicating with a god or goddess or, in the case of us Zaalians, try to reach for something as elusive as magic. Eventually most of us gave up, except for Esther. It took her over five years to regain her powers. But Esther's half magus and not capable of doing death magic during battle. The guards at Tavan were reputed to be the best at extracting magic from others—they had trained to be vaids."

Healers? I feel slightly sick. *How can* healers *commit such a monstrosity?*

"They often reduced the girls and women to husks," Falak continues, her voice hard. "So many lost their minds. Those of us here are lucky we're still functioning. Raja Subodh was as surprised as anyone else when Esther began seeing living specters again."

There's a long silence. Then:

"I think we need to focus on the first problem at hand—which is defense," I say. "Most of you use lathis easily and can fight one-handed with them. But you also need to start getting used to shields. Magically reinforced shields are much heavier than regular ones. Did the guards have an armory here? With magical weapons?"

Sami nods. "There's a pile of weapons lying in a room here, gathering dust. We've not used them, though—except for the lathis. The maces were too heavy for most of us to wield. And Esther Didi banned the use of swords a few years ago, after a couple of women got seriously injured. We melted them down and reshaped them to use as kitchen knives."

I bite back a curse. Then again, the way things were, there probably *wasn't* enough time to learn how to use new weapons.

"Can the lathis be reinforced somehow?" I ask. If I shattered Roda's weapon without my daggers, then it has no hope of withstanding a Sky Warrior's atashban.

Sami and Falak frown at each other, as if having a silent conversation.

"We can use some Jwaliyan iron to reinforce them," Falak finally says, turning to me. "One of the women is a good smith."

"I've never fought with a shield before," Sami says. "But how hard could it be?"

"Don't knock yourself in the head with one and you should be fine," Roda says, receiving a light kick from Sami in response.

"Sami!" Falak admonishes. "She's injured!"

"Oh, please, Falak Didi. I have a hard head." To demonstrate, Roda rises to her feet, still slightly wobbly, but standing without any help. She turns to me.

"Don't underestimate us, Star Warrior. We are stronger than we look. We want you to use your magic on us. Right, Legion?"

A few cheers rise behind her. But not everyone looks as eager. A few of the older women avoid my gaze; clearly my magic has made them nervous.

"I think we need to see what can be done to ensure practice happens in a more, uh, controlled environment," Falak says, watching me closely. "We'll make *sure* Kali joins in on every one of our practices. Will that work for you, Star Warrior?"

Perhaps. Perhaps not. But right now, I know it will do no good to express my doubts.

"Maybe Kali can give you some tips to regain your magic," I say instead. "Also, please call me Gul, Falak Didi. All of you. I feel strange being given honorifics or titles I don't deserve."

"Very well, Gul." A smile flashes across Falak's stern face: a wink of sunlight through a cloud.

"Sounds good to me—Gul." Roda nods.

Everyone turns to face Sami, who appears to struggle with herself for a moment. Then she sighs. "Fine," she says. "Gul."

8

GUL

I'm in a nightmare again. When I wake, my throat is raw from scream- ing, my jaw aching from being clenched tight. Fingers brush my wet cheek, a soft voice whispering that I'm safe.

Cavas. Here again.

"Sorry I woke you," I say.

"You didn't wake me. I barely sleep most days. Too many nightmares of my own."

His thumb lightly strokes my lower lip, and despite the pain, warmth unfurls in my belly. His other hand holds mine, firm and steady, almost lulling me to sleep again.

"I hear you did magic today at practice," he says.

I force my body to stay relaxed and not freeze the way it wants to. *Of course. That's why Cavas is really here. To make sure I stay on track for his revenge plan.*

Remorse follows shortly after I have the petty thought. *Goddess, I hope he didn't hear that!*

But there's no shift in Cavas's expression, which remains curious and a little worried.

I release a breath and shrug. "I did. I mean, I didn't kill anyone yet."

"I know this is hard for you," Cavas says, his frown deepening. On closer observation, I notice that his eyes are bloodshot and that there are bags under them. "Also, I don't want you to feel like I'm only here to talk to you about this."

I stroke his arm, trying to distract him from the guilty flush flooding my face.

It works. "I . . . It's hard sometimes," he says, watching my hand. "I talk to Esther Didi and my mother from time to time, but it's not the same. You're the only other person who was *there*. When Papa was killed."

"I know," I whisper.

Trust Cavas to make me regret every spiteful thought I've had about him in the last few seconds.

"Sometimes I wish my brain was like a slate," he says. "That I could take a cloth and sponge it clean again. Right now, all I'm doing is making futile attempts to revise the past. Or write a future that involves so much violence it terrifies me. When we first met, I didn't get why you were hell-bent on taking revenge on Raja Lohar. I mean, I understood on a basic level, but it wasn't the same as it is now—like a hook under my skin, constantly prodding me to take action."

I say nothing. Who am I to lecture Cavas on the perils of revenge?

And so, a moment later, when he tries to pull away, I tighten my hold on his arm.

"Wait," I say, moving to make more room on the bed. "Stay awhile." Then, realizing what I implied, I hastily add: "Only to sleep. Nothing more."

"You mean, I can trust you to be honorable?" His eyes sparkle with amusement.

"I thought I could keep watch over you for a change."

He hesitates and then lies down next to me, flat on his back, his hand still clasped in mine. Eventually, I fall asleep, waking up only when dawn breaks, Cavas's side of the bed empty, but still warm.

"Will you help me?" I ask Kali quietly as we eat a simple meal of bajra roti and black lentils. Cavas and Esther, having finished their lunch, are outside now, checking the boundary for faded specters.

"Of course I will," Kali says at once. "What do you need me to do?"

I tell her about my old practice sessions with Amira in Javeribad. "She'd shoot a spell at me and I'd have to repel it with magic. I'm planning to do some easy spells—you know, blasts of air and stuff. Have the women deflect me without magic as much as possible."

In Javeribad, Amira didn't exactly hit me with killing spells, either, I reason. *Only magic that knocked me off my feet.*

"Sounds good." Kali uses the last bit of roti to wipe her plate clean. "Though you do realize you'll have to use death magic during practice at some point. The Sky Warriors won't be hitting us with air."

I say nothing, watching Roda and her friends talking and laughing a few feet away. Kali's right, of course. Most of these women have never faced an atashban. Those who fought against the Sky Warriors twenty years ago are probably dead by now, and those who remain are having trouble regaining their drained magic. Speaking of which—

"Sami told me she had felt a few sparks when she tried doing magic," I tell Kali. "I think some of the others might have as well. Could you work with them? Give them a few tips? I mean, Cavas and I practiced again this morning, but we still have a lot of work to do before we can combine our powers properly. Anything could help. I might feel better about shooting attacking spells at them if they could defend themselves."

"I'm happy to try," Kali says.

She's staring at the mess hall's newest arrival: Sami. As if sensing

Kali's gaze, Sami looks up. A shy smile lights up her face—quite at odds with her typical gregarious cheer. Next to me, Kali's pale skin flushes a light pink.

Interesting.

Kali raises an eyebrow at me. "If you grin any more widely, your teeth will fall out."

"Says the woman whose eyes are about to pop out of her own head."

Kali's face doesn't light up with its usual humor. She frowns at her empty plate. "There's a war at hand, Gul," she says finally. "We don't know what will happen tomorrow."

The old Gul—the one who plunged headfirst into so many things without thinking of the consequences—would have argued, would have asked Kali if a fear of the future meant that we ought to stop living today. But her quiet words make me hold my tongue, weigh me down in a way I did not anticipate.

Kali waits in silence until I finish my meal. "Shall we go, then?" Her face is calm again. I nod.

We walk in silence toward the courtyard outside the temple at the west end of the city. Since we're a little early, I use a bit of chalk to draw a large circle on the ground—big enough for three people to stand inside it and spar. The roof of the activities building is much too small to train fifty women at once, so I suggested a different training ground for the women. Moments after I pocket the chalk, the Legion begin arriving in small groups.

Their eyes narrow against the afternoon sun, and their gazes study me from head to toe. By now, everyone knows what happened to Roda on the roof, and even the skeptical ones are curious.

Footsteps hammer the earth; I glance around to see Esther arriving with Cavas.

"I think he should watch us, since you both are training together," Esther says. "Is that okay with you, Gul?"

I nod. Cavas gives me a slight smile.

Grateful that I can blame the sun for my flaming cheeks, I turn to face the women again. My heart beats so quickly I'm certain they can see it pumping through my clothes.

"Thank you for being here," I begin. "And thank you for trusting me to lead you in this war against the usurper queen Shayla. I am not going to lie or pretend I have everything figured out. I really don't."

No one talks anymore. But I can feel them listening. Kali gives me an encouraging nod.

"I'm hoping I can rely on you to guide me," I continue. "Esther Didi, Falak Didi, Kali—you are more experienced than I am at leading groups into battle. Will you advise me?"

"Of course," Esther says at once.

"I'll help you, Star Warrior," Falak says, looking pleased.

"Why else do you think I'm here, silly girl?" Kali nudges my elbow.

I release a breath. "All right. The first thing we need to work on is defense against magical spells. Some of you mentioned that you occasionally felt sparks of power emerging when you tried to meditate. But if you still want to try to see if you can access your powers, Kali can help. Kali?"

Kali is as short as I am, but as always, when speaking to a crowd, she appears taller, her voice magnified in the practiced way of leading the novices at the Sisterhood during training.

"I was in a labor camp the way you were," she says. "With a little luck and a lot of help from a brave woman and a braver girl, I escaped the place. With patience and meditation, I regained my powers. I can't guarantee you will do the same. But I can try to help you. If you want me to."

"Yes!" Sami looks a little flustered when every gaze focuses on her. She clears her throat and smiles. "I mean, of course we appreciate the extra help."

Kali begins to smile back—for real—before a frown overtakes her face again. She nods coolly, not seeming to notice Sami's crestfallen expression.

On instinct, Cavas and I lock gazes. He raises an eyebrow, as if to say, *What's up with them?*

I mouth, *Later.*

"Anyone interested in trying to regain their powers can stay back once Gul finishes her session," Kali says. "Gul?"

"Right." I give Sami my best smile to make up for Kali's indifference. "Why don't you divide into pairs? I'll cast a spell, and you try to defend yourselves against it as best as you can. You can throw your spears or knives at me, can do anything to protect yourselves."

Roda and Sami are the first to volunteer. I raise my daggers and without warning shoot a blast of air, making Sami duck under the white light. It's soon clear that Roda and Sami are much better at dodging spells than sending retaliatory attacks—or that's what I think until Roda eventually throws a rock that I'm forced to blast away, and Sami sneaks up from behind, slamming a lathi against the backs of my knees.

For a moment, I lie on the ground, slightly dizzy, and find their worried faces looking down at me. I can't help but laugh. "Am I dead or something? That was good!"

I get up, shaking off my stupor. "I think working in pairs might be your best option when it comes to fighting Sky Warriors."

It's the right thing to say because Roda and Sami look pleased and the women behind them suddenly look a lot more confident. I am about to raise my daggers again in attack when Kali stops me.

"Wait," she says. "Could you come here for a bit, Gul?"

"I'll be right back," I tell the women before walking to where Kali and Cavas are now standing. "What's up?" I ask them.

"I don't think you should practice against all twenty-five pairs of women on your own—even if it is simply shooting air," Kali says. "Cavas agrees with me."

"The morning's meditation session was pretty draining," he says quietly. "I'm exhausted. I'm sure you must be, too."

I'm about to argue when I feel the pinches of another headache creeping up the back of my skull. My nose, stupid thing, must be bleeding again. When I brush a finger against my nostrils, I find that true.

"Let me take over," Kali says. "You need to rest. Conserve your energy."

"I've only worked with one pair so far." Desperation creeps into my voice. "It's too early in the lesson. They'll think I've betrayed them. Or that I'm weak. I'm supposed to be their leader!"

My words—and the truth in them—surprise me. I didn't think I cared that much about being shunned by the Legion. But I'd forgotten what it feels like to be listened to, how good it feels to be looked at with an expression that isn't frank hostility. Also, deep down, I secretly miss doing magic that isn't whispering. My death magic can be unstable and terrifying, but it's also the only time I don't feel completely powerless.

"What use will you be if you can't fight later?" Cavas tells me now. "Good leaders know when to attack, yes. But they also know when to retreat."

"It won't look like that to the Legion," I point out. "As is, they don't trust me to do magic during practice."

And are you doing magic, Gul? Really doing the sort of magic they'll face? a voice taunts in my head. I push it aside.

"Gul—" Cavas begins.

"How about a compromise?" Kali cuts in. "You practice with twelve pairs, Gul, while I practice with thirteen."

"I take thirteen or you don't have a deal."

Kali rolls her eyes. "Fine. Thirteen for you, then."

By the time practice ends, blood has stained the collar of my tunic and I'm ready to collapse on the ground. But none of the women have been injured with more than bruises and scrapes. And there's something in the eyes of the Legion that I hadn't seen before.

Respect.

"Same time tomorrow?" I ask them.

"Yes, Gul!"

"Yes!"

"Yes!"

Voices echo, one after another, each one lightening my mood. Slowly, women begin trickling away. About thirty remain behind to try to access their magic with Kali.

"We're going to try to meditate now," Kali says, giving me an approximation of her usual smile. She looks nearly as exhausted as I do.

I nod. Most of the women who want to try to regain their lost magic are younger, like Roda and her friends. Sami is there, too, and despite her indifference, I know Kali is aware of this, her face paler than usual.

"Good luck," I say, not knowing if the words are for the women, Sami, or my troubled gray-eyed friend.

That night, when I head to bed after dinner, Cavas follows without a word. I say nothing when he slides under the covers next to me. Nor when he reaches out and takes hold of my hand.

"What does it feel like to have a complement?" he asks.

"Strange," I say. "I didn't know—couldn't even sense you were in my head. Seeing the sky goddess and everything."

"If you don't want me to, I won't. I'll make up an excuse."

"I don't really mind. What about you?" I turn my head to see his expression. In the darkness, I can't see much, except for the shadowy outline of his profile.

"I don't mind, either."

"Are you sure?" I face the ceiling once more. My heart pounds in my throat. "I mean, I know I'm not the easiest person to be around. If you want to be with someone else . . ." My voice trails off as the bed shifts, Cavas's breath warm against my cheek.

"Why would you say that?" he demands. "Do *you* want to be with someone else?"

"No! It's . . . I was just thinking about what you told Subodh the night the bounty hunters attacked. About finding a replacement and . . . Never mind. Forget I said anything."

He sighs. "Gul, all I know is that every time I've tried to leave you, something has stopped me. And that something isn't our magical bond."

What is it, then? I want to ask.

But I'm too afraid to say the words out loud. Too afraid to broach a conversation alluding to a future neither of us can see. Cavas doesn't elaborate on his statement, either.

"Is it okay if I sleep here?" he asks after a pause. "If you're uncomfortable, I can go—"

"No. Stay."

Cowardly though I may be about discussing my feelings, I know I don't want to be alone tonight.

"Might as well save yourself a trip later, when I have a nightmare," I add.

He laughs. "Right."

There's a long silence, during which I hear nothing except for our breaths. Then:

"Ready?" Cavas asks. His voice trembles and I know he's thinking about the night ahead, full of unseen terrors that we both have to meet.

I squeeze his hand in response. "Ready," I say, my eyelids drooping.

I wake again that night, screaming. But this time, Cavas is there. He murmurs reassurances in my ears and presses a chaste kiss to my temple. This time, when I nestle my head against his shoulder, I fall right back to sleep.

9

CAVAS

A week into my training with Gul, Subodh says we will move into the next part of the lesson: using weapons.

"Ideally, I would wait a month before attempting this, but you both have progressed more quickly than I anticipated," Subodh explains.

Our time is also running out. Last night, before dinner, I saw another specter fade—so quickly that I thought I was dreaming until I saw the too-wide gap between the two golden bars. I had to race to find Subodh and Esther to make sure the space was covered again. For now.

"We'll start by moving into battle stances." Subodh glances at Gul, who has brightened up slightly, her seaglass daggers sheathed on a belt around her waist. "I see you have brought your weapons as I asked."

"Yes," Gul says. "But I still need a shield. And Cavas doesn't have any weapons."

I swallow hard. I've been dreaming about this moment for months. Fantasizing the numerous ways in which I could wield a spear or a sword.

So why does my heart feel like it's going to beat right out of my chest?

"You're right," Subodh says. "That's why I've had this brought in.

Turns out the Legion *didn't* melt all the weapons in the armory to make kitchen knives."

He rises to his hind legs and strides to a small table near the altar. Plucking off the cloth covering the surface, he reveals an array of weapons, including two daggers with hilts of white jade, a sword of watered steel, a spiked Ambari mace, and two round leather shields embedded with chips of white marble.

"The leather shields are lightweight and less brittle than wood. The sangemarmar in them will help deflect most magical spells," Subodh says. "I wasn't sure what weapon you preferred."

"I'm not sure myself," I admit.

"Daggers aren't bad," Gul says. "They're lightweight and easy to throw or stick into someone who gets close."

I unclench my jaw. Despite my talk of revenge, a small part of me still wants nothing to do with magic or with this war. Yet I can no more run from it than I can from the mixed blood flowing through my veins. I'm about to pick up the daggers when something else catches my eye—a thin spear resting to the side, its tip sharpened to a fine silvery point.

Bypassing the daggers, I lift the spear. It feels strange in my hand and oddly . . . right.

"Interesting choice," Subodh tells me. "A man named Javer often preferred spears in battle. Until he became a saint, of course."

I look up with a start. "Sant Javer fought in a war?"

"Several wars. He gave it up later. He, too, was half magus." If raj-singhas were capable of smiling, Subodh would be doing so right now at the shock on my face. "You didn't know, did you?"

"I didn't. Did you?" I ask Gul.

"No," she says. "But it makes sense, doesn't it—why both magi and non-magi worship Sant Javer?"

I say nothing. I don't tell either of them that, while meditating for the very first time, I initially focused on various gods and goddesses, even Prophet Zaal, to access my magic. But it wasn't until I thought of Sant

Javer that I finally felt something bright and light erupting through my skin. Gul's eyes meet mine and she gives me a small smile. I try not to think too much about last night—or how I simply *followed* her to her bedroom without thinking.

Oh, you were thinking. Of tangled bodies. Tangled sheets.

Of reaching into Gul's mind to find out if she, too, feels about me the way I feel about her: a strange emotion that goes beyond admiration. Beyond magic and lust.

I was surprised by the words that spilled from my mouth last night—by the truth I heard in them. But I'd only ended up making Gul uncomfortable. Heart sinking, I push the thought away.

"Legs braced apart," Subodh says. "Yes, that's right. Keep your weapons raised and your eyes open."

I force myself to breathe slowly. *Ready?* Gul mouths. I nod.

"Now go deep into your heads, the way you did with your eyes closed," Subodh says. "Seek out the power that rests within."

Within seconds, Gul's body begins to glow, her eye sockets emitting a blinding white light. It takes me longer—much, much longer—despite focusing on Sant Javer, and even then my body is barely lit.

Why isn't this working? I wonder. *What am I doing wrong?*

I suddenly understand the anger I'd seen on Gul's face when she was taunted about her inconsistent magic—the shame that overcame her whenever words from the prophecy loomed over her head. I long for movement—to throw the spear, to lash out, to do *something*, though I've never used a weapon before, though I grew up avoiding every fight that ever broke out in the tenements.

Gul's seaglass daggers gleam in her hands. Green light shoots from the spiral tips, the way it did inside Raj Mahal, seconds before slicing through the necks of the crown prince and his brother. But this time, instead of molding the light into a weapon, Gul focuses it into a glowing emerald sphere. Her eyes reflect the orb and its crackling energy.

Can you hear me? she asks.

Yes, I respond.

Cavas?

Saints. She still can't hear me. Gul guesses this from my expression because soon enough, she adds: *See the glowing ball? That's a shield spell. I want you to amplify it.*

After several desperate attempts at telepathy, I resort to speech: "I can't. I don't know how."

"Gul, bow your head to pay your respects to the sky goddess," Subodh growls. "Draw your magic back inside by pressing your hands to your heart. Slowly now. It will hurt."

Gul bows her head respectfully and presses her hands against her heart. The ball of light turns nebulous like smoke, then slides back into her body in swirling ropes of light. It must hurt, the way Subodh said it would, because she's wincing at the end, her lips taut against the pain.

Subodh turns to me, cold fury etched onto his scarred face. "What happened, boy? Why did you let her go so far?"

"I'm sorry. I didn't know," I say tightly. "I mean, I tried to tell her that I couldn't amplify her magic."

"It's my fault," Gul says at once. "I couldn't hear him. My mind is still . . . blocked somehow."

Something shifts on Subodh's face—for a moment he looks exhausted, resigned. Then his yellow eyes glass over, his expression neutral once more.

"No matter, we'll try again," he says. "This time, I want you to meditate with your eyes closed, Cavas."

I do this—and instantly see a difference. Within seconds I'm transported to a darkened version of the temple we're in right now. Subodh isn't here, but I can see Gul quite clearly, glowing white with magic, her daggers in her hands. Two statues occupy the temple's inner sanctum: the sky goddess and Sant Javer.

"Gul?" I say, my voice still hesitant.

"I can hear you!" she exclaims. "Finally! Looks like you need to have your eyes closed, huh?"

"Probably not a smart thing," I mutter.

A dimple flashes in her right cheek. "Never mind. I am going to cast a shield spell. I want you to strengthen it."

"Fine. But don't blame me if nothing happens."

I raise my spear in the air, aligning it so that my magic will meet Gul's halfway. I pause. "What now?"

"Pour your magic out," Gul says. "It's there on you—I can see you glowing. Imagine yourself focusing it into a spear or an arrow if that helps. I'll do the rest."

I can see myself glowing, too, my skin emitting a white light that smarts my eyes. Within the brightness, though, I see something else: like a vein bubbling under my skin, a pulsing bit of light at my elbow. The first time I try to touch the light physically, it scalds my fingers, nearly making me drop my spear.

"Use your mind, Cavas," Gul says softly. "Use your mind to do the pushing."

"All right," I whisper.

Go, I tell the throbbing flame that now reappears on my wrist. *Strengthen Gul's magic.*

For a moment, nothing happens.

"Harder," I hear Subodh's voice, as if from a distance. "Push yourself harder, Xerxes-putra Cavas."

Maybe it's because he calls me by my full name—the one that links Papa to me. Or maybe I'm simply fed up with that mocking bit of light on my arm. My muscles tense as I focus, my heart pumping so hard I'm sure I've popped an artery by now.

But it works.

I feel my magic move down my arm in a crawl, then a rush of burning heat, emerging in drops of gold from the tip of my spear. Small globes form, magnetically drawn to the green sphere of light floating over Gul, creating sparks wherever they join.

My head begins spinning as our magic merges. Without touching

Gul, I hear the thoughts flickering through her head—*attack, attack, attack*—and the roar of blood in her veins. As Gul spins her daggers, focusing our combined powers in a jet of light at the table holding weapons in the corner, I grow dizzier, my knees buckling.

The next thing I know, I'm opening my eyes again—and lying on the floor, my head feeling like it's been hit repeatedly with a hammer. Gul's and Subodh's faces hover above, their worried murmurs filtering through to my ears.

"Was I dreaming or did we really destroy that table?" I ask hoarsely.

"We really did it." Gul helps me sit up, her fingers lightly checking for bumps on my skull. "Look." She points to the space where the table holding weapons once stood—everything now lying in a pile of wooden chips. "I think it took a toll on you, combining your powers with mine."

"Which is normal," Subodh says, his voice revealing neither pleasure nor displeasure. "The main thing for us to work on is keeping your eyes open during battle, Cavas."

I feel my shoulders sag. "I know."

Ahead of me, Gul and Subodh stare at each other without a word. They're probably holding a silent conversation with whisper magic again.

"That's enough for today," Subodh says. "Go eat breakfast. We can try again tomorrow."

The morning sun glows hot as we step out of the temple. Within a moment or two, my head begins aching—though that might have more to do with how I hit it on the floor than with using magic.

"What were you talking about?" I ask Gul. "You and Subodh."

I watch a flush creep up her cheeks and wonder if she's going to tell me the truth. "He was reprimanding me," she says finally. "For not using my magic properly."

I frown. "What do you mean? You *were* using magic. I felt it."

"I was." She clenches her jaw. "But Subodh wants me to use my magic the way I did in Raj Mahal—every bit of it, no matter what the consequences are for me or you."

"Wait. You were holding back?" I frown, puzzled. "Why?"

"You could hear my thoughts more clearly when our magic combined, couldn't you?" Gul asks.

I hesitate before nodding.

"Well, I heard you, too." For the first time, I note that her face looks slightly ashen, as if our combined magic took a toll on her as well. "I could *feel* you getting dizzy. If I had put any more power into that spell, it could have been worse than simply seeing you faint, Cavas."

I take a deep breath. *Don't lose it, don't lose it.* "You can't fight this war if you're so scared of hurting me."

"Do you *want* me to hurt you?" she demands. "Do you want to die at my hands before taking your revenge?"

"Javer's b—" I break off before finishing the curse. "This isn't about that!" *Not completely, anyway.* "I mean that this is your war, too, Gul! Whether you like it or not."

My rising voice silences her. It silences me as well when I see how badly she's shaking. *Well done, fool. Now you've terrified her.*

"Gul," I whisper. "Gul, look at me."

She does, but her jaw remains taut.

"We *have* joined powers in the past," I remind her. "My eyes were open then, and I didn't faint, either. The only difference was that we were touching—and now we're trying to merge powers at a distance."

"So you mean that proximity helps," Gul says, frowning.

"Maybe. Look. This is new to me, too. But you can't expect us to get everything perfect the first time. You told me that you went through two months of training with Amira before you could use death magic properly. Isn't that right?"

The logic in this must have hit home, because she doesn't retort.

"We're in this together, you and I," I say, meaning it. "No matter what happens. No matter what others say."

I gently cup her face in my hands. I'm tempted to kiss away her frown, but I sense that now isn't the right time. Instead, I simply rest my forehead against hers. To my relief, she doesn't pull away.

"I won't use magic if there's any danger to your life," she says. "Do you understand?"

My heart skips a beat. I imagine my spear, burning with magic and then dimming, dimming, my power gone. I imagine the Scorpion at a stone's throw away. I imagine General Alizeh, her back turned to me, a perfect target turning into a lost opportunity—because Gul refused to wield her powers.

Do you really need Gul, though? a traitorous voice whispers in my head. *Murder doesn't need magic. Seek out the general yourself. Kill her when you get close.*

I force a smile, grateful that Gul still has trouble accessing my thoughts.

"So I guess I'll have to make sure you do use your magic," I say out loud.

10

CAVAS

The next day, Subodh moves our lessons into the temple courtyard, where he has set up a series of wooden targets.

"How do you do it?" I ask Gul. "Keep your eyes open?"

"Well, what did you see when your eyes were closed?" she says.

"A darkened version of the temple in Tavan. You were there. So were the sky goddess and Sant Javer."

"Imagine that with your eyes open. Daydream a little."

I know her last suggestion is a joke, but I use it, and surprisingly, it works better than I expect. My eyes remain open, capable of seeing everything around me, but my mind is elsewhere—in an odd, empty space of calm, seeking something. A voice.

Gul's voice, to be specific.

Are you there? I call out.

Yes, she says, her voice fainter than normal but still audible. As I focus more, I can feel other things: magic, fiercely restrained, a seething energy under my fingertips. *We're aiming for the first post*, she tells me.

An attacking spell. It makes me a little nervous, combining my

83

powers with Gul's already deadly magic in this regard. But I breathe deep and aim for the sthirta that Subodh had talked about. At the very last second, I close my eyes very briefly. This time, I don't faint or fall. I only feel magic unraveling from me like a chain.

Open your eyes, Gul says.

I obey and see a swirl of golden light combine with the glowing green sphere that now hangs suspended over Gul. She raises her right arm, and the sphere turns into an arrow, skewering the first wooden target, shattering the disc into chips.

I'm grinning. *We did it. We did it.*

But Gul must feel otherwise, because the smile she gives me in response is weak. From the cool gaze Subodh directs our way, I sense he feels the same, even though he nods and says, "Well done, Cavas. Xerxes and Harkha would be proud to see you."

It's strange to hear my mother's name spoken out loud. Stranger to see her appear somewhere in the distance behind Subodh, as if summoned. She smiles at me, a mix of pride and fear on her face. As I begin turning away, I spot a blue-clad figure behind a dhulvriksh, watching us. It's one of the Legion's soldiers. The woman named Roda.

Then Subodh turns his attention to Gul, and my grin fades.

"From what I've heard, you shouldn't have needed a complement's powers for that meager display, Star Warrior," he says. "You should have reduced a single target to dust on your own. With a complement's power combined, *all* three targets should have been destroyed. Esther told me that you've also been doing only simple demonstrations of magic for the Legion during practice. This won't be enough for a war—and you know it."

Gul's jaw tightens, but she says nothing in response. It's true, of course. Gul has done worse damage with magic on her own.

"You must get over your fear of hurting others, child." Subodh's voice is iron, wrapped in silk. "Remember that Cavas is strong. So are the women who've dedicated their lives to the Legion. Come now, let us try again."

But no matter how many times we try, the result is much the same, sweat soaking our clothes at the end of the session.

"I'm trying, Cavas," Gul speaks quietly so that Subodh can't hear. "I swear, I am."

"I know you are," I say. As her complement, I'm acutely aware, not only of the fiery magic in her blood but also her fears and her truths. "But Subodh is right, Gul. Your heart isn't in the spell, somehow. Something's holding you back. It's me, isn't it? You're still afraid of knocking me out."

She says nothing.

"I can place a bale of hay nearby and try to aim for it when I fall," I offer.

But Gul only looks more dejected at my joke. "I'm heading to breakfast," she says. I think I see tears gleaming in her eyes before she abruptly turns away.

I let her go. It isn't a good time to tell her that my mother and Roda witnessed her embarrassment. Subodh, I suspect, already knows about both. Those great yellow eyes of his miss no one, living or dead. Now they're focused on the golden bars guarding Tavan and the shadows of the specters circling them.

"How much longer do we have?" I ask him once Gul is gone.

"I don't know." Subodh turns to face me. "You and Gul are doing better than I expected. But she's still not willing—or able—to use the full extent of her power. If we are attacked tomorrow, it won't be enough."

A pair of flags hang limp over the temple's spires, not the slightest breeze stirring them.

"I could try to talk to the specters," I say. "Try to persuade them to stay longer."

"Esther knows Tavan's specters best," Subodh says quietly. "If she can't convince them, no one can. You and Gul focus on training. And regardless of what happens, don't get separated during a battle. You are stronger together than you are apart."

I swallow hard, wondering if the Pashu king somehow senses the thoughts I've been having recently about seeking out General Alizeh and killing her myself. After practicing with Gul today, the idea has grown only more tempting. But Subodh doesn't expound on his warning, so, a moment later, I say:

"Thank you for your help. Without your knowledge about meditation and complements, Gul and I would be lost."

"You're welcome. Though I don't think it's true that you and Gul would be completely helpless. The Pashu are a much older race than humans, yes, but we are only marginally more knowledgeable. Perhaps it would have taken you both a little longer to figure out your complementary bond, but you would have reached there eventually."

"I wish someone knew how to rid us of the Scorpion."

"A throne's conquest isn't necessarily a victory. The day she overthrew Raja Amar, Shayla claimed the title of Sikandar, or Victor, as you say in the Common Tongue. Yet, if things continue as they have been over the past week or so, it won't be long before her own people call her Sitamgar."

Oppressor.

I recall the last few lines of the new prophecy that the living specters have been singing over the past few days. "Is the specters' prophecy true? Is Amar still alive?"

"Yes," Subodh says after a pause. "It took me a couple of months to confirm this, but yes. He's in hiding right now."

"Are you sure it's him and not an impostor?"

"His mother would know, wouldn't she? Amba was the one who told me."

It's startling to hear Queen Amba's name spoken out loud and with such familiarity. Amar's haughty mother, Lohar's first queen, was intimidating on her best days, terrifying on her worst. But there's a strange, distant look in Subodh's yellow eyes—one that tells me he isn't thinking about living specters anymore.

"You knew each other?" I venture. "You and Rani Amba."

"We did. At one time. Amba wasn't a queen then, but a noble-woman's daughter. She had come of age the summer we first met. A few years later, her mother, the last remaining member of the Chand gharana, bound her to Raja Lohar."

The Chand gharana is an old magi clan whose descendants claim to trace their bloodline back to the moon goddess Sunheri. For centuries—some say since the time of the first queen of Ambar—Chand gharana members have been binding with the royal family. Queen Megha was the only one to break tradition, taking no mate from the clan.

"Amba and I stayed in touch the first year after her binding," Subodh continues. "Sent each other letters by shvetpanchhi. Then she abruptly stopped writing. My own shvetpanchhi was found shot by an arrow somewhere outside Ambar Fort. I didn't expect her to reach out to me after so many years. But she has. To protect her son, of course."

Bitterness enters his voice, leaving me at a loss for words. It's the most I've heard the Pashu king speak about his past. I'm still mulling over what to say when he turns and begins walking back toward the temple.

My stomach growls loudly, and with a sigh, I head to the mess hall, hoping breakfast hasn't already ended. Inside, Gul is sitting with a few women from the Legion. She smiles when she sees me enter, and I can't help but feel relieved. Clearly, whatever the women said has put her at ease.

Roda raises her eyebrows when she sees our exchange. Someone else's comment leads to laughter and Gul's lowering her head in embarrass-ment. I feel my own ears turning red. Gul and I do not hide the fact that we both sleep in her room and on her bed. And though we haven't done anything except sleep so far, I am aware of the sort of conjectures appearances can lead to.

Later that night, I wake sweating after a nightmare . . . only to turn around and find Gul watching me. "You don't scream," she says quietly.

"No." Sunheri's light pours in through the window, casting gold over us both. "You didn't sleep?"

"I couldn't. Sometimes I think it's easier not to."

I know exactly what she means. Unwilling to let my thoughts take me to darker places, I focus on Gul's face: her delicate features, the dent in her stubborn chin. I reach out to brush a lock of hair out of her eyes. I allow my hand to linger, to trace the shell of her ear with my fingers.

"You have piercings." I'm surprised to feel the shape of them, the slight dips of flesh along her ear and in the center of her soft lobe.

"Ma had my ears pierced when I was very small. Later, when I was fifteen, one of the girls at the Sisterhood pierced my nose. I don't use them very often." She closes her eyes as my fingers gently tug on her earlobe, her lashes fluttering against her cheeks. The three silver beads she always wears around her neck rest in the hollow of her throat.

"Your necklace . . ." My voice trails off.

"My mother's. Well, the beads at least. I picked them off the ground after she died." Her eyes open, bore into mine. "I don't want to think about that now, though."

Neither do I. Which is why, when she inches closer, I let her, parting my lips when I feel hers brushing mine. Kissing her feels like tasting a rose, like cool water poured down a parched throat. Warmth prickles the back of my neck and my cheek, my skin coming alive under her calloused fingers.

When we break apart for air, I say, "It feels like I've been waiting forever to kiss you."

"Three months and sixteen days. The last time was in Chand Mahal."

"You kept count?" I ask, amused. "Am I going to find a tally somewhere in this room?"

"You weren't the only one waiting."

She trails kisses over my throat. I shiver.

Two can play that game.

I sit her up and push aside her heavy, fragrant hair. Fitting my mouth to the soft curve between her neck and shoulder, I allow my teeth to lightly graze her skin, making her gasp.

She doesn't stop my hand from moving down her back or from drawing the sleep tunic she wears up and over her head. Her skin looks like honey, darker in some places, lighter in others. Her arms twitch at her sides and I wonder if she's refraining from crossing them over her chest. Her small breasts slope downward, peak into dark-brown tips, and then dip into perfect curves.

Before I can touch her, though, her strong hands slide up my torso and tug impatiently at my tunic.

"Fair's fair, pretty boy," she says, a smile belying her mocking tone. "I'm not the only one getting naked."

I pull off my shirt and toss it to the floor.

She grins and soon our clothes are flying everywhere until we're fully bared to each other.

I fidget, resisting the urge to hide under the covers as Gul's gaze travels over my protruding collarbones and too-thin torso. Her eyes are full of awe, a wonder I don't understand.

She brushes her fingers up my arm, over the slight curve of my bicep. I mirror her movements and soon the awkwardness between us melts into curiosity—an exploration by eager hands and lips as we fumble our way into fitting our bodies together.

Later, we lie in bed, sweat-limned and glistening in the moonlight.

She might have whispered a good night. I might have responded in kind.

Sleep follows.

Neither of us dream.

11

GUL

Subodh is the first to figure out that things have changed when Cavas and I combine our powers during training the morning after . . . and turn our targets into dust.

"You are lovers now," Subodh declares, sniffing hard. "Yes. The air reeks of it."

I will the ground beneath my feet to turn into quicksand and swallow me whole. Cavas must be equally embarrassed, but he doesn't break eye contact with the Pashu king.

"Is that a problem?" he asks coolly.

"Not really," Subodh replies. "Considering that the only other complements in history, Sunheri and Neel, were also lovers. Such a bond strengthens both trust and magic; it will likely help you communicate over greater distances. Of course, should you choose to part ways or take other lovers, it will weaken the way it did for the moon goddesses."

"What makes you think we'll do such a thing?" My sharp tone makes Cavas turn and raise his eyebrows in warning.

Subodh looks unperturbed. "You are still young. You will meet others. You will change your minds several times over."

"Or maybe we won't," Cavas interjects. "Maybe the things you said won't make a difference."

On instinct, I reach out to slip my hand into his.

"You're offended, which is understandable," Subodh says. "Under normal circumstances, I wouldn't comment on this. But as your trainer, I have the duty to explain what can affect your powers. Love is a strange thing. I've seen it grow between people; I've seen it fade. Staying in love is often a choice." There's a distant look on the Pashu king's face, turning it unreadable. "But I might be wrong. Perhaps you both will turn out different. Only time will tell."

My mind stews over Subodh's words throughout training—even when Agni and Ajib interrupt the session by galloping around us and kicking up clouds of dust.

"They're chasing a living specter," Cavas explains, his expression forcibly cheerful. "Nothing serious."

Translation: *No breach by Sky Warriors so far.*

After Subodh dismisses us for the day, Cavas and I walk back to the barracks for breakfast. I must have been walking faster than normal, because Cavas calls out to me a couple of times, jogging to catch up.

"You're angry," he says.

"I'm not!"

"Yes, you are. You're brooding over what Raja Subodh said."

"I'm not!" *Liar.* "I'm . . ." I sigh and then admit the truth. "What if he's right, Cavas? What if we do . . . fall apart?"

I don't mention love. Or hint to the anxiety that's now rushing through my veins at the idea of being separated from him. But, though Cavas is my complement, he does not try to find out what I'm thinking now that our session is over.

"You're the Star Warrior," he says. "Your power is too strong to be affected by the loss of a mere complement."

"Don't joke about such things. These days I can't even blow up a target the way I'm supposed to."

"A temporary setback. You can't produce the same results every time, Gul. Everyone has bad days."

Yet I can hear the frustration under his reassuring words, see it in the frowns he's no longer able to smooth away.

"I know I don't have the luxury of bad days, Cavas. We could be breached at any moment." *And I'm still not ready.*

"Gul . . . Gul! Listen." Cavas cuts across my path, gently placing his hands on my shoulders. "No single battle has ever won or lost a war. And I believe that no matter what happens, you won't let us down."

He does believe this. Maybe it's a part of his being my complement, but now that he's touching me, I can *feel* his trust, prickling against my skin like his magic. Our gazes lock the way they did last night, right before we sank into each other, and I sense something else. An emotion close to lust, but not quite.

"Gul, I—" A pair of screams rise in the air, cutting Cavas off.

My skin breaks out in goose bumps, while Cavas spins in the opposite direction to watch the shimmering golden bars, an ominous, never-ending line.

"What is it?" I ask when he's silent for a moment too long. "What happened?"

He slowly turns around to face me again, his lips leeched of color. "Another living specter has disappeared."

12

GUL

Flowers that bloom in the desert during the Month of Song begin wilting eleven days into the Month of Sloughing. It's around this time that Esther accosts me and Cavas in the mess hall, a grim expression on her face.

"Here," she says, handing me a little cloth bag, the kind used for storing herbs or medicine. "Drink this with your morning tea every day."

"What for? What is this?" I ask, confused. Behind me, Cavas groans, covering his face with his hands.

Esther's lips purse, and I'm not entirely sure if it's because she's annoyed or suppressing a smile. "These are herbs to prevent accidental children during a war. They'll work no matter when you take them. Just be careful with the doses—I've marked out how much you need to take here on this cup."

The words take a moment to sink in. When they do, I can barely look her in the eye. I snatch the packet and the wooden cup from her hands and slip them into my pocket. It's not exactly a secret that Cavas and I share the same bedroom, though it's only recently that we became lovers. Even so, conjecture is different from reality, and the realization of how *visible* we've been this whole time is freshly appalling. I was so wrapped up in Cavas and basking in the high of my new feelings that I completely forgot about the living specters who come spying on us occasionally. Clearly one of them must have told Esther.

Queen's curses, was it Cavas's mother?!

The slim possibility of Cavas's mother having witnessed our nighttime activities live makes me want to sink into the ground. A moment after we get served our food—roti, yellow daal, and pickled honeyweed—Kali comes to sit next to us.

"You may want to close your door," she tells me, smirking. "Walls have ears, you know."

I elbow her hard. "We do close the door!"

"Don't worry." Kali grins openly now. "I'm the only one who can hear you. And only occasionally. I've learned to stuff my ears with cotton before sleeping. I told Esther to give you the herbs."

"How are your sessions with the women going?" I force myself to change the subject. "Have they been able to regain some of their magic?"

"Not really," Kali says, concentrating on her food. "Most don't have the patience required for meditation."

"What about Sami?" I ask, spotting the young woman a few feet away, talking to Roda and Falak.

"She's the only one who has shown some aptitude," Kali says, her expression neutral. "She accidentally grew some flowers out of the sand yesterday. There might be some earth magic in her. Not of much use in battle."

"Rajkumari Malti was—*is*—pretty strong with her earth magic," I say, remembering the little princess with a pang. What must be happening to Malti now—with Shayla on the throne? "She was more than likely capable of burying people alive with mere taps of her feet."

"Well, Sami is nowhere near that point," Kali says. "None of them are."

94

And I doubt they will be. Though she doesn't say the words out loud, I sense the implication from her tone.

"The Scorpion has probably placed Rajkumari Malti in shackles by now," Cavas mutters.

His pronouncement sounds bleaker against the backdrop of eating and chattering women, some like Roda laughing without a care in the world.

Instead of watching me train with the Legion, today Esther and Cavas decide to patrol the borders again to check how many more specters have gone missing.

The women pick up on my mood, wincing whenever I snap at them for their mistakes.

"You're not perfect, either, Star Warrior," Roda points out finally. "You could cut us some slack."

There's a warning in her tone—one that reminds me how fragile my new bond with the Legion is. I'm about to lash out—with a combination of words and magic I've so far held back—when Kali's cool voice interrupts.

"Gul, why don't you take a break? I'll handle the remaining session."

I stalk off, the desert air doing little to cool my burning cheeks.

Moments later, I feel lower than I did this morning, when Cavas told me about another living specter disappearing. A shadow falls across my face, shielding me from the sun. Sami.

"Are you all right?" she asks. "You aren't yourself today."

"I'm worse than I ever was," I admit. *And I'm still not exposing you to the sort of magic you'll be facing in battle.* "Why do you still want me to lead you?"

"Because, when you're good, you're really good, Gul. Even Roda said so. I've seen you in a battle—a real battle. I feel safer having you and Cavas with us."

95

I find myself smiling faintly. Sami didn't add *ji* after my name. And her confidence has buoyed my spirits.

"How are your sessions going?" I ask. "Kali says you have some earth magic in you."

Sami's face brightens. "I grew *flowers*! Out of sand!" She sighs, wiping the sweat off her forehead. "But Kali always seems annoyed with me for some reason. I don't think she likes me."

No. She likes you too much.

"Kali's best friend, Amira, would get annoyed with me frequently," I tell Sami. "We eventually learned to, er, like each other."

"Kali talks about Amira a lot." Sami's muscular body tenses. "Are they . . . close?"

"The way sisters are," I say truthfully. "Kali and Amira kept each other sane in a labor camp much like this one until Juhi rescued them. They would give their lives for each other."

"The way I would for Esther Didi or any of the Legion," Sami says, releasing a sigh. She looks into the distance behind me. "Do you really think that Kali—"

A sharp neigh pierces the air, cutting Sami off.

It's Agni, galloping toward us.

"Agni! Agni, what's wrong?" I ask. Kali and the practicing women have fallen silent, watching us both now with apprehensive faces. I ignore them and focus on the mare, who is snorting, her back slick with sweat.

It's all right, I whisper through our bond. *What is it? Tell me.*

It's Ajib, Agni responds. *He slipped past the southern boundary—must have found a gap in the bars—and into the desert outside. I called for him to come back, but he didn't.*

My stomach plummets. Ajib isn't a stallion who wanders off easily; he is as even-tempered as Agni is fiery. It's possible that something—or someone—drew him outside. Another whisperer, perhaps. Yet, if Ajib can't find a way back in, it means the magic spun by Subodh and the living specters must still hold to some degree.

Or someone else got to him.

Are they outside? I ask Agni. *The Sky Warriors?*

Yes, she replies. *About fifty soldiers. There's a boy with them as well. He can see living specters.*

A seer. I bite back a curse.

"I need to find Subodh or Esther," I tell Sami. "Ajib found a way out of the southern boundary and into the desert. There are fifty Sky Warriors out there *and* a seer!"

"Raja Subodh was on patrol duty, but he should be back by now," Sami says. "I'll come with you."

"Can we do something?" It's Falak and some of the other women who have broken apart from the practicing group, their weapons in hand.

"Stay alert. Keep your weapons with you at all times," I tell them, trying to sound calm despite my quaking insides. My gaze falls on a frowning Roda. "And I'm sorry. I behaved abominably at practice today."

Roda nods, but her expression remains the same. "Go on, Star Warrior."

And so I do, with Sami and Kali in tow, nearly running into Subodh and Esther at the temple entrance.

"Where's Cavas?" I ask, looking around.

"He should be back any moment," Esther says. "He was patrolling the northern boundary with his mother."

Subodh and Esther listen to my story about Ajib's disappearance and also to what Agni said about the Sky Warriors congregated outside.

"Fifty," Subodh mutters, as if calculating something in his head. "We will need to send a message to Rani Sarayu and—" His voice cuts off abruptly. Without warning, he lunges forward, his body uncoiling to sprint across the courtyard.

When I see the reason for his distraction—Cavas racing toward us, carrying his spear and shield—I run as well, my pulse pounding in my ears.

"There's . . . breach . . . northwest boundary." Cavas can barely get the words out. "Nearly four specters disappeared at once . . . There's a wide gap between the bars. There are Sky Warriors outside and Ambari foot soldiers—all geared for battle." His face is as ashen as mine feels. "There must be a hundred of them."

I bite back a curse. A hundred Sky Warriors and foot soldiers at the northern end and fifty or more at the southern end—that's thrice as many as us. Without another word, Subodh gallops toward the reservoir, likely to talk to the Pashu queen, Sarayu.

"Is that the only breach?" Esther asks Cavas.

"Yes," he says. "Though there might be more now that I don't know of."

Esther nods and then turns to the Tavani women.

"Saavdhaan!" Esther booms for the Legion's attention in the Common Tongue, the silver stars on her forehead gleaming in the afternoon light. Within moments, the women form into three columns, the familiar instruction making it almost feel as if we're back at lathi practice.

"Can you hear me?" Esther shouts.

"Yes, Commander!" the Legion roars.

"The war has begun and the enemy is at our boundary. We must outwit, outmaneuver, and do our best to evade any attacking spells."

"Yes, Commander!"

The Legion are surprisingly calm. On Esther's command, they draw their lathis, now reinforced with gleaming iron tips; they hold up those old, rusting, magic-repelling shields, almost as if it's second nature to them.

"Do not fear the enemy's greater numbers. There will be Sky Warriors, yes, but also foot soldiers like yourselves. You are the Legion of the Star Warrior. You have been practicing for this very moment for the past two decades. So tell me now: Whom do you fight for?"

"The Star Warrior!" the women bellow.

"What do you fight for?"

"Freedom!"

"One of us must fight three of them," Esther says. "Have we trained for this?"

"Yes, Commander!"

"Is victory ours or the kabzedar rani's?"

Voices merge in a resounding chorus, followed by a familiar chant:

The sky has fallen, a star will rise!
The sky has fallen, a star will rise!

"I will take the right flank," Esther commands. "Kali will take the left. Falak, you'll be in charge of the command center and the reserve army."

I frown, seeing the look that passes between them and Falak's sharp nod.

As I make a move to step forward, Esther pulls me back. "No, Gul. You and Cavas stay back with Falak. You are not to go into battle until she says so."

"But—"

"No buts," Esther says firmly. "If Rani Shayla targets anyone first, it will be you two. Whatever happens, you cannot get caught. So don't do anything rash. And always stick together."

Ignoring my protests, she turns back to the Legion and shouts: "Charge!"

13

GUL

Esther, Kali, and half of the Legion march to the north end of the city, toward the training center and the barracks. Agni stays with me, her presence allowing me to maintain a semblance of calm in front of the reserve army.

As we wait, Falak paces back and forth without looking at anyone else, and I can tell she hates being left behind as much as I do. But Kali is the only one in Tavan, apart from me, who can fight with death magic. She can help hold off some of the Sky Warriors' worst spells. Maybe.

"Is *she* there, too?" I ask Cavas in an undertone. "Shayla?"

"I don't know," he replies, equally quiet. His face is taut in a way I've seen only once before—when he told me he'd signed up for King Lohar's army. "General Alizeh is, though."

My already tense insides coil. "Cavas, I know what you're thinking. But, please, by all that's holy, don't do anything rash."

"Like killing her, you mean?"

He holds up his spear, as if examining it, the newly sharpened tip reflecting in his cold brown eyes. He does not look at me.

"Cavas, you can't!" As dearly as I agree with his sentiment, Alizeh is a seasoned Sky Warrior. She'll kill Cavas before he knows what happened. "We need to stick together and protect the Legion as much as possible. Now *isn't* the time for revenge."

"It doesn't matter," he says, locking gazes with me. "If I get close enough, I won't even need magic to kill her. I won't need you."

My face smarts as if slapped.

"Cavas, listen. I *know* how it feels," I speak quietly, though I want to shout. I sense that some of the reserve army is watching us, trying to listen in. "I felt the same way whenever I saw Raja Lohar or whenever I heard his name. But I was shortsighted. I didn't see how my actions would affect the people around me. I didn't—"

"Saavdhaan!" Falak's sharp command severs all thought. I inhale sharply upon spotting several figures racing toward us. It's Sami and some others from Esther's contingent, their faces and tunics splattered with blood.

"Esther Didi's dead!" Sami cries out. "Kali's trying to hold them off. But they're coming, Falak Didi! They're coming!"

The shock of Sami's announcement hasn't even registered when Falak takes control. "Arms at ready!" she shouts. "Keep your shields raised high!"

"Stay close," I tell Cavas. "Don't leave my side!"

Though he doesn't answer except for a nod, his brown eyes hold none of their earlier animosity. I force myself to breathe in and out, visualizing the sky goddess in my head. Slowly, but surely, my heart rate grows steady and I enter a state of sthirta. Everything else in the real world moves at half its normal speed. My magic surrounds me, suspended in the air like shimmering, rainbow-hued particles of indradhanush—metal drops ready to be shaped, to change color at my command.

I turn to Cavas, whose eyes are glowing white.

Can you hear me? I ask telepathically.

A few seconds go by before I hear his answer. *Yes. Are you planning to attack first?*

Do we have a choice?

Ambari foot soldiers in russet tunics and brown leather helmets are now racing toward the temple, headed by a pair of Sky Warriors on steeds. I recognize Captain Emil in his blue-and-silver Sky Warrior garb, and next to him, General Alizeh in white, the cloth winding her helmet flying behind her.

I raise my daggers and shoot a beam of green light at Captain Emil, neutralizing the attack from his atashban. To my left, Agni rears on her hind legs, scaring off one foot soldier and trampling another who attempts to throw a dagger at me.

Up ahead, Falak slashes out with her spear, killing a burly foot soldier and then spinning around to knock heads with another. The Legion's reserve army follows her lead, its lathis rotating in deadly arcs, and soon enough several bodies are strewn across the ground, the foot soldiers knocked out cold. In fact, I'm surprised at how inexperienced some of the soldiers are. I can tell they have never seen battle before, their terrified faces appearing barely older than mine.

Gul! To your left! Cavas's voice rings in my head. His magic merges with mine like a jolt, much stronger than expected. I spin and throw up a shield, barely deflecting twin spears that two other soldiers aim our way.

Don't lose focus, Cavas says. *They may be young, but they're armed.*

I heed his warning. The foot soldiers might be magi, but not all are capable of death magic. Of the lot here, few are able to throw up magical shields. The Legion are more than a match for the foot soldiers, their lathis cracking over heads. The only attacking spells come from General Alizeh's and Captain Emil's atashbans—and Cavas and I block each one.

They thought . . . weren't strong enough . . . them. Cavas's voice, so clear in my head before, begins fragmenting, some words fading before I can hear them. The battle has forced us to drift a few more feet away from each other, though I can still catch glimpses of him between other fighters. I'm still close enough to feel Cavas's anger—and his triumph—when Alizeh snarls out loud with frustration.

Don't move too far, I warn him. *Our magic needs proximity to work.* I also want to tell Cavas that the battle isn't yet over, that things could change at any time.

But before I can, General Alizeh raises her atashban and aims it behind her, at a sky-blue figure leaping into the air—a Legion soldier, whose spear misses the general's ear by an inch. There's a single, terrible flash of red light and the Tavani woman drops to the ground, her body trampled by Alizeh's horse. Before I can react, Alizeh forces her horse in a circle, shooting her atashban simultaneously. Three more Legion soldiers fall in quick succession, no match for her deadly skill.

Shield! I call out to Cavas. *Amplify!*

But there's no answering energy—no sign of Cavas's power merging with mine. I throw up a shield on my own, somehow protecting myself and another woman behind me from the stray red beams of Alizeh's rapidly shooting atashban.

Cavas! My heart quickens, panic rising. *Cavas, where are you?*

I spin around—and spot Cavas aiming his spear at General Alizeh, shooting a spell at her.

"No!" I scream out loud. *Cavas, what are you* doing?

It's a mistake. Distracted, I break out of the meditative state, everything around me rapidly returning to normal speed.

General Alizeh easily sidesteps Cavas's attempted attack. Her spell slashes the air like a whip, a flaming coil aimed right at Cavas's shield. "Gul!" Sami shouts before I can neutralize Alizeh's attack. "Behind you!"

Narrowly missing the sharp edge of a spear, I shoot at a pair of foot soldiers, targeting their legs instead of their hearts. The soldiers—boys who look no older than thirteen—flee, abandoning their weapons and shields. But by the time I turn around again, Cavas has disappeared—and so has Alizeh.

I force myself to breathe deeply and focus on the image of the sky goddess again, trying to find the sthirta Subodh had always stressed during practice. To my relief, everything around me slows again.

Cavas? I call out. *Cavas, can you hear me?*

Sand erupts in clouds around the fighters—more spells from atashbans blurring my vision. I lose sight of Agni, though I still hear her neighing in the background. I'm about to plunge into the melee when I think I hear my name. Feel the skitter of a heartbeat other than my own.

Cavas, where are you?

My voice is a lone scream in my head.

"Cavas!" My magic erupts from my daggers with a *boom*: a veil of red light that obscures the sun for a brief moment. "Cavas!"

Bodies part, making way for me. In the dusty haze rising around us, I can no longer distinguish one face from another. But I can see color. A figure in white astride a horse, dragging along a prone body on a rope.

Before I can move, something hits me from the side like a battering ram. A spear cuts through the air overhead, while I hit the ground, teeth rattling within my jaw. I turn to the person who pushed me out of the way—Sami, her face terrified. "Gul, you can't follow them! We'll lose you, too, otherwise!"

"She has Cavas! General Alizeh—"

A roar cuts off my voice, making my hackles rise. Subodh races on his hind legs toward us, a giant mace in his hands. Behind him, a flock of screeching shvetpanchhi streak the sky, diving down to peck at the soldiers' hands and faces. Rani Sarayu's army of birds. Captain Emil struggles to control his skittish horse from bucking him off. He raises his atashban, aiming right at the rajsingha's heart.

I'm about to hit Emil with a spell when Subodh leaps into the air—all ten feet of him—and gives the captain what appears to be a light smack on the cheek with his mace. The impact throws Captain Emil off his horse. His face bleeding profusely now, the captain raises his atashban again. But instead of shooting the way I expect him to, he shouts something inaudible, slashing the air before him. In the distance, I see them again—Alizeh and Cavas, growing smaller and smaller as they move past the boundary.

"Cavas!" I shout, racing toward them, the battle around me forgotten. "CAVAS!"

White light erupts from Captain Emil's atashban, followed by a darkness so thick that it obscures everything. My lungs seize at the smell—sulfur and smoke and the coppery odor of blood. Tears flow out of my eyes as I cough. I fight the pair of arms that go around me, but they're much too strong.

"Don't, Gul!" Sami's voice sounds as tearful as I feel. "Don't go farther! That smoke is poisoned!"

The smoke dissipates to reveal bodies lying on the ground: a woman in blue with stars on her forehead and two Ambari foot soldiers. In the distance, I watch Subodh twirl a mace with his powerful arms, crack it over a Sky Warrior's head. Falak snarls, fighting one of the last remaining foot soldiers. Everywhere is chaos and blood and noise.

"Retreat!" Alizeh's voice, magnified by magic, makes my skin crawl. "Infantry, retreat!"

But when I finally break free of Sami's grip and go to look, I don't see her anywhere. Neither do I see Cavas.

The foot soldiers disappear as soon as the general calls for a retreat.

"Most of them weren't even magi," Subodh mutters after sniffing one corpse. "Probably poor tenement dwellers who were persuaded into battle for a few coins."

Pain flares sharply within me as I think of Cavas, my heart pulsing, my breaths turning short. Cavas, captured by the Sky Warriors and taken to the usurper queen. It will be difficult to catch up with them now.

Unless . . .

I race to Subodh, gasping out the words in the wrong order: "Rani Sarayu . . . can she . . . Cavas . . . rescue."

New lines etch Subodh's scarred face. He shakes his great head. "I've been trying to contact Rani Sarayu myself. I have been doing so even before we learned of the breach. But her birds can't find her yet. It might still take a few hours, perhaps a day. By then, it will be too late. I'm sorry. The boy is lost to us."

"No, he's not! I won't let him! I'll go after him myself!"

"And it's exactly what they want!" A shadow cuts across my path, familiar hands falling firmly over my shoulders. It's Kali, her pale face streaked with someone else's blood. "Think, Gul. They failed to capture you, so they've captured him, instead. They *want* you to follow them to Ambarvadi."

"That is what I'm supposed to do anyway, isn't it? To go back there and fight them!"

Too late, I feel the shackles of Kali's immobility spell, the sort that not only restrains my limbs but also freezes my tongue.

"I'm sorry," she whispers. "But you need to calm down first. The other women are scared."

My eyes move from side to side, taking in tired, blood-streaked faces, frightened expressions.

They are looking for a leader, Subodh whispers through our bond. *If you react this way, you will die before Cavas can be saved. And you will kill everyone else who fought for you.*

His words claw at me, forcing me to think.

Ask Kali to unfreeze me, I whisper back to Subodh. *Please. I won't do anything rash. I swear on the sky goddess.*

Subodh stares at me briefly and then nods at Kali. A moment later, my tongue unrolls itself, my limbs feeling strangely loose.

"We can't stay here much longer," Subodh says. "Tavan is no longer hidden from outsiders. We'll have to take the risk of crossing the desert now and finding Raja Amar."

The golden bars that once surrounded the city, making it invisible, have now mostly disappeared, many living specters fading as soon as the breach occurred. Wails rise around me, but they aren't coming from the remaining women of the Legion or Kali. *It's the specters*, I realize. Those who have still not faded.

I wonder if Cavas's mother is among them—if she, too, blames me for losing her son.

Have *you lost him though, Gul?*

While my heart skips a beat, my mind protests at the impossibility of communicating with Cavas from such a distance. A few feet is the farthest we have been apart while meditating. There is no way of knowing if our bond can navigate the miles that the Sky Warriors have already put between us.

Step back, little one. The voice in my head isn't mine, but my father's. *Allow yourself to look at the bigger picture.*

I close my eyes and breathe deep. The memory of Papa's voice allows me to detach momentarily from my fears and reassess the situation. General Alizeh has captured Cavas *alive*. She and Shayla will likely keep him that way for now—if only to gain information about me and the rebellion.

Cavas is alive. I focus on the thought again, repeat it to myself the way I would a spell.

Without the strain of battle, it's easier to breathe deep and find sthirta, to feel the magic humming in my body. I spot the sky goddess watching from a distance, her skin the color of a sky blurred with rising dust and blood, as I call out to Cavas: *Cavas. Are you there?*

Long moments pass by.

There is no answer.

14

GUL

Of the fifty Legion women who lived in Tavan when I first got here, only twenty remain after the breach. A pair of them now prepare the fallen for burial—Esther, Roda, Nav, and others—cleaning their faces as best as they can before wrapping them in shrouds. The rest of us dig burial pits in front of the temple, where we had practiced fighting with magic. After today's battle, we know we will not remain in Tavan any longer.

"The city is not safe," Subodh says. "We need to leave soon—tomorrow at the latest. Traveling at night will be our best option. There is no telling when the Sky Warriors will return."

They won't return now, I think wearily. *They have Cavas. They know I will come to them.*

Subodh glances sideways, and I wonder if he heard my thoughts through our bond, but his great yellow eyes are wet, and I realize he isn't looking at me.

"Let me," he tells Falak, rising to his hind legs and walking over to where Esther's body lies. Subodh's forehead gently brushes hers before he lifts her up in his arms. Esther is a tall woman, but in Subodh's arms, she looks surprisingly small. A soft white glow surrounds them both.

"You were born to this earth and you died for it, Ghiyas-putri Esther." Subodh's deep voice intones a single line from the Holy Scroll: one used for fallen soldiers at funerals.

"You were born to this earth and you died for it," voices around me echo.

"Sky goddess, accept your child and her immortal soul," Subodh says.

The women repeat his words, tears pouring down their faces.

The back of my throat pricks. As Subodh lowers Esther into the ground, the other fallen women begin glowing with the same white light. For a brief, startling moment, each face looks completely at ease, as if they aren't dead but merely asleep. As the prayers for the fallen continue, I allow my own tears to fall. Picking up shovels like the others, I help them pour sand over the bodies in the burial pits.

The Legion of the Dead.

I hear Roda's voice—so clear in my memory—and I nearly drop my spade and spin around to see if she's still here. But she isn't, of course. Roda died trying to keep me safe. Something soft and wet nudges my shoulder—Agni, whose mane I bury my face into and sob, clinging to her the way I always have, whenever I couldn't share my pain with anyone else.

Once the burials are over, Kali calls out to me.

"Gul," she says. "Shouldn't we bury *them*, too?"

Something within me seizes when she points out the fallen Ambari foot soldiers. It's not sorrow. Not anger, either, exactly. *It's discomfort,* I realize. A feeling that makes me cringe at the flies that have started buzzing over many of the corpses.

"It doesn't seem right, leaving them like this," Kali continues. "Some were only children. Some weren't even magi."

"I am not touching them," Falak says. "Those *children* killed Esther. They killed Roda, Nav, Rohini, and so many others."

The other surviving women have similar hard looks on their faces. They will not touch them.

"I'll help you," I tell Kali. I think about how Cavas might have been one of these soldiers. How he would have done anything—even join King Lohar's army—to save his father's life. Who am I to judge someone else's desperation?

"I'll help, too." Sami steps forth with a shovel, ignoring Falak's glare.

Subodh works with us as well, using magic to burn holes in the ground for the Ambari soldiers, while Kali, Sami, and I heft each body in and shovel sand over them. There is no time to clean the bodies the right way or to cover them with shrouds, but we do our best.

Forgive us, sky goddess, I think. *Accept their souls.*

As he moves from body to body, Subodh also murmurs quietly, as if talking to someone.

"I'm checking to see if there are any living specters among them," he says when he catches me staring.

"Are there any?" I ask.

"A few," he admits. "I tried to recruit them to our cause, but I think I frightened many of them off. I don't have Esther's touch."

"Were there . . ." I lick my lips. "Were there any among the Legion?"

"Only one." Subodh pauses. "Most of the Legion died doing what they had always dreamed of—fighting for the Star Warrior."

My stomach churns. I can't bear to ask Subodh who the latest living specter is. I say nothing throughout the rest of the burials, pouring myself into shoveling sand over the bodies. Exhaustion creeps up my bones, but my insides remain as tightly wound as thread over a loom.

"Guilty, are you?" The voice that whispers into my ear belongs to a man. Only, no man—no living human—is next to me.

"Latif?" I ask hesitantly. "Is that you?"

"Pleased to finally make your acquaintance," the living specter replies. Grass sprouts from the ground—a trail that I follow away from the funeral proceedings.

"You haven't faded," I say. I don't know why, but somehow, I feel relieved about this.

"I haven't."

I blink back tears. "Esther's gone," I say. "So Indu has . . . has she . . . ?"

"She has faded, yes." Latif's disembodied voice is filled with sorrow. "Indu's greatest wish was to protect her sister. With Esther gone, Indu simply . . . broke apart."

I'm startled by the added grief I feel over not being able to hear Indu's strange singing or see her thick white fog again.

"What about Cavas's mother?" I ask, bracing myself for the worst. "Is she still here?"

"Yes, Harkha is still in specter form. The last I saw, she was chasing after her son as the city fell."

"But if she fades . . ." I can't say the rest of the words.

"She hasn't, as I said before," Latif says, his tone matter-of-fact. "We specters have our own ways of communicating with one another. I would know if Harkha was gone."

Breath rushes from my lungs. The grass forms a circle around me, sprouting around my sandaled feet. "That's remarkable. Your magic," I say, pointing to the patch of green in the dry earth.

"A fading remnant of an old life," he replies, and I recall that Latif was once head gardener at Ambar Fort.

"It's remarkable how you're still here, though," I reiterate. "You haven't faded while the other specters have."

"Their ties to the world weren't as painful as mine are—and therefore not as strong. Some would argue that this makes me weaker than they are, of course."

"What keeps you tied to the living world?"

"Ambar," he says simply. "Or Ambar under a good king. Sant Javer once said that his version of paradise was a garden and that, when he died, he wanted to enter it. When I was alive, I used my earth magic to emulate Javer's vision and tried to create the most beautiful garden I could think of. My playground was Ambar Fort, and so I had the tools I needed, every plant and flower at my disposal. But my little paradise was a sham, of course, built on the broken backs of non-magi and nurtured with the blood of enslaved Pashu. My heart remained uneasy as a young man, grew bitter and angry as an older one. So, in some ways, it doesn't surprise me that I'm still here. Waiting."

"Subodh says that I'm Ambar's only hope," I say. "Yet I can't promise a victory. I can't promise that I'll stay alive—or that my death will have any meaning."

"Your death could have some meaning to the rest of Ambar. You could be the martyr they could rally behind. But this kingdom has remained far too long without a living hero. People need to see you fight and live and thrive—even if Cavas doesn't."

Brutal as his words are, at least he isn't hiding the truth from me.

"It won't ever come to that," I promise. *If I have to die to save Cavas, I will.*

I ignore the prickle of warning in my chest, one that suggests I may not be able to live up to my vow.

THE THRONE OR
THE GRAVE

12th day of the Month of Sloughing
4 months into Queen Shayla's reign

15

SHAYLA

The nightmare is still brimming in my vision.

It comes to me from time to time, clouding my dreams ever since I made my first kill. An island in the middle of an ocean, black waves wild in a red sky. My arms sluice the water, strong and fast, the way they did when I swam through muddy Ambari ponds as a girl. On the island, there's a tree, skeletal branches extending like a hand uncurled in an offering. Hanging from the branches, clustered like jackfruit, are human heads with closed eyes and gaping mouths, in some cases, hollows where the noses are supposed to be—noses that I'd cut off while executing royal orders. Until last night, though, I never had the courage to speak up.

"What is this?" I asked in the dream. "Who are you?"

A small boy's eyes opened, two hollows bleeding red over his cheeks. I blinded this one before killing him—a nosy servant who saw me slipping a drop of poisonberry extract into King Lohar's morning milk.

"I am part of the tree of your sins, Megha-putri Shayla—and I am not even your first kill," the boy said. "Its roots run deep, more and more heads having appeared over the years. But the time has finally come. The tree can bear you fruit no longer."

If the boy were not already dead, I would have killed him then, all over again.

"Greater sinners than I continue to live. To thrive, despite everything they've done!" I told him.

"Their time will come," the boy said. "As will yours."

As he spoke, the Tree of Sins parted its branches, revealing a hollow within, shaped perfectly to fit a human head. Mine.

I woke with a start, my scream held back only by long hours of training and a sheer determination to never show any kind of weakness. Not to the cadets at the Sky Warrior academy. Certainly, not to the guard who now stands outside my door, day and night. The rising sun gleams red in the glass panes that make up Lohar's old bedroom. Dark clouds shroud the sky, cresting like the waves from my dream.

"The throne or the grave," I whisper, suppressing a shudder. "The throne or the grave."

Years ago, while training at the academy, fourteen would-be Sky Warriors were asked a single question: "What wakes you up in the morning?"

The other cadets spoke of their parents, their mates, the dream of a good home. When my turn came, I said, "The throne."

Two words, no explanation.

My fool instructor thought I was pledging my loyalty to King Lohar. Some of the other cadets laughed, saying that the only way I could get close to the king was by being his whore. Only Alizeh looked at me and saw what lurked under the mask I wore.

The truth. My ambition.

Now, over three decades later, the men who called me a whore are dead—perishing in the early elimination tests, their severed feet stuffed into their mouths.

My instructor had disparaged me for my conduct. "Killing your opponents does not mean you should desecrate a body."

"I only do to them what they did to me when I was alive," I said.

When they rendered me immobile with magic and crushed my teeth with their boots. When they stripped the clothes, and then the skin, off my back, leaving other scars that no amount of magic can undo.

The instructor fell silent. He said nothing about the deaths that happened afterward, not even when he found the last body scattered in pieces across the compound: ears, nose, fingers, limbs.

A knock on my door interrupts my reverie. "Ambar Sikandar! I have news!"

I sit up on my bed. "Enter, Captain."

A tall figure steps in; newly promoted, the Sky Warrior is bright-eyed and brimming with excitement. She gives me a deep bow.

"General Alizeh and Major Emil have returned, Ambar Sikandar," she says. "I apologize for disturbing you, but you asked me to come to you with the news right away."

"It's quite all right, Captain." I make my voice pleasant, which isn't entirely difficult when called by my new title. Ambar's Victor. "Ask the general to report to me as soon as possible."

The captain bows again. "My rani."

The sun begins pouring into the room, slowly leeching away the shadows of my nightmare. Of the past.

I toss aside the blanket and bedclothes, slipping out of the simple white tunic I always wear to bed. I pad barefoot across the thick paisley carpet to the giant almari in the corner that holds the royal wardrobe, opening the doors with a snap of my fingers. I don't rush to cover myself out of modesty upon hearing Alizeh's familiar tread. Alizeh has seen me at my best and at my worst. I have no secrets from her.

"Ambar Sikandar," she says, her soft voice neutral, the warning there undetectable to anyone who does not know her well. "You honor us with your presence."

Ah. So we are not alone.

116

Calmly, I continue to dress, slipping into the sleeves of my angrakha. This one has my new emblem embroidered over the collar and the hem: my mother's trident merged with a Sky Warrior's atashban. Leaving the ties open, I turn to find my most loyal adjutant and behind her the obsequious form of Ambar Fort's high priest—Lohar's most trusted advisor, Acharya Damak.

As always, the acharya is dressed in cream-colored robes of the finest silk. Jade beads garland his neck and wrists and swing delicately from his lobes. The acharya isn't as well dressed as he is well preserved. Under a head full of silver hair, his skin remains as taut and unscarred as the day I first saw him at court twenty years ago. Now his pale-green eyes rove over my bare legs, scan the scar over my torso, and linger on my naked breasts.

"Rani Shayla," he says. "My apologies. I will come at another time."

"Don't pretend to be squeamish, Acharya. I've seen you salivate over me in the past." I tie the strings of the angrakha over my left shoulder—the way Ambari royals do. "There was a reason you barged into my chambers with the commander of the armies. Get to the point."

"Ambar Sikandar," Damak says delicately, as polished as always, his eyes narrowing ever so slightly. "The zamindars are getting obstreperous again."

"Obstre-*what?*" Alizeh asks, frowning.

"Noisy," I translate. *Difficult to control.* "I'll have it taken care of, Acharya Damak."

The acharya coughs. "That's what I wanted to talk about. Perhaps it isn't wise to send out soldiers to, uh, persuade the landlords. My rani, might it not be wiser to meet with some of them? See them face-to-face, perhaps give them some gifts?"

"*Gifts?*" Ice stems from my voice, making the acharya wince. "The punishment for sedition is death, Acharya. Our treasury isn't meant to appease wealthy old farts with gold lining their tunics. Funds are low as is, thanks to the past raja's misappropriation of Ambar's assets."

"Not every zamindar is wealthy, Rani Shayla," the high priest says, frowning. "In the city, more and more people talk about how you increased the pay for the Sky Warriors and gave them new homes in the Walled City, mere days after taking the throne. There have been whispers of discontent among the army—from as far away as Amirgarh. Soldiers have been demanding a pay raise. Many of them are related to the taxed farmers and landowners, you know."

"And how am I expected to *gift* these people?" I ask. "Surely you don't expect me to empty my own pockets."

"You could use the weapons in the royal armory," the acharya suggests. "The maha-atashbans can be melted down, the gold and firestones embedded in them extracted and sold for a profit. I know of buyers in lands across the Yellow Sea, in the Brimlands, too. That's what Ra—er—the conjurer Amar was initially planning to do."

"The conjurer was also planning to dismantle the flesh market and free every single human and Pashu still under indenture in Ambar," I say, acid seeping into my voice. "Did you know this, Acharya? Your servants, those pretty girls you bed, gone—like this."

I snap my fingers for emphasis, making the high priest wince. "Those giant atashbans that you so cavalierly suggest melting away—and my Sky Warriors—are the only reason Ambar still remains free from external attack. I am not going to dissolve both because a few zamindars and their progeny think of the state's land—*my land*—as their own."

Clearly, killing the zamindar in Dukal had not been enough to silence people about the new land tithes. The Sky Warriors have brought me rumors of secret meetings to discuss the new prophecy, of magi gathering in pockets in different parts of the kingdom, some even conspiring with non-magi in plotting to overthrow me.

"But the land *does* belong to the zamindars, Ambar Sikandar!" Sweat beads Damak's unnaturally smooth forehead. "The laws were laid out by Rani Asha herself during the formation of Svapnalok."

"What laws are you talking about? The ones that were rewritten after

Ambar separated from Svapnalok, to segregate non-magi filth into the tenements?"

The acharya's mouth opens and snaps shut again.

"There's no need to be coy, Acharya. Laws can change." I slip on a pair of lightweight black trousers that are cinched at the calves. "Under my rule, any zamindar unwilling to pay tithes will be punished severely. The land under his jurisdiction will be annexed by the state, the revenues going directly to the royal coffers—after a fixed portion is taken by the farmers cultivating the land, of course."

"Ambar Sikandar, I strongly discourage that idea. It will be seen as a grave injustice! As rani of Ambar, you are the shadow of the sky goddess on this earth."

"I am no shadow, you fool!" I snarl. "As rani, I am Ambar's very head—equal to a god myself. Isn't that what you claimed was written within the Holy Scroll while legitimizing the usurper Lohar's rule and, later on, his edicts to open the labor camps and indulge in unnecessary wars?"

The acharya swallows audibly in the silence. "My rani—"

"Enough. Don't bore me with things I already know. Do you have anything else to say?"

Acharya Damak doesn't blink. Ever the politician, he bows again. "Nothing, Ambar Sikandar."

Once the acharya leaves my chambers, I turn to Alizeh again.

"You have news," I say. "What happened in Tavan?"

"The raid went well," she replies. "We lost soldiers, of course, but that was to be expected with untrained children and dirt lickers conscripted to the cause." Though the words are delivered casually, I sense Alizeh's disapproval; she doesn't like to lose *any* soldiers on her watch.

"Don't make excuses, Alizeh. You and Emil were more than adequately equipped to deal with the Star Warrior and her magically impotent army," I say coldly. "So? Did you get her?" With the girl in my hands, at my beck and call, I can crush any budding hopes of a "true king."

Alizeh grits her teeth. "We nearly captured her, but the rajsingha Subodh and his bird army interfered. That said, we *do* have something that's guaranteed to bring the Star Warrior to us. We have her dirt-licker lover. You remember him, don't you?"

"How could I forget?"

Xerxes-putra Cavas. His signature, endorsed in perfect Vani within our army records at the Ministry of Bodies. The signature had allowed us to track him—and the girl—to Tavan, though it had been hellish to breach the invisibility barrier. But that isn't the only reason I remember this dirt-licking stable boy.

I have been called many things over the past three decades. Terror. Witch. Scorpion. Molester of underage boys. In truth, the boys who came to me were willing, of age or older, drawn to my face and my body despite the rumors surrounding me, their lust always overcoming their fear. And I took advantage of this whenever I could, drawing in General Tahmasp's attendant to me, extracting every bit of information from the boy before I disposed of him.

They were mostly the same, these whimpering adolescents.

Except for one.

Since I first saw him, the stable boy's stiff body revealed how repulsed he was by me, despite the atashban pricking his throat. It was the first time in a long while that I remembered my early years at the academy. The unwanted touch of an instructor's hand curving my rear. The laughs of the male cadets rattling through my head as my body lay paralyzed on the floor.

If I hadn't hated Xerxes-putra Cavas already for his filthy blood, I would have hated him for reminding me of how weak I once was. I avoided him afterward, choosing instead to pursue boys who sought me themselves for the promotions I could get them at Ambar Fort, and for the coins I poured over their bare bodies once we were done.

But then *she'd* come into the palace—the girl from Lohar's death prophecy with her wide gold eyes and wild magic, making herself a threat where there was none in the first place.

And it was thanks to a boy I'd stupidly chosen to ignore.

I don't make the same mistake twice. The rajsingha's spells around Tavan were stronger than I anticipated, protecting the invisible city from unfriendly attacks over the past twenty years. But then the living specters began to fade.

My redheaded hound from Jwala had advised me well—another teenage boy who thought himself too charming for his own good. I rewarded him by branding his neck with my emblem. He was mine now, regardless of the black flames tattooing his arms. The Jwaliyan queen be damned.

"Where is our Jwaliyan hound?" I ask Alizeh now.

"He tried to escape on our way back to Ambarvadi," Alizeh says. "Captain Emil caught and shackled him. He's in the kalkothri now, along with the dirt licker."

I push aside the last lingering image of the Tree of Sins. "We'll deal with him soon enough."

I put on my belt and sheathe my daggers before taking hold of the atashban I always keep in my room, its black arrow tip gleaming in the sunlight.

"It's time to pay the dirt licker a visit."

16

CAVAS

I wake up to darkness, my head sore, my tongue stuck to the roof of my mouth. For a second, I wonder if I've been gagged, but then gasps unfurl, along with panic.

What have they done to me? Where am I?

Movement brings answers: the flash of damp stone on three sides and iron bars on the fourth, illuminated in the brief glow of blue shackles on my wrists and ankles. Needles of dizzying pain follow and I curse myself for moving too quickly.

What possessed you to think you could kill General Alizeh? The voice in my head sounds like a mix of Papa's and Ma's. *Why did you leave Gul alone?*

I was a fool, that's why, I want to reply.

With Gul by my side, *finally* doing the kind of magic that could maim and kill, I had felt strong. Invincible in a way I never had before, our combined powers a drug in my veins. I was sure we could take on the general and her whole army together, if needed.

As the battle waged on, though, my initial adrenaline wore off, replaced by exhaustion and nausea. I forgot that as strong as they are, magi pay a price for their power. It was a struggle to stay connected to Gul, to hold firm when I felt her terror and fatigue melding with mine. At one point, I spotted General Alizeh fighting a few feet away from us.

And that's when I did the most foolish thing of all.

Knowing that Gul couldn't always hear my voice through our bond, I sneaked away, pursuing the general on her white steed, aiming a spell at her with my spear. It was a mistake. Without Gul to amplify my magic, the spell was no better than an irritant, a whiff of air that the general swatted aside. Then she pursued me, shooting a series of rapid spells that first broke my weapon, then my shield, and then a final spell that would have killed me if she wasn't simply planning to knock me out cold.

I try to moisten my lips, but grit coats my tongue and it feels like I've swallowed a mouthful of ash.

"Ca . . . as?" a familiar voice echoes in the dark.

"Ma?" I whisper. "Is that you?"

I move again—on purpose—and glimpse her gray face in a glow of painful blue light.

"Ca . . . as." My mother's voice is soft, urgent. "You . . . serious danger."

"Why is your voice breaking?" I demand. "What's going on?"

"No . . . time—" My mother gasps, as if struggling for air. The shackles' light flashes again, and I see that bits and pieces of her body are missing. A finger on her right hand. An ear, an elbow.

"Ma, what's happening to you?"

Saints above, let her not fade. Not now!

In the dark, I hear her take a breath. "Stay . . . alive . . . don't . . . let . . . her . . . kill . . . you."

Her, meaning the Scorpion.

"And remember, you . . . Gul—" Her voice cuts off abruptly, as if swallowed by the air.

"Ma?" I call out. "Ma, are you there?"

But there is no answer, and even without the glow of the shackles' light, I realize she has disappeared.

My thoughts come one after another, each adding to my panic: *What happened to Ma? Why couldn't I talk to her?*

Overhead, I hear footsteps, the screech of an old door opening and closing. The air around me smells damp and musty, like the inside of a waste pit. Underneath that, there's another odor. Smoke—which finally allows me to guess where I am.

I've heard enough stories about Ambar Fort's kalkothri: an underground dungeon so well protected that it gets consumed by fire if a single prisoner tries to escape. Designed by the Chand gharana, the builders of Rani Mahal, the kalkothri has evolved per the whims and fancies of different Ambari rulers. During King Lohar's reign, the dungeon was expanded farther, spanning the length between the two palaces at Ambar Fort.

The kalkothri was where the king kept his "amusements"—humans and Pashu bought at the flesh market to fight in the cage—along with criminals who needed interrogation. Now, the faintest brush of light touches the corner of the bars of my cell. I watch it grow in intensity until a blue-white lightorb floats outside the bars. Underneath are three figures: a prison guard dressed in gray; General Alizeh, in white; and beyond that, the usurper queen, Shayla, herself in head-to-toe black.

Unlike her predecessor, who bedecked himself in colorful clothes and jewels, the Scorpion's attire is fairly simple: a form-fitting angrakha and trousers, and boots made of armored leopard hide. Her only two concessions to her status appear to be the gold dusting her cheeks and the simple crown on her head, a large firestone gleaming like a bloody tear at its center.

"Admiring my crown, dirt licker?" the Scorpion says. "I had it forged after salvaging my mother's firestone from the kabzedar Lohar's turban ornament."

She holds up a hand and I see a ring on her index finger with a firestone cut in the same shape. "I discovered recently that there had been a matching necklace, too. My mother had it made using only stones that worked together best to amplify her powers. So many jewels. Every bit gone to pay for the excesses of the usurper and his clan."

Had I not been placed in magical shackles, with two of Ambar's most lethal women standing before me, I might have wondered where this discussion on jewelry was leading. But I recognize the glint in the Scorpion's pale-brown eyes. The one that forewarns terrible things.

"Did you know that it was a non-magus vaid who lied to Rani Megha, who told her that I was born a boy and not a girl?" she says. "He should have been grateful, felt privileged to be serving Ambar's greatest monarch. But instead, he listened to my father. Together, they kept me from my mother—from my true heritage. And then, there was you. A foolish dirt licker who tried to help a girl from a stupid prophecy do the same. I, who am now your rani, your goddess, Ambar's true sikandar."

A second later, General Alizeh's hand is at my throat, her palm nearly crushing my windpipe. If I didn't think I was going to die before, I certainly feel like I'm going to die now, the lightorb blurring overhead. Sound fades from my ears. Then, without warning, the general's hand leaves my throat. Air rushes back into my lungs, burning my insides like grain alcohol. I cough and cough, tears streaming down my cheeks.

They'll kill me now—and why shouldn't they? I didn't think before pursuing General Alizeh on the battlefield. I deserve death for my stupidity.

Stay alive, Cavas.

I don't know if it's Ma's voice in my head or my own. But it forces me to gather my wits. I recall whatever I know about the Scorpion and how she likes to play with those she tortures.

"You called Raja Lohar a kabzedar," I speak, even though the act feels like swallowing thorns. "But you're no sikandar. If you think the people of Ambar will accept you as their rani, you are mistaken."

My words earn me a fist to the jaw and then a boot to my mouth. I feel a tooth dislodge, spit it out along with a wad of bloody saliva.

"Enough, Alizeh."

The Scorpion touches my face with a finger, tracing my jaw slowly.

"Interesting," she says now. "He plays for his survival the way our little hound does—but with taunts instead of flattery. I have to admit, dirt licker, I find your method *much* more interesting. Raise the wall to my right, sentry."

The guard thumps his staff on the floor, a boom echoing through the dungeon. The stone wall to my left rises in the air, the grind of gears rattling my ears. I see prison bars again, and beyond them a red-haired boy in shackles, black flames tattooing his sun-browned arms. A royal messenger from Jwala.

"He's a seer, dirt licker," Shayla informs me. "Half magus, half non-magus. Able to see the living and the dead. Three months he stayed here, working for me, tracking living specters . . . only to betray me at the very end."

I force myself to stay calm. I don't know if the Scorpion is aware of my half magus blood, but for now I try to look as puzzled as I can. The Jwaliyan messenger's terrified brown eyes lock with mine and I wonder how much he knows—if he heard me talking to Ma earlier.

"My queen, surely I can be forgiven simply for wanting to be at your side—for wanting to be the first to give you the good news," the boy speaks in Vani, his voice dripping honey. His accent only adds to his charm, almost making the listener forget about the patchwork of red and mauve bruises marring his skin.

The Scorpion's head crooks sideways. She steps out of my cell and into the boy's—an act that fills me with more trepidation than when she was inches away from my face. She tilts his chin up with a finger and leans forward until they're close enough to kiss.

A muffled scream gurgles in the boy's mouth as the Scorpion forces the arrow tip of her atashban between his lips. The messenger's cheeks glow orange for a second before blood begins pouring from his ears. Shayla withdraws her atashban, allowing his lifeless body to fall to the floor. Bile rises to my throat, along with the urge to throw up.

"I can't abide liars," the Scorpion says calmly. "Lying was General Tahmasp's specialty, did you know? He even lied to himself, pretending he'd found love with a dirt licker's mate, when, in reality, he raped her. Over and over, until she had you, Xerxes—or is it Tahmasp-putra Cavas?"

I want to scream. To tell her to shut her vicious mouth. But all that emerges from my mouth is a whimper as the truth of my paternity embeds like thorns under my skin. The Scorpion leans over, plucks something from the messenger's hand. A small, but lethal-looking, turban pin.

"Silly boy. Does he not know I anticipate everything?"

Stay alive. Stay alive. Stay alive.

As if sensing my thoughts, the Scorpion gives me a smile and walks back into my cell. She laughs when I try to jerk away from the long fingers tugging back my hair, thrusting my chin upward.

"Ask him everything you can about the girl and her plans, Alizeh," the Scorpion says. "Break him until he bends wholly to our will."

She rises to her feet and walks out of the cell, her boots gently tapping the dungeon's stone floors.

Next to me, General Alizeh puts aside her atashban and withdraws what looks like a pair of garden clippers, only smaller, thicker. "Tell me about the girl, dirt licker. Where is she now? What were your plans?"

"I don't know," I say truthfully, my voice thick with blood and drool. "As for our plans, clearly, they didn't work, did they? I'm here with you."

"Don't be a fool, boy. There's an easy way to do this and there's a hard way. Change your allegiance to Rani Shayla. Beg for the Ambar Sikandar's pardon and you might still live."

Let me live and both you and your rani will regret it, I want to tell her. *Stay alive, Cavas.*

"Killing me won't help your cause," I say. "I'm your only hold on Gul at the moment. If you kill me, she will never come to Ambarvadi the way you want her to."

Alizeh's face is studiously blank, but her eyes sparkle with malice. "Is that so? Hold up your left hand, dirt licker."

I don't have the chance to obey. My left hand magically rises, palm facing the floor, fingers spaced evenly by a firm, invisible hand. Slowly, ignoring the screams that pour from my throat, the general uses the clippers to pull out the nail from my middle finger, tearing it right out of the nail bed.

I pass out by the time General Alizeh removes my second fingernail. When I finally come to, she is gone, darkness—blessed darkness—surrounding me again. I didn't tell her anything about Gul . . . Or at least I think I didn't. My left hand throbs and I wonder if she has removed every nail. Ignoring the shock that goes through me from lighting up the shackles, I see that she hasn't. But the sight of my blood-encrusted middle and index fingers has me heaving, the taste of vomit still lingering in my mouth.

"Cavas?"

A hiss of pain: the barest hint of a sound. I freeze in place.

"Cavas?" the voice persists.

"Ma, is it you?" I ask, my voice hoarse.

"It's Juhi."

Her name shocks my system, makes my chest swell. "You're lying."

"Ask me a question, then." The woman's voice, though still quiet, has a familiar arrogance.

"Where did we meet for the first time?" I ask.

"Outside Sant Javer's temple in Ambarvadi. It was dawn. Gul was there, too. You both argued."

I release a breath I didn't know I was holding. "Where are you?"

"Follow the sound of my voice."

It takes me a while to move, needles pricking my skin, my shackles lighting the way to a wall. There, I notice a slight gap between two of the stone blocks. A pair of black eyes gleam in the flash of blue light. I press my cheek to the wall's cool surface.

"How is Gul?" Juhi asks.

"Safe," I whisper. She must be, for the general to torture me for her whereabouts. "I can't believe that you're here, though."

A hoarse sound that might be a laugh. "That I'm still alive, you mean. Death would be a blessing in this place. But Rani Shayla doesn't bestow it easily. Even daily torture isn't as bad compared to the healing. Yes, she'll eventually send a vaid to heal your injuries. And then, right after, have a Sky Warrior cut into you again."

I fall silent for a long moment. "Who else is in this prison?"

"Right now, it isn't full—if the guards' gossip is to be believed. Raja Amar had initially signed an order to free the cage victims being held here. After Shayla took the throne, she overrode the order, deciding she was better off reselling them at the flesh market. Didn't make much off them, from what I hear. The mammoth turned out to be a liability, trampling half his handlers. He had to be put down. The peri she sold escaped his merchant owner by killing him in the first week. The merchant's family demanded compensation from Shayla, which she, naturally, didn't give. Now, apart from the shadowlynx, which even the guards are afraid to approach, this prison holds only me, Amira, and you."

"Amira's still alive, then." Relief briefly flickers in my ribs. "Gul had nightmares about you both."

I wonder if she's still having them. I wonder who's taking care of her now.

"Amira's alive," Juhi says. "And she will probably remain so until Gul is captured."

"*If* Gul is captured," I correct. "She won't make it easy. She's stronger than she was before. I've felt her magic."

"Which is why they got to you first, didn't they? So that they could draw her here to Ambar Fort?"

"That was my fault—*I* went to attack Alizeh," I say, my guilt like salt rubbed over an open wound. "Gul's too smart. She won't take their bait and pay the price for my stupidity!"

"Oh, Cavas, I wish I could believe you. But you don't believe yourself."

In the darkness, something prickly crawls across my foot, a bloodworm that I kick off in the sharp blue light of the shackle.

"I wish I could tell her not to come," I say.

"Can't you?" Shrewdness returns to Juhi's voice, reminding me why I didn't trust her the first time I met her—why I still don't feel wholly comfortable confiding in her.

"What do you mean?"

"You said you *felt* her magic. That's very specific."

We're complements. It would be easy to say aloud. But the prison's walls likely have ears and I don't want my words falling on the wrong ones.

Juhi seems to understand. "Try," she whispers. "Try to tell her."

I close my eyes, breathing deeply, my mind entering that eerie, meditative space that makes my skin glow, that takes me back to Tavan's darkened temple. I make my way to the shadowy sanctum, where Sant Javer waits alone, watching me calmly. I hesitate, feeling shy. Gul, I know, has spoken to the sky goddess several times, but I've never done so with the saint I've worshipped since I was a boy.

My tongue eventually unties itself and I wish him an "Anandpranam."

"She isn't here, my boy," Sant Javer says softly. "She hasn't been here for a while."

My already fraying nerves teeter on the edge of breaking. "Gul?" I call out. "Are you there? Gul!"

The pain makes it difficult to concentrate and so does the distance. Barely a moment goes by before I'm opening my eyes again, my head resting against the wall where I collapsed.

"Juhi?" I whisper.

"Still here," she says. "You began glowing for a bit and then you collapsed. What happened?"

"It didn't work," I say. "I couldn't reach her."

And I'm terrified that if I do reach Gul, all I'll hear in return is silence.

17

GUL

Gul? Are you there?

"Gul!"

Kali's voice shakes me from my stupor, her strong hands gripping hold of my shoulders before I fall face-first into the sand.

"Tired?" she asks, sounding weary herself.

"A little."

I pinch my arm, the pain steadying me somewhat, jerking me into wakefulness. When Subodh first broached the idea of leaving Tavan at nightfall, I didn't think much of it. The city wasn't my home, and after Cavas's capture, less so. After a day of mourning and packing our belongings, we finally left the city this evening. But traveling the desert at night is easier said than done. Despite the threat of the Sky Warriors hanging over my head, exhaustion eventually began creeping in and I found myself yawning from time to time.

I must have blanked at some point, because I can't remember when the desert scenery shifted from the parched, cracked ground outside Tavan to an ocean of sand or when the sky shifted from navy to black, sequined with thousands of stars. There is no Sunheri to light our way tonight, the first day of a new moon cycle. I adjust the blanket around my body, trying to warm my frozen nose against it.

"Sorry," I tell Kali, my voice muffled against the blanket. "Were you calling for me before?"

"A few seconds ago," she replies. "You were dozing. Many of the women are tired, too."

Tired, shivering. Stumbling, as if weighed down by our meager belongings, a small sack of food and a waterskin each. Agni and Subodh trudge ahead of everyone else, carrying tent poles and other heavy equipment.

"I thought I heard . . . ," I begin, my voice trailing off.

"Heard what?"

"Nothing." I stifle the hope before it roots in my brain and refuses to leave. Cavas and I never practiced communicating at long distances. There's no way I heard his voice. "I must have fallen asleep, like you said."

"You're not the only one." Kali rubs her eyes. "I feel like I'm about to collapse. But Subodh says we're nearly there."

Nearly at the dunes that lie to the west of Tavan—slippery hills of Dream Dust that shift with the wind, muddling travelers, sometimes burying them alive. People avoid the Dunes if they can—and this includes the Sky Warriors and dealers who sell the Dust at exorbitant prices on the streets of Ambarvadi.

Which is why the Dunes are also the fastest way to cross the desert and find Raja Amar, I remind myself. Subodh won't tell anyone Amar's exact location—"a precaution in case we get captured," he explained.

Moments later, I hear Subodh speak: "Let's stop here for now. The Dunes aren't much farther."

As sighs of relief echo through the camp, he rises on his hind legs and raises his front paws, casting a web of light around us.

"That should protect us tonight," he says. "My shield won't turn us completely invisible, but we will remain hidden from a distance. Also, the living specters will sound an alarm if any danger arises."

Specters like Latif, who have still not faded, who for some reason remain loyal to our cause.

Kali magicks a lightorb, the heat of it breaking the night's cold stillness. Soon enough, we gather around the bright sphere hovering a few inches over the ground, warming ourselves. Agni lies down sideways, resting her head on the cool sand next to me, her eyes fluttering shut as I stroke her mane. I know she won't sleep like this for long—not when we're so vulnerable out in the open—but for now I want her to rest as much as she can.

I take a small sip from my waterskin and chew on a roll of cold, stale bajra roti, slathered with butter and jaggery. The butter must have melted when we first started walking, but I can taste the salt from it mingling with the cane sugar.

"My mother used to make this as a snack for me when I was a little girl," I tell Kali, the memory surfacing seemingly out of nowhere. "It was the only way I would eat bajra roti back then—with a dollop of butter and jaggery on top."

I can still recall Ma sprinkling the millet flour over a flat wooden surface, rolling out roti after roti, cooking each on the tava into perfect, round pillows. Papa ate his bajra roti exactly the way I did, and Ma would laugh whenever she saw us, grease dripping down our chins. A year ago, the memory would have made my heart seize painfully. Today I simply feel myself basking in its warmth.

Falak, who overhears me, says, "My ma did something similar. She would also mix her jaggery into the karela she cooked for us. Didn't do much for the taste, though."

A few laughs emerge at the mention of the bitter gourd. I force a smile. I don't deserve the Legion's kindness or their compassion. It's because of *me* that they're in this state—because of my refusal to do proper death magic during practice. But today I don't have the courage to point that out.

"I'm not a fan of karela, either," I admit.

"It's supposed to be good for you," Kali scolds.

"Oh? Then why don't *you* eat it?" Sami raises an eyebrow, her bright-brown eyes sparkling. Everyone laughs, including Kali.

As the conversation goes on, I find myself dozing again. I'm about to lie down next to Agni when a keening sound rips the air.

The lightorb warming us vanishes.

It's Ajib, standing only a few feet away from us, his eyes red and wild, saliva foaming at his mouth. I find myself rising to my feet before a shadow blocks my path. Agni snorts angrily, neighing a warning.

Stay back, she tells me.

It's Ajib! I protest.

That isn't Ajib!

To my left, Subodh growls, "Do not go any closer. The stallion is too far gone for us to help him."

As he speaks, Ajib rises to his hind legs, hitting the magical barrier so hard that I hear it vibrate.

"We can't leave him like this!" Kali says sharply. She unsheathes her dagger, the blade glowing red.

Subodh roars at the same time that Ajib releases another terrifying neigh. Beyond the magical barrier, a shadow leaps, spiraling horns rising over its head: a shadowlynx that digs its claws and teeth into the stallion's left flank.

A pair of hard hands grip me by the biceps, hold me back from leaping forward.

"I'm sorry, Gul." Sami gasps. "You can't save him! It's too late!"

I twist away from her and run toward the stallion, Kali next to me, our daggers raised over our heads.

A booming sound erupts, throwing us backward, flat onto the ground. By the time we rise again, the shadowlynx is licking its black paws, its eyes gleaming in the reflected light of our burning daggers.

Subodh towers over us both, his giant mace glowing red. "Stay here, you two. Nothing can be done to save that horse."

"You stopped us!" Kali screams at him before I can. "Why did you stop us?"

"Because if not the shadowlynx, then the Dream Dust would have killed you!" Subodh thunders. "Do you think we face only one enemy in the desert?"

In the silence that follows, we hear the shadowlynx making quick work of Ajib's remains. Wind howls beyond the barrier, sand rising in the air.

"Sleep," Subodh says. "We have a long day ahead tomorrow."

In the moonlight, Kali is as pale as bone, her gray eyes blank.

"Subodh," I begin. "He shouldn't have—"

"No," she cuts in quietly. "We aren't shadowlynxes or dustwolves, who've developed some sort of immunity to the Dream Dust. Subodh was right to stop us and to protect the other women. I should have been more careful. It's . . . it's Ajib. That horse stayed with me the whole time when Juhi first rescued us. He sensed my pain and fear faster than any human did."

I say nothing in response.

What if it had been Agni who was affected by the Dust? What would I have done?

As if sensing my thoughts, the mare nudges my shoulder. I wrap my arms around her neck and bury my face there to hide my tears.

The rest of the night passes by in relative peace, Sami being the first to fall asleep. The others soon follow. Three people don't sleep—Kali, Subodh, and I—each of us watching the shifting dunes of sand that lie ahead.

Eventually, Subodh turns to us both. "Sleep, both of you. I will wake Falak when it's time to change the watch."

I expect Kali to protest, but she nods without argument. I, myself, am too exhausted to argue. I fall asleep almost instantly, my sleep surprisingly untouched by dreams, waking only when patted lightly on the shoulder by Falak.

"It's time to wake up," she says, her breath sour, her voice like gravel.

"It's still dark," I mumble.

"It's nearly morning. We need to start moving soon."

To my surprise, many of the women are up already, some making tea with the aid of the lightorb's heat.

I notice Kali and Sami sitting on the ground, teacups in hand, talking seriously to each other. Not wanting to disturb them, I make my way to Falak and pack our equipment quickly, working in silence as snippets of quiet conversation float in the air.

Dawn breaks by the time we begin moving again, mauve shading the sides of terra-cotta clouds, their peaks and curves seeming to blend into the Dunes at this distance. The sun crawls up the sky, a hot orange ball that sears the inside of my eyelids red if I look at it too long.

Farther ahead, the clouds disperse. The sun rises, and so does the heat. We draw our dupattas over our heads, veiling our faces against the glare. Sweat gathers in the soles of my jootis and beads down my back. My chapped lips burn. Here, there are no trees, no cacti, no honeyweed bushes. Only hills upon hills of golden sand. At midday, Subodh pauses behind one of these hills for a short break in its shade.

"We aren't far," he says. Beyond the hill, I spy shifting peaks of sand, Dust swirling around them. "I suggest you eat now."

"We might not eat again," I hear one of the women mutter behind me. I chew on a meager quantity of dried dates and take small sips from my waterskin for sustenance.

As we eat, Subodh places his paw on the ground. Bright-blue light emerges from the spot, and sand erupts around the rajsingha, nearly making me tumble over. The reason for the disturbance is a bird—a shvetpanchhi with a bloodied wing, a scroll falling from its beak and into the sand. Without a word, I rush to Subodh, who now leans over the bird, gently brushing its wing with his front paw.

"Rest, old friend," the Pashu king tells the shvetpanchhi. "I will make sure you are sent back to Rani Sarayu. You have risen above and beyond your duty."

I hesitate a few feet away. "Can I help?" I ask.

"Not unless you have knowledge of animal-healing magic." Subodh's great yellow eyes focus on me. "This bird was attacked by arrows yesterday while flying back from Ambar Fort."

A chill goes through me. "Ambar Fort? What—why? You're writing to someone there?"

"Rani Amba," Subodh replies. "It's how I've kept track of everything that's been happening with Raja Amar these past few months."

He was Pashu. A rajsingha, if you want to get specific. I recall the words Queen Amba had spoken months earlier, expressing her annoyance with Lohar's third queen, Farishta, who'd called Subodh a lion.

"Rani Amba knew you were alive this whole time?" I ask the Pashu king.

"Not until four months ago. She thought, like everyone else, that I'd been killed during the Battle of the Desert. We started corresponding again only after you arrived in Tavan." Subodh picks up the tiny scroll the shvetpanchhi dropped. "A dangerous scheme in many ways. But Amba has always been clever. She releases two or three birds at once to confuse the palace's spies. Here, she attached a decoy letter to the shvet-panchhi's leg, enclosing the real scroll in its beak."

He breaks open the seal—two full moons stamped into marbled blue-and-gold wax. Scanning the letter quickly, he hands it to me. "What do you think?"

The letter itself is short and, as expected from someone being spied on, cryptic. There is no salutation.

"'The shifting hills hold your answers, if you can find your way through them,'" I read out loud. "Does she mean the Dunes?"

"She does, indeed." The sand around Subodh glows blue again. "It's not the first time the both of us have had the same idea."

He carefully places the injured shvetpanchhi onto the sand and, surrounded by that eerie blue light, makes a sound akin to a bird—an odd, high cry that reminds me of the first time he and Rani Sarayu communicated through Tavan's reservoir.

Drishti jal. I recall the substance Subodh used to form the connective link and wonder now if that's what he's using again. The shvetpanchhi remains strangely calm for a bird being sucked into the sand, and once it's gone, Subodh turns to us.

"The Dunes are a place of deadly magic," he says. "They can trick you into moving one way instead of another. They can lead you back exactly where you began. They can show you falsehoods—including people who no longer exist in this world."

A visible shudder goes through the group.

"The only way we can get through the Dunes unharmed is with the aid of one who can see through their magic," Subodh says. "The only ones who can do so are those capable of meditating with their eyes open."

Every head swivels in my direction. My skin feels prickly and exposed despite being fully clothed.

"You knew," I say. "You'd planned this."

"This route through the Dunes? Yes, I did."

"Rani Amba suggested the same route. How can you be sure that it isn't a trap and that there aren't Sky Warriors or bounty hunters waiting for us at the other end?" I demand.

"There might be," Subodh agrees. "We'll have to take the risk, though, won't we?"

The silence around me is broken only by Agni's snort.

"What must I do?" I say at last.

"Ask the sky goddess for her guidance. Once we are in the Dunes, we won't be able to see one another. But you will be able to see the way through them." He holds up a coil of rope. "We will all be tethered to you."

I take the rope with shaking hands. The last time I dived into a dust storm, we lost a horse, and Kali, Cavas, and I nearly died. Now I'll be leading more people into a place even deadlier.

They trust you, Savak-putri Gulnaz, a voice whispers in my head. Subodh. *And I do, too.*

How can you trust me so much? I betrayed you.

Do what you did during our training sessions. Think of your complement. What would Cavas say if he were here?

"He'd say, 'Stop overthinking,'" I say out loud, ignoring the puzzled glances from the women.

But Subodh beams and that strengthens my resolve.

I breathe deep—in, out—the way I always do during our practice sessions, imagining I'm back once more in Tavan's quiet temple. As in a daydream, my eyes remain open while everything around me slows to half the normal speed.

Sky goddess, I call out, *are you there?*

I'm here, daughter. Do you see me?

I feel her presence rather than see it, a magic that draws me in like iron shavings to a magnet. The goddess, in this form, isn't human, but a flame that glows bright blue, floating a few feet in the air above our heads.

I see you, I tell her.

Good. Tell the Pashu king and Kali to join you in creating a shield to protect the women. Once that is done, you must follow me, no matter what happens.

As she speaks the ominous words, a swirl of dust makes the blue flame flicker.

Don't lose faith, daughter, the goddess urges. *My flame only remains as strong as your faith in your magic. If you lose that now, you'll lose everything.*

I feel myself teetering the way I did as a child among the high branches of a tree, too afraid to jump to the ground.

"Raja Subodh, Kali," I say in a voice that sounds hollow to my ears. "Throw up shields over the Legion. We need to move quickly."

As they tie ropes around the women, I cast a shield spell, the orange glow from my daggers extending outward, somewhere to the middle of the snakelike line. I feel the reassuring brush of Kali's magic as she casts her shield from the line's center and then watch Subodh raise his mace in the air, covering the end with another spell.

"We should cover our faces, too," Falak calls out. Shouts of agreement ensue, and we adjust our dupattas, veiling our noses and mouths with the cloth.

I secure Agni to the end of the line and fix the dupatta I've tied around her face, praying it doesn't move.

Follow the tug of the rope, I whisper to the mare. *And keep your eyes closed. I don't want Dust getting into them.*

She nickers softly, telling me she understands.

Once Agni is settled, I turn to the Legion. "Follow me! Hold on to one another as best as you can! And try to keep the Dust out of your eyes!"

The first few steps into the Dunes are no different from moving to another part of the desert, with the exception of the wind, which feels a lot stronger. A few more steps in, though, tears stream from my eyes, the wind howling so loudly I can't hear myself speak.

It's only the blue flame that remains constant, despite the eddying Dust, seeming to repel it no matter how strong the wind blows.

But then, I see my father walking toward me, his arms stretched out, his gray lips spread in a smile.

Papa?

The blue flame's magic tugs on mine continually, drawing me away as I make a move to join him. *Leave me*, I am about to snarl when someone pinches my arm.

I turn, locking gazes with a pair of dark-brown eyes. Falak—who is now gesturing to one of the women behind us—Kali—trying to hack away at her rope with the tip of her spear.

"Let me go!" Kali's voice reaches me in slow increments of sound. "It's Juhi Didi! Amira!"

Dust dreams. The realization turns Papa's image into swirling sand again.

Protect, I think instinctively, and the shield I've cast over the Legion automatically grows, moving over my hallucinating friend, then the two behind her, over and over, until I reach Subodh himself, feel the barest brush of his magic against my own.

Focus on the road ahead, Star Warrior, I hear him whisper. *I'll see you at the other end.*

Time seems to slow and simultaneously speed the farther we move into the Dunes. I continue following the blue light, nauseated and terrified, wondering if I'm going to collapse then and there, when the sand begins tapering off, revealing hard earth. It's here that I allow myself to sink to the ground, my cheek pressed to its hot, fissured surface. Words and conversation slip into my mind in fragments:

". . . nose . . . bleeding."

A hand opens my mouth, dripping bitter liquid over my tongue.

". . . calming draft. Gul? Gul, can you hear me?"

When I finally do wake, the sun is exactly in the middle of the sky, its light piercing my eyes like needles.

"Where are we?" I mutter. And then, on a whim: "What day is it?"

"It's been a week since you entered the Dunes," a disembodied male voice says. Latif. "I thought you'd never come out."

"How did *a week* pass us by?" I say, a second before a terrible exhaustion creeps up my body, sinking into every muscle, every bone. A horse neighs outside. "Wait, is that Agni? Is she—"

"Your mare is well. As for a week disappearing . . . well, time passes differently in the Dunes," Latif says. "Usually, people die, lost in the shifting hills. You lot were lucky; most of you only fell unconscious. Your shield protected everyone from the worst of the damage, Star Warrior."

"I'm not the only one who threw up a shield," I tell him.

As I speak, I grow aware of another presence—and turn around to find Sami patiently waiting for our conversation to end. She hands me a small, uncorked jar. Yellow fumes smelling of sulfur rise from its narrow neck. When I bring it close, it makes my eyes water.

"What *is* this?" I say.

"A reviving draft. Come now, drink up."

"I'm supposed to *drink* this?!"

"You've been drinking it hourly for the past day. It's a good thing I packed some of Esther Didi's medical supplies before we left Tavan. Otherwise, you and Kali would still be asleep."

Despite the draft's retch-inducing taste, I feel a lot sharper than I did before, my mind and body already more alert.

"Kali. Is she okay?" I ask.

"She is," Sami says, looking relieved. "Your shield protected her—and us—from falling into a deep sleepstate."

"Told you," Latif sings out.

"Only your shield held up during the storm," Sami explains. "Kali's shield failed midway. So did Raja Subodh's." Sami blinks rapidly, her eyes wet with tears. Without thinking, I place a hand on her wrist.

"I'm fine, Sami." Around us, women sip water, some still packing their equipment.

Sami takes a deep breath, her smile taut, forced. "I won't cry, I promise. I'm too excitable for that. It's a fault of mine. When Kali woke up, I overwhelmed her with questions about how she's doing. I'm sure she hates me right now."

"I'm sure she doesn't hate you, Sami. She's probably just tired." I suppress a frown. Sami may be "excitable"—even exhausting in her enthusiasm—but I doubt that mere grouchiness from Kali would make her dissolve into tears. "Where is Kali now?"

"In Falak's tent." Sami gestures toward it. "Want me to take you there?"

"It's better if I see her alone."

To my relief, I find Kali sitting up in the tent, sipping tea.

"You're up!" she exclaims when she sees me enter. "Sami didn't say!"

"I only woke a few moments ago." I pause. "So. You and Sami. What's going on there? Before we entered the Dunes, I thought you both were getting along. Now she's suddenly miserable again and ready to cry at the very mention of your name."

"Why do you think I'm the reason for her misery?" Kali's cool voice belies the tremor in her hands.

"Don't act coy with me, Kali. If you don't have feelings for the girl, cut her loose. But make a decision one way or another. Don't play with her emotions."

"Go," Kali says, her face paler than I've seen it before. "Before I throw you out."

"Fine!"

I duck out of the tent, expecting a blast of heat. Instead, I feel the cool presence of a specter in the air.

"You might have poked an armored leopard there," Latif comments.

"Good," I say, not bothering to rebuke him for eavesdropping. "Someone needed to."

"Raja Subodh will be happy to see you up and about. He's talking to Harkha now."

My heart skips a beat. "Cavas's mother? She hasn't faded yet?"

"She's still around, Star Warrior. Your other half still lives. But then, you would know, too, wouldn't you? If you reached out to him."

"We've never—"

"—tried communicating at long distances, yes," Latif cuts in. "But there's always a first time, isn't there? Try it at night, when everyone's asleep. And do it with your eyes closed. It might make things easier."

My heart skitters. I'm debating on how to respond to the specter when I hear someone call my name.

It's Subodh.

"You're up again," he says, walking over to me. "The great animal spirits be praised. If you're feeling better, we should start moving again. It isn't safe to stay here too long."

"I'm ready."

Exhausted as I am, I am not imprisoned the way Cavas is.

At midday, we begin trekking farther north, away from the desert and closer to civilization. A village appears in the distance: small houses and thatched huts, the curving white roof of a temple, a faded blue flag snapping in the wind.

"Where are we?" someone mutters.

"We're outside the village of Sur," Kali says, raising a hand to shield her eyes from the afternoon sun. "I recognize those banyan trees."

"The village won't be safe," Subodh says. "Rani Shayla is sure to have informers there. We must stick to the outskirts as much as possible and try not to be discovered."

My mouth feels dry even after sipping from my waterskin. At the Sisterhood, Juhi always told us that the best way to hide was in plain sight. But I have doubts we'll be able to pull this off with me, Kali, twenty other women, and a horse. Subodh will stick out as well. Pashu take pride in never being able to disguise their true nature or form, though in this instance, some shape-shifting might be useful.

"We'll get caught before we take two steps," Falak echoes my thoughts.

"Perhaps." Subodh raises his spiked mace and props it against one shoulder. "Be prepared to fight."

18

GUL

Falak leads the way, with Subodh in the rear, while we keep our weapons close, my hands constantly brushing my daggers' hilts. We walk. And walk. No one crosses our path—not an animal, not even a bloodworm. The silence is absolute, every scrape of feet on the ground booming in my ears.

"I don't like this," Kali whispers to me.

"Neither do I," I say.

It's nearly sunset, the sky a dusky rose, when a woman in front of us screams. "Raja Subodh!"

I rush forward, my daggers growing hot in my hands, and pause next to the woman, whose finger points out something farther ahead.

It's a horse's carcass, the body ripped open, apparently by wild animals. Flies buzz around the corpse, the stench of it nearly making me hurl. I take a step backward. To my surprise, Subodh walks over to the horse and sniffs around its ears.

He gestures me and Kali over. "Look." He points to the dried blood next to the corpse. "What do you see?"

Kali and I hold our dupattas over our noses. Though every instinct urges me away, I force myself to look . . . and see patches of green tainting the blood, a faint glow rising from them. *Magic.*

"Dustwolves couldn't have left that there," Kali murmurs. "Is it a trap?"

"More like a diversion," I say. "Someone doesn't want us going farther."

"Not us, necessarily." Subodh's large paw delicately nudges a scrap of cloth still hanging to the horse's saddle. "Blue and silver. These are Sky Warrior colors."

"Do you think it's Am—" A whinny breaks off my sentence: Agni, galloping past the dead horse, her body vanishing into thin air.

"Agni!" I shout. "Agni, no!"

But, where Agni went, I can't go, a bout of dizziness striking the moment I try to follow.

"An enchantment," I mutter. "I can't move any farther."

Subodh walks past the horse and sniffs carefully. "Yes, I can sense it," he says. "It's an enchantment that will repel both humans and part-humans. It won't let me through, either. If Agni does not return in the next few moments, then we will have no choice but to turn back and find a safer place to camp for the night."

"I'm not losing Agni to some enchantment!"

"Perhaps you won't," Subodh says, his yellow eyes focused somewhere beyond the spot Agni disappeared into. "Enchantments don't work the same way on animals the way they do on humans and Pashu. It's the reason Agni alone was able to move forward. Let's wait for now and stay alert."

I take a deep breath and focus on Agni's form, picturing her in my mind. *Agni, are you there?* I whisper.

A long silence. I'm about to call for her again when Agni speaks: *I'm coming. Stay where you are.*

"She's coming back," I say out loud, squinting at the hazy blur behind the dead horse, my eyes watering from the effort. It's why, when Agni steps back through the airy barrier, it takes me a moment to see the figure walking beside her. A skinny man of medium height, a cudgel in one hand, wild black hair curling around his head and chin. It's the first time I'm seeing him without a turban, but those eyes are unmistakable—as brilliant as yellow firestones in a dark mine. Though we crossed the desert solely to find him, meeting Ambar's true king is a shock, as if I'm still inside the Dunes.

"Pashuraj Subodh." King Amar bows deeply. "You came."

"Raja Amar." Subodh's bow is equally deep. "I am glad to see you are not only alive but also well. I'm surprised you took the risk of crossing the enchantment and coming out here yourself."

"Your Jwaliyan mare was pretty convincing. So was the living specter who accompanied her. He described a rajsingha, about ten feet tall, and a girl with black hair, gold eyes, and a starry birthmark on her right arm."

Amar locks eyes with me. To my annoyance, my heart skips a beat.

Agni moves forward to nuzzle Amar's cheek with her nose, making him laugh and stroke her in response.

I raise my eyebrows. *What in Svapnalok are you doing?* I ask her through our bond.

Getting on the raja's good side. You should, too.

Don't tell me that you could see him across that enchantment! And what's this talk about a living specter?

I couldn't see him. Latif told me he was there, she says cheekily.

Of course, Latif was there. I grimace. *Why couldn't* either *of you tell* me *that?*

Agni snorts. *Cheer up. I didn't die, did I?*

"The mare—Agni—is Gul's companion," Subodh tells Amar now.

"I see that," Amar says. "Even at Ambar Fort, she controlled my sister Malti's rambunctious pony with little effort. It's good to see you again, Gul ji."

"It's good to see you, too, Raja Amar," I say truthfully. The passing reference to Princess Malti makes my heart seize. With Shayla on Ambar's throne, I don't know when I'll see the little girl again. *If* I ever will.

Amar smiles at me. "More like a raja without a crown or a kingdom."

I feel another presence by my side. "Did you ask *him* to stop using the honorific on you?" I can hear the smirk in Sami's tone.

"Ambari royals are ingrained with superfluous formality," I mutter, avoiding the question. *Or at least* this *royal.*

I don't like to think of the one and only time Amar called me by name—only my name—in the gardens at Ambar Fort. He knew me as Siya, then, not Gul, but I'd never forgotten the moment or the longing and hope in his eyes. It would have been easy for me to love Amar—and equally easy for me to kill him later at Raj Mahal, if not for Cavas.

"The dead horse isn't real, I take it," Subodh says.

"It isn't." Amar waves a hand over the corpse, which disappears briefly to reveal the skeleton of a bird long dead, draped with a bloodied horse blanket—and then reappears again. "I conjured the skeleton into a horse to drive away Sky Warriors. It took some time, but I don't think I got the dustwolf's tooth marks right."

"You didn't," Subodh says. "The bites weren't as clean."

"Rani Ma said you'd notice," Amar says, eyeing the Pashu king. "She sent me a message a couple of days ago that you were headed this way. She also said I should trust you."

The last sentence hovers in the air, the hesitation in it unmistakable.

"We have a truth seeker among us," Subodh says, gesturing to Kali. "You may ask her if we are trustworthy."

"Yes, we've met." Amar's eyes flicker to where Kali stands. "Well, my mother trusts you and that certainly counts for something. She isn't easy to convince."

If Subodh is moved by that statement, he gives no indication of it, his face as impassive as always.

"How did you end up here, this close to the desert?" I ask Amar to change the subject. "Was it a coincidence?"

"It wasn't," Amar says. "I began tracking your movements, Gul ji, as soon as I was crowned king. It was easy enough, with Cavas's having enlisted in the army. His signature allowed me to track you into the desert. But I didn't anticipate leaving Ambar Fort or being on the run myself."

He pauses briefly before continuing. "One night, while I was visiting my mother and Malti in Rani Mahal, General Shayla and five Sky Warriors ambushed me. I was a fool. The palace vaid told me there were suspicions that Shayla had poisoned my father, but I still went to her when she said she needed me for something urgent. Moments after I left my mother's chambers, I had to duck an atashban's spell. I managed to evade them and run to the servants' quarters downstairs. In the corridor, there's a ramp that leads to a window with a drop of two hundred feet onto the grounds surrounding the palace."

A shiver runs down my spine. I know exactly which window he's talking about, having discovered it on a nighttime venture when I pretended to work at the palace.

"As you can imagine, I jumped," Amar continues. "Unlike many other magi, I never instinctively grasped the art of breaking a fall by floating on air. Conjuring was the only magic I knew well—the only magic I could think of using to protect myself.

"As I tumbled to the ground, I shot spells in the dark, multiplying the grass on the ground below, made it thick enough to soften my fall. Luckily, I didn't break any bones. Do you remember Yukta Didi, Gul ji?"

I nod. The shrewd old servants' mistress always watched me as if she knew more about me than she let on.

"While the Sky Warriors scoured the grounds for me, I slipped back into Rani Mahal and found Yukta Didi's quarters. She knew that Ambar Fort was no longer safe for me with the Sky Warriors under Shayla's control. I used magic to turn myself invisible and Yukta Didi smuggled me out in a basket of trash headed to Ambarvadi. She told me later to make my way here, to this place, where she knew the sarpanch."

The sarpanch? I frown in confusion. Villages and towns had their own governing councils called panchayats, which were made up of five councilors, including the head councilor or sarpanch, elected locally from the area. But Sur and Dukal lay in opposite directions, half a day away from this spot. The nearest town was farther away. Unless . . . *wait. Can it be?*

"This place you speak of," I say. "What is it?"

"Let me show you."

Amar turns around and slowly raises his arms. The air in front of us ripples, the scene shifting from cracked, endlessly dry plains to a cluster of houses and decrepit buildings garlanded with marigolds, the sounds of children chasing one another rising distantly in the air.

A small crowd of adults waits several feet away from us—turbaned men in worn tunics and dhotis, and sari-clad women holding sickles and hoes in their hands. Their exhausted faces tell me who they are, along with the familiar distrust I see in their eyes.

Non-magi.

"Welcome to the southern tenements," Amar tells us.

19
GUL

Air brushes my cheeks like fabric as we cross the enchantment's barrier, reminding me of—

"The rekha!" I say out loud, making Kali jump back with a start.

Ignoring her confused look, I turn to Amar. "This barrier. It's similar to the rekha at Ambar Fort, isn't it?"

"Yes. Only this one's stronger. As I recall, a certain serving girl crossed the last one far too easily." Amar smiles, reminding me again of the prince who preferred reading to ruling, the boy more interested in learning about the venom-extracting properties of blood bats trapped in royal cupboards. However, the lightness soon fades from his eyes.

"I never wanted to make the rekha at Ambar Fort, or keep women away from Raj Mahal's grounds. After I became king, I lifted the spell, thinking I'd never have to do something like that again." He grimaces.

"Well, this rekha is an improvement to the previous one. It restricts humans and part-humans of all genders equally," I joke, trying to lighten the mood.

Amar gives me a wry smile. "It's the least I can do to protect the people here." He gestures to the tenement dwellers standing nearby, their farm implements still raised like weapons.

"Sarpanch ji," Amar addresses someone in the crowd. "Please come. These are friends of ours."

A man slowly detaches from the throng. He's short and sturdy, with a round, scowling face and thick white sidelocks. Lines fan out from the corners of his eyes, an indication of someone more prone to laughing than frowning. But the head councilor of the southern tenements isn't laughing now. He hesitates for a moment, his eyes on Subodh, before determinedly stepping forward, his palms pressed together in greeting.

"Anandpranam," he says, his voice neutral. "I'm Sarpanch Parvez. It is my honor to welcome the Pashu king, the Star Warrior, and her army to our home." As he speaks, four others step forward—a man and three women, who gather around Parvez, holding tall bamboo lathis. "These are my fellow councilors."

I keep my smile fixed and try not to look like I've forgotten the councilors' names the second after Parvez introduces them to us. I'm not the only one fighting exhaustion. Several women from the Legion are slumping their shoulders. Kali is blinking rapidly again.

"We can set up tents with your permission, Sarpanch ji." Subodh's rumbling voice makes a few non-magi step back fearfully. "We don't want to cause you any inconvenience. Perhaps by the reservoir?"

Sarpanch Parvez's mouth tightens, but he nods briefly. "I'll take you there. Our people will help you with your belongings."

Several non-magi step forward, offering to take some of the load off Subodh, who gracefully accepts. I fall into step with Kali as we walk to the reservoir, noting the suspicious looks on the faces of many of the tenement dwellers.

"They don't seem very happy with our arrival," I say quietly.

"No," she agrees. "I guess they're worried. First harboring Raja Amar, and now us. Especially if you consider what happened in Sur."

"What happened in Sur?" I ask, nonplussed.

"Didn't Raja Subodh tell you? Well, it happened a couple of months ago, when we were still in Tavan. After the zamindar in Sur refused to pay the increased land tithe, many of the farmers joined him. Naturally, Rani Shayla sent her general to arrest everyone. They were tied on stakes and burned without a trial."

I taste blood on my tongue and realize belatedly that it's from biting the inside of my cheek. Swearing seems pointless right now.

"I wonder how they agreed to let us stay now," I murmur, watching the head councilor slowly make his way to the reservoir. Unlike the other councilors, Parvez actually uses his lathi to support himself. At one point, it looks like he's about to trip, when the other male councilor places a hand on his shoulder, holding him upright.

"With great difficulty," another voice says. I turn to face Amar, who gives us a wan smile. "And it's thanks to Councilor Rayomand over there. He and Sarpanch Parvez have been bound for several years now. Councilor Rayomand persuaded his mate and the other councilors to take me in. He doesn't believe in divides between magi and non-magi."

As if sensing our stares, Councilor Rayomand turns around and gives us a brief, whiskery smile.

"The sarpanch is a good leader, but he can be abrupt at times, and intimidating," Amar continues in a quiet voice. "Rayomand is better with people."

"What about you?" I ask curiously. "How do the people here feel about you?"

Amar shrugs. "I guess they trust me a little for now. They took me in only because the sarpanch and Yukta Didi knew each other as children. Back in those days, it wasn't so strict—the mixing of magi and non-magi—at least here in the south of the kingdom. Yukta Didi was like a sister to Sarpanch Parvez. They stayed in touch after Parvez was moved to the tenements and sent letters to each other by shvetpanchhi. The sarpanch trusts Yukta Didi, and the tenement dwellers trust the sarpanch. Though, now that you're here, Gul ji, they might trust me more."

"What do you mean?"

"You're the Star Warrior, remember?" Amar says, as if this should be obvious. "For the longest time, you were only a legend to everyone, a myth. It's important for people to see that you are real. Do you know how many shrines appeared in your name almost overnight after Shayla usurped the throne? Even here, in the tenements, there are a few shrines dedicated to you and Cavas. That you love a boy raised by non-magi and fought to save him at Ambar Fort matters to many here."

My heartbeat quickens. People are rooting for me and Cavas. But Cavas is in captivity now—and who knows how long he'll survive?

"Cavas is . . . he's—he's . . ." I can't say the words.

"I know," Amar says softly. "Shayla made sure everyone knew Cavas was captured and imprisoned. If she means to scare people with her tactics, then she needs to think of something else. People are *angry*, Gul. I've never seen them like this before. One bad ruler after another, with no real break in between—they feel like they've lost their voices."

"When we speak about *people*, whom are we talking about? Magi?" I ask, raising an eyebrow. "If that's the case, I'm surprised they *had* voices. They never raised them for non-magi, neither for the marked girls who were imprisoned in labor camps."

Amar flushes. "I know," he says after a pause.

I say nothing, and we continue the rest of the way to the reservoir in silence. Despite my anger, I feel a little guilty for snapping at him. Amar didn't order the murder of my parents. Back then, as King Lohar's third son, he had little power of his own.

I turn to face the body of shimmering water ahead of us and grow still, struck by the colors of the setting sun reflected on the reservoir's surface, vibrant oranges and pinks brushing the sides of darkening palm trees.

"In the morning, you will be able to see the flower bushes by the reservoir bank," Amar says. "Non-magi are ingenious, really, the way they've found ways to grow things without magic. They dig these pits and fill them with manure and compost and seeds right before the Month of Tears. The manure attracts termites, which tunnel underground to build nests. After the rain falls, the termite tunnels hold water for a long time, allowing plants to grow."

Amar's voice rises in volume the way it does whenever he's excited about something. Soon enough, we draw other interested stares.

One of the female councilors, a stern-faced woman in a purple sari, taps him on the shoulder. "We could use an extra hand in the garden. If you're interested, Raja Amar," she says.

"Y-yes, C-councilor M-maya," Amar stutters. "Of course. Though, you'll have to forgive me for making mistakes. I don't have earth magic in me like my sister—" Amar's voice breaks off and he presses his lips together.

My anger toward Amar feels pointless now—a prickly emotion that gets overwhelmed by grief.

The councilor nods, sympathy flickering in her dark-brown eyes. "Mistakes aren't fatal as long as there's a willingness to learn. See you at dawn."

"I'll be there, Councilor Maya." Amar bows, an act that I can tell surprises the councilor and the others—not for the bow itself, but for how naturally Amar performs it, as if the councilor were a revered elder or one of his own family members. It doesn't surprise me, though. Of all the royals I met at Ambar Fort, Amar and Malti were always the nicest, never acting like they were better than the people who worked for them.

The rest of the evening passes by in a blur of activity: setting up tents, building a proper wood fire for the night. A few men and women from the tenements approach shyly, offering to bring us dinner.

"It isn't much," the oldest woman tells us. "Only roti and kadhi."

"Roti and kadhi sound wonderful after a week of dust and dates," Falak says, making everyone laugh.

"Can we help you?" Kali asks the woman, making a move to rise to her feet.

"Don't be silly, child," she says. "As if we'd make our guests work for us! Sit, sit. We'll bring you the food."

Dinner takes place on blankets under the stars: soft, warm bajra rotis, which we rip into like dustwolves, and steaming white kadhi spiced with mustard, chilies, and honeyweed. I note from the corner of my eye that the old woman brings Subodh a different, covered plate. A meat dish, I guess, from the sudden sparkle in the Pashu king's eyes.

"May I join you?"

I startle at the sound of Amar's voice, find him standing near me with a plate in hand. "Of c-course," I say, moving aside to make room.

Why am I nervous?

"Are you enjoying your meal, Gul ji?" Amar asks pleasantly.

"Gul, please, Raja Amar."

"What?"

"Please call me Gul. I'm not used to honorifics."

"Siya didn't mind it when I called her Siya ji," he says, slyly referring to the false name I used at Ambar Fort.

"Well, Siya had appearances to keep up, didn't she?" *Siya had a king to kill.*

The humor drains from Amar's face.

"Are you thinking of ways to punish me if we win the war?" I ask, forcing lightness into my voice.

"I should, shouldn't I? You had every intention of killing my father . . . even if you didn't really kill him in the end." Amar sighs, staring into the bonfire's dancing flames. "I didn't mourn his death, Gul. As a son, I should grieve for my father, no matter how bad our relationship was. When he died . . . there was only an overwhelming sense of fear. I never wanted to be king. I never planned for it. But this land . . ." He reaches behind us to gather a handful of earth, red dust coating his palm. "I've loved this land since I was a boy. The land, in turn, has loved me back and responded willingly to my magic whenever I conjured."

As he speaks, his hand glows, particles of dust rising, molding into a miniature version of Rani Mahal. A perfect, tiny replica of rose-colored stone and glass that crumbles to dust again with a softly whispered word.

"I think of Rani Ma," he continues. "Of Malti. Rani Janavi and Rani Farishta, who were always kind to me, regardless of their arguments and rivalries with my mother. What kind of person would I be if I abandoned them?"

"Honor above all else?" I ask, echoing his words from a long time ago.

He meets my gaze without fear. "My mother always told me that without honor, there is no respect nor trust. I want my people to trust me, Gul. It's the only way we will win this war. It's why I'm so grateful that you're here. You are bringing together the people of Ambar in a way no one could have anticipated."

It's the second time today that Amar has mentioned my importance. It also explains why he doesn't want to punish me. I fit neatly into his ascension plans.

"Getting magi and non-magi to unite will be difficult," I warn. "Even with Cavas—it took me ages to gain his confidence."

"We don't have a choice. The first lesson of statecraft is to look for weaknesses within your kingdom and fix them. The second lesson is to look for weaknesses without, to use them to your advantage and expand your territories. If Ambar crumbles from a civil war, the kingdoms surrounding us will swoop in to scavenge the pieces. You can be sure of that," Amar replies grimly. "That's why I've been working hard to get in touch with the queens of Jwala and Samudra these past months."

"Is it safe to contact them?" I ask, surprised. "Won't they give information about you to Shayla?"

"The Brimlands might—considering that Shayla still holds the king's daughters Rani Janavi and Rani Farishta captive. It's why I haven't contacted them. As for the others, I don't think they will—yet. I sense they don't particularly care for Shayla, but everyone is aware of her military prowess. From what I can gauge, they're playing both sides now and watching what unfolds. More recently, I was able to get a message to the kingdom of Prithvi as well."

"I thought Prithvi's wall was inaccessible!"

"How do you think someone brought a mammoth into Ambar's flesh market this year? Walls form cracks, as do kingdoms. We are only as strong as we are united." He turns to watch Subodh, who has now settled by the reservoir bank, lapping at the water. "I wonder why the Pashu king aids you so much."

"He has relationships with the women of Tavan," I say at once. "The Pashu do not tolerate injustice. Everyone knows that. They came to the aid of . . ." My voice trails off.

"They came to the Samudra king's aid to fight *against* Ambar in the Three-Year War," Amar finishes. "The Pashu aren't saints, Gul. Raja Subodh has been alive for far longer than us or our parents. To continue living among humans *after* being freed from my father's spell is odd. No ruler feels that kind of obligation unless he anticipates an advantage of sorts."

"Perhaps not," I say, though I hate the thought of it. "As you said, Raja Amar, it's a war. Not everyone fights honorably."

"Sometimes I wonder if I'm being foolish," Amar admits. "Being so honorable."

"Someone needs to be. How else would the world believe in goodness?" I pause before adding, "My heart tells me that Raja Subodh is like that, too. That honor rules him as much as it does you."

Amar does not respond to the comment and we lapse into silence. Next to me, Kali rises to her feet and moves to the other side of the fire to sit next to a surprised and wary Sami. Farther ahead, the councilors are talking to women from the Legion, and children are chasing one another in the sand.

Yes, I think. *I'm glad Amar is honorable.*

For I, most certainly, am not.

"I should go get some sleep," Amar says once dinner ends. "I was up since before dawn. Shubhraat, Gul."

I think I wish him a good night in return.

I know I should do something useful right now—like planning more training sessions with the Legion and teaching them to ward off unfriendly spells. The faster I train them, the faster we can get to Ambarvadi and rescue Cavas.

But what if there's an easier way? One that requires no death magic. One that requires no one else except me.

I stare out at the reservoir, not moving from my spot, until Falak shoos me away, telling me to get some rest.

In our shared tent, Kali and Sami are sleeping, heads turned to face each other, as if they were in conversation before. I lie down on my pallet, close my eyes, and breathe deep. In. Out. In. Out. My heartbeat slows and once again I'm within the quiet, familiar darkness of a temple. The sanctum holds two statues—the sky goddess and Sant Javer. The saint's presence gives me hope. Maybe Latif was right. Maybe this form of communication *could* work.

"Cavas," I call out. "Cavas, are you there?"

There's a moment when I think I see an answering flicker of light, hear a susurrus in response. But before I can press any further, my eyes open the way they do after a dream—to the prick of sunlight against my lids, the sound of chatter and crackling fire, the air thick with the smell of spices and steeping tea.

TWO HALVES OF
A WHOLE

20th day of the Month of Sloughing
4 months into Queen Shayla's reign

20
CAVAS

Cavas, are you there?

Gul's voice floats in my brain, a talisman I struggle to hold onto, as my own answer dissipates with another shock from the shackles around my wrists.

In the kalkothri, I've kept track of time by the meals I'm provided—a portion of stale bajra roti, dates that are more seed than fruit, and a small jar of water once every day. The vaid arrives shortly after the ninth day's meal, carrying a fanas to light the way into the dungeons, his white turban and angrakha glowing in the dark. As healers go, he looks fairly young, the brown skin of his forehead taut and unwrinkled, his sideburns and mustache holding the barest tinge of gray. Up close, I can also see the engraving on his silver turban pin—a pestle and mortar girded by a two-headed snake—a symbol I've seen painted only on hospital buildings and apothecaries in Ambarvadi.

"I'm Vaid Roshan. Easy now," he says when I try to sit up. "Those shackles are meant to restrict movement. Sudden jerks will activate their magic and damage your nerves. Hold up your hands for me. Slowly, please."

I do so and am surprised to find that the shock, though still there, is more tolerable: a faint buzzing against my skin instead of a hundred needle pricks.

The vaid stares blankly at my nails. "This is going to hurt," he says.

A moment later, his entire body begins glowing nearly as brightly as the fanas light. Magi healers rarely came to the tenements, and this is the first time I've seen one perform magic. With warm hands, the vaid applies pressure right below the cuticle of my middle finger.

It hurts, as he said. Nearly as much as it did when General Alizeh extracted them. But my nails grow back, healthy and whole, sealing over the throbbing tips of my fingers.

"The general will be here soon," the vaid says, carefully wiping the blood encrusting my hand with a clean cloth. I think I see a glint of sympathy in his dark-brown eyes before footsteps echo on the stone floor outside.

The healer makes a move to leave as General Alizeh steps into my cell with another Sky Warrior. She raises a hand. "Hold on, Vaid Roshan. We might be doing consecutives today."

Vaid Roshan says nothing, but his jaw tightens ever so slightly.

"So, boy." Alizeh kneels before me, her gray gaze level with mine. "Are you willing to speak?"

"About what?"

She smiles, almost as if she expected my rudeness. "About the girl, of course. About that army of hers. What are they planning to do next?"

When I say nothing in response, the general's smile sharpens. "Do you know what a consecutive means, dirt licker?" She holds up the hand the vaid healed a moment earlier. "It means I break you over and over. And Vaid Roshan heals you every time that I do. Break and heal, break and heal. Our prisoners aren't able to say what's worse."

"I can't tell you anything that you already don't know." My pulse beats in my throat.

"Don't be foolish, boy. Why live through this nightmare while she roams unrestricted? Tell me and I'll set you free."

From the living world, you mean, I think. Or mean to. The words spill from my mouth, making the general's hard eyes grow harder.

"I see what Rani Shayla meant when she said you'd be difficult." Alizeh rises to her feet and holds out a hand to the other Sky Warrior. "The pliers, Captain Shekhar."

This time my screams come quicker, every nerve on edge—my body anticipating the pain, fearing it. But the trouble with pain is that your body gets used to it. I don't pass out when the general pulls out my second fingernail and then my fifth, not even when she sinks two daggers into the flats of my palms, pinning me to the earth floor. She asks me a question, breaks a finger, makes the vaid heal it, then asks the same question again.

What's the girl planning next?

In the space between the consecutives, I float, imagining that I'm on a bed of grass, green and lush like the gardens at Ambar Fort. And then the pain of breaking or fixing follows and everything around me burns.

I look forward to the in-between moments, when I feel nothing. Moments when I think I hear my name. At times like this, I pretend my father is still alive. I talk to him, asking him if he has taken his medicine. Sometimes I scream for him over and over even though I know he's gone. I call out for my mother as well and, once, think I hear an answering sob. When the pain is at its worst, I find myself inside the familiar confines of a dark temple.

Sant Javer waits alone in the sanctum. Yet something else lingers in the air—the smells of sun and salt, of chameli on a cool, moonlit night.

"Gul was here, wasn't she?" I ask, looking into the saint's kindly eyes.

"Some time ago," he replies. "She was looking for you."

"Some time? How *much* time?!"

"Forgive me, child, but I don't know. Here, in this space, time is impossible to keep track of."

I spin around. "Gul! Gul!"

The darkness swallows my shouts, leaves me gasping for breath. There is no response.

"You would know if something happened to her," Sant Javer says.

Sure, I think bitterly. If Gul were dead, the Scorpion would be celebrating by now.

"I don't know how much longer I can hold on," I say. I can feel the waves of pain from the consecutives pricking through, even in this state of sthirta. "If I can stay alive."

"For your own sake, you must," Sant Javer says grimly. "If you don't, they will turn you into a living specter the way they did Latif, the way they did so many others, chained to this earth, unable to move on."

"If I die, then Gul will not come." I don't want her here in this hell with me, sharing my nightmare.

"Do you really believe that, Cavas? Do you really believe that Gul is the type to abandon the people she loves?"

My heart skips a beat at the word *loves*. "They're going to kill me."

"They will not kill you as long as they believe you still have something to give them," Sant Javer says. "Revenge has many forms, child, and not all of them involve killing people."

I'm about to protest this—*revenge was what got me here in the first place*—when my eyes flicker open, blurry figures outlined in the harsh rays of a lightorb.

"He's awake, General," a weary voice says. Vaid Roshan. "But I fear the revival draft won't last long. He needs to rest if he is to be questioned again."

General Alizeh's white uniform reflects the too-bright light, making my eyes water. I would close them again if I could—if I didn't feel the vaid's magic holding them open, clamping the lids in place.

"Is she here?" Alizeh asks someone standing to her left.

"She's here," the guard answers.

The *she* in question is a person I never expected to see this far below

Rani Mahal, the two moons tattooed on her chin nearly obscured by the hoop of her elaborate, pearl-encrusted nose ring.

Mourners in Ambar wear gray during the first year of a family member's passing. Lohar's first queen, Amba, doesn't. She is dressed, instead, in her usual finery—shadowlynxes and leaping deer embroidered in gold on a pale-green sari, her pallu neatly in place over her head. It's only when the queen's indifferent yellow gaze meets mine that I notice her swollen eyes, the weary lines around her perfectly painted red mouth. I also note the absence of the gold dust that once visibly marked her cheeks, indicating her royal status.

"I will not touch him," she says coldly.

"Oh, you will, Rani ji." Alizeh's addition of the honorific is more mockery than respect. "Unless you wish to lose your last remaining child as well."

Princess Malti. My stomach sinks. Are they holding her captive, too?

Queen Amba is well accustomed to hiding her feelings. It's not until I feel the brush of her fingers against my arm that I realize how much General Alizeh now controls her, how quickly the tables have turned on Ambar's old royals.

"I was kind to you before, boy," the general tells me. "I gave you many chances to tell the truth. Now I will drag the truth from you with the help of our friend Amba, here."

The quiver from Queen Amba's fingers is slight and would have been undetectable if my skin wasn't overly sensitized from the consecutive rounds of torture.

"Where is the girl they call the Star Warrior?" Alizeh asks me. "Where do she and the old Pashu king plan to go next?"

I consider telling them the truth again: that I know nothing. Rani Amba can easily vouch for it. But, if they realize how useless I am, they will kill me, drawing Gul to the palace simply to avenge my murder.

They will not kill you as long as they believe you still have something to give them.

Sant Javer was right. If I want to protect Gul, dying isn't an option. Also, his last comment about revenge awakens my curiosity: an old friend stirring after a drowse.

What if my best revenge now is to survive—no matter what they put me through?

"Amirgarh." I name a town that lies in the western part of Ambar. A town that I'm certain has never come up in conversation with either Gul or Subodh.

"Lie," Amba says flatly.

"Is that so?" General Alizeh's eyes narrow. "Hold out your hands, dirt licker."

The shackles around my wrists force them upward. Once again, pain washes over my body, my screams ringing in the silence. There's a moment when I think I see a shadow rise overhead, the lightorb flickering in response. I'm bracing myself for more pain to follow when my body finally gives up and everything turns dark.

In my dream, I'm walking through Ambar Fort again, following Sunheri's path around the perimeter of the wall with blood-encrusted fingers. Strangely, no specters are here today. None, except one, her touch as warm as it is cool in the real world.

"Are you trying to get killed?" Ma's reprimand, clear and strong, is music to my ears. "Why did you lie with a truth seeker present?"

"I thought you were fading," I say, still marveling at her presence. "But I can see you now."

"I will never fade. Not until I'm certain you're safe. And while you can see me now, you won't be able to for long. Cavas, there's something in that prison. A magic that prevents living specters from staying within the cells for more than a few moments at a time. I bet that you don't have spectral dreams anymore."

"I don't." I frown as the realization sinks in. "But how am I having one now?"

"I'm not sure. It might have to do with the fact that you're teetering on death's edge," Ma says, her voice tightening with despair. "Listen carefully. Get out of that prison. Get on the kabzedar rani's good side. Stall her until Gul gets here."

"The Scorpion will never believe I changed allegiances!"

"A person will do anything when tortured badly enough," Ma says sharply. "Pretend . . . must . . . my sake!"

Ma's voice crackles, breaks off as my eyelids flicker open, preventing me from asking her any other questions.

"Ma?" I call out. "Ma!"

"She isn't here, Cavas," a quiet voice says from beyond the far corner of my cell. Juhi. "Thank the gods for Vaid Roshan. That man saved you from being finished off for good."

I brush a hand over my aching ribs—whole, where I'm certain they were broken before.

"I had a dream," I tell Juhi. "That's how Ma and I talked. Apparently, there's magic here that prevents living specters from staying for too long."

"Not surprising. Magi from the Chand gharana were far more inventive than any of Rani Asha's own bloodline," Juhi comments. "What did your mother tell you that made you so angry, though?"

"What do you mean?"

"You were mumbling in your dream. I thought it was a simple nightmare, but then I heard you say something about changing allegiances."

A long silence falls between us, interspersed only by my rattling breaths.

"My mother told me to get on the Scorpion's good side. To get out of prison any way I can," I say flatly. "I don't see how, though, with a truth seeker monitoring my every move."

"Well, what in Svapnalok possessed you to lie in Amba's presence?"

"I wanted them to think I had something to hide," I explain. "If I told them the truth—that I know nothing—they would have killed me and used that to lure Gul here."

A lull follows after that comment, one that tells me that Juhi is thinking.

"Amba cannot refute the truth if you tell bits and pieces of it," she says at last. "I have lived with a truth seeker long enough to know this. In fact, it might be better if you persuaded Amba to be your ally."

"She reviles the thought of touching anyone with non-magus blood. Why would she be on my side?"

"You both are fighting the same enemy. Why wouldn't she?"

My response gets drowned by a man's bloodcurdling scream followed by the sound of a yowl.

The shadowlynx.

"They usually drug it with sleeprose. I suppose the guard on duty forgot to dose it today," Juhi says dryly.

It must be the case, because amid the shadowlynx's roars, a woman begins laughing out loud. Amira.

"What's Amira—"

"Shhh!" Juhi says. "Someone's coming!"

She's right. Soon enough, my eyes pick out the faint glow of white light from the distant corridor. Moments later, a small lightorb hovers outside my cell. Underneath that stands—

"Rajkumari Malti?" Thankfully my shout gets drowned out by the commotion at the far end of the prison corridor. I crawl closer to the bars. "Is that you?" I ask, my voice much lower.

Apart from a slight pallor, Princess Malti looks well enough, her yellow ghagra and blouse glowing sun-bright in the darkness of the kalkothri.

"How did you get past the guard?" I whisper.

"He was distracted by the shadowlynx," she says, her voice calm, matter-of-fact. "It bit off one of his legs when he went in to feed it."

I think I hear a gasp from Juhi's side of the wall. So that explains Amira's laughter. Her spiteful laughter.

Malice glitters in Princess Malti's dark-brown eyes as well, the shadow of her dead father momentarily reflected on her seven-year-old face. But Malti isn't King Lohar—and that is evident from the question she asks me next.

"Are you hurt, Cavas?"

"Vaid Roshan healed me," I reply, holding up my hand.

She frowns, as if she doesn't believe me. I force a smile despite knowing how difficult it is to maintain a charade in front of a child as perceptive as Malti.

"Is Siya here?" she asks.

Siya, who? I almost ask before the memory returns. Siya was the false name Gul used while infiltrating the palace.

"She isn't," I tell Malti. After a pause: "Her real name is Gul."

"Gul," Malti repeats. "That's the name General Alizeh uses when she asks me questions about her. She makes Rani Ma check and see if I'm telling the truth."

Malti's about to say more when a pair of hands curl around her shoulders, pulling her back. I stare at the long, slender fingers, the signet ring embellished with unpolished yellow and blue firestones.

"Rani Amba," I say, raising my gaze to meet hers. "Anandpranam."

Her cold yellow eyes stare at me from under the lightorb. "Malti," she says calmly. "How many times have I told you to never leave my chambers without me?"

Malti bites her lower lip, saying nothing.

"Come," Queen Amba tells Malti. "We must go now."

"So you're going to run away, then." A month ago, I wouldn't have dared to speak that way or to look Queen Amba in the eye. But now I'm thinking of my conversation with Ma and Juhi. As Juhi said, Amba would be a good ally to have, if I can persuade her to be one. But first I must pique her interest—or rouse her anger by challenging her pride.

"Watch your tongue, fool boy. Lest you lose it at my hand." The tremble along Amba's normally firm mouth tells me that the threat is as meaningless as her finery.

"I heard your ancestors were the ones who built Rani Mahal," I say. "The Chand gharana, wasn't it? A noble house named after the yellow moon itself. Bold, considering no one really knows if you can trace your bloodlines back to Sunheri."

Malti makes a small sound of pain. The queen's grip on her daughter is so hard that her knuckles have paled. Amba relaxes her hands. In the distance, I hear the shadowlynx's roars echoing in its cell, but that doesn't intimidate me as much the woman now watching me.

"What else have you heard?" the former queen asks.

"I heard that your palace wasn't called Rani Mahal," I force myself to speak over the pain. "That your ancestors put up a fight when Asha, the first rani of Ambar, wanted to take it—and that they lost."

"We did not lose." Her voice is clipped. "We acquiesced to a peace treaty that agreed to Rani Asha's binding with one of my ancestors. Since then, many royal bindings have involved a member from the Chand gharana."

"And now you have—what's that word you used—acquiesced again?" I allow contempt to fill my tone. "Your family handed over your ancestral lands to someone—and now you're handing over a whole kingdom to someone else?"

"Mind your tongue!"

"I can and I will," I say. "As long as you back me up during the next interrogation."

"I am not going to lie to save your sorry behind, half magus. That's not how truth seeking works."

"I'm not asking you to lie. You'll only need to *accept* my truth for what it is. Help persuade the Scorpion to get me out of this prison," I urge.

Silence fills the space between us. In the dim light, I see her frowning, as if mulling over what I said.

"We'll see," she says.

Then, with a final tug on Malti's shoulders, both woman and girl sweep away.

21
CAVAS

"Where is the girl named Gul, also called the Star Warrior?" General Alizeh asks me again the next day.

Amba's finger rests against the pulse on my wrist, her gaze focused somewhere on the stone wall behind me.

I take a deep breath. "I don't know," I say honestly.

"Truth."

I hear the snap of Alizeh's neck turning to stare at the former queen. Her gray eyes narrow. Amba's hand—the one that isn't touching me—is upraised and glowing gold, the only way to know a truth seeker's own truth.

"He's useless then," says the Sky Warrior next to Alizeh. The one named Captain Shekhar.

"I doubt it," I say boldly. "I know Gul better than anyone else. I may not know exactly where she is, but I can make an educated guess."

Again, Amba says, "Truth."

"I want to get out of this dungeon," I tell Alizeh. "For that, I'm willing to do anything."

"Truth," Amba confirms.

"Oh really?" Alizeh asks. "Are you willing to surrender? Pledge loyalty to Rani Shayla?"

"I am." *For now.*

There's a slight quiver against my skin. "Truth," Amba says after a pause.

General Alizeh doesn't notice. She's eyeing me the way a farmer would eye an old barrow that has suddenly become useful again. "Tell me then, dirt licker, where do you think she might head next? Whether or not we let you out of the prison depends on the information you give us."

I'm sorry, Juhi.

"The last place Gul lived in was Javeribad, with the Sisterhood of the Golden Lotus," I say. I hear a sharp intake of breath from the cell to my left. "It seems safe to say that's where she would go, wouldn't she? To get more support for her cause?"

"Truth," Amba says.

General Alizeh's mouth twists into the approximation of a smile. "Javeribad. You have been useful, dirt licker. In all this time, neither of the two witches imprisoned here gave a hint about where the Sisterhood is. Raise the wall," she tells Captain Shekhar.

The captain smartly taps his atashban against the wall dividing my cell from Juhi's. So far, the only bits of Juhi I've seen have been her midnight eyes or a lock of blue hair against a bruised brown forehead. Today, as the stone wall lifts, I see a wild-eyed, blue-haired woman behind bars, a muddied tunic hanging off her emaciated body, fury lining every bit of her worn face.

"Traitor!" she snarls, spittle flying everywhere. "You have betrayed her in the worst way possible!"

I jerk back as she slams her forearms against the bars.

"I'm going to kill you!" she screams, uncaring about the shackles glowing on her wrists and ankles. "*Kill you!*"

"Oh look. She's upset," Alizeh says lazily. "Lower the wall, Captain."

The captain hastens to do exactly that, while Juhi continues to scream in the background. In the second before the stone shields her from view, the purported rage vanishes from Juhi's face. She gives me a firm nod before shouting curses at me again. My heart slowly resumes beating normally. If I thought Juhi was angry, then surely that display must have convinced General Alizeh.

It does. Without torturing me this time, the Sky Warriors exit the prison, Queen Amba following in their wake. Once their footsteps fade away, I attempt to reach Gul. The consecutives must have weakened me far more than I'd anticipated, because even with my eyes closed and Vaid Roshan's healing, it's difficult to reach sthirta, to grow calm the way I'm supposed to as the temple materializes around me.

"Gul!" I call out as loudly as I can. "Gul, it's me!"

I shout over and over again until I think I feel a shift in the air, hear a distant, yet distinct reply.

"Cavas? Cavas!"

A spasm of pain takes over—aftershocks from the torture sessions, Vaid Roshan calls them. I force myself to focus on Gul's voice, to hold on to the threads that still keep me in my meditative state.

"Javeribad," I spit out. "Create a diversion in Javeribad. Do it as soon as you can."

22

GUL

Create a diversion in Javeribad.

The words rumble in my head as I jerk awake, my skin covered with goose bumps. Next to me, Sami snores, still fast asleep, but Kali is gone, her sheet tossed aside, her pallet still warm.

Picking out voices rising from beyond the tent flap, I slip out, a blanket wrapped around my shoulders, the cold air nipping at my nose. The sky is still dark, the main fire long turned to ash. But a little farther away from the area where our tents are set up, I find Subodh and Amar standing on two sides of a small lightorb, tension clear on their faces. Kali wavers between the two, her hands held out as if to keep them apart.

"What happened?" I ask, the strain of my dream showing up in my voice. "Why is everyone awake?" *Is it morning already?*

"I'm glad you're here, Savak-putri Gulnaz." Subodh's voice is little better than a growl. "We're here to decide—once and for all—if I am trustworthy or not. Isn't that so, Raja Amar? Perhaps then you will see no need to have me followed around by a small child—whom I frightened off, by the way, simply by shaking myself dry after a bath."

176

ward off the shivers that have taken over my body again as I recall the vision I had of Cavas.

As Subodh, Kali, and Amar settle by the lightorb, their faces shrouded by firelight and shadow, I tell them about my dream, words spilling out in a rush.

"It was strange," I say. "I mean, I've been meditating each night, trying to reach Cavas, ever since we got here. Each time, I've been unsuccessful and have fallen into a dreamless sleep. But just now, it was different. I don't know if it was a dream or simply wishful thinking."

"Perhaps it isn't," Subodh says, his eyes like molten firestones. "What did Cavas look like? What did he say?"

"I couldn't see him clearly. So many shadows were surrounding him; the look of them made me nauseated. He told me to create a diversion in Javeribad. To do it as soon as I can."

"Are you certain? Those were his exact words?"

"Yes."

Flames lick at the lightorb, popping and crackling, the silence around us broken only by the distant crowing of landfowl. Morning will be here soon.

"And you're certain it was Cavas," Amar says. The doubt in his tone makes me bristle. "Why would he tell you to go to Javeribad?"

"I'm not sure, Raja Amar. I didn't have time for an extended conversation."

Amar does not seem perturbed by my sarcasm. "I should write to Rani Ma. Ask her what exactly is happening at Ambar Fort. It would be a while before I got her answer, but that would still be more reliable."

More reliable than a sixteen-year-old girl's fevered nightmare, you mean. I grit my teeth.

"Actually, complements can communicate telepathically at great distances," Subodh says. "It's a fairly reliable system, when done awake. Try to reach Cavas again, Gul. See if he gives you the same message."

A part of me hesitates. I *have* communicated with Cavas telepathically but never successfully from miles away. However, Amar's skeptical expression makes me change my mind. "All right," I say, forcing myself to sound more confident than I am.

Unwilling to chance my concentration being broken by any real-world distraction, I close my eyes and breathe the way Subodh taught us during our first lesson. I'm back again in the darkened temple, the sky goddess alone in the sanctum. There is no sign of Sant Javer.

"Cavas?" I call out. "Cavas, can you hear me?"

"He isn't here, daughter."

I turn to the goddess and look into her eyes, which now reflect the dawn breaking outside the southern tenements.

"I *was* dreaming, then."

"What is meditation if not dreaming? What is dreaming if not living on a higher plane of existence?" the goddess replies. "What do you think you saw, daughter? What do your instincts tell you?"

My heart convulses now, too afraid to hope. "I want to believe what I saw. But you told me already that Cavas isn't here."

"He isn't here *now*, my child. But he was here before. And so were you."

I stare at the goddess, her smile cryptic. "You mean, it was real. I heard him."

"Yes, you did. But there are shadows around him," the sky goddess warns. "He needs to get out of that kalkothri. The only way he can do so is by giving the right information about your movements. If the Sky Warriors don't find you in Javeribad, I'm afraid he will not last much longer."

When I open my eyes, the sky is awash with color: an early-morning palette of pinks and yellows breaking through a gray sky. "Was I gone long?"

"Not long," Kali says. "Did you see Cavas?"

"No," I say. "But I saw the sky goddess. She was there the last time, too, when I heard him. She confirmed he was there."

"What if it's a trap?" Amar demands. "You weren't actively meditating when you heard Cavas. A living specter might have spoken to you in the night and you might have mistaken him for Cavas."

"That isn't likely, Raja Amar," Subodh says before I can retort. "Living specters can only disguise their voices to match the dead—not the living. Also, I know for a fact that Latif watches over Gul's tent each night while she sleeps. He would have known if any mischief was afoot."

My eyes widen. *Latif watches over me?* I whisper to Subodh.

As Cavas's mother watches over him at Ambar Fort, he replies.

Out loud, he says: "Latif, please come forward."

I frown, wondering how they communicated without the green swarna I always saw in Cavas's hand—when I spot it glowing on the ground, right next to Subodh's front paw.

A moment later, a sly voice speaks: "You called, Pashuraj."

Even now, after so many days of living among specters, I can never quite get rid of that crawling sensation under my skin in the presence of one.

"Please tell us about what's happening at Ambar Fort," Subodh says. "Or what the specters know."

"Harkha stays there to check on Cavas, of course," Latif says. "She never leaves the place. She told me that the kalkothri is difficult, nearly impossible for her to access. Magic built into its walls prevents living specters from entering the space for more than a few seconds at a time. The only time Harkha can talk to Cavas is in a spectral dream—when his interrogators nearly beat him to death."

No one speaks for a long time after that statement, not even a frowning Amar.

"The sky goddess told me that Cavas won't survive if he stays imprisoned for much longer," I say. "I have to go to Javeribad!"

"Absolutely not!" Kali snaps. "You'll only get captured or killed."

"But—"

"Esther *died* to keep you safe," Kali goes on brutally. "So did many

181

others from the Legion. For someone so reluctant to put others' lives at risk, you seem to have no concern for your own!"

My face burns. I want to defend myself. I also want to sink through the ground.

Surprisingly, Latif speaks up for me. "Come now, Kali. Going to Javeribad is dangerous, but surely, there must be ways to mitigate the risks and allow Gul to make an appearance—safely—before whisking her back here."

"There *is* no way." Kali shakes her head. "It's impossible!"

"I imagine if Juhi ji had thought the same thing years ago, you and your friend, Amira, would still be languishing in that labor camp," Latif's soft voice continues. "Most likely you'd be dead by now—or living specters yourselves."

Now it's Kali's turn to be speechless and unable to look anyone else in the eye.

"The other issue is Cavas himself," Amar says, breaking the silence. "Let's say—hypothetically—that your insane plan works and they let Cavas out. For our purposes, it will mean that he will become an informant. The question is: Will he still remain on our side?"

"Of course he will!" I say. "Why would he *ever* switch over to Shayla's side?"

"Human desires are unpredictable. They shift, and with them so do prophecies. You should know that better than anyone else."

"I believe we can risk Cavas not turning on Gul so soon, Raja Amar," Latif says—again coming to my defense. "Not unless he has developed a taste for sadists."

Amar's head snaps sideways at being addressed so directly. He squints, as if that will make him capable of seeing the specter any better.

"Also, Cavas might have used Javeribad as a ruse to get out of prison by hinting that Gul was going to the village to see someone there," Latif continues.

"The Sisterhood of the Golden Lotus," I murmur. *Or the Sisters who remain, anyway.* "I need to warn them that the Sky Warriors are coming."

"You can do that by shvetpanchhi," Amar points out. "Why go yourself and put everything at risk?"

Everything meaning Ambar. *His* kingdom.

"Because if the Sky Warriors don't see me, they will kill Cavas," I say sharply. "And I am not going to let that happen."

"You'll only put yourself in unnecessary danger. If something happens to you, the entire rebellion will fall apart!"

"We're perpetually in danger now!" I also want to add that I don't care about the rebellion if Cavas's life is at stake. But Subodh's thoughts brush mine, giving me pause.

Savak-putri Gulnaz. The Pashu king's voice in my head is calm, almost akin to a purr. *Don't lose your temper. Remember, Amar is still your king. There are ways to get what you want. Use your mind.*

I take a deep breath. "Ambarnaresh," I address Amar by his future title. "I don't mean to be insolent. Perhaps sending the Sisters a warning by shvetpanchhi is a smart idea. But I still need to go to Javeribad." *Do it as soon as you can.* "Perhaps there is a way to do it—as Latif said? A safe way?"

Amar's mouth flattens. "Let's ask *Latif* if he has any ideas, then."

"I agree," Kali says, the color having returned to her face. "Especially how he plans to *get* to Javeribad faster than a shvetpanchhi or a horse."

"I do have some ideas," the specter says from somewhere above the lightorb, his voice perfectly mimicking the mocking tone of Amar's and Kali's voices. "It will require planning, naturally, but with the Pashu on our side, we can pull off a quick visit to Javeribad. It might even be safe."

"*Might?*" Amar says sharply. "That's not good enough!"

"*Might* is what I can guarantee in these circumstances, Raja Amar. No plan is entirely foolproof. Something can always go wrong."

As Latif relays the details of the plan, I watch everyone's expressions.

Subodh is as neutral as always and Kali is frowning thoughtfully. Only Amar's face remains hard.

"What do you think?" Amar asks when Latif finishes speaking. "Raja Subodh?"

"I think it could work," the Pashu king says.

Amar raises his eyebrows skeptically. "Do you really think so? So much could still go wrong! What about you, Kali ji? What do you think?"

"It's risky," Kali says. "But it could work—*if Gul does exactly what she's told.*"

"I will," I say at once, holding out a hand, linking it with Kali's.

"No matter what?"

"No matter what," I say honestly.

Kali releases me.

Amar says nothing, but I can see he's still reluctant. It frustrates me to the point that I want to shake him.

You must not judge him harshly, Subodh whispers, as usual sensing my hostile thoughts. *He worries for you as you worry for Cavas.*

He's not worried for me! *He's only thinking about what I symbolize to the Ambari people.*

Do you really believe that's the only reason, Gul?

I think of Amar at Ambar Fort. That moment in the garden when he told me to challenge his father for trying to bind me with the crown prince. I'd seen longing in Amar's eyes back then. Sometimes, when he looks at me, I think I still see it.

I take a deep breath, wondering if Amar's first instinct was right. If this is simply a trap and it *is* wiser to avoid going to Javeribad. But even as the thought arises, I push it aside.

Cavas's life is at stake—and it's the only thing that matters now.

The morning boasts a blue sky thick with clouds, their edges tinged navy like cotton dipped in ink. I dig my knees into Queen Sarayu's feathered back, worried that I'll fall off even though I'm securely strapped to her with ropes. Kali clutches my waist as we rise into the clouds, squealing when a particularly dark layer soaks us right through. We both gasp upon emerging overhead, our eyes smarting in the sunlight.

"Are you all right back there?" a voice asks, sounding like a hundred birds singing in my ears.

"Y-yes." I will my teeth to not chatter and fail. "Y-yes, R-rani S-sarayu."

A few thousand feet in the air and shielded by clouds, the Pashu queen soars on her eagle wings, unfurling her peacock feathers as I imagine a ship's sail would. My stomach swoops when a pair of birds pass us— Brimmish falcons, I realize, from their glistening brown and green feathers. My arms, wound around the simurgh's neck, tighten before I realize what I'm doing.

"Goddess! I'm sorry, Rani Sarayu!"

"You aren't hurting me, Savak-putri Gulnaz. I meant it when I told you to hold on tight."

"You aren't to let go of her under any circumstance!" Kali says in my ear for probably the hundredth time. "Remember the plan."

"I do," I mutter.

Latif's plan was simple: "Fly to Javeribad, but do not land there. Hover over the village until you find the Sky Warriors—look for the screaming and mayhem, it should be easy—and venture close enough to let them see Gul seated on Rani Sarayu's back. The moment they see Gul, you are to fly back home. This will minimize your risk of capture—and you'll also prove Cavas right. You are *not* to dismount—either of you. *No matter what you see happening down there.*"

It was the only time I heard Latif sounding stern and forbidding— like a parent warning an errant child. To ensure our security—but mostly our compliance about dismounting—Latif had suggested strapping us to Queen Sarayu with ropes, an act that annoyed Kali as well as me, but it was the only thing that finally persuaded Amar to let us go.

As we fly farther north, my heart rate begins returning to normal, and

I slowly grow aware of the ropes chafing at my thighs. When Latif first suggested flying to Javeribad by simurgh, I thought he was joking. The Pashu don't like being treated as beasts of burden. When the stately Queen Sarayu actually agreed to take us to Javeribad, I was baffled. It made me consider again what Amar said about the Pashu and their motivations behind aiding us in this war.

Subodh had proved himself, of course. *But what about Rani Sarayu?* I wonder. *What does* she *want from this war?*

"I don't like this," Kali mutters, distracting me from my thoughts.

"You should open your eyes," I tell her. "The land actually looks beautiful from up here."

There is something remarkable about seeing Ambar spread beneath us: a patchwork of scattered green squares quilting a sea of flat, sandy plains and russet hills. Between the clouds, I glimpse passing towns and villages, the temples and havelis shrunk to the size of toys.

But as we move farther north, the air around us shifts. Clouds disperse and the sun burns like the top of a stove. No one speaks now, but I can sense that Kali is as alert as I am. Ambarvadi spreads ahead of us, its magic a glowing dome of pink over the city. Farther ahead lie the gleaming spires of Ambar Fort. *Cavas.* As the thought enters my head, Queen Sarayu heads west, toward Javeribad.

"Remember the plan," Queen Sarayu says. "Do *not* engage the Sky Warriors in battle. The point of this rather dangerous excursion is for Gul to be seen *without getting caught.* The moment a Sky Warrior recognizes her, we fly away. Keep your shields up at all times. And under no circumstances must either of you dismount."

As she speaks, pressure builds at the back of my throat—an instinctive protest I crush before it lands on my tongue. Dismounting would mean getting captured, jeopardizing everything Subodh, Amar, and the Legion have been working so hard toward: a united Ambar. And, selfish as I am, even I can't afford such recklessness.

Moments later, my ears start closing up as we begin our descent toward Javeribad.

"Shields up," the Pashu queen announces. "And hold tight."

My stomach turns seconds before I see the village's familiar kidney-shaped lotus pond or the column of smoke rising farther—from the temple housing Sant Javer's shrine.

23

GUL

Queen Sarayu swoops into a descent and then hovers over the temple. Kali and I hold our daggers at the ready, watching everything happening below through the orange veil of our shields.

Screams float upward as fiery bodies roil the earth, while a few brave villagers desperately attempt to douse the flames with rugs and blankets.

"Goddess, is that the *priest*?" Kali's voice is tight, horrified.

It *is* the priest, his partially burned dark-blue robes the only part of him that remains recognizable among his many injuries. Besides the priest, others have been burned—worshippers, whose faces the fire has melted like wax, and a young apprentice, who, despite his injuries, pours a bucket of water against a burning wall, barely dousing the flames.

Water, the one substance that cannot be conjured out of thin air.

"The pond's on the other side of the—"

"*No*, Gul." Kali's hard voice cuts me off. "We are *not* to land or to interfere in any way. We can't do anything right now except look for the Sky Warriors!"

I bite back my protests. Kali's right, of course. We have three things to do: *Find Shayla's minions. Let them see me. Fly back to safety.*

And so, I turn away from the burning bodies.

From the sooty children wailing next to their mother's corpse.

From the now-felled banyan tree outside the temple, a hundred years' worth of wishes tied to its branches in faded scraps of cloth, the woody flesh at the bottom of its trunk mangled, splattered with human blood.

Heat gathers around my birthmark and crawls up my limbs, my daggers emerald-bright under my shield.

Use me, my magic urges. *Do something.*

I can't. I don't.

When I was five, my mother walked into our yard barefoot, accidentally stepping on some broken glass. I didn't even know she was hurt until I saw her red footprints and ashy complexion; she made no sound as she walked back inside, or later, when Papa carefully extracted the bloody shards from her foot, her lips held so tight they might have been sewn together.

Today I hold myself together the same way, sweat limning my shoulders and ribs, my knees digging deeper into Queen Sarayu's feathery back. I mentally thank Latif for his foresight; without the ropes binding me to the simurgh, I would have surely slipped off and fallen.

Or jumped off.

"Where do we go from here?" Queen Sarayu asks, her soft voice audible despite the chaos below.

"We head west of the temple," I say, my throat feeling like it's been scraped with sandpaper. "That's where the orphanage—where the Sisterhood's house is."

We fly over a burned copse of trees and a line of soot-covered water bearers straggling up to Sant Javer's pond, buckets in hand. Javeribad's streets are deserted, stray dogs left barking outside shuttered huts. The milkman's cart lies overturned in a puddle; what happened to its owner I can only guess from the bloody footprints staining the ground nearby.

I'm about to look away, nauseated, when I spot the whip of a dark braid. A racing figure that looks a lot like—

"Prerna!" I shout. "Goddess, is that you?"

The girl's head snaps up at the sound, the surma rimming her eyes dripping black trails over her cheeks.

It *is* Prerna. A novice at the Sisterhood—a girl I once shared a dormitory with. Today, I barely recognize her, thanks to the bruises swelling on her face.

"Gul?" Prerna gasps, her voice barely audible. "Kali Didi? Is that you?"

"Where are the Sky Warriors, Prerna?" Kali's voice is firm and clear, much calmer than mine would have been. "Are they at the house?"

"They c-came there f-first. They were l-looking for Gul," she stutters, her voice growing louder as she speaks. "When they couldn't find her, they attacked . . . So w-we f-fought them."

At this point, Prerna bursts into sobs. "They k-killed Urvashi . . . I was l-lucky. They only kicked me in the face a few times. Uma Didi told me to r-run. One of the Sky Warriors f-followed me to the temple, b-but the priest hid me and refused to let him in. S-someone threw a rock at the Sky Warrior, hitting him on the head. So I started r-running again!"

My heart sinks. It's easy to guess what happened at the temple: the Sky Warrior's rage, the atashban's deadly fire catching onto the thatched roof, the straw knit into its mud-brick walls. But the Sky Warriors were no longer there. Which means—

"They're somewhere else," Kali tells me, her voice low, urgent. "We need to find them, Gul. *Now.*"

"That's good enough, Prerna," I call out. "Get away from here. Head to the northern tenements and find a woman named Ruhani Kaki. She'll help you."

I've barely spoken the words when a blast shatters the air up ahead, black smoke blooming from the general area of the village square.

Queen Sarayu swoops west as I dig my knees into her back. Behind me, Kali keeps muttering: "Don't engage, don't engage."

I don't know if the warning is for me or herself.

As we approach the square, we notice a familiar white figure on horseback, speaking to a Sky Warrior in an angry voice: ". . . mad? I've *told* you a hundred times to not overreact, Captain Shekhar, not in a place of worship—especially not when we're on the lookout for that stupid Star Warrior!"

"Ayye, General!" I shout as loudly as I can. "Up here!"

Her head audibly snaps as she hears my voice; it's the last I see of her before Kali shouts "Retreat!"

My ears begin popping again, my body frozen against the cold air, as Queen Sarayu zooms back toward the clouds. A moment later, though, the Pashu queen lets forth a frightening shriek.

"She's been hit!" Kali shouts before I can ask what happened. "Rani Sarayu, you need to rise higher! Higher!"

Blood seeps from one of the simurgh's brown wings, drop after drop of loamy black. Somehow, she rises up and out of the range of the atash-bans. Her feathered body grows warm and then hot with magic. Clouds gather around us, their moisture soaking our skin. A drop of blood falls on one of the cottony tufts, coagulates to gray. Before my stunned eyes, the clouds coat the wounded wing like one of Esther's poultices, stanching the flow of dark blood.

"That should hold for a while," Sarayu says, her calm voice revealing no hint of pain. "The cloud cover will shield us adequately from sight."

And it does, for so long that I begin shivering from the cold. I'm thinking there is no end in sight when we begin descending toward the southern tenements and land with a terrible thud.

The next few moments go by in a blur: Hands unstrap Kali and me from our harnesses, help us down before wrapping us in blankets.

"You need a change of dry clothes," someone says, but I barely hear their words.

I'm watching Subodh, who gallops past us, toward Sarayu, who is wheezing now, her wound having opened again. Subodh presses a glowing paw against her injured wing.

"Sami!" he roars. "Drishti jal!"

Sami races forth with a vial of the substance, a scared look on her face.

I watch as Subodh makes Sami tip a drop of the drishti jal into his mouth before spitting it out again in a thick glob of saliva onto the sand. He uses his other paw to make a paste out of the two and smear the mix onto Sarayu's injury.

"A bandage," he instructs now, his voice calmer. "Quickly!"

This time it's Sarpanch Parvez who appears, clean rags in hand. "I can help, Pashuraj," he says quietly. "I know something about healing."

Quickly, efficiently, with a finesse I don't expect, the head councilor lifts Queen Sarayu's injured wing and binds the wound.

"It will take some time to heal," Subodh says. "The drishti jal and sand will help knit the wound together. My saliva thickens it so that it will not run down her wings."

"Maybe we should ask Raja Subodh to bottle up some of his spit to keep for later," Kali jokes under her breath. "Who knew it would be so useful?"

I try to smile and fail. Queen Sarayu could have died on the way here. It's a miracle that she survived, that we returned the way we did.

From behind Kali, I notice Amar approaching us, a frown on his face.

"You're back," he says, relief clear in his voice. "How did it go?"

"Clearly it was successful," I say bitterly. "I didn't engage any Sky Warriors in battle even when they shot Rani Sarayu. I didn't die—though so many people in Javeribad did. The great symbol of your rebellion, your most treasured weapon—the Star Warrior—is still safe, Raja Amar."

Amar steps back, red blotches appearing under his beard.

"Gul, that was uncalled for!" Kali says.

"Sorry," I mutter, not meeting Amar's eyes.

"Is that how you apologize to someone?" Kali demands. "Like you don't mean the words?"

"Leave it," Amar says, silencing Kali. "It's fine. You've both had a rough day."

No. It's not fine. I'm being absolutely awful to Amar and he deserves a proper apology. But if I look at him right now, I'll only burst into tears.

Who am I really angry with? I wonder as their footsteps recede. *Amar? Or myself?*

For weeks, *months*, I'd struggled against using death magic, never wanting to wield my powers until absolutely necessary. But today, at a time when my magic *could* have helped people, I was the one who remained helpless, held back by a promise I made of my own accord.

Ultimately, our main mission was successful. I went to Javeribad and showed my face to the Sky Warriors. They'll now know Cavas was telling them the truth. He won't be tortured anymore. He'll be released from prison.

That's what matters, right?

The question nags at me as other images flood my brain: Sant Javer's shrine in flames surrounded by corpses and wails; Prerna's bruised face, her sobs searing my insides. There's also the reminder that now, despite his so-called freedom, Cavas must pretend to switch loyalties. Under Shayla's watch, he must do whatever he can to prove himself to her.

A cold that has little to do with my cloud-soaked body snakes through my limbs, causing my teeth to chatter.

"Gul!" a woman cries out. Sami, who rushes over, wrapping an arm around me. "You're shivering. Come with me at once!"

Alone in the tent, I strip off the wet clothes, slip into a dry tunic and leggings, and toss my damp hair into a braid. I will myself to remember the way Cavas looked at me. Like I wasn't simply a girl he was lusting after, but something more—something as wispy and wonderful as moonlight itself.

"Cavas will never betray me," I whisper. "No matter what happens."

A cackle sounds in the otherwise empty tent, raising the fine hairs on my nape and arms.

"Is that a specter? Is it you, La—oof!"

The tent flap snaps across my face, obscuring my vision. As I push aside the canvas, I realize the voice I heard couldn't have belonged to Latif. It simply wasn't deep enough. By the time I step out, the specter is gone, the prickling under my skin the only evidence of one having been there.

24

SHAYLA

"Ambar Sikandar, I can explain."

"I would hope so, Alizeh. It baffles me how you and your soldiers managed to set fire to a whole village but were *still* unable to catch a sixteen-year-old girl!"

We are in the study adjoining my bedroom in Raj Mahal—a room where Lohar used to gather classified reports when he was alive. Unlike the rest of the palace, this room isn't built for spectacle. A large mahogany table and three comfortable chairs are its only furniture, along with a small wooden cabinet holding enameled boxes of paan and an ornate, rock crystal hookah. Today, like every other day, the table is piled with scrolls: briefs about what's happening in the kingdom, but most overwhelmingly, about what happened in Javeribad.

Perspiration coats Alizeh's forehead, her throat bobbing as she swallows. While a part of me wants to throttle her, another part knows that I can't. Not yet. I force myself to breathe deeply.

"Tell me what happened," I say. "From the very beginning."

Alizeh's words emerge in a rush: "We went there on the dirt licker's information yesterday, as you know. After making inquiries, we discovered that a group of women and girls lived in the village orphanage. We went in for questioning. We did it the usual way."

With threats, instead of treats.

"We put down most of them, but the cook slipped away. Another girl escaped into the shrine in Javeribad. Captain Shekhar followed. He demanded that the priest hand her over. The priest refused. Some of the villagers began protesting as well." Alizeh licks her lips, and I know this story isn't going anywhere good. "Captain Shekhar says someone threw a rock at him. So he shot his atashban, setting the priest and a few others on fire. The shrine caught fire, too, but the captain says that was entirely an accident. I've punished him, Ambar Sikandar. Twenty lashes."

I say nothing, though I'm certain that my eyes reveal my fury. It is one thing to punish zamindars and farmers who do not pay the increased land tithes. But destroying religious shrines is another matter altogether. People get sensitive about their gods and saints. Incensed enough to wage war against their queen.

"If this happens again, Alizeh, I will lash you myself and replace you with another, more effective general," I warn. "Your subordinates should be under your control at all times."

Alizeh's only response is to swallow once, audibly, and say, "Yes, Ambar Sikandar."

"What happened next?" I ask. "How did the girl escape you again?"

"She was flying a bloody simurgh! They never landed, the cowards. I shot the simurgh, though," Alizeh says viciously. "Hit it right in the wing. I sent out a couple of trackers to follow it. They lost its trail east of Dhanbad."

Alizeh winces when I raise my hands, but I use them only to clap twice. The guard outside comes running into my study.

"Fetch Damak and Amba," I say. "At once."

"Yes, my queen."

Acharya Damak is the first to arrive, all silk and slippery smiles, his eyes nearly as cold as mine. Amba takes a little longer to come, wearing a sari of deep pink and gold. The serving girl I've assigned to watch the former queen day and night enters my study quietly behind her and nods once at me.

Nothing out of the ordinary to report, then.

I lean back in my chair. For once, Amba hasn't been sending out unsanctioned shvetpanchhi or hatching another escape plan. Her hands tremble slightly as I watch her—hands that I once broke before having the vaid fix them again. As the old Vani saying goes: *Spare a snake and it might still prove useful.*

"Now that we're all here," I say. "I am going to put forth a plan. You will advise me to the best of your ability, Acharya. And you, Amba, will make sure he isn't lying."

Amba's mouth stiffens. She doesn't argue the way she did the first time I made her use her powers. With her broken hands.

"Yes," she says now. A pause before adding: "Ambar Sikandar."

I nod, satisfied.

The acharya holds out a hand. Amba places her left hand on his arm and raises her right hand, the palm glowing gold.

"I am planning to let the dirt licker out of prison and transfer him to a room in Raj Mahal, guarded around the clock," I say. "I want to use him as an informant. Tell me, Acharya. Is it a good idea?"

The acharya frowns, saying nothing for a long while. Then: "It could be a good idea. If executed properly."

"Truth," Amba says.

"Explain," I tell him.

"Don't limit his role to a mere informant. Use him as leverage instead. There are some political advantages to be seen out in public with the half magus." Silk knits itself into Damak's voice, the way it always does when making dangerous propositions. I'd heard that voice several times before at court, whenever the acharya advised Lohar.

"What kind of political advantage?" I ask, my voice equally silky.

The acharya's unctuous smile does not slip. "Think about this, Rani Shayla. Shrines are sprouting across the kingdom, dedicated to the girl and her dirt-licking lover. If you show the people that the girl's lover is now on *your* side, his loyalties completely bound to you, there will be confusion among magi and non-magi. As the old Ambari saying goes, *To stop a sand dune, you must build a barrier.* Xerxes-putra Cavas can be your barrier and protect you from much of your subjects' wrath."

"Truth," Amba says.

I grow silent, alternating between watching Damak and Amba, wondering if they're both conspiring to hatch a plot together. But Amba simply looks as if a pile of dung is under her nose—she must be gagging at the thought of a dirt licker living inside the king's palace—and the acharya's pale-green eyes are clear of any deception.

"You may have a point," I say after a pause. "It will be dangerous, bringing him out of the dungeons."

"When has danger ever stopped you, my rani?" the high priest questions.

True. When has it?

"You may leave," I say, which instantly makes Amba drop her hand back to her side.

"I will arrange for his security," Alizeh says once they're both gone, almost tripping over herself in her eagerness. "Watch him myself, if needed."

"There's no need, General." My cold voice makes Alizeh wince. "Your job is to keep the city and your troops under control. Do it well. And bring me daily reports."

If Ambarvadi falls, we are done for, I think. And Alizeh, despite her faults, has the cunning and cold brutality necessary to keep invaders away.

"Captain Emil can watch the dirt licker, along with two others," I say after a pause.

"Yes, Ambar Sikandar."

It will be risky, bringing Xerxes-putra Cavas out in the open. Riskier than anything I've ever done. The boy may not have any magical powers apart from seeing living specters, but he was born with the cunning that every dirt licker possesses. The sort that can keep mothers apart from their daughters. The sort that can kill queens if underestimated.

"Ask Emil to bring me the dirt licker now," I tell Alizeh. "And make sure he doesn't smell like sewage."

25

CAVAS

When I wake up again, it's to the sound of screaming.

Gul! I think instinctively before realizing that it isn't Gul's voice I hear but someone else's—someone whose cell lies farther away from mine.

Amira.

I sneak toward the wall, despite the stinging shackles, and place my mouth close to the thin opening there.

"Juhi ji?" I whisper, the sound almost drowned out by another gut-wrenching cry of pain. "Are you there?"

There's a long pause before I see those black eyes again, a flash of bright-blue hair. "I'm still alive," she says hoarsely. "If that's what you're asking."

"What happened?" I ask. "Why are they torturing Amira? Is it the same reason they tortured you yesterday?" Juhi had fallen silent for so long after the torture session that I worried the guards had killed her.

"I suppose," she replies. "A group of masked figures broke into the Ministry of War in Dhanbad, tied up its employees, and trashed it. They defaced the door with curses for the new queen and the symbol of a golden lotus."

The same lotus etched onto Juhi's and Amira's palms.

"But you didn't . . ." I hesitate. "Did you?"

"Of course not!" Juhi says, her voice rough. "Secrecy was paramount to the Sisterhood's survival. Whenever we attacked, it was with purpose, with a goal in mind."

"You mean other women attacked the ministry?"

"I don't know who they were—if they were even women. The Sisters I know would never engage in such attacks. The last I knew, they were still in Javeribad. But perhaps I'm wrong." Her voice turns bitter. "I've been wrong about so many things in the past—"

Her voice cuts off abruptly as a pair of footsteps clatter in the hallway. A lightorb glows over Vaid Roshan, who rushes past without looking into our cells. Amira's screams soften to a whimper that fades as voices rise in argument, clear and distinct in the silence of the dungeons.

"You must cease the consecutives at once." Vaid Roshan's voice is as tight as wire. "You will kill her at this rate!"

"We're only doing our job," a guard snaps back. "Hey! You can't touch her without permission!"

"I am doing *my* job, which is ensuring she remains alive," the vaid says in a cold voice. "You don't want me to have to tell Rani Shayla that a Level One died because the guards got carried away during interrogations. Do you?"

There's a long silence, broken only by an occasional moan. The vaid's threat seems to have worked. Shortly afterward, the guards march past our cells, running their lathis across the bars, spewing filthy, unimaginative curses, most of them involving women.

"A Level One?" I whisper to Juhi.

"From what I can gather, it means a prisoner they can torture but not kill yet without the rani's permission. I must be a Level One for now. So must you."

At the end of the hallway, Vaid Roshan takes on the dulcet tones of a healer's reassurances, and despite everything, I find myself collapsing against the wall with relief. For now, at least, Amira will face no cruelty.

"That vaid is a miracle," Juhi says. "It's a wonder he's still alive."

"The Scorpion can't kill every human with a conscience."

"Yes, but she can mold them to suit her purposes. Force them into doing her bidding even if they don't want to. Promise me you'll be careful once you get out of here, Cavas. That you'll do your best to stay alive."

"*If* I get out, you mean."

I don't know if Gul heard my message. If my attempt at meditation had simply passed her by like a fevered dream.

"You will," Juhi says quietly. Something rattles like marbles across the floor in her cell. "Sometimes, I scry the future by using pits from the dates they give us to eat. They don't work as well as my cowrie shells, but they're adequate. You won't be here much longer."

My insides tighten. I'm about to ask how she can be so sure when I hear footsteps again. This time, they aren't hurried, but quick and efficient. A lightorb pauses outside my cell, revealing two figures: a prison guard in gray and the Sky Warrior who held me back in Raj Mahal as my father died. I recognize him by his silver hair and soldierly features, by the single red atashban on his uniform that marks him as a captain.

"Xerxes-putra Cavas," he says. "The rani has sent for you. Get up. Hurry, now."

I get up as quickly as I possibly can without triggering the shackles. To my surprise and relief, the captain points his atashban at my ankles, removing the shackles there in a warm spiral of golden light. He also waits for me to move forward, not shocking me the way the prison guards or General Alizeh would have to make me go faster.

"The shadowlynx needs feeding," the captain tells the guard. "Make sure that's taken care of."

"Y-yes, Captain Emil." The guard's leering face loses color. He's probably remembering how the shadowlynx took a piece out of another guard's leg three days ago.

"What are *you* looking at, dirt licker?" the guard snarls suddenly.

A glob of spit lands on my cheek, dribbling down to my chin. Now that I'm getting out of prison, it barely registers.

"Stand back," Captain Emil says before raising a hand to the bars, turning them blue. Cool air wafts into the cell, filling my lungs.

"Careful when you step out," the captain says, his voice drawn tight with the caution of someone more worried for himself than those around him. "I've lifted the spell that triggers the agnijal, but don't touch it in any case."

I lower my gaze, noticing the thin channel of liquid at the threshold of my cell—agnijal, gleaming like oil under the lightorb. Ten times more flammable than grass-oil, agnijal is a substance that is said to light up at the slightest touch. I notice it flanking the sides of the hallway, a design that effectively blocks in—and kills—the prisoners if someone tries to escape, while still allowing the guards to leave unscathed.

A few feet from the staircase leading out of the kalkothri, I'm struck with a sudden bout of dizziness, one that would have made me collapse if not for Captain Emil's tight grip on my arm.

"Easy, boy," he mutters. "We're passing through a patch of Prithvi Stone. Slowly, slowly—that's it."

I force myself forward, one step at a time, my vision refusing to clear until I reach the very top of the staircase, daylight flooding the corridor, pinching my eyes into a squint. I raise my shackled hands without thinking and nearly tumble back down from the shock on my wrists. A lathi pokes me between the shoulder blades—the guard has followed us out.

"That will be all," Captain Emil tells him. Two burly Sky Warriors emerge from the shadows, their atashbans raised. "His guard is here. Keep walking, boy. The effects of the Prithvi Stone will wear off soon."

They lead me to a small room at the side, to a bucket of water and soap, and a shaving blade small enough to be useless as a weapon. A folded pile of clothes has been placed nearby: a clean, navy-blue angrakha and narrow white trousers. My convoy does not leave the room even when I pause.

"Hurry up." Captain Emil's tone is brisk. "You can't present yourself to the rani looking like that."

That's when I see the mirror and the creature reflected within. Emaciated, bearded, with hollows for cheeks and eyes. The only things that look familiar are the blue bands glowing at my wrists.

"My shackles," I say. "I can't . . ."

Annoyed, the captain presses a hand against my wrists. The shackles disappear.

There are no marks on my body thanks to Vaid Roshan's handiwork. To my interrogators, the marks don't matter, though. The healer doesn't modify memory, and the brain remembers every scar.

The guards do not flinch or wrinkle their noses when I toss aside ragged clothes that smell of urine, feces, and blood, or when I wash my body, which smells much the same. My new clothes hang loose on my frame. I pull the trousers' drawstrings tight and tuck my cracked soles into a pair of new leather jootis.

Captain Emil nods. "Shall we go, then?"

The shackles reappear on my wrists.

My security convoy leads me down a long stone corridor, then up a set of glass stairs. Strange marble palm trees form the pillars of another hallway, this one with glass on both sides, revealing the lawn and garden outside Raj Mahal. The floor sparkles in the sunlight, appearing to shift like sand when I move. The lobby with the sword chandelier has been restored, no evidence of the battle that took place there several months ago.

What date is it now? I wonder. I've lost count of the number of meals

I received in prison—the only way I used to keep track of time. *How long have I been locked up?*

I get my answer upstairs, in an enormous room, its glass walls shimmering with rainbow hues, its marble floors furnished with plush, paisley-patterned rugs. The number twenty-three glows gold on a chart at the back, next to an illustration of a tree repeatedly growing and shedding its leaves. *Day twenty-three, Sloughing. Which means I was in prison for twelve days.*

I pause a few feet from the Scorpion, who sits at a mahogany desk, writing with an ink-stained sangemarmar pen. Queen Amba stands beside her, almost sentinel-like in her posture.

"Ambar Sikandar," the Sky Warriors chorus.

Shayla looks up, her cold eyes landing squarely on mine, and I suddenly remember why I feared her as a stable boy. Why the sour smell of sweat rises from my armpits now as she gestures us over and then asks me to sit in a chair.

"Xerxes-putra Cavas. Classified as a dirt licker in our official records, though you are really a half magus thanks to your rapist sire's blood. Tell me now. Can you see living specters?"

I swallow. It would be foolish to lie about something so obvious. "Yes. I can."

"Amba," the Scorpion says.

Queen Amba's anklets are the only indication of her movement. She places a hand on my arm.

"Are there any living specters around me now?" the Scorpion asks.

I turn around, looking, praying my mother hasn't followed us here. "No, Rani Shayla."

"Truth," Amba says.

"Will you be loyal to me as you told General Alizeh?"

Until it no longer suits my purposes. "Yes."

A pause. The barest score of nails against my flesh. "Truth," Amba says.

The Scorpion smiles with one side of her mouth, a strange look in her eyes. "Yes, you will be loyal to me," she murmurs before her voice shifts, turns to honey. "But are you mine, Xerxes-putra Cavas? Mine and mine alone?"

Bound to the palace. Shackled to her whims.

"Whom else can I belong to?" I ask quietly, before adding, "My queen."

I don't need to prick my ears to know that Amba will verify this truth in her bland voice.

I force myself into stillness as the Scorpion rises from her chair and walks around the table. She pauses right in front of me and then bends her head before tilting my face upward. Her fingers lightly brush my newly shaven cheek, gently tug on my lobe. The other side of her mouth lifts, gold dust gleaming on the apples of her cheeks.

"Yes, you are mine. All mine," she says before biting my lower lip. I taste bile at the back of my tongue. When she lifts her head again, traces of my blood are on her teeth. "And soon, everyone will know this." She tosses me a scroll of paper. "Can you read this?"

"Yes," I gasp out, not even thinking of lying.

"Truth," Amba says, her cool voice and touch grounding me.

"Good." The Scorpion smirks at me. "Memorize this by tomorrow. If you miss a single word, I'll take a bite out of your tongue. Understand?"

"Yes, Rani Shayla." I'm surprised I can speak, let alone sound as calm as I do now.

"Truth," Amba says.

"Take our guest to his new accommodations," the Scorpion tells Captain Emil. "And make sure you don't let him out of your sight."

26

CAVAS

My room isn't anywhere near the Scorpion's, thank Javer, but somewhere on the floor underneath, through a series of passageways that I try to memorize—and forget the moment I make the next turn.

Some spy I am.

My heart almost jumps to my throat when a gray figure floats in from one of the doors. My mother, her eyes fiery with triumph. She raises a finger to her lips as we pass her by and I blink once to show I understand. Unaware of our exchange, the Sky Warriors press forward until we reach a small room at the very end, furnished with a simple bed, table, and chair. An unlit fanas hangs in a nook in the wall, the wick hissing to life the moment we step in. There are no windows in the room. Nothing except stone, as if simulating my old cell underground. One of the Sky Warriors steps in with me and settles into the chair, while another stands guard outside my door. When it comes to keeping an eye on me, they're taking the Scorpion's orders literally.

"I will return tomorrow," Captain Emil tells me. "If you need anything, simply ask Captain Shekhar over here."

Captain Shekhar sneers at me the moment Emil leaves the room. "Don't look at me, dirt licker. Unless you'd like me to rearrange your face."

There's an old Vani saying: *Dogs bark, dustwolves bite.* I sense that Captain Shekhar, with his bloodshot eyes and gold-plated canines, hovers somewhere between the two.

I undo the scroll the Scorpion asked me to memorize and read it carefully. A few lines in, my stomach begins churning. The speech implies that my feelings for the Scorpion are deeper than mere loyalty—that I've not only switched allegiances but also hearts. I refrain from wiping away the feel of her kiss from my mouth. Though we don't speak, I know the Sky Warrior is watching my every move, ready to report back my expressions to his queen. One way to convincingly lie to someone is to believe a little in the lie yourself. I know this from years of lying to my father and the stable master, Govind. I wonder where Govind is now, if he's still alive.

A cool draft of air enters the room. Without glancing sideways, I know it's my mother—having slid through the gap between the closed door and the floor.

I rise to my feet. "I need to use the toilet."

The captain points to a chamber pot in the corner of the room.

"Do you have to watch me?" I pretend embarrassment—which isn't really that difficult if I put my imagination to work.

The captain grimaces. "Oh, all right. But be quick about it."

I wait until the door closes behind him and then turn to my mother. "What news?"

"Gul went to Javeribad," she whispers. "But you must have guessed already. It's why they let you out. In the meantime—"

Sharp raps on the door cut off her words.

"Are you done?" Captain Shekhar shouts, sounding suspicious.

I sigh, glancing at the empty chamber pot. "Not yet," I shout back.

"Stay alive," Ma whispers. "Do nothing to rouse the Scorpion's suspicions."

Once Ma disappears, I call the captain back in.

"It w-was a f-false alarm," I pretend to stutter, bracing myself for a blow. "S-sorry."

He rolls his eyes. "Get to it," he tells me, pointing at the scroll.

"Y-yes, Captain."

I settle down on the bed and begin reading under the Sky Warrior's watchful gaze. It's going to be a long day.

Sometime during the night, I wake from a doze. In the dim light, I see that Captain Shekhar is asleep, his parted mouth drooling, his right hand on his atashban.

Now is as good a time as any.

I put aside the scroll and close my eyes. It's a risk to do this with a Sky Warrior so close.

But it's the only opportunity I've got. I breathe deep, my pulse slowing as the darkness behind my eyelids shifts, turning into a temple's carved pillars. Figures form before the inner sanctum: a smiling Sant Javer, the sky goddess and—

"Gul!"

She hits me with the force of a dust storm, her hair smelling of the desert, of the sun itself. It's strange how I can touch her in this meditative state. Hold her, even. Though the touch itself feels different—less *real* and more like the remnant of an old memory. For the first time in many days, I feel myself relax.

"You're here!" she says, still watching me as if I'm a dream. "Are you okay? Did they let you out?"

"They did. I'm still being guarded, but I'm inside the palace now. I saw my mother, too."

It's strange, being able to see Gul in my mind, to talk to her from inside this fort when she's miles away from me.

"I can't believe this actually worked—that I can *talk* to you!" Gul shakes her head. "Listen, Cavas. Right now, we're in—"

"Don't," I interrupt. "Don't tell me where you are. They make Rani Amba verify my truths. I don't want to have to lie—or have them figure out we're complements."

Gul frowns, but her mouth clamps shut. She nods.

I take a deep breath. Might as well get to the important stuff. "The Scorpion wants me to give a speech tomorrow."

"What kind of speech?"

"About how I've switched my loyalties and everything." I don't tell Gul about my meeting with the Scorpion, about how she bit my lip. But she senses something is off, because she steps back and looks up into my eyes with a frown.

"Something happened," she says. "Something you're not telling me."

Pain begins to throb in my temples, steady as a hammer. I don't know if I can hold on much longer.

"It doesn't matter. Remember: Whatever happens, this"—I press her hand to my heart—"will always be yours." I expected to sound awkward, even nervous while expressing my feelings to Gul for the first time. But the truth gives my voice clarity, a strength I've never felt before.

Gul's lips tremble. "Cavas—"

"Trust me," I whisper, the last thing I say before the temple vanishes and I'm back inside the room with stone walls.

A moment later, when Captain Shekhar wakes with a sneeze, he finds me up, reading his queen's scroll by the dim fanas light.

27

GUL

As a child of four, there were rare instances when I would wake shaking in the middle of the night, having dreamed of being wrenched away from my parents by Sky Warriors, a scream still encased in my throat. The night Cavas tells me about his forthcoming speech, I wake the same way, my body quivering, gasping for breath. Glancing over at Kali and Sami, who are still fast asleep, I open the tent flap and quietly head out to find Subodh.

Please be awake, I think, relief rushing through me at the sound of a pair of voices carrying in the silence, including Subodh's distinctive rumble.

"How much longer will we continue sacrificing ourselves for human wars?"

The tension in Queen Sarayu's voice gives me pause, my feet slowing several yards away from the reservoir. I watch them sitting side by side, Pashu king and queen, rajsingha and simurgh, their furry and feathered forms silhouetted by a gibbous yellow moon.

"We *are* part human," Subodh says. "Pashu have fought against injustice since the time of the great animal spirits."

"The great animal spirits are remembered by none except the Pashu. Humans today don't know they existed," the simurgh retorts, her voice sending chills up my spine. "And Pashu have fought in a human war before, remember? We lost so many of our people to it."

"Which is why I need you to help us with this one. To free Pashu who were captured and enslaved during the Battle of the Desert. Once he is king, Raja Amar will sign an order to free all Pashu who are under indenture contracts with humans. But we need to help him win the throne first."

"Wars are *your* specialty, Raja Subodh. Why do you need my help? Take over the throne in my stead and help the humans yourself."

"You know I cannot do that, Rani Sarayu."

"And as queen, I cannot in good conscience risk more Pashu lives. I promised I would help you during this war—and I will. With messenger birds. With food and water for your armies. But I will not give you my soldiers. I cannot subject them to the terrible fire of human atashbans again."

I bite my lip. It's my fault that Queen Sarayu went to Javeribad and got injured. My fault again that we will lose this war. But before I can say anything, Subodh speaks again:

"You're punishing me, aren't you?"

"I am not, old friend." Queen Sarayu's grief is palpable. "I waited more than twenty years for you to return and take over your father's throne. I kept convincing myself and everyone else that you would change your mind. Fool that I was."

I find myself holding my breath in the silence that follows.

"I am going to get some sleep," Queen Sarayu says at last. "You should talk to Savak-putri Gulnaz. The poor girl has been waiting in the cold for quite a while."

My heart skips a beat as the simurgh turns her bright-eyed gaze at me; of course she heard me approach. It's likely Subodh did as well.

"Shubhraat, Rani Sarayu."

"Shubhraat, Raja Subodh."

Cordial though their farewells are, I still feel the weight of the conversation hanging in the air as the simurgh hobbles to the nest the tenement dwellers made for her comfort from clean honeyweed bushes and the softest grass they could find.

The awkward silence continues as Subodh faces me, his great yellow eyes scanning me from head to toe.

"You meditated," he says to my surprise. "And successfully."

"How did you—"

"You're still glowing a little."

I am, I realize. There's a faint light emitting from every part of my skin. "Did that tip you off to my presence?"

"Not really. It was your tread. Humans aren't quite capable of silencing their feet. Now tell me. What happened?"

I recount the meditation session—how I saw Cavas and what he said to me.

"I'll ask Latif and the specters to check on this," Subodh says once I finish. "You should be proud of yourself, Gul. This is useful information."

"Sometimes I wish I *didn't* know what was happening tomorrow." My triumph of having successfully communicated with Cavas has been completely overshadowed by the fear of his upcoming speech. "It's a strange feeling."

"Knowledge has its own price." Subodh studies the moonlight patterning the reservoir's surface. "We always regret the things we're desperate to know."

Almost instinctively, I turn to look in the direction Queen Sarayu headed, the nest utterly still in its silence. "Rani Sarayu—"

"Was right," Subodh says. "As usual. I have always been more of a wanderer than a ruler. Kingship was thrust upon me when my father died, and I never enjoyed the burden. Raja Amar is different, though. If he wins this war, he can do a great deal for this kingdom."

"How *are* we going to raise armies, though?" I ask. Without the Pashu on our side, our chances of winning any kind of war appear slim.

"I have a plan in mind," Subodh says. "In fact, I want you to join Raja Amar and me in our tactical meetings from now on. It would help to have Kali and Falak there as well. We need to persuade non-magi from the southern tenements to join us in the war effort, and it would be better if they see you there."

"I'll be there," I say at once. "Are we planning to invade Ambarvadi?"

"Eventually. But to do that, we need external support."

"External support? You mean from other cities in Ambar?"

"Partially, yes. I will let Raja Amar address that in the morning. In the meantime, I want you to start training with the Legion again. *Properly*, this time. Expose them to the sort of magic you'd use against an enemy."

I nod, guilt knifing my gut. "I will," I promise.

"Also . . . I want you to temporarily block your mind from Cavas's."

"*What?*" I feel my jaw drop. "But *why?*"

"It will be too dangerous now, with his being so closely watched by Rani Shayla and her guards. Cavas may have escaped detection this time, but he may not be able to again. Rani Shayla likely already knows that Cavas is half magus. We don't want her knowing you both are complements as well. For the time being, it's better that Cavas sends us messages through his mother or another living specter."

"Won't they see him if he talks to the specters?" I argue. "How is that not dangerous?"

"Yes, but though dangerous, it is still easier for Cavas to communicate with a specter over directly communicating with you. He hasn't yet learned to meditate properly with his eyes open. If the wrong person finds him in a state of sthirta and wrenches him out of it, I fear it could damage his mind permanently. It could also affect you. Tell me something. Were you and Cavas able to touch each other when you meditated?"

"Yes . . . though it wasn't exactly the same as touching in real life. I could still tell I was in some sort of dream state. If that makes any sense."

"It does. Touches in a meditative state are not the same as physical touches—your bodies still remain exactly where they are. Yet your *minds* are still deeply connected and, therefore, at their most vulnerable. If someone on Cavas's side attacks him, there's a possibility that they could reach you, too, and scar your mind in irreparable ways."

I grow quiet. A part of me continues to battle, to resist, the idea of not being able to see Cavas, to touch him in this small way. I don't care about myself. But if Cavas gets hurt . . .

"Fine," I say, hating the word. "I won't communicate with him."

"Good. I'll send a message to Harkha to relay the same information to Cavas." Subodh pauses. "You should get some sleep. The night is still long."

I walk back to the tent without a word, knowing I won't be sleeping anytime soon.

28

CAVAS

Captain Emil makes me recite the speech to him the next morning, one eye on the scroll, another eye on my expressions.

"You know the words," he says when I finish. "You even sound like you mean them."

"I do mean them," I lie. "I'm loyal to Rani Shayla."

The captain stares at me. Something akin to disappointment flickers in his eyes, but it disappears so quickly that I can't be too sure. "Come along," he says.

Instead of going upstairs to the royal chambers, we make a left at the staircase, heading deeper into Raj Mahal, through another set of hallways held up with giant marble pillars shaped like palm trees. Indradhanush knits a rainbow-hued metal web through the glass roof, casting a shadowy lattice over the floor. Guards appear, posted every few feet, their spears embedded with firestones, their eyes the only part of them that moves under their dark-blue turbans.

The hallway ends in gold doors made with paneled mirrors, flanked by two hard-faced Sky Warriors. They nod at Captain Emil and move aside one of the panels, revealing another, smaller door.

Hot air cloaks me the moment I step outside, following Emil down a set of stairs. A pair of sleek white mares are tethered to a carriage made of polished wooden doors and a glass roof, dazzling indradhanush spiking its giant wheels. Unlike open-air Ambari carriages with their colorful umbrella roofs, this carriage is from the Brimlands, one of the many that the king sent as gifts to celebrate the binding of his second daughter, Farishta, to Lohar a few years ago. The only change to the carriage is the new emblem now painted over its doors—an atashban crossed with a trident. Next to the carriage stands a familiar figure, a man whose eyes widen ever so slightly when he sees me. Apart from this, though, Ambar Fort's stable master doesn't speak nor give any indication of our former connection.

"Captain Emil," Govind says with a quick bow. "The carriage has been modified as requested."

"Thank you, stable master," Emil says before turning to me. "Go on. I will take off your shackles once you're inside."

Climbing into the carriage shackled is a lot more difficult than I anticipated, pricks of pain jolting my wrists every time I make a move. Eventually Emil gets impatient, and Govind rushes forward to push me in. As he does, he presses something small and hard into my palm. I keep my expression neutral as my pulse kicks up a notch. My fingers roam over the familiar surface of the coin—a green swarna to communicate with living specters. Govind's specialty.

I sense the magic in the carriage's walls the moment I climb in—thick as the air outside, nearly as suffocating. Sweat forms a layer on my forehead and nape. I look out the open window and breathe deep.

"Don't even think of escaping." Captain Shekhar has stepped in. "You'll kill yourself before you know it."

So a barrier of sorts. I wonder now if this is what the rekha felt like to the women at Ambar Fort—an invisible cage that bound them to Rani Mahal. Words from the Scorpion's speech buzz in my head, and the physical shock of Emil removing my shackles barely registers.

The carriage bounces over the steep inclines of the Walled City, and from there, it glides smoothly toward the city of Ambarvadi, its roads and alleys spreading out like a web. Throngs of people line the main thoroughfare, pointing at the carriage, speaking in loud voices. Taking advantage of the Sky Warriors' distraction, I finally slip the green swarna into the pocket of my angrakha.

The deeper we go in, the denser the crowd seems to grow. Outside the sky goddess's temple, the main square is packed with bodies, their disjointed voices pouring in through a crack in the carriage window:

". . . not the rani, no. Only more Sky Warriors."

"Are they planning to shoot someone here, too?"

"Hold on! There's someone else in the carriage!"

"Is it him? The half magus?"

Before I realize what's happening, a number of people begin calling my name. There are several instances, however, where I see people, mostly older men and women, snapping their fingers twice in the air over their heads as the carriage passes by—an act meant to ward off any living specters that I may attract.

"Look at them, dirt licker," Captain Shekhar sneers. "Look how scared they are of you and your half magus blood."

Captain Emil raises a hand, and the carriage's windows snap shut, turning their shouts into a faint buzz.

"Not every Ambari is as superstitious, Xerxes-putra Cavas," he counters. "In fact, you have grown quite popular recently. You and the so-called Star Warrior."

I say nothing, avoiding his shrewd gaze. I've heard about this, of course. Sarayu's birds brought us information in Tavan about shrines popping up across Ambar for Gul and me. But back then, cut off as we were from the rest of the kingdom, it was hard to believe any of those stories. It's a shock to see how much things have changed. How—despite the finger-snappers—people who would have once spit on my face for crossing their path are now chanting my name like a prayer.

A moment later, the faint sound of Ambari bugles penetrates the carriage. The crowd gasps, its many heads bobbing like fish, struggling to see over one another and catch a glimpse of the Scorpion making a public appearance.

And what an appearance.

Seated on a howdah, atop an enormous Ambari elephant, the Scorpion wears her crown and black armor, her black atashban strapped to her back. There is no mahout guiding her steed. The Scorpion guides the elephant herself with a whip and goad, once making it trumpet loudly from behind a cavalry of armed Sky Warriors. The closer she gets, the more imposing she looks, and groups of people begin calling for her:

"Rani Shayla! Rani Shayla!"

"Ambar Sikandar, grace us with a look!"

She turns to face her supporters, the sun hitting her angular, gold-tinted cheeks, her full red lips curling into a wide smile. As the procession moves farther, passing us, Emil opens a small window in the roof.

"Follow them," he tells our driver.

Our carriage falls behind the trumpeting elephant, the driver slow, carefully keeping his distance. Guards flank us from every side, keeping the crowd from jostling the vehicle as we make our way to the main square, where a small stage has been set up in front of a sea of buzzing spectators.

"It's like attending a spectacle at Raj Mahal," Captain Shekhar mutters.

As Shayla descends from the elephant, the crowd strains at the rope cordoning them into a rectangle, forcing the armed guards stationed every few yards to push them back. An onyx throne emerges from the center of the stage. Next to it stands Acharya Damak. Even in this heat, the high priest of Ambar Fort looks cool, his skin and white robes unmarked by sweat.

"Rise as one for Megha-putri Shayla, rani and sikandar of Ambar," the acharya says, his voice magnified by magic. "Rise as one, for Ambar. For the true queen."

"For Ambar!" the crowd chants. "For the true queen!"

Not everyone speaks up, though. In pockets here and there, many remain stubbornly silent. The Scorpion notices, her smile growing more fixed, her eyes dangerously narrow. She raises a hand to silence the crowd.

"Ambaris," she says, her magnified voice gentle, almost motherly. "I thank you for your love. Yet I can also see the distrust on some of your faces, which is understandable. You do not know me well, thanks to the usurper who killed my mother, Rani Megha, and later imprisoned thousands of women—magi and non-magi—simply for the birthmarks on their bodies."

Applause rings from a few sections within the crowd.

"The time has come now to take back what was stolen from us," Shayla continues. "To restore Ambar to its former glory. The time has come to weed out dissent and rebellion, to uproot everything that would lead to bloodshed and war. Restraint will be required on your part. Moderation, where none was before. There will be those who call me harsh for my measures—evil, even. However, there are those who have come to their senses. Who now understand what is true and what isn't. Let me introduce you to the throne's newest friend, Xerxes-putra Cavas."

The crowd's many heads turn as I get out of the carriage and walk up the stage, Captain Emil a few steps behind me. Acharya Damak gestures me forward and then, with a neutral expression, lightly taps my throat with a finger. The magic tingles, coats the inside of my mouth like mint. When I speak, my voice emerges ten times louder than normal.

"I begin by thanking Rani Shayla," I recite. "If not for her kindness and magnanimity, I would not be standing here today. I would still be supporting the alleged Star Warrior, a witch who first drew me in with jantar-mantar and evil magic and then bent me to her will."

I hear several emotions in the whispers that break out among the audience: shock, disbelief, triumph, anger. Swallowing the hot bile rising to my throat, I plow forward:

"She claims to be the prophesied savior of magi and non-magi, and of women falsely persecuted for accidents of birth. It took me a long time to understand that her end goal wasn't to free Ambar of tyranny but to simply fill the shoes of a tyrant herself. For this, she committed regicide and murder. And I let her, bewitched fool that I was."

Silence fills the air, a single moment of hushed anticipation.

"It's Rani Shayla who freed me," I say, turning to the Scorpion seated on her throne. "Rani Shayla, to whom I now pledge my allegiance and loyalty forevermore."

An invisible hand pushes me forward, the magic forcing me to bow first and then prostrate at the Scorpion's feet.

"Rise, Xerxes-putra Cavas." The Scorpion's voice sounds like a caress. She reaches for me as the magic forces me to stand. A hand curls around my cheek, tilts my chin up ever so slightly. "I will always reward loyalty."

I try to brace myself, but I'm still unprepared for the kiss, the hard mash of her teeth and mouth against mine. Shouts emerge from the crowd, swarming my ears in a low buzz. Two weeks ago, before I got captured, I might have considered how I could use this moment to my advantage. Like the Jwaliyan seer, I, too, might have imagined pulling out the pin decorating my turban and sinking it into a vein climbing the Scorpion's neck. Right now, though, with the Scorpion's hand cupping my cheek and the other curling my throat in a near choke hold, I'm struggling to breathe.

Stay alive, Cavas.

Something clatters over the platform, finally breaking the kiss and forcing us apart. As air fills my lungs again, the hand at the back of my neck tightens, holding me in place. The tingling in my throat subsides.

"Don't move, dirt licker," the Scorpion says under her breath.

And that's when I notice the shoe—a dusty, old jooti lying upside down, barely a foot away from where we stand. I watch as the guards drag forward someone—a man with graying hair and a mustache, his mouth open in a snarl.

"Traitor!" he shouts at me. "You've betrayed Ambar and non-magi! You've—"

Red light flashes past me, silencing him. A Sky Warrior next to the Scorpion's throne lowers his atashban, watches expressionlessly as blood gurgles from the man's mouth, pours dark and red from the hole in his chest. Seconds later, the guards drop his body to the ground.

"Any other comments from the audience?" the Scorpion asks.

There are none. No chants, no murmurs, not a sound except for the gentle tapping of the high priest's sandals on the wooden platform.

"Let it be written that on this twenty-fourth day of the Month of Sloughing, Xerxes-putra Cavas pledged his unflinching loyalty to Rani Shayla," Acharya Damak says, his voice holding the barest trace of a quiver. "Let it also be known herewith that anyone showing allegiance to the so-called Star Warrior and her supporters will be condemned for treason against the crown."

As he speaks, a pair of Sky Warriors raise the dead man in the air with magic and impale his body through a spike emerging from the ground near the sky goddess's temple.

"This man's body will remain here as an example of what happens in the event of treason," the acharya continues, his face as expressionless as always. "Long live Rani Shayla!"

"Long live Rani Shayla!" the crowd chants, though their faces tell a different story. Many turn away when their gazes meet mine, and many others stare back, defiant and angry. But no one makes further attempts at challenging the usurper queen in this moment, and I know that no one will.

In the distance, I catch General Alizeh staring at both me and the Scorpion, her mouth curled with disgust. Is her contempt for the Scorpion, now reduced to keeping me—the Star Warrior's half magus lover—at her side? Or was it our kiss that repulsed the general? I think back to all the times I'd seen Alizeh watching the Scorpion. The expression on her face

I'd always chalked up to frenzied devotion. *But it wasn't just that*, I realize now. General Alizeh was in love with the queen. And the Scorpion did not love her back.

Revenge has many forms, child, and not all of them involve killing people.

Triumph flares in my belly, followed by a dizzying bout of nausea, the horrible urge to throw up right on the stage.

Who am I? I wonder. *What am I turning into?*

"Looks like you've done a good job, dirt licker," the Scorpion tells me softly. Her hand is still warm on my neck. "They believe you completely."

Of course they do.

They don't see the atashban Captain Shekhar points between my shoulder blades as we march to the carriage, or the shackles Captain Emil places me in once I sit down. They don't, for one moment, realize that behind my closed mouth, a bit of skin has come loose from biting the inside of my cheek. A carved silver cup appears in my hands, the madira within it a deep, bloody garnet.

"Long live the queen!" Captain Shekhar empties his cup in his mouth, alcohol dribbling down his chin.

Distaste flickers across Captain Emil's face—though I'm not sure if it's directed at Captain Shekhar or his words. I turn away before his gaze meets mine and raise my own cup to wash away the taste of the Scorpion's kiss.

I doze intermittently on the way back to Ambar Fort. When we get to my room, Captain Shekhar barely settles in his chair before sleep hits him like a pile of rocks. I would have fallen asleep as well if not for Ma, who floats in through the door seconds later, making me glance up, surprised.

Ma? I mouth. *What in Svapnalok—*

"Don't worry," she says in a soft voice. "I mixed a bit of sleeping draft into his cup of madira on the way here. He'll be out for now."

I wait for a long time, watching the captain. But when he shows no signs of moving, I allow myself to relax.

"What is it?" I whisper. "Is something wrong?"

"Not at the moment, no," Ma floats over to my bed, settling down next to me. "But I came to warn you—you need to stop communicating with Gul."

"*Wha*—" I begin, but Ma presses a cold hand over my lips, encasing my shout within.

"Hush, child. It's only temporary. Right now, Pashuraj Subodh believes it's the most prudent thing to do. I agree with him. Now, do you promise you won't yell?"

I nod. Warmth pricks over my mouth and jaw again, and I release a ragged breath. I want to scream at my mother. To slam my head against the wall.

"I don't understand," I say instead, through gritted teeth. "Why stop? It's our bond that got me out of prison in the first place."

"It's also your bond that puts you both in danger. When you meditate, you emit a glow, son. If someone catches you, it would be disastrous—not only for you, but also for Gul."

Pain pricks the center of my palm. For a second, I feel exactly the way I did when General Alizeh impaled my hands with her daggers. I unclench my fingers, observe the crescents imprinted into my newly healed skin.

"What do I do?" I ask tonelessly.

"If you have messages, send them through me or one of the other specters. It's for your own safety, Cavas. Cavas? Are you listening to me?"

I don't push off the hand she uses to shake my shoulder, don't wrench my forehead away from the brush of her cold kiss. I remain silent, as still as a temple god, unresponsive to her questions and her sad "Shubhraat."

It's how she finally leaves me: cold, brittle, and alone, anger spooled tight around my heart.

29
GUL

When morning arrives, Kali and I head out for a quick wash and breakfast by the reservoir.

"I can't believe Subodh told you to stop communicating with Cavas!" she exclaims, nearly spitting out the date she was chewing. "Isn't it dangerous for complements to be kept away from each other like that? What is he thinking?"

"Because it's more dangerous for Cavas right now to enter a meditative state than to talk to a living specter," I say, unable to curb my bitterness.

Kali sighs. "I don't know what to say, my girl. I'm so sorry."

"It can't be helped." I force myself to change the subject. "Tell me about you. How are things with Sami?"

She shrugs, raising a cup of tea to her lips. "Good."

I raise an eyebrow. "That's it? That's all you're going to say?"

But Kali merely smiles in response, and I decide to leave her alone for now. I much prefer this Kali to the sulking figure I'd seen over the past month. As if sensing the topic of our conversation, Sami looks over in our direction and gives Kali a dazzling grin. I turn away, envy spiking my heart. A moment later, Kali's pale hand covers mine.

"Cavas is smart," she says gently. "He knows how to cover his tracks."

"I guess. I feel so helpless right now."

"Don't be negative," Kali chides. "Let's see how today's meeting goes before we lose hope."

Mention of the meeting reminds me of someone else, and I finally do what I've been avoiding for the past three days.

"Raja Amar," I begin, waiting until he looks up from his tea. "I want to apologize for my behavior three days ago. I behaved like an a—atrocious donkey," I amend quickly. "I'm willing to accept any punishment you give me."

Amar raises his brows. "*Any* punishment?"

"Uh . . ." *Queen's curses.* What have I gotten myself into?

Then Amar's mouth twitches, and he bursts out laughing.

"*Atrocious donkey*—Gods!" he exclaims. "What happened to plain old ass?"

I can't help it. I laugh as well, the knot in my chest unraveling.

"You're forgiven," Amar says. "Provided you attend our meetings and train with the Legion."

"Thank you, Raja Amar. You won't have to force me to do either of those things," I tell him sincerely.

"Call me Amar. I know I'm supposed to be king of Ambar and many terrible things in the future, but I, too, would like a friend."

"You're ridiculous." I smile. "Amar."

The meeting takes place after breakfast in a small temple at the heart of the southern tenements, squeezed between a ramshackle building teeming with people and the ruins of an old haveli. Sunlight pours in from a hole in the roof, but apart from that, the temple is well-maintained, its bells hung with new ropes and oil lamps surrounding the statues of the sky goddess and Sant Javer in the temple's inner chamber.

Before the inner chamber sit the tenements' five councilors, Sarpanch Parvez at their center. He presses his hands together in greeting. "Anand-pranam."

"Anandpranam," we chorus.

"Please have a seat."

I settle gingerly on the hard floor, expecting the sun's heat to have penetrated the stone, but it's surprisingly cool to the touch.

"You wanted to speak to us, Raja Amar," Sarpanch Parvez says. "You said you have a plan."

"Yes," Amar says. "The plan, as you may have guessed, is to launch an attack on Ambarvadi. The Pashu queen has been kind enough to offer her birds as messengers and food and water to our armies—once we have them."

"You have no plan, then," a female councilor—the one named Maya—says bluntly. "Unless you intend to conjure an army out of thin air."

"I could do that, but it would only be a temporary solution," Amar says calmly. "We would still need human forces. Over the past few months, I have been writing letters and sending my mother's shvet-panchhi to various places in the hopes of gathering some aid." He holds up a scroll. "My negotiations with the queen of Jwala have gone well so far. She has offered to support us in any way she can."

"And you believe her?" Councilor Maya's skeptical tone makes me bristle. "How do you know she isn't already allied with Rani Shayla?"

"The Jwaliyan queen has known me since I was a boy," Amar replies. "She allied with my father, yes, but she never really liked him. My mother, however, made sure that she liked me and my two brothers during her earlier visits to Ambar. I wrote to her on a hunch. She says she was forced to send a messenger to Ambar at Rani Shayla's request. He hasn't returned yet, which makes her fear he has been killed.

"Jwala's relationship with Ambar is, naturally, complicated because of the many rigorous contracts that my father forced the queen to sign. Now, with my father no longer here, it's possible she may be able to help more than she might have when he was still alive."

"But—"

"What do you need from us, Raja Amar?" Sarpanch Parvez interrupts with a glance at Councilor Maya.

"Your support. An army of men and women willing to fight, if the need arises. I know that I don't have the right to ask for your help—"

"You don't," Councilor Maya interjects.

"Councilor Maya!" the sarpanch admonishes.

"Sarpanch ji, we can no longer tiptoe around this. He is not Ambarnaresh yet," she points out. "Besides, you have the same concerns I do. Magi have used—and misused—non-magi in the past. They let their jealousy drive us to the ground and nearly demolish us. Why in Svapnalok should we help them? What will they give us in return?"

"I appreciate your honesty, Councilor Maya," Amar says.

When the sarpanch attempts to speak again, Amar raises a hand. "Please. I mean it. Loving a kingdom doesn't mean turning a blind eye to its problems. The Code of Asha says that a monarch must listen to their happiest *and* their unhappiest subjects to rule a kingdom wisely. If I am to be king later, I must learn to take criticism now. So please go ahead, Maya ji. I'm listening. Tell me what you'd like me to do."

"I would like to know if you'll restore us to our former positions," she says. "Will you get us out of the tenements? Will we and magi be equals in deed as on scroll?"

"I will do that and more," Amar says. "I want to build my government the way Ambar's first queen did—with magi and non-magi ministers at the helm."

"Will you sign a magical contract to that effect?" Councilor Maya demands. "Right now?"

There's a long silence. Triumph glitters in Councilor Maya's cold brown eyes. Even the other councilors frown.

Then: "Could someone please pass me a parchment?"

Amar's words make me stiffen. Subodh turns his head sideways, as if trying to communicate with him. But Amar's serious yellow gaze is fixed on

Councilor Maya, who hands him the parchment and watches as Amar raises his quill and signs his name at the bottom of the blank page.

My throat closes when I see the ink glow green for a brief moment.

"The magic in this ink will hold me to my word," Amar explains. "If I fail to live up to it, I will die."

The non-magi council break into heated whispers. Finally, Sarpanch Parvez looks up.

"We can't let you do that," he says. "Yukta is like my sister. She sold herself at the flesh market because she didn't have a choice. She would never approve of such a binding contract."

"Neither would your mother, Raja Amar," Subodh warns.

"Yukta Didi doesn't make decisions for me. Neither does Rani Ma," Amar says firmly.

"Raja Amar, you do realize what this is," Councilor Maya says, her voice tight, oddly anxious for someone who has been granted an impossible wish. "We could write anything here. Saints, we could make you abdicate the throne and declare a non-magus monarch if we so wished! You can't possibly trust us!"

"But I *do* trust you, Councilor Maya. You, your fellow councilors, and every non-magus in the southern tenements kept me safe when you could have given me up to Rani Shayla for a great reward. If not you, then whom else can I trust?"

The councilors say nothing, but they're watching Amar now like the rest of us, hanging on his every word.

"Without trust, there is no faith," Amar says. "Without faith, there is no hope. If we are to bring back the Ambar of old, the great kingdom of our ancestors, we need to start somewhere. I choose to start with placing my trust in you."

The sarpanch and other councilors congregate, having a hushed conversation. Long moments later, they break apart.

"We will draft a contract separately first before placing the final words on the parchment," the sarpanch says. "I'm sure that non-magi across

Ambar will want to have a say in this as well, especially our brothers and sisters in the northern tenements."

"Very well," Amar says. "Is there anything else?"

"Yes," the sarpanch says. "You said you want us to fight for you. But who will lead us in battle? And when?"

"Pashuraj Subodh and the Star Warrior will lead you in battle," Amar says, glancing at me and Subodh. "I hope you think that is all right."

I swallow hard, wondering if the councilors will reject me on the spot. But each head is nodding. The relief on their faces scares me more.

"Mind you—I will not force my people to fight," Sarpanch Parvez says. "But I will not stop anyone who wishes to join your cause, either."

"What about you, Sarpanch ji?" Amar asks. "Are *you* with us?"

The sarpanch frowns. "I have lived through segregation, a famine, two droughts, and a hundred changes to the tenement laws by two monarchs. I am not sure I'm doing the right thing by placing my trust in you, Raja Amar. I'm simply following my instincts. They may fail me, for what I know, and I may be written off as another foolish old man. But for today, I am with you. For better or worse."

"And I am with the sarpanch," Councilor Rayomand says in his gentle voice. Two of the women councilors echo the same sentiment. Only Councilor Maya says nothing, though her expression appears less hostile than before.

"We will spread word about the army," Sarpanch Parvez says. "Will you accept anyone?"

"Yes. As long as they are of age or over," Subodh says. "I'll be at the reservoir if they need to find me."

As we walk out of the temple and back into the bustle and heat of the crowded slum, I fall into step with Amar. "That was reckless of you. How do you know they won't misuse that parchment?"

"You mean as reckless as you when you wanted to go to Javeribad?"

My mouth opens and then clamps shut, a stinging retort held back. He's right, of course. Who am I to lecture him?

Amar sighs. "I'm sorry. I shouldn't have said that. I now have an in-kling of what you were going through. Some things are worth risking our lives for." He pauses. "Speaking of which, do you know what hap-pened to Cavas? Have you been in touch?"

I hesitate for a moment before filling him in.

Amar frowns. "A speech," he muses. "She'll attempt to discredit you, you realize. Make Cavas do it, more likely."

"I trust Cavas," I say, a little more forcefully than I want to.

"As you should." Amar watches me for a moment, worry lining his forehead. "Well, I'd better go now and see if Councilor Maya needs any help with the garden. Perhaps I can conjure a mango tree to please her."

We part ways. I head to the reservoir, where I find Subodh standing next to Queen Sarayu's nest—empty, save for a few bones and the old bandage we used for her wing.

"What happened?" I ask. "Where's Rani Sarayu?"

"She was feeling better, so she left for Aman," Subodh says, gesturing to the reservoir. "She never likes staying away from her subjects for too long."

The silence between us stretches and I know Subodh is thinking about his conversation with the simurgh last night.

"Have you ever thought of going back home?" I ask.

"What is home, Gul?" the Pashu king asks wearily. "Where is it, I wonder, for a rajsingha who always felt better fighting than ruling—who endangered his own subjects in a war that wasn't his to begin with?"

I think back to something Subodh whispered to me months earlier. "Is that what you meant when you told me that you've made bigger mistakes in the past?"

"It is. And I continue making them today. Thank the great animal spirits for Rani Sarayu. Without her I would have done the same thing all over again. She is a better ruler than I'll ever be. In any case, today is not about me and my problems. I think the meeting with the non-magus council went well, don't you?"

"Don't you think it's dangerous, what Amar did?" I ask. "What if someone misuses that parchment? Councilor Maya—"

"—is someone we should risk placing our trust in," Subodh says quietly. "Besides, what other choice do we have?"

We lapse into silence for a moment. "Do you think non-magi will sign up to fight?" I ask.

"I think they will. Though I'm not sure how many. They'll likely be intrigued once they see the Legion training together."

"Maybe you're right," I muse. "But *where* will we train?"

The tenements are crowded and, even with only twenty women, it will be difficult to find a large enough space for everyone to practice at once.

"Falak might be able to help," Subodh says. "She worked side by side with Esther when it came to training the women."

Falak does have a solution.

"Not a problem," she tells me. "For many years, Esther trained a few of us at a time on the roof of the infirmary. We can do the same here, in front of your tent. Two facing you off *here*." She draws a circle on the ground with chalk to mark the spot. "You'll probably need to put up magical shields to protect anyone else from getting in the way of a lathi or a spell. You're using death magic, correct?"

"Yes." I can no longer avoid the inevitable. "Kali and Raja Subodh will put up the magical shields."

Moments later, I raise my daggers and face two lathi-wielding women—Sami and Falak herself. My mouth flutters as I exhale, a sound that makes them both smile.

"Keep your shields ready," I tell them. "You are free to use anything you like to defend yourselves."

Their smiles disappear the moment I release a jet of green flame. Sami flattens herself to the ground, her shield covering her head. Falak does a little better, standing firm the way the commander of the Legion should, and holds up her metal shield to deflect most of my spell, which singes off the tip of her shoulder-length gray braid.

"Again," I say. "Falak Didi, you were great. Sami, see if you can stand up this time. Throw rocks at me if you want to. But try fighting back, however you can."

It's not what Amira would have done. Amira would have mocked and taunted, would have smirked as she repelled Sami's rock back with magic, aiming it right at her skull.

I, on the other hand, shatter the rock with a well-placed spell and then nod.

"Not bad," I say. "Now see if you can put your shield to use. Deflect the spell back at me so that I have to fight it. At the same time, throw a rock. See if you can slow me down."

Without losing a breath, I shoot another spell at them, this one turning into a swarm of green arrows.

When neither Falak nor Sami move, I wonder if I'm going to have to find myself another new commander of the armies and Kali a new girlfriend.

Then, at the very last second, Falak takes both of their shields and holds them up together side by side. From behind the extended barrier, Sami deftly throws a series of rocks aimed at different parts of my body.

Protect, I think, forced to shield myself from my own deflected spell. The shower of rocks, however, continues, finding my left shoulder and my right knee, which both explode in agony, nearly toppling me to the ground.

Sami definitely has excellent aim.

Tears reflexively leak from my eyes, but I'm grinning so wide that no one else notices. Or cares.

"Fantastic!" I shout, my ribs swelling at the sight of their beaming faces. "Teamwork is key here. Don't look at magic as something insurmountable, but simply another weapon you need to fight."

They may no longer have their magic, this Legion of mine, but they still have their wits. As we practice a few more times, I note a small crowd of non-magi gathering by our campsite, their eyes widening every time Falak and Sami deflect my spells, gasping when I'm forced to spin out of the way of a spear that would have otherwise lodged itself in my throat.

"Well done, again, Sami," I call out. "Now let's take a break before you both finish me off."

The two women laugh and so do our onlookers—as if the very real possibility of our dying during a spar were a myth.

Strange, I think. Only a few weeks ago, such a scene would have been unimaginable to me. Right now, though, anything seems possible, including saving Cavas and winning this war.

As Kali hurries over to check on our injuries, a young woman from the cluster of watching non-magi walks up to Sami.

"You really weren't fighting with magic?" she asks, her voice barely a whisper. "You and that other woman?"

"We weren't," Sami confirms. "My magic—and Falak Didi's—was drained away years ago in Tavan."

The girl stares at Sami's starry tattoos, her eyes widening. "Can I learn to fight like that?"

"Of course you can," Sami says with her wide smile. "We're hoping you will, actually. You and any other friends of yours."

"One moment." The girl rushes off and returns with two more women. I write down their names and ask them to come in for training tomorrow.

"We'll have to plan this properly," I say. "If more people show up, there will be no place to fight."

"Raja Amar said he's working on something," Kali says.

"Is he planning to conjure an arena?" I ask, making her laugh.

Yet, despite the lightness of the moment and the general triumph of the day, darkness hovers at the back of my mind.

It's not until the evening that news about Cavas arrives—brought in by a living specter with a hard, oddly familiar voice.

"He promised allegiance to our new rani, of course," the specter says. "She kissed him to seal the deal. It went on for rather a long time."

Trust me, Cavas said. *Whatever happens.* The words mingle with others from his speech: *witch, jantar-mantar, regicide, murder.*

I stand stiff and pale-knuckled, ignoring the concerned gazes of my friends and my army.

"The crowd reacted in various ways," the specter goes on. "Some cheered, some looked disgusted, but most were confused. I have to say she's clever, the kabzedar rani. Showing the whole kingdom that the Star Warrior's lover is now hers."

My nails dig into my palms. What did I expect? That Shayla would leave Cavas untouched?

"Populous as it is, I hardly think the capital constitutes Ambar as a whole," Latif smoothly puts an end to the whispering caused by the other specter's remark. "Thank you, Roda, you have been most useful."

Roda? I look up, shocked. "Did he say—"

"Roda, yes," Subodh answers. "She became a living specter when we battled the Sky Warriors in Tavan."

"Don't mind her," Latif says, his presence like a cool breeze at my side. "She's merely angry at being killed off so early. Spite and mockery, unfortunately, are common traits among specters who die young."

Like Indu, I think, remembering the little girl's scornful voice. Yet I can't feel angry with Indu now or, for that matter, Roda. It was my ineptitude that cost Esther and Roda their lives.

"Stop it," Sami tells me.

"Stop what?"

"Being so hard on yourself. Ah, ah, don't deny it," she says when I open my mouth to respond. "You have a tendency to beat yourself up over what happens to others."

"She does," Kali says, joining in the conversation. The two women give each other conspiratorial smiles.

"It isn't funny," I say angrily. "People are dying."

"And you can't blame yourself for every death," Sami says, her tone surprisingly stern. "Roda was part of the Legion. She knew that there would be danger and that some of us would die in battle."

"Not everyone expects death. Some expect only victory."

"And you can't hold yourself accountable to every expectation," Kali says. "Some will expect victory followed by a parade of dancing dustwolves. What will you do then? Whisper a few into swaying with clay pots over their heads?"

Kali shifts into a dancing pose—a really bad one, with flying arms, widened eyes, and bared teeth to mimic a dustwolf's snarl.

A snort erupts from my mouth, the prelude to a laugh that brings tears to my eyes. Next to me, Sami clutches her stomach, her laughter reduced to gasps.

"Queen's curses, Kali. That was awful," I say upon recovering my voice.

"Good," Kali says, smiling. "Now let's go have dinner."

That night, I dream of blood pooling the marble floors of Ambar Fort. Of the Scorpion parading Cavas from city to city, slowly peeling off bits and pieces of his flesh, only to reveal a stranger underneath. When I wake this time, it's to the tang of metal in my mouth, the sharp pinch of a bitten tongue. No one's here to comfort me. Nor to stop me from plunging deep into a meditative state if I wanted to.

I step out of the tent, sweat drenching the front of my sleep tunic.

"You need to trust Cavas," I tell myself. "He knew what he was going into. You can't put him in any more danger than he already is."

I repeat the same thing, over and over, until I grow exhausted again, ignoring the shivers that run through my body and Roda's scornful laugh floating overhead.

SNAKES AND SPECTERS

23rd day of the Month of Dreams
6 months into Queen Shayla's reign

30

SHAYLA

"Threat of a mutiny in the Amirgarh cantonment?" I toss the scroll the messenger brought in this morning back on my desk. "What nonsense is this?"

"The infantry are demanding wage increases," Acharya Damak says in his slippery voice. "Similar to the kind you gave the Sky Warriors."

"The Sky Warriors keep the whole kingdom safe," I snarl. *They keep me safe in this pit of vipers.* "Besides, the treasury is nearly empty. How am I supposed to increase the wages of peasant soldiers at a time like this?"

"Ambar Sikandar, it isn't only the peasants who are revolting. Many of the infantry soldiers come from the families of zamindars, merchants, and wealthy farmers. They have now banded under the leadership of one Brigadier Moolchand, brother to Zamindar Moolchand, who was executed for sedition in Dukal."

"Sounds like a family trait," I mutter, turning to the sound of new footsteps. "Alizeh. Good, you're here."

"Ambar Sikandar." Alizeh bows smartly.

"There's a brigadier named Moolchand in the Amirgarh cantonment," I say. "Bring me his head on a pike."

To my surprise, Alizeh hesitates. "I don't think that's a good idea."

"What do you mean? Do you know him?"

"I haven't met him. But I'm aware of his threats of a mutiny," she admits. "He wrote to me two weeks ago. I wrote back to assure him that our rani always has the army's best interests at heart. In the meantime, I dug a little more into his background and found that he has fought in nearly every war Ambar has been involved in. He's well respected in army circles." Alizeh's voice falters when she sees the furious expression on my face, but she goes on. "Killing him may not be wise."

"The general's words hold merit," Acharya Damak says, his shifty eyes sliding between me and Alizeh. "Imprisonment perhaps would be better. And only as a last resort."

"Imprisoning the snake only defers the problem," I point out. "Cutting off its head is more effective."

Yet who is *the real snake here?*

I continue watching Alizeh, whose face has frozen into an expressionless mask.

"My rani, the move will be taken badly by the soldiers," the high priest says. "They aren't civilians threatened easily by a fear of death. They will walk to the scaffold with their heads held high. We should invite the brigadier to Ambarvadi. Placate him with a gift or two."

Selective bribery. As much as I hate the idea, I have to admit that Acharya Damak makes sense.

"Fine, then." I lean back. "Since you're so eager to gift the brigadier, perhaps you could contribute that jade necklace, Acharya."

I try not to sneer when the high priest's hands flutter protectively over the string of beads circling his neck. "Ambar Sikandar, this necklace is priceless! A gift from Rani Megha herself for my services to the kingdom!"

"And now Rani Megha's daughter asks you to give up that gift as a further service." My smile sharpens. "What will it be, Acharya Damak?"

Slowly, almost as if it physically pains him to do so, the high priest removes the necklace and places it on my desk. Priceless and unblemished. The exact shade of Damak's watchful green eyes.

"You may go now," I tell him. "You have been of great service to Us."

The royal Us. One I haven't used before. It feels good to deploy it now, to watch Acharya Damak's stiff bow and hasty departure.

"He's probably off to hide his matching earrings," I jab. "What do you think?"

"Shayla, what are you doing?" Alizeh demands. "I know you don't like the acharya, but is it wise to make him an enemy?"

It's been a long time—years, really—since Alizeh has called me by my name. Far too long since two lonely girls held each other after a long, terrible day of practice at the Sky Warrior academy.

"I should be asking you what you're doing, Alizeh," I respond, my jaw tightening. "You *knew* about the threat of a mutiny in Amirgarh and didn't tell me. It makes me wonder where your loyalties truly lie."

Alizeh's pale skin mottles red. "I am loyal to you, of course. I've always been loyal to you!"

"Because if you want, Alizeh, I can take away your house in the city," I snarl. "Cut your pay and distribute it among the soldiers, if you wish."

"I don't fight for you because I want those things! But I *am* commander of Ambar's armies, Shayla. That's the position you gave me! What kind of leader would I be if I kept running to you every time a problem arose?"

The kind that cautions her queen about a situation that might cost her the throne, I think. But I hold in my words. I did not like the look on Alizeh's face when I asked her to bring me Moolchand's head. There was resistance there. Resistance I've never seen before when it comes to me. Instead, I employ an old interrogation tactic. One that involves long periods of silence, flustering a subject enough to confess more than they initially intended.

"I'm worried," Alizeh says. "I've never seen so much . . . anger from the public before."

"The dirt licker has done well to keep the anger at bay."

Xerxes-putra Cavas has surprised me in that sense. He speaks with an eloquence that fails most ministers and has convinced every town and village we have gone to that he's on my side. Everywhere we go now, people watch him with suspicion, snap their fingers to ward off specters when his carriage passes by. Sometimes, I find myself believing the boy, too. Until I see the hint of fear in his eyes. The revulsion that never really goes away.

The boy is merely doing what he can to save his own hide. He holds loyalty to no one—not even the so-called Star Warrior.

It's only this last thought that keeps me from slitting his throat whenever he gives his speeches.

"Write to the brigadier," I tell Alizeh. "Invite him to Ambarvadi as a guest of the queen. We will see if the acharya's precious jade beads shut him up. Also, send Captain Emil here."

"Yes, Ambar Sikandar. Of course." I note the relief that overcomes Alizeh, the increased energy in her stride on exiting the study.

Captain Emil arrives shortly, his Sky Warrior uniform as crisp as his bow, his hammered gray hair reflecting silver in the glow of the lightorb.

"Ambar Sikandar."

"Have a seat, Captain."

I ignore the discomfort on his face. Emil has always been more at home on a battlefield than in a stuffy sitting room.

"I want you to look into recruiting mercenaries from the Brimmish desert." I get directly to the point. "About a thousand. Perhaps two thousand if you can. Let me know how much they cost."

Ruthless and bloodthirsty, Brimmish mercenaries are loyal to no one except those who pay them in full. Even the usurper Lohar had refrained from using them during the Three-Year War against Samudra, preferring Jwala's less brutal, more controllable army instead. But, after my last interaction with the Jwaliyan queen's copper-haired messenger, I can no longer count on her as an ally. Moreover, if Brigadier Moolchand turns out to be one of those honorable bastards who refuses bribes—and if a mutiny does happen—then I will need backup.

A small frown appears on Emil's face. "I don't mind, Ambar Sikandar. But recruitment usually falls under the purview of a major or General Alizeh."

"The general is to know nothing about this," I say. "I will make you a major if that makes things easier."

I raise my atashban and point it at Emil's chest, noting the swallow bobbing his throat. The tip of my weapon glows orange instead of red, light spiraling to the single atashban embroidered on Emil's chest, replicating it thrice.

Emil stares at me. "You're serious. You're making me a major."

"When am I ever not serious?"

Emil's stern mouth trembles. "S-sau aabhaar, Ambar Sikandar."

I feel my shoulders relax. Emil may be as stolid as the wood that makes up my desk, but he's loyal to whoever sits on the throne. "You're welcome. Any updates on the dirt licker?"

"No suspicious activity as of yet or communications with living specters as far as we can tell. I have someone watching him around the clock."

I nod once. "You may go. And remember our need for secrecy . . . Major Emil."

"I'll remember, Ambar Sikandar."

A sharp knock sounds on the door, making Emil pause midbow.

I frown at the Sky Warrior who barges in, pausing short of a scold when I note the fear etched over his young face.

"Ambar Sikandar, sorry for the intrusion," he begins. "But a terrible thing has happened."

My gut clenches: a pathetic reaction I thought I buried along with my tormentors at the Sky Warrior academy.

"Tell me," I say, my voice hard.

"There was a disturbance at the Ministry of War office in Ambarvadi. A group of non-magi loadbearers barged in with lathis and sickles, demanding payment for their services."

First Dhanbad, now Ambarvadi. "Go on."

"Captain Farid and I were called in to stop them." He swallows. "There were too many, so the captain sent me to get reinforcements. By the time we returned, though, it was too late. We found Captain Farid's corpse nailed to the wall outside the ministry."

I stay very still, aware of the two Sky Warriors and their too-watchful eyes. "Where are the dirt-licking loadbearers now?" I ask.

"Fourteen of them have been arrested. General Alizeh wants to know what you want us to do with them."

I give him a smile that feels cold, even to me. "Doesn't the general remember? There is only one punishment for murder."

The burning happens in the heat of the afternoon, in the city's main square, the loadbearers tied to their pyres, screaming curses at me as the red flames of the Sky Warriors' atashbans eat away at their clothes, skin, and flesh, eventually leaving nothing behind except for ash and bone.

I sit astride my horse, watching the crowd that has come to see the mass execution, evaluating the terror on every face.

It should be satisfying, I think, *to have them understand what the consequences are for crossing their queen.*

But somehow, it isn't, the smell of burning flesh lingering in my senses long after I've returned to Ambar Fort and changed my clothes. I know I'll dream of the Tree of Sins again tonight—though that's the least of my worries.

I ask an attendant to send Xerxes-putra Cavas to my study. When he arrives, he's wearing a clean black angrakha and dhoti, my emblem embroidered over his chest in a red that perfectly matches his turban.

"Rani Shayla." The boy bows in the servile way of his kind.

"Sit."

He sits, barely batting an eye. Whatever public perception may be of us outside Ambar Fort, he still remains a valuable and dangerous prisoner.

"It's been two months since the incident at Javeribad," I tell him now. "And you have not yet told me what you anticipate the alleged Star Warrior's next move to be."

He hesitates. Being outside the kalkothri has done little to improve his pallor, though he looks less emaciated than before. "I assume she will come to Ambarvadi, Rani Shayla. Perhaps to Ambar Fort."

He has never called me Ambar Sikandar. Not once.

"An obvious assumption that a small child could have made," I sneer. "It's a good thing you're useful to me in other ways, or I would have rid myself of you long ago."

He says nothing in response, keeping his gaze focused somewhere along my chin.

I should dismiss him now, but something within me hesitates.

"Tell me," I say. "What do the people think of me?"

I pretend not to notice the way his head snaps up or the tightening of his jaw.

"Do you want the truth?" he asks.

This time, I am the one who is surprised, though I hide it with a raised eyebrow and a silent nod to speak further.

"People fear you," he says. "They know that any rebellion on their part will be crushed."

"And rightfully so."

The boy says nothing at first. Then: "My father said once that terror does not inspire love."

No. Of course it doesn't. But terror wins thrones. Terror keeps kingdoms in check.

"Well, it's a good thing, then, that I don't need their love, isn't it?"

I hate the tremor that has entered my voice, the way my fingers have curled into fists. The boy's throat bobs. For a moment, I think I see an emotion other than revulsion flicker across his handsome features. *Pity.*

"Get out," I snap, making him jump. Rising to his feet, he bows again before hastening from the room.

A wasted opportunity, a small voice says in my head. *You should have used that pity of his, tried to get him on your side.*

But I no longer have the patience to play coy or to hide behind false tears. Tyrant though I may be, I know this: Victors write the final story.

And I have never been good at losing.

31

GUL

"Saavdhaan!" Falak hollers. "Left! Now right!"

Twenty women from the Legion and eighty non-magi swing in unison, their lathis swiping left and then right. A hundred bodies in perfect sync.

"Form the simurgh!" Falak commands for a battle formation mimicking the wingspan of a simurgh in flight. A haphazard, but passable, V takes shape. Yet the moment Falak asks them to charge forward with their lathis, the trouble begins; many of the new recruits stumble into one another or accidentally hit someone with their staffs.

I bite back a groan. If Kali and I use magic on them right now, it'd be ten times worse. Pasting a smile on my face, I approach a non-magus boy and girl of my age, carefully spacing them apart, before moving on to an elderly man with a giant mustache.

"Kaka, are you all right?" I ask gently.

"I poked myself," he admits, revealing an inflamed left eye.

I nod. He's not the only one. Many non-magi who signed up initially dropped out of lathi training once they realized how difficult—and injurious—it could be to spin around a six-foot wooden stick, even during non-magical combat. To my surprise, though, many more stayed and showcased good fighting skills with time and practice. They're strongest when fighting in pairs or threes, dodging most of the spells Kali and I send their way.

"Gul!" a voice shouts.

"Make sure you get that eye looked at, Kaka," I tell him before heading to the back of the formation, where Kali and Falak are standing.

"What is it?" I ask.

"This isn't working," Falak says, her voice low, clipped.

I blink. "What do you mean it isn't working? The last practice round may not have been that great, but they've progressed significantly in two months."

"During exercises, yes. But these people won't be able to fight in a battle! Not the way we want them to. Half will be wiped out by Ambari forces, the other half will likely throw down their weapons and desert."

"You can't know that!" It's an effort to keep my voice contained to the three of us.

"Gul, Falak is right when she says it will be difficult to teach them the intricacies of lathi during an actual fight," Kali says. "If we had more time, say a year or two, maybe things would be different."

I feel myself deflate. I know she's right. Time is a luxury we don't have. It is miraculous enough that we've had these two months and that we've found a place to practice within the southern tenements itself—a long strip of land that curves along their outskirts, protected by another one of Amar's clever magical boundaries. Everyone who is non-magus can cross the boundary without problems, making it easy for them to go to work every day. Magi and half magi, on the other hand, can cross the boundary using only the little wooden, disc-shaped charms that Amar provided us shortly after he secured this patch of land.

Now, after the trouble we went through, my two generals—the only women I can count on to lead us to victory in this war—are telling me the whole exercise is pointless.

"Excuse me," Sami says, interrupting my dismal train of thought. She gives us a sheepish smile. "Didn't mean to bother you. But you were talking for such a long time, we were wondering if practice was dismissed for today."

I raise my eyebrows at Kali and Falak, who studiously avoid my gaze.

"Also," Sami continues. "I couldn't help overhearing what you said. And, if you don't mind, I'd like to offer an opinion. An alternative, if you will."

"Go ahead, Sami," I say.

"Instead of complicated battle drills that take years to get right, how about focusing on the basics? Apart from training, in a real battle, soldiers need grit: a willingness to keep fighting, through pain and hardship. And an ability to duck those nasty spells Gul and Kali send our way, of course."

For the first time today, the smile stretching across my lips feels genuine. Falak looks thoughtful, as if considering Sami's words.

Kali, however, frowns. "I worry that the basic drills will turn boring soon. Not everyone will be satisfied with simple advance and retreat exercises."

"Then someone should coach those people separately," Sami says patiently. "The way you coached us to access our magic in Tavan."

"That does make sense," Kali admits. "But who will do the extra coaching?"

"I will," I say at once. "I have plenty of time in the evening after our council meetings."

"*And* working with Raja Amar in the vegetable garden. *And* helping out at our campsite by the reservoir," Kali adds with a scowl. "Do you want to wear yourself out?"

When I say nothing, Kali mutters something that sounds like "hopeless."

I don't care. Working myself to the bone is the only way I can distract myself from brooding over what is happening right now across Ambar, with Cavas and Shayla visiting every town and village, presenting a united front.

The nights, on the other hand, remain interminably long, leaving me clawing at the air, restless despite the long hours of work and training. One time, I gave into temptation, breaking the rules despite what Subodh told me, and meditated, calling out for Cavas in the darkened temple.

But there was no answer. Nothing except the sort of void that comes from being depressingly alone. My sole source of information about Cavas now is the living specters—more specifically Roda, who seems to relish relaying any moment of intimacy between Shayla and Cavas.

Tonight, she appears right in the middle of dinner, announcing her presence with a thunderous cracking sound over the reservoir.

"What news, Roda?" Subodh asks, his gaze focused on an invisible point in the sky.

"Rani Shayla met with the leader of the Amirgarh army this morning," Roda reports in a bored voice. "He talked about a mutiny. She offered a bribe. He refused, so she got annoyed and had him thrown into the dungeon—after feeding his sword arm to a shadowlynx."

"Sounds exactly like something Rani Shayla would do," I whisper to a grim Kali.

"An army mutiny at Amirgarh?" Amar, who had been exhausted throughout today's council meeting, is suddenly alert. "Who was the leader, Roda ji?"

A giggle. Roda clearly loves having an honorific placed after her name. "His name is Brigadier Moolchand, Raja Amar. Apparently, he's the brother of some zamindar from Dukal. The brigadier and Rani Shayla talked about the zamindar as well. He accused the rani of killing him unfairly."

I suppress the chill that goes through me. From somewhere in the recesses of my brain, I recall another night in a village, more than two years ago, when Zamindar Moolchand flashed an oily smile at three strange women, offering them shelter in his haveli. *My only brother is in the army and no longer lives here*, the zamindar said.

"It isn't surprising that the army is growing restless," Sarpanch Parvez tells us. "I've news from many non-magus loadbearers who have been languishing for months now without any pay, since before Raja Lohar died. They were planning to head to Ambarvadi, too, to talk to someone at the Ministry of War."

"She had them burned alive." Roda's disembodied voice is eerily casual about this. Or probably desensitized by the number of people Shayla has killed so far. "They got a little too excited, those loadbearers—killing one of her Sky Warriors and nailing him to the ministry wall."

Grim faces around me turn grimmer. "If she thinks executions are going to stop us, she needs to think again," Sarpanch Parvez proclaims to loud cheers and applause.

Only Amar continues to frown, and I wonder if he feels as uneasy as I do about this. "I suppose the incident could work in our favor," he says. "If Shayla continues to oppress every dissenting voice, she'll turn the fearful ones angry as well."

"Not everyone is dissenting, Raja ji." Roda's tone turns snide. "*He's* on her side, isn't he? The Star Warrior's discard. The one whom people call the half magus traitor. He goes wherever she takes him to kiss her behind and lick her boots—when he isn't kissing or licking her elsewhere."

The specter's voice cuts off as a streak of green light splices the sky—a spell I shoot with my daggers before Kali grips hold of my arm, pulling me down.

"He isn't a discard!" I snap, hating the fact that I can't see the snickering specter. "And neither is he a traitor!"

"Any other news, Roda? Once you're finished taunting Gul, of course," Subodh says.

There must have been a warning embedded somewhere in that calm voice, because when Roda speaks again, she's oddly subdued. "Bounty hunters were spotted near Sur recently. They were asking the villagers questions about the southern tenements. Too many questions."

"The damn barrier must have drawn attention," someone grumbles.

"Yes, but at least it keeps us safe." We turn to the speaker—Councilor Maya, who scowls at us. "What are you looking at me for? It's the truth. Raja Amar may be magus, but he's not all bad."

Amar's mouth twitches under his beard.

"Anything else, Roda?" Subodh asks.

"Nothing, Pashuraj. Unless you want to know about the exact way Acharya Damak likes to pluck out his nose hairs—"

"That's everything for today," Amar cuts in. "Thank you, Roda ji."

A whiff of cold air passes by, indicating the specter's exit from the reservoir. Soon after, I leap to my feet, leaving my partially eaten food on my plate. Kali's and Falak's voices steam my ears as I walk to the training ground.

"You do realize she's making most of those things up, right?" Kali says. "She's doing this to rile you and you know it!"

"I can't help it!" I force myself to take a deep breath. "It has been more than two months since I've been able to see Cavas or talk to him!"

"Roda likes to stir trouble, Gul," Falak says. "She was like that even when alive."

I breathe deep, trying to cleanse my brain of images of Cavas and Shayla. I find some relief moments later, sparring with a few non-magi who arrive for extra practice on our training ground. But when the time comes to settle back in our tent, sleep eludes me.

It gets worse when, next to me, Kali and Sami first begin whispering to each other, giggling, and then—unmistakably—kissing.

On a normal day, I'd be amused by this development, ready to tease Kali about it the next day. Tonight, all I want to do is storm out of the tent. I force myself to stay put.

"We should sleep," Sami whispers finally. "We'll wake Gul."

I wait in silence until their breaths turn deep, until all I can hear is the sound of stray dogs barking in the distance. Minutes trickle by. Perhaps an hour.

I can't take this anymore. Once snores begin rising from Kali and Sami's end of the tent, I slip out.

The camp is quiet, everyone slumbering after a long day of activity. Subodh's long body is in repose, silhouetted against the moonlit reservoir. I glance around warily, wondering if Latif is around, lurking somewhere, watching me the way Subodh asked him to.

If so, the specter doesn't stop me as I tiptoe out of camp and make my way through the tenements' winding lanes, past the darkened buildings and ruined havelis, around a few men snoring peacefully on netted cots outside, to a small, makeshift shed behind the vegetable garden. Inside the shed, I find Agni—not asleep, as I anticipated, but wide awake. She snorts, her ears perking up the moment she sees me. I raise my finger to my lips.

Quiet, I tell her through our bond. *We don't want anyone else waking up.*

Agni does as I ask, her body vibrating with the same sort of restlessness that I feel. Soundlessly, I lead her out of the shed, away from the buildings, to the stretch of land where we train in the mornings. I don't bother with a saddle, sliding onto her bareback the way I did as a novice at the Sisterhood whenever we went off on our nighttime jaunts, my seaglass daggers secure against my hips.

The barrier prickles my cheeks—a warning—but in this moment, I don't care. I simply want to get away for a short while—away from the rumors and conjecture, from the many curious gazes, from the living specters I'm forced to rely on for information but can never really trust.

Soon we are off on a gallop against the dark, barren land, nothing ahead of us except an endless starry sky.

Finally. Agni's voice is a sigh in my head. *I can run again.*

"Me too," I gasp out loud. My heart races. There are no magical barriers here. No protection against wild animals, spies, or bounty hunters.

In fact, what I'm doing now is equally dangerous, possibly more so than trying to communicate with Cavas. "Tell me if you see or sense anything strange," I tell Agni.

Don't worry. I don't smell any humans nearby.

After a while, we slow down, pausing seemingly in the middle of nowhere, thhor plants and honeyweed bushes our only companions, along with a full yellow moon.

"I'm so tired, Agni," I say as I dismount. "I don't know what's really happening there. What Cavas is doing. What *she's* doing to him. Amar keeps saying we need to wait. That we can't attack Ambarvadi yet. And I know it's logical. Many non-magi aren't trained soldiers, and Shayla has armies above and beyond the Sky Warriors. I . . ." My voice trails off.

Do you love Cavas?

Agni's question—so strangely human in nature—sends my heart racing. "Why do you ask?"

If you love him, then you should trust him.

"I trust Cavas," I insist, annoyed by the comment. "I don't trust *her.*"

Loving someone means you worry for them, Agni comments. *I worried for you when you were at the flesh market. I wanted to come get you. But I waited. I trusted Juhi to get you out. Now you must trust yourself to get Cavas out.*

I wrap my arms around Agni's neck and press my cheek against her velvety skin. "I'm sorry I worried you."

Agni snorts, as if laughing at me. *Come now. We have been here too long.*

I say nothing more. I climb on Agni's back without complaint, staying as silent as possible as we head back to the tenements.

And find the way back in to be blocked.

Two men on horses stand before us, the ends of their turbans covering their faces, talwars glinting in their hands. I unsheathe my own daggers without thinking, my body humming with magic and anxiety.

"Look at what we have here," one of them says.

"A girl on a horse. Alone."

"Looks like she has gold eyes, too." The first man's mask falls off, revealing a grim, weather-beaten face. "Like Rani Shayla said in her reward proclamation."

Bounty hunters.

I bite my tongue to curb my rising fear. It would be easy to kill them. To call on the sky goddess again, to channel her power through my daggers, letting it emerge in the form of an unforgiving red chakra.

But this isn't something I want to do. Not unless I absolutely need to.

"Stay away," I tell them in a hard voice. "Unless you want me to blow you up."

The men say nothing, but I can sense their wariness, see the way their gazes flicker repeatedly to my green daggers, now sparking at the tips. I know I need to play upon every myth about the Star Warrior, to keep bluffing for as long as possible, until I can find a way past them and through the barrier.

Feint left, I tell Agni through our bond—which she does, instantly making one of the men move in that direction, before galloping right instead.

The first man, however, is smarter. Expecting the move, he blocks my way again, this time slicing at me with his glowing red talwar.

Protect, I think, raising my arms, but the bounty hunter's spell is stronger than I anticipated and my shield barely deflects the sword's deadly red edge. Working the whole day without a break has done me no favors, either. Soon my temples begin to pulse, and I grit my teeth against the pain. We parry for a while in this way, my shield spells growing weaker each time.

Get off, Agni says suddenly. *Get off now.*

"What?" I am so exhausted that I forget to keep my voice contained to my head. "What are you talking about?"

"Talking to ghosts, girl?" the man sneers. "Or perhaps a living specter?"

"You mean me?" a disembodied voice says out loud.

Latif!

Several things happen at once:

Off! Agni bucks, the action startling me enough to slide off her back.

As the bounty hunters converge, their horses begin bucking in the same exact way, as if being drawn by an invisible force. Or possibly a living specter.

"Hurry, girl!" Latif shouts.

"Don't let her get away!" the first bounty hunter hollers, trying to control his horse. His companion is thrown off, landing on the ground with a thud.

"I think I broke something!" he groans.

"Fool!" the remaining bounty hunter snarls, leaping off his horse the way I did and landing on his feet.

Run, Gul! Agni screams before charging at the bounty hunter to block his way.

I run, though I hate leaving Agni.

I run, forcing myself to ignore the awful sounds that rise behind me—mingled shrieks of human and horse, a cracking sound that might very well be someone's bones.

I'm nearly at the barrier to the tenements when pain sears across my ribs, so sharp that I fall to my knees. But no blood comes off on my hands, nor is there a single cut on my skin.

My headache spikes. I felt like this only once before. Inside a stable in Dukal, when a Samudra woman with black eyes tried to silence a mare for trying to protect me.

"Agni!" I wail. "Agni, no!"

But as I double back to get to her, someone begins dragging me in the opposite direction, toward the barrier. The hands that grip my ankles are like ice and inhumanly strong. The southern tenements' barrier cloaks my skin—a curtain of air and sound that blocks everything, except the final sight of Agni rearing on her hind legs, blood running down her flank.

Latif holds on to me, pulling me farther as I continue making futile attempts to shoot him.

"Stop, girl!" Latif says in a harsh voice. "Stop screaming!"

In my head, something snaps—the tether, I realize, that has always joined my mind to Agni's.

"Agni!" I shout, though nothing answers me now except silence. "Agni!"

My fists pound the earth, over and over until I collapse, grief searing my chest, my knuckles bruised and throbbing.

"She's gone," Latif says softly. "But she protected you. She killed them both."

"I should have died," I say, my voice raw. "Not Agni."

He does not protest this, nor does he try to comfort me.

I'm not aware he has left until I feel another presence by my side. A shadow that's too big, too tall to be anyone except the Pashu king. Next to him is another presence—a human, whose hands gently sit me up.

Amar's yellow eyes, so hard and serious during the day, are full of compassion. "What happened?" he asks.

The story pours out of me, haltingly at first and then in a torrent. The moment they hear that Agni's body is outside the barrier, Subodh and Amar exchange quick glances. Without another word, Subodh stalks away, disappearing through the barrier.

"He'll be fine," Amar tells me when I grow tense.

I say nothing, my gaze focused on the expanse of plains that shows me nothing of what is really on the other side.

Eventually, a limb appears, followed by a mane, Subodh gently drawing back Agni into the tenements with his forepaws.

"I buried the men," he says. "Made sure they went deep into the earth where no one will find them. The horses are gone. Perhaps they'll find better owners."

Agni's lovely red coat glistens with sweat and dark patches of blood. Subodh carefully closes her bulging eyes.

"I want to wash her," I say. "I don't want her looking like that."

A bucket appears in the air before me, water sloshing within. Latif's cold touch brushes my fingers as he hands me a cloth that I use to gently, carefully clean Agni's body. We bury her here, in this space where I train, marking the grave with a small, horse-shaped stone that Amar conjures out of thin air. I think I hear Amar say my name a few times, before sensing what feels like a pair of invisible fingers brushing my mind—*Subodh*, I realize, attempting to create a bond.

Not now, I beg. *Please.*

Eventually, their voices and footsteps fade, and I'm left on my own, my fingers smelling of dirt, of the sweat and blood of the only creature in this world whose love I never doubted.

32

GUL

The next day, Kali asks me if I want to spend the morning in our tent.

"What for?" I ask.

"To mourn," she says. There's now a permanent indent between her brows that wasn't there before.

"One day won't be enough," I tell her, strapping my daggers to my waist. "And I can't mourn when there is still so much work to do."

"If you say so. I won't be at practice today; Raja Amar has called me to the temple for some work. Will you be all right?"

"I will."

It's easier said than done. The whole day, I carry the knowledge of Agni's death, feel the iron grip of it tightening my ribs whenever I unsheathe a dagger during training and go deep within to produce an attacking spell.

Halfway through practice, a small boy comes racing toward us.

"Star Warrior," he gasps, nearly out of breath. "You're wanted at the temple."

Falak and I glance at each other and I nod. "Go through the regular drills. I'll go see what's going on."

A crowd has gathered outside the temple, murmurs rising to questions as they see me climb the stairs, still wearing my sweaty practice uniform.

And soon I see why.

Two strangers stand at the threshold, talking to Amar. Men from northern Ambar, their vibrantly patterned turbans wound in tight coils around their heads, making them stand out here amid the southerners, who stick to plain colors and a more relaxed style of wrap. As I approach, both men fall silent and gape at me, probably startled by my disheveled appearance.

"Gul, this is Sarpanch Alok and Councilor Cama." Amar's voice breaks our staring game. "They're delegates from the northern tenements."

Non-magi. That explains how they got through Amar's barrier. I turn to face the men who lived where Cavas once did and say, "How do we know they aren't spies? Or bounty hunters?"

"I had Kali question them," Amar says calmly. "Raja Subodh helped."

"I think we should take this inside," Councilor Maya abruptly cuts in. She turns to the gaping crowd. "Brothers and sisters, we are among friends here. Please, go about your work, and do not worry."

Though her voice is kind, there's a firmness that brooks no argument. Soon the crowd begins to disperse, and after ensuring that no one remains lurking, we head into the temple's inner chambers.

"I suppose Latif and the specters are stationed outside?" I ask Subodh.

"The way they are during every meeting," he replies.

A day earlier I might have asked a question about Roda or mockingly suggested that she be put on guard duty. But now, with Agni gone, my grievances against the former Legion warrior feel petty. Pointless.

Trust me, Cavas said the last time I saw him. I hold on to those words, encasing them with every happy and safe memory I've ever had.

Cavas is not yet a memory. He's still alive.

The ferocity of that final thought must reflect on my face and in my eyes, because the two non-magi councilors from the north, who have been staring at me since I got here, look away.

"Thank you, brothers, for making this perilous journey here," Sarpanch Parvez begins once we're settled. "We know how bad the roads have become—with Sky Warriors on the loose, shooting anyone without impunity, and now bounty hunters and thieves, who have taken it upon themselves to loot villages and towns in the name of unearthing the Star Warrior."

"We no longer worry about such dangers," says the head councilor of the northern tenements. "We thought the kingdom was bad under Rani Megha and then Raja Lohar. But this rani is much worse than the others. Already, many are starving in villages and towns outside Ambarvadi because of her tithes. If nothing is done, we will die."

I feel my heart sink at the utter resignation on Sarpanch Alok's face. The councilor next to him—Cama, I think his name is—looks equally tired.

Amar's face tightens. "We hope it will not come to that."

"I suppose that's why we're here, isn't it?" Councilor Cama's voice is like gravel: pebbled and prickly, ready to draw blood at the turn of skin. "My own reason for being here is more personal. It has to do with the half magus traitor, Cavas."

"Call him a traitor again and I'll slit your throat," I say. My seaglass dagger glows green in my hand.

"Gul!" Kali admonishes. "Put that down!"

But I don't. I look right into Councilor Cama's dark eyes, which are now narrowing with distaste.

"Don't be foolish, girl. He has moved on from you the way he moved on from my own daughter," he says with a sneer. "He now warms the queen's lap as her pet dog."

I stare at him uneasily. "Was your daughter's name Bahar?"

The councilor's face turns ashen. "How do you know that?"

"Cavas told me." I swallow hard. "He said she was taken away because of her birthmark. It . . . it bothered him. A lot."

The councilor doesn't speak for several moments.

"After Rani Shayla shut down the labor camps, I thought I could find my daughter again," he says finally. "I thought I could bring her home. We didn't know where she was initially. After making inquiries, the palace simply sent us a scroll saying that Bahar passed away at the labor camp outside Havanpur. A scrap of parchment with her prisoner number and the day she died. We don't know where they buried her. *If* they buried her."

I close my eyes.

"Rani Shayla had promised us relief for our dead—a compensation for our grief over the past few years," Bahar's father continues bitterly. "But when we went to see her at Ambar Fort, they unleashed the makara guards on us. We knew then that there was not going to be any change. Not with *her* on the throne."

He looks toward Amar. "We received word from Sarpanch Parvez about your pledge to agree to our demands. If this is true, then we are willing to support you, to fight for you in this war."

Far from looking pleased at this news, Amar looks grimmer than ever.

Councilor Rayomand notices. "Raja Amar, are you well? You don't seem happy."

Amar sighs. "The more I think of it, the less I like this idea of a civil war. Innocent people slaughtered in a battle for ascension. Yet, at the same time, I know Shayla isn't going to give up the throne without a fight."

"I . . . I need to think about this, to see if there is a way to spill as little blood as possible."

Then, quietly, so that only I can hear, he whispers, "I think you and Cavas should start communicating again."

"Isn't that dangerous?" I whisper back, even as I tamp down the swelling excitement in my chest.

"It is. But I don't think we can rely on the specters alone. It's why I think you should let *Cavas* initiate the communication and not reach out to him yourself."

Is there a point to giving me freedom if I'm to be held on a leash? I wonder.

But I don't ask the question out loud. I see the warning in Subodh's gaze—he and Amar must have discussed this beforehand—and the avid interest on the faces of the non-magi councilors. Any argument on my part will reflect badly on Amar and could be detrimental to his fragile hold on these new alliances with non-magi.

"All right," I say quietly. "I'll wait for Cavas to make the first move."

For now.

33

CAVAS

At the palace, Ma and I fall into a routine of sorts. She usually comes to see me in the middle of the night, when Captain Shekhar briefly falls asleep, and I tell her anything I've overheard the Sky Warriors talk about that day.

"They mentioned a mutiny at the Amirgarh cantonment," I whisper to my mother. My eyes remain on Captain Shekhar, who sits slumbering a few feet away. "Also talked about a brigadier named Moolchand, who might be leading the mutiny."

"Yes, we know," Ma says. "One of the specters found out yesterday and sent the information. Anything else?"

I shake my head.

Instead of disappearing the way she normally does, Ma lingers. "I have some news . . . good news for you. Raja Amar believes you and Gul should start communicating again."

"*What?*" My voice is loud enough to alarm both me and Ma. We glance at Captain Shekhar—staring at him for long moments until he releases a snore.

"Quiet, son. And don't be hasty." Ma's voice is so soft I can barely hear it. "Raja Amar wants *you* to initiate the communication, not Gul. Use the opportunity wisely. Don't enter the meditative state unless it's safe for you to do so."

Barely a second after she disappears, the dozing Sky Warrior wakes, and I pretend once more to be fast asleep—though inwardly I want to punch something.

It's been a little over two months since I gave my first speech in Ambarvadi and last saw Gul in a meditative trance. Who knows if I'll be able to do it again—with no practice whatsoever? How do they expect me to help Gul or fight when the time comes?

What I *am* doing now is helping the Scorpion.

Giving speeches in whatever village, town, or tenement she takes me to. Deflecting the hate she receives onto myself. Facing bewildered Ambari citizens everywhere. Some days I'm not sure if I'm doing a good enough job. The only thing I've been thankful for is that the Scorpion hasn't tried to kiss me again after the first speech in Ambarvadi. Now, she simply nods once my speech is over, as if impatient to get away, and most of the time, that is exactly what we do. I haven't forgotten the man who spoke out in protest in the capital, and I can tell that neither has Queen Shayla.

We no longer encounter such people in public.

Instead, I see small signs of dissent. The faces in the crowd who do not cheer for their new queen. Scattered groups of people wearing mourning grays. Broken shrines lying untouched, in heaps of rubble and crushed flowers.

After Ambarvadi, the town of Havanpur made the boldest move yet. As I made my speech, fireworks lit up the sky, forming a giant eight-point star and the words *The true king waits*.

It was the first time I saw fear—real fear—on the Scorpion's face. She issued an order to give up the culprit to her or she would shut down the black market—the town's biggest source of income. No one spoke, and in retaliation, she pulled someone from the crowd and raised an atashban to his head. Havanpur's governor eventually stepped forward to take the blame and save the man, getting promptly arrested.

When I open my eyes again, it's morning, and Major Emil is hovering over me, shaking me awake.

"Hurry, boy. We're late and the rani isn't in a good temper."

Is she ever in a good temper?

I rise and wash my face, slipping into the latest costume they've laid out for me: another costly silk tunic and dhoti set, this one in pure saffron, with a matching orange-and-white turban. Major Emil turns sideways to give me some privacy to change out of my underclothes and then watches in silence as I wind the turban around my head.

"Where are we headed today?" I ask.

"Amirgarh," Emil says. He looks grimmer than usual.

I feel my throat tighten, then swell at the sound of the name.

"Isn't Amirgarh an army cantonment?" I ask Major Emil. "Why go there?"

He gives me a cool look, as if he doesn't quite believe my ignorance. "The rani wishes to address her subjects there, per usual," he says.

Yet, as we prepare to leave, I can tell this trip is going to be different. Outside, next to the four carriages Govind and his stable boys have brought out, wait four guards normally stationed at the gates of Ambar Fort. With green scales and elongated, crocodile faces, the makara stand nearly a head taller than the tallest Sky Warrior of the group, liquid orange flashing intermittently between their wrinkled brown eyelids.

"Don't look at them directly and you'll be fine," Major Emil mutters.

My skin breaks into goose bumps. The makara, after all, are Pashu, who were captured by Lohar after the Three-Year War, much like the gold-skinned, winged peri. The makara guarding our carriage hisses as we approach. Emil goes in first, fists clenched, entering the carriage as if it were the inside of a lion's mouth. Despite the major's warning, I glance up at the makara, who stares right back at me, teeth bared.

"I saw Rani Sarayu," I whisper, my voice so soft that I barely hear it myself. "And Raja Subodh. They're still out there. Fighting."

The makara grows very still, nostrils flaring. Then, an atashban pricks between my shoulder blades—Captain Shekhar nudging me inside.

"Idiot," he says as he climbs in behind me. "Why in Svapnalok were you staring at that vile thing? Do you want to turn to ash? They're barely controllable as is."

I say nothing, fully aware of Major Emil's gaze.

The makara shuts the carriage door, causing it to rattle slightly, before climbing to sit up front with the driver. Soon we are racing across the barren plains to the west of Ambar Fort. In the distance, I see Prithvi's wall, the magic from its silvery stones making my skin crawl, even from here. The rocking motion of the carriage has a soporific effect. I'm nearly dozing when Captain Shekhar suddenly opens the window, letting in the hot afternoon air.

"The town of Meghapur is approaching," he says. "You're from here, aren't you, Major Emil?"

"Yes." Major Emil's voice, though polite, is curt. Tension radiates from him, more so now than before.

Captain Shekhar doesn't seem to notice. "Isn't Meghapur known for its herb and spice market? How they grow here, in this arid climate, baffles me."

"Meghapur's main crop is roopbadal—and that grows in any kind of soil," Emil says. "A bit of rain during the Month of Tears and you have an herb that tastes savory when cooked in oil, sweet when cooked in water, and spicy if left out overnight in brine."

"Roopbadal, huh? I thought Meghapur was known for other, *faster* crops," Captain Shekhar sneers.

Major Emil says nothing in response, his frown deepening.

Meghapur's agricultural bounty, however, appears to be a thing of the past. We cross field upon fallow field, plows and sickles strewn across the ground, gathering dust. The town appears deserted as well, its streets empty and shops boarded up, the havelis forsaken with nary a horse nor bullock cart in sight.

"What happened here?" Captain Shekhar asks. "Where is everyone?"

"Most are gone," Major Emil says flatly. "Harvest was poor this year and they couldn't pay the increased land tithes. I was at the border crossing near the Brimlands over a month ago, and people from Meghapur were leaving in droves. Along with others, of course."

Silence falls over the carriage.

"Your family," Captain Shekhar begins. "They—"

"I have no family," Major Emil cuts in. "Not anymore."

"Didn't you have a daughter—"

"That's enough, Captain."

Emil's forbidding expression wipes the smirk off Shekhar's face.

The major looks out the window, so still that his profile looks like it's carved from stone. The carriages approach a stone archway covered with white paint, depicting Ambar and Meghapur's various crops and spices. Up close, I see the peeling and cracks, the rough stone under what once was likely a layer of sangemarmar. A Sky Warrior from the carriage ahead of us steps out, waving an arm for us to halt.

Major Emil leans out the window. "What is it?" he asks.

"Rani Shayla wishes to speak to the governor," the Sky Warrior says. "He's uncle to the new brigadier in Amirgarh."

"Does the rani need anything from us?"

"She requested Captain Shekhar's presence. The governor claims to be loyal to the rani, but these days you can never be too sure."

We watch from a few feet away as a small man prostrates before the Scorpion, laying his turban at her feet—a sign of ultimate submission. Shayla nods and raises a hand in blessing. Words like *honor* and *guest* float our way as the governor gestures to a haveli nearby that looks relatively inhabited, if not well cared for. The Scorpion's stiff shoulders belie the giant smile pasted on her face. She doesn't trust him—and neither do the rest of her guards.

"Go on, Captain Shekhar," Emil says. "I'll keep an eye on the half magus."

After the captain leaves, silence falls over us again. I clear my throat before speaking. "Captain Shekhar said you had a daughter."

Major Emil says nothing. The space outside the haveli is empty now, the Scorpion and her three Sky Warriors having followed the governor inside. The makara guarding the Scorpion's carriage patrols the front door.

"I don't know what happened. But I know what it feels like to lose someone." As I speak, I sense my mother sit down beside me, her cool gray hand resting next to mine.

Emil's mouth is pressed thin under his perfectly groomed mustache.

"She was a small thing," he says slowly. "Hardly bigger than my forearm. She'd barely left the womb when the midwife saw the birthmark on her right shoulder. We were forced to give her up. The grief killed my mate eventually. When I went to look for my daughter a week after her mother died, she wasn't at the same labor camp anymore. General Tahmasp had her transferred somewhere else. That was around sixteen years ago. I don't know what happened to her. If she's still alive."

Ma's hand curls around my now tightened fist.

"My papa said that when my ma died, she went to live among the stars," I say after a pause. "I sometimes gaze into the sky looking for her. For him, too, now. I feel them there."

Something flickers in Major Emil's eyes—grief, bitterness, perhaps regret. Then his face grows smooth again, turning once more into the perfect, expressionless mask of one of the Scorpion's most loyal soldiers.

34

CAVAS

A long time goes by before Captain Shekhar returns—thankfully, with food. I force myself to eat slowly and not inhale the honeyweed pulao and spiced mango preserves. Though I'm no longer starved at the palace the way I was in the kalkothri, during trips like this, food remains scarce, dependent on the Scorpion's own hunger, which is surprisingly limited. We set off for Amirgarh again at breakneck speed—so fast that my stomach heaves, and I wonder if I'm going to throw up. Major Emil looks equally green around the gills.

"What did you feed the horses?" he demands. "Enhancers?"

"Funny you should mention that." Captain Shekhar's eyes are more bloodshot than usual, his broad face flushed with excitement. "See this?"

He holds up a small, oblong fruit akin to a date and thrusts it in my face. "Know what it is, half magus?"

"A ber?" I guess, though the fruit is a strange combination of yellow and purple rather than the usual red.

"A ber he calls this, Major Emil! This isn't a ber, boy!" Captain Shekhar booms. "This is tez! Grown only in Meghapur, during the Month of

Tears, ripening at the end of the Month of Dreams, which is about now." The captain holds the fruit up to his eye. "Put this in a horse's mouth and it runs at twice the normal speed. Mix a little in your morning curd, and your magic becomes twice as strong. Better than any amplifier."

"I hope you remember that tez is banned for human consumption, Captain," Major Emil says sharply. "Tez shouldn't be given to horses, either—unless it's an emergency."

The captain pockets the tez fruit, his smile like a blade. "Well, it's a good thing for us that Rani Shayla plans to lift the ban, isn't it? Allowing us to fight the way we want to. The way we should during this *emergency* that will be a civil war."

Both men glare at each other; clearly the captain is enjoying his one-upmanship on the major right now. Emil says nothing, his face taut. Disapproving though he might be about tez, he knows he can do nothing about it if the Scorpion herself allows the drug.

With tez aiding the horses, we reach Amirgarh in the early evening, lanterns flickering to life on tall poles as our carriages drive down its streets, toward the fortress in the center.

Hundreds of armored men and women march out into the courtyard in perfect unison, their boots thumping the dusty ground, their long sleeves rippling bloodred in the air. Hard faces glare at us, and I pinch the inside of my arm, the pain grounding me enough to stop trembling.

The new brigadier, a broad-shouldered and bull-faced man, gives the Scorpion an oily smile. He is nearly as servile as Meghapur's governor, bowing deep, stopping short of placing his turbaned helmet at her feet.

"Saavdhaan!" he booms.

The army stands at attention.

"Sena pranam!"

The soldiers point their spears at us, the tips glowing red. My heart balls in my throat. But then they shift positions again, shooting sparks into the air. They follow this up by thumping their breastplates twice—the Ambari royal salute.

"Sena pranam, Ambar Sikandar!" the army shouts.

The Scorpion thumps her own breastplate in return, her smile hard, approving. "I salute you, in turn, soldiers of Amirgarh. As part of our army, you have always been Ambar's backbone. It's because of you that we can hold our heads upright, raise them high. However, it has come to my attention that we, the people of Ambar, face a threat from our very own now. *You*, who took vows to protect the sky, to keep safe Ambar's head—its queen. You, who pledged your *lives* to protect the kingdom, which is now going through financial difficulties. Are you truly bothered by a few delays in payment?"

I frown. This wasn't Shayla's usual speech, which solely focused on defaming Gul. This is something I've never heard before. But it seems to be working. Though most of the soldiers are still stone-faced, a few now begin to frown, as if considering her words.

"Raja Lohar emptied our coffers. We now face a threat from a girl who calls herself the Star Warrior, a savior of the people, when all she wants is to usurp the throne. We also face external threats from kingdoms that were once our allies. Soldiers, your allegiance is to Ambar, to the uniform you chose to wear for life. Yet, if you wish, you may choose to leave now. Defect, if you will."

Not a breath nor a whisper breaks the silence that follows. The Scorpion's words have cleverly positioned the army's soldiers between a wall and a steep cliff. Defection from the army means certain death. No one moves.

Shayla's smile sharpens. "Good. I see you are still loyal soldiers, who were not swayed by traitors like the former brigadier, Moolchand, who came to see me at Ambar Fort and demanded a bribe."

She does not notice the frown on the new brigadier's face, nor the way he steps forward and then hesitates, as if to stop her from saying anything else.

What mistake did the Scorpion make? What did she say that was changing the fear on the soldiers' faces to confusion and disbelief?

But I don't have time to ponder these questions. A moment later, my name is announced, and I step forward to give my usual speech. The moment I finish, Captain Shekhar hustles me back into our carriage. He hands me a bundle, this one containing a clay pot of sweet curd and another pot of vegetable pulao. Though the food smells delicious, I can barely taste it.

Something's wrong. I feel it in my gut.

We don't spend the night in Amirgarh. Instead, we speed back to Ambar Fort, the Sky Warriors constantly watching the landscape for traps or danger.

"Sleep, boy," Major Emil tells me. "It's going to be a long night."

But sleep remains elusive. My body thrums with the same sort of restlessness that I'd felt during the battle at Tavan.

Dawn breaks across the sky by the time we get back to the palace. I feel myself droop, falling into bed moments after Captain Shekhar and Major Emil escort me back to my room, my exhausted brain finally shutting down. I'm quite sure I wouldn't have woken again had it not been for the hands on my shoulders, a voice I never expected to hear in my room.

"Wake up! Wake up, boy!"

My eyes snap open, looking right into Queen Amba's. Instantly, I glance to my left. A snore rises from where Captain Shekhar sits on his usual chair. Behind him, the door is open by a crack, its edges glowing slightly—probably a remnant of the spell Queen Amba used to get in.

"Rani Am—"

"Shhhhhhh." She raises a hand to her lips. "Listen now and listen well. She's hiring mercenaries from the Brimlands. I overheard her talking to Major Emil upstairs."

She? Is she talking about the Scorpion?

It has to be. There is no other *she* whose mention could blanch the color off Queen Amba's lips.

"Why would she hire mercenaries?" I ask quietly. "She has a whole army."

"An army that might have seen through her lie about bribing Brigadier Moolchand," Amba says, grim satisfaction lining her face. "Remember now: mercenaries from the Brimlands. Inform the living specters about this and ask them to tell my son and the Pashu king. I would have done it myself, but none of the specters are answering me right now."

"What about my mother?" I glance at the snoring Captain Shekhar, marveling at the strength of whatever sleep spell Rani Amba has put him under.

"She was my usual contact. Honestly, she was the only specter who answered me," Amba admits. "But Harkha isn't here at the moment and, as a seer, you might have better luck communicating with the others. I'm being watched more closely than ever. I found my last shvetpanchhi dead, its blood soaking my pillow. It's with great difficulty that I got this moment alone."

I grow silent, my gaze flickering to her hands on my body, touching me. A moment later, she drops her hands, her face turning impassive, as she shields whatever is human in her behind a regal mask.

"Hurry," she whispers.

Then, with barely a brush of her silk jootis against the floor, she's gone. Carefully watching Captain Shekhar, who's still snoring, I reach into my pocket for the green swarna Govind gave me.

"Ma?" I whisper, rubbing the surface of the glowing coin. "Are you there?"

There's no answer. Nothing, which is strange since my mother has been here every time I've called, was there with me nearly the whole way to Amirgarh.

Until she wasn't.

I frown, wondering what she had seen—if she'd had to deal with another emergency.

"Latif?" I rub the coin again. "Any specters around?"

Seconds later, a voice brushes my left ear.

"Anandpranam, handsome."

The specter does not show herself to me, but I know I've never spoken to her before.

"Can you pass on a message to the other side?" I tell her. "The kabzedar rani is hiring mercenaries from the Brimlands. The army at Amirgarh may still mutiny."

A cold hand strokes my neck. I suppress a shiver. "Is that everything?" the voice whispers.

"Is . . . is Gul okay? Have you seen her?"

The hand stills, nails scoring my skin like ice. "Last I saw, she was batting her eyes at Raja Amar, wrapped up in his arms."

Liar, my mind says at once.

"What need would I have to lie, handsome?" The specter giggles. "It's not like I'm going to get anything from *you*." The last word is filled with so much venom that I feel myself jerking backward, inching toward the wall.

"Please!" I force myself to breathe deeply and not snap at her the way I want to. "Will you give them the message?"

There's no answer. Not a sign that a living specter was here except for the crawling sensation that has yet to leave my skin.

I glance once more at my guard, but Captain Shekhar is still fast asleep.

I have to risk it. Just this once.

With a deep breath, I close my eyes and slowly go inward.

It takes a while for Gul to hear my voice. Or, perhaps, to respond to it. She doesn't throw herself at me the way she did the last time. Instead, her eyes remain watchful, skeptical. My mind, fueled by the specter's poison, instantly forms an image of Gul and Amar embracing.

"What happened?" Gul asks abruptly. "Why did you call me?"

"Mercenaries," I reply, my voice equally curt. "The Scorpion's hiring

them from the Brimlands. We were at Amirgarh last night, and she sus-
pects the army there might mutiny."

A frown. "Interesting."

Interesting? *That's all she has to say?*

But Gul doesn't seem to notice my scowl. "Delegates from the northern tenements came to see us," she says after a pause. "One of them was
Bahar's father."

"Did he tell you something?" I blurt out. "Is that why you're acting
so cold? Or is it Raja Amar? Are you with him now?"

Her eyes widen. "Where in Svapnalok did you get such a ridiculous
idea? Of course I'm not with Amar!"

"A specter told me," I admit. "It's why I meditated. I . . . I couldn't
stand the thought."

"Was the specter female and flirtatious?" she demands.

"Yes," I say, surprised.

"Roda," she growls, her scowl at once confusing and heartening. "Of
course she'd tell you a stupid thing like that. She's been telling everyone
for weeks now about how you've become Shayla's lover."

"What?"

Gul's laughter does little to hide her relief. "You should see the look
on your face. Like you're about to puke."

"The Scorpion kissed me," I admit. "And I didn't kiss her back. It
happened only once, I swear."

"It doesn't matter," Gul says, her face a strange mix of anger and sorrow. "I wouldn't blame you for anything you were forced to do in order
to survive. I paid the price for listening too much to that specter, anyway. I lost Agni."

She tells me about the bounty hunters, the terrible chase back to the
southern tenements. "Agni said you love me," Gul says finally.

The vulnerability in her voice surprises me.

Didn't I already tell her my heart was hers?

But maybe these things need to be spelled out more clearly.

"I do love you," I say honestly, without embarrassment. "I realized it when Papa refused to run away and told me to go back and save you from Ambar Fort. He told me that if I didn't, I would regret it for the rest of my life."

"You did regret coming for me, though," she points out.

"I did. Mostly because I regret Papa's death. But I don't regret you being here. Or feeling the way I feel about you. Does that make sense?"

A slight smile, which I take to mean *maybe*.

"Do *you* love *me*, though?" I ask the question simmering in my mind. "You never said."

Gul's eyes widen as I step forward, but she doesn't move away.

"I once said I would give up my mission of killing the king if it meant saving you," she says. "Wasn't that enough?"

I raise my eyebrows. "You mean the time you shot me with a spell? *That's* what you meant? Javer's beard, you could have been less convoluted!"

She rolls her eyes, but this close I can feel what's going through her mind. The heat of embarrassment. Another feeling that has my insides turning to mush.

"I thought you changed your mind with that good-looking conjurer king by your side," I say.

"Well, it's good that I'm not drawn to you for your looks or your magic, isn't it?"

Her teasing smile melts against the pressure of my lips, her arms tightening around my neck. A warning ticks in the back of my skull, but I can't seem to remember what it's about.

Until I feel an invisible hand pulling me backward, a voice snarling "dirt-licking traitor" in my ear.

I wrench myself from Gul, a red haze of pain searing my head and torso. "Go!" I tell her. "*Go!*"

Gul shouts something in return, but I can't make out what it is.

Seconds later, I'm back in the windowless room at Raj Mahal, my head bleeding as I lie on the floor, Captain Shekhar's boot repeatedly slamming into my ribs.

My second time being imprisoned makes the Sky Warriors go twice as hard with their interrogations.

"Where did you get that magic?" Captain Shekhar demands. "Who did you steal it from?"

When I say nothing, he kicks me in the ribs again. Though pain blurs my vision, I sense another presence inside the cell—one that I instinctively know is more dangerous than Shekhar.

"Shall I make him light up again, General?" the captain asks, panting, the manic gleam in his eyes making me wonder if he's been ingesting tez. I whimper as pain shoots through my right hand, the sound of my index finger breaking only barely registering in my head.

"That's enough, Captain." Alizeh flips my green swarna in the air, slaps it against the back of her palm. "Tell me, dirt licker, where did you get the green swarna—a classified contraband item? You, who are not allowed to communicate with specters? Also, since when do half magi glow with unexplained magic?"

When I say nothing, her nails dig into my skin. "Do you know what we do to traitors here?"

"Hang me, then," I spit out. "What else can you do?"

Light flickers around the edges of my mind, gentle yet persistent, followed by a voice that I shut down before it floods my brain. I cannot have them guess about my connection to Gul right now. I cannot glow—even by accident.

"I think it's time to start the consecutives again," General Alizeh says.

They break my fingers first, then my already injured ribs. Then Alizeh presses the burning tip of her atashban to my forehead, peeling off my skin. I would scream, but my voice is gone by then and all that emerges from my mouth are grunts. Between moments of consciousness and unconsciousness, I hear Vaid Roshan urging General Alizeh to go slow. That there are some injuries even healing cannot cure.

"I thought you had a stronger stomach for such things, Vaid ji," the general tells him.

"Healing isn't butchery, General."

The silence that fills my cell afterward makes me wonder if General Alizeh shot the vaid then and there, furious with his cold rebuke. But then I feel her boot again, pressing into my diaphragm, the searing pain that follows, threatening to knock me unconscious once more.

"Heal *that* then, Vaid ji."

By now I am spitting blood. My vision is so blurred that I can barely see the shadow hovering overhead.

"Easy," says the vaid softly. "She's gone now."

He sits me up. "Unfortunately, this is going to hurt more than what she did."

Healing me hurts Vaid Roshan as well. As my vision clears, I see the sweat pouring down his face, the glow around him flickering as blood trickles from his left nostril.

"Leave that," I say quietly when he goes to heal the nail on my big toe, broken in half and pulled out with a pair of lethal tongs. "Use some herbs instead."

He nods, his shaking hands moving to the side of his body, where he carries a satchel with several small clay jars. Scooping out a pasty substance, he applies it carefully to the bloody nail before bandaging it.

"Why?" I whisper. "Why do you help me now? You don't have to."

The healer raises his tired eyes. The blood under his nostril has been wiped away, but I still see a trace of red on his pale-brown skin.

"There are others like me, within the palace and without." He speaks so softly that I can barely hear him. "Magi who believe in the Star Warrior and the true king. Magi who believe in you, Xerxes-putra Cavas."

His words make the fine hairs at the back of my neck rise. I squash down the hope they bring by shaking my head. "People hate me. They think I'm a traitor."

"People are smarter than you think," he whispers. "They—"

His voice breaks off at the sound of raucous laughter outside my cell.

"What are you going to do, old man?" a guard calls out, his voice carrying in the silent corridor. "Bite me? Shoot me with that stump? Oh wait. You can't hold a talwar anymore, can you?"

I release a breath. They're taunting the old army brigadier, who lost his arm to the shadowlynx.

"Give me your hands," the vaid says out loud. I press them together, allowing him to shackle them again. I know that the disgust on Vaid Roshan's face isn't directed toward me. "Feet."

Once I'm shackled, he turns my hand over gently, before dropping a single green swarna into my palm.

"From the stable master, Govind," he says quietly. "We guessed this might happen at some time."

"But this place . . . I can't communicate with living specters here. They're blocked out."

"That's true," the vaid says. "It's the old magic in these walls. But if you rub the swarna and whisper a specter's name, they will still be able to sense it. They'll know you're in danger."

With that final bit of advice, the vaid rises and leaves me to my thoughts, taking with him the lightorb that illuminated the cell.

I turn to the wall next to me. "Juhi?"

A moment later, I hear a scraping sound, see the partial outline of a face in the sudden flash of blue from her shackles.

"They found you out, did they?" Juhi sighs, and I wonder if she was expecting this outcome.

"It was my fault," I admit. "I . . . I took a living specter for her word. I should have trusted Gul."

"Loving someone is often easier than trusting them."

I curl my fingers around the green swarna, feel the reassuring weight of it in my palm. "Do you think they will kill me soon?"

"Not if I can help it," Juhi says grimly. "They're so focused on you right now that they've forgotten me and Amira. Forgotten what we can do."

Instead of reassuring me, Juhi's words only fill me with dread. Being imprisoned can play tricks with desperate minds, can make them believe in the impossible. I don't ask Juhi what she's planning to do. Or how she assumes Amira is in any shape to help her—and us—right now.

All I can do now is lie in a corner of my cell, the green swarna pressed to my mouth, whispering my mother's name like a prayer, hoping that my stupidity did not cost us this war.

35

GUL

Hands lightly slap my cheeks, a voice urging me to wake, to focus on the world outside the dark corners of my mind. My eyes open to a worried face.

"Gul, are you all right?" Falak asks. "Gul!"

"Why am I lying on the ground?" I say, forcing myself to sit up. *What was I doing before I slid into the meditative state?*

"You were having breakfast with us when you said you had forgotten something in your tent. You were gone so long that Kali sent me to look for you. When I came, you were thrashing about on the ground. And you were glowing."

Yes, I remember now. The faint call of Cavas's voice fluttering through my head. The skip of a heartbeat, the sudden, desperate urge to be alone with him. To ask him everything. And I had.

Cavas took me by surprise, telling me he loved me. And fool that I was, I chose to kiss him instead of telling him that I loved him, too.

That's when I heard that awful voice. *Dirt-licking traitor.* And though

Subodh warned me how dangerous it was to be found connected to Cavas at a time like this, I reached out to him again and again.

Until the scene shifted and the temple shrank, its carved pillars turning into stone walls, iron bars gleaming in dim blue light. I squinted, trying to see where I was, but the darkness was almost absolute, the figures within wispy shadows.

Shall I make him light up again, General? an unfamiliar voice asked.

That's enough, Captain. It was General Alizeh. *Tell me, dirt licker, where did you get the green swarna—a classified contraband item? You, who are not allowed to communicate with specters? Also, since when do half magi glow with unexplained magic?*

Do you know what we do to traitors here?

Hang me, then.

The last three words—spoken by Cavas—made me cry out. My voice lifted the darkness, revealing a lightorb hung suspended between stone walls, a red-eyed man wearing Sky Warrior blue and silver, and General Alizeh, her uniform so white it hurt my eyes. They were standing over a figure lying on the ground, blood covering his face and soaking the front of his clothes.

I think I must have said something, must have shouted his name, because suddenly Cavas's eyes widened, and I was thrown back out of the vision, as if by an invisible hand.

I close my eyes briefly. The cost of my wish being granted doesn't come with surprise but a heavy dose of guilt.

Once again, I've put someone I love in terrible danger.

"I need to see Subodh and Amar," I tell Falak. "Where are they?"

We find them at the temple, talking to Sarpanch Parvez and Councilor Maya. Neither Subodh nor Amar seems surprised by what I tell them.

"I wish that Cavas had waited," Subodh says. "Roda delivered his message to us a few moments earlier."

"Can you blame him?" I demand. "Roda shouldn't be allowed in here anymore!"

"Could you give us a moment?" Subodh asks the two non-magi, who nod before exiting the temple.

Subodh turns to me. "Listen, Gul. I understand your anger, but you need to remember that Roda is a living specter now, bound to this world with the sort of restlessness we, the living, can't imagine. She doesn't have to remain loyal to us, but for some reason she is."

"Why didn't Cavas send the message through his mother, though? Isn't she looking out for him at the palace?"

"Not now," Subodh says. "At the moment, Harkha is in Jwala."

"Jwala?" I ask, surprised. "But why?"

"To deliver our message to the queen there," Amar replies. "The tenement councilors pointed out to us that shvetpanchhi are too noticeable—and easier to kill off. Unlike Ambar, the Jwaliyan queen still keeps half magi and non-magi courtiers. The Jwaliyans are not overtly fond of living specters, but they will accept them as messengers."

"You really believe Jwala is on our side?" I ask skeptically. "Especially when the queen is still publicly allied with Shayla?"

"I can't be sure," Amar admits. "My mother always called Jwala a vessel with a round base, tilting whichever way suits it most. But I also got *this* letter a week earlier."

I frown at the scroll, unable to decipher the curving script of the unfamiliar language. I'm about to ask Amar what it means when I notice the emblem at the bottom: crafted from green strands of mermaid hair intertwined with gold, a sword that splits into four blades when unleashed on an enemy.

"Is this from Samudra?" I look up from the split-whip, astonished. "Or am I dreaming?"

"It *is* from Samudra," Amar says, looking happier than I've ever seen him. "Written in the hand of Queen Yashodhara herself. Until now, I've been communicating with only her first minister."

Queen Yashodhara. Juhi's own sister, who gave Juhi up as collateral to King Lohar during Samudra's bitter cease-fire and treaty with Ambar more than twenty-two years ago. When Juhi staged her own death to escape Ambar Fort, she never got back in touch with her family in Samudra. Though she had spoken only once to me about her experience at Ambar Fort, I know Juhi had felt betrayed by her sister, anguished in ways she'd never revealed to the rest of us.

"You told her Juhi's alive," I say, feeling furious. "Didn't you?"

"I had to, Gul. There was no other way she would have agreed to help us. Now that my father is dead, Samudra's old treaty with Ambar is defunct. Samudra can send us troops—can help us in other ways, too, if we so wish."

"How do you know help is what she'll give you?" I challenge. "The Samudra queen might have been waiting for years to exact revenge." According to the history scrolls published by the Ministry of Truth, the southern kingdom suffered more casualties in the Three-Year War between Ambar and Samudra.

"She might," Amar agrees. "Then again, she might not. I would like to give her the benefit of the doubt."

"I have to agree with Gul on this," Subodh says. "You can't be so trusting, Raja Amar. They're queens who rule other kingdoms. Their help will not come without a cost."

"No," Amar says grimly. "Which is why I've given them both a test."

We both fall silent.

"What sort of test?" I finally ask.

"I've asked each queen to send me a promise in writing, magically signed and sealed, asserting that they will support my claim in the event of a war and that they will accept me as the next ruler of Ambar, without attempting to annex my kingdom. In return, I will release Jwala from its debt to us—which, when I was last informed, was in the range of a hundred thousand swarnas. And I will ensure that Juhi, the princess of Samudra, is rescued from the prison at Ambar Fort. Alive."

It's a tall order. A risk that could backfire on him completely. Also—

"I thought you wanted to avoid a civil war," I say. "What made you change your mind?"

"That's what I *did* want," Amar says. "If I had a choice, there would be no bloodshed whatsoever. But now that Shayla's hiring Brimmish mercenaries, I can't take any more chances. It's one thing to fight with Ambari troops. But the mercenaries fight without a conscience. The king of the Brimlands pays an annual tribute to keep them at bay. Shayla is a fool if she thinks that she can control them or that they will leave Ambar in anything except ruins. Cavas's imprisonment also changes things. I can't let people continue to think he's a traitor when he was really helping us. And the only way I can do it is by coming out of hiding. Ambar needs to see that its king is still alive. And that he supports Cavas."

My skin prickles—probably because it's the first time I've heard Amar refer to himself as a king. His eyes flash now, harder than firestones. His face, hollowed by the sparse diet of the tenements, holds no trace of the helpless prince I once saw at Ambar Fort.

Quietly, he settles cross-legged on the floor before unfolding a bit of parchment and laying it flat across the stones. It's a map of Ambar, with the kingdom's various towns and villages, the capital city of Ambarvadi and Ambar Fort marked with glowing green stars. Next, he pulls out a sheaf of blank parchment and a pen, dipping the nib into a jar of muddy ink that glows green every time he scribbles a word.

I watch him write out the first couple of lines, my eyes widening. "Amar . . . what in Svapnalok are you doing?"

"Writing another letter," he says, without looking up. "It's time to reintroduce myself to the one who usurped my throne."

THE WRATH OF
A QUEEN

3rd day of the Month of Birds
7 months into Queen Shayla's reign

36

SHAYLA

Having to imprison Xerxes-putra Cavas in the kalkothri again does not surprise me. Neither does the fact that he's still loyal to the girl. What does surprise me is the odd ache in my ribs, a feeling I last experienced before killing my father—one that I've since identified as disappointment. So I do what I did that day. I shrink the ache into something insignificant and bury it deep. The hollow that it leaves behind, I fill with rage, inflicting that on everyone who comes to see me in the morning.

The serving boy who brings me chai far too hot to drink.

The Minister of Treasure, who tells me our firestone mines are depleting so quickly that they will run out by the end of this year.

Acharya Damak, who advises me against dismembering the dirt-licking half magus's body and displaying a part of it in every corner of the city.

Unlike the others, though, the high priest does not cower.

"Use the half magus, Ambar Sikandar," he urges. "Find out where his magic comes from. Perhaps there's a connection to the alleged Star Warrior."

"With your immense knowledge, it amazes me that *you* aren't aware of where his magic comes from, Acharya," I say. "Don't make me bring Amba up here and unravel your silky tongue for a single fiber of truth."

Acharya Damak pauses. "I can think of only one thing . . . though it's too foolish to be considered."

"Nothing is too foolish when it comes to the so-called Star Warrior."

I have not forgotten the way the awful girl's magic repelled mine seven months ago—nor forgiven myself for underestimating her the way the usurper Lohar did.

"They could be complements," the acharya says.

"Complements?" I ask, incredulous. "Are you serious?"

"Yes, Ambar Sikandar."

"You do realize, Acharya, that the only complements anyone has ever heard of are the two moon goddesses. And they don't exist."

"I said it would sound foolish, Ambar Sikandar."

"And I'd rather you focus on reality instead of myths." The acid in my voice makes Acharya Damak wince. "What other news? Has Amba been sending out any more birds?"

The high priest looks relieved by my sudden change of subject. "None that I or my servants know of, Ambar Sikandar. The dead shvetpanchhi we placed in her bed has scared her for the time being."

I nod. If I had a choice, I would toss Amba, her daughter, and Lohar's two other former queens in prison, too. But Amba and her child are still well loved by the people of Ambar. And imprisoning Janavi and Farishta would likely have the Brimmish king launch an attack on us.

"Very well. You may go, Acharya Damak. You have been surprisingly useful today."

In the afternoon, there's another knock on my door.

"Enter."

"Ambar Sikandar."

I force a smile when I see Alizeh. As angry as she's made me with her past incompetence, I don't want to alienate my old friend completely.

"What news?" I ask.

Alizeh does not smile back. Instead, there is a worried expression on her face, one that makes me snap, "Go on. Spit it out."

"There have been . . . birds, Ambar Sikandar."

Shvetpanchhi and crows, hawks and pigeons. Hundreds of birds— according to Alizeh's sources—flying over the capital, swooping through windows, dropping scrolls across desks, into buckets of milk, onto un- suspecting heads.

"This one came into my office at Ambar Fort this morning," Alizeh says, holding out a scroll.

Instead of snatching it from her the way I normally would, I stare at it for a moment, my insides crawling with bloodworms. The shadow of a tree on an island hovers at the back of my mind.

Slowly, I take the scroll and begin to read:

I, Amar, son of Amba and Lohar, hereby declare that I am the rightful king of Ambar. I challenge the usurper, Shayla, daughter of Megha and Afrasiab, for the throne. I also demand the immediate release of Balram-putri Juhi, Shiamax-putri Amira, and Xerxes-putra Cavas—Ambari citizens who have risked their lives to remain loyal to their true king and are being held by the usurper in captivity.

Ambaris, our history isn't without its flaws. We are no longer the king- dom established by the First Queen Asha: a place where all were treated equally, regardless of class, gender, or magical ability. But where there is sor- row and loss, there is also hope in the form of the Star Warrior, born with the sky goddess's own blessing, and in the form of our Pashu friends, who have always fought with honor. Rise with me, Ambaris, if you, too, hope for a better future.

The more I read, the more I smirk. By the time I reach the end of this so-called proclamation, I'm laughing out loud.

"He expects people to believe this pompous garbage?" I toss the scroll aside. "What does he plan to do about an empty treasury and our depleting firestone mines? Is he going to conjure his way out of trouble?"

Alizeh takes a deep breath. "Ambar Sikandar, you'd be surprised how many people believe him. During patrol today, I passed a group of people outside the Ministry of War in the city, shouting slogans in his favor. They've set that stupid prophecy to song. I had to shoot my atashban twice in the air before they dispersed."

"Any arrests?"

"If I'd arrested them, it would have led to a riot."

A tick goes off in the side of my cheek. As angry as her words make me, I know she's right. "Did you have this tested?" I ask, tapping the scroll.

"I did. The parchment is conjured from the branches of a dhulvriksh. Likely from the south of Ambar. Perhaps Dhanbad. Perhaps Sur. I've asked our soldiers to comb through the area, check every hut and haveli."

"The conjurer won't hide where our soldiers have strongholds, Alizeh. He'll hide where no one will think to look and put up magical barriers to protect himself." The more I think about it, the more it makes sense. "Consider this. Who in Ambar remains completely invisible to the rest of us? And, no, I'm not talking about living specters."

Alizeh's eyes widen. "Non-magi. But they hated old Lohar more than we did. Why would they harbor his son?"

"For the promise of more than what they have now. For rights and freedoms that no monarch in their right mind would give such people. They're desperate enough to believe him."

"Perhaps," Alizeh says, her skeptical tone annoying me.

"Have someone check the area," I say. "If we attack them now and capture the conjurer king, his supposed revolution will end before it begins."

Alizeh clears her throat. "What if you changed tactics?"

"What do you mean?"

"You could hold a janata darbar in Ambarvadi. Hear the people's grievances like the ranis and rajas of old."

A public court? I bite back my laugh when I see the expression on Alizeh's face.

"You're serious," I say. "You really want me to hold a janata darbar."

"Why not?" Alizeh's eyes grow bright with excitement. "You shut down the labor camps, didn't you? Remind the people of that. Listen to their grievances—or at least pretend to."

"The usurper Lohar didn't keep a hold over his kingdom by coddling dissenters!"

"Yes, but times are different now. The people of Ambar are angry and the conjurer is acting like he's their only savior. You need to beat him at his own game."

I frown. Alizeh's points do have merit. What harm could there be to hold court? To play magnanimous queen for a while?

"Very well, then," I say. "I'll tell the high priest to make arrangements."

Which I do, calling him back the moment Alizeh leaves the room.

Acharya Damak frowns. "Are you sure you want to do that, Ambar Sikandar?"

"Are you telling me I shouldn't, Acharya?" I ask pleasantly, though I'm feeling anything but pleasant.

He pauses. "Ambar Sikandar, there have been letters—"

"—from the conjurer," I cut in. "I know. General Alizeh told me."

"Did she also tell you about how high the janata's emotions are running right now?" he demands. "After what happened outside the Walled City—it's too much of a risk, my queen."

"What do you mean?" I demand. "What happened outside the Walled City?"

His silver eyebrows go up. "You mean, the general didn't tell you?"

"Stop playing the question game, Acharya," I snarl.

Quietly, the high priest pulls out a scroll from his robes. It's a portrait. A nearly perfect drawing of me atop an elephant, crushing the heads and bodies of men, women, and children. Three words title the portrait: SIKANDAR YA SITAMGAR?

Victor or Oppressor?

"When did this go up?" I ask.

"Two days ago," the high priest says. "The entire southern wall of the Walled City was covered. General Alizeh ordered the guards to remove them. I grabbed a copy . . . in case."

In case General Alizeh didn't tell you. In case I needed it later to curry favor.

Yet, as much as I long to throttle Damak, I can't help but wonder why Alizeh didn't come to me first. Why she suggested a public court when there are so many angry emotions running against me.

"Did you know, Ambar Sikandar," the acharya says, his quiet voice barely breaking the silence, "that Rani Megha stopped the tradition of a janata darbar in Ambar because a group of non-magi tried to assassinate her? They nearly succeeded, too."

My blood runs cold. I study the portrait again, the bright colors, the sheen of gold on the parchment, which unlike the conjurer Amar's letter is of fine quality, the faint buzz of magic on its surface. A non-magus didn't make this poster. A magus did. Which means that I am hated even more than my mother. Possibly more than the usurper Lohar.

Aware of the acharya studying my every move, I look up again.

"The conjurer Amar's letter suggests origins from the south of Ambar. I wondered if he might be hiding in the tenements there."

The acharya frowns the smallest of frowns. "It's possible, my rani. There were traces of sand on the last bird that visited Rani Amba—the one we shot down."

"General Alizeh does not think it wise to attack the southern tenements."

He raises an eyebrow. "Do you really trust her, my queen?"

I don't, I think. *I barely trust you.*

Then again, I am not the first monarch to feel that way about the people surrounding them—and I will not be the last.

"Mistrust is good, Acharya," I say. "It keeps us ranis on our toes."

Once he leaves, I call for Alizeh again.

"I want you to take your strongest cavalry to the southern tenements. I also want speed. Immense speed. Good thing I trusted my instincts and ordered several cartloads of fresh tez from Meghapur's governor last month. The crop arrived earlier this week and is ready for use in the palace cellars."

A single blink of the eyelids. "*Tez?* But, Shayla, what about—"

"Do I look like I want an opinion from you, General?" I hold up the poster that Damak gave me, watch Alizeh's eyes widen. "Do I look like I want anything other than your unquestioned loyalty?"

"Shayla, I was planning to tell you. I swear—"

"I am your queen." The scroll sails across my desk, falling at Alizeh's feet. She doesn't look away, red blotching her pale cheeks. "I am your queen and yet again, you choose to hide these things from me."

"I didn't tell you because I knew this is how you would react!" Alizeh protests. "Shayla, you know I'm always on your side."

"And yet you suggested I hold a janata darbar—a public court that could expose me, putting me at risk of an assassination, as it did my own mother!"

I wait for Alizeh to fight back. To give me the explanation I so desperately want to hear. But she simply stares back at me, her lips so tight that they're colorless.

"Well?" I demand. "Do you have nothing to say for yourself?"

"You suspect me," she says, her voice trembling. "You think I would . . . you think I'd . . . you aren't simply a queen to me. You know this. You know I—"

"General, you forget yourself." I keep my voice as cold as possible, ignoring the sudden spasm her words cause beneath my ribs. "Remember why I appointed you and only you to this position."

There's a long silence, followed by a flash of pain in Alizeh's gray eyes. "I apologize, Ambar Sikandar," she says stiffly.

"Find the conjurer Amar and the so-called Star Warrior," I order.

"Turn every house in the tenements upside down; burn them if you need to. He wrote Ambar a letter, didn't he? Now Ambar's queen will give him her reply."

"But the half magus Cavas—"

"Do you *really* think an imprisoned traitor is a priority right now?"

"As you wish, Rani Shayla." Alizeh's voice is flat, giving no indication of her personal opinion—exactly the way I want.

It makes me wonder why I hate it so much.

"Go then, General," I tell her. "Make sure you don't let me down."

37

GUL

Five days after Amar told us about his plan for the letters, he presents it at the council meeting. As expected, pandemonium breaks out.

"It's too dangerous!" Councilor Maya exclaims.

"Impossible," Councilor Rayomand murmurs.

"I have to say that I agree," Sarpanch Parvez adds, the furrows between his brows deepening. "Is it really wise to bring the Sky Warriors *to* us, Raja Amar? It's not the soldiers I worry about, but non-magi civilians under my protection."

"Listen," Amar says, pointing at the parchment laid out over the ground in front of the temple. "Today is the second day of Birds. I plan to send out the letters on the third. It will take the Sky Warriors about two days on horseback to ride from Ambar Fort to the southern tenements. They will need to stop at some point. They will likely camp out somewhere here." A glowing red star appears at a spot somewhere to the left of Ambarvadi and the southern tenements. "We could attack them then. Take them by surprise while they sleep. We probably won't need that big an army—"

"If I may interrupt, Raja Amar." Latif's voice appearing out of no-where never fails to jar the senses.

"Yes, Latif ji." Amar speaks with barely held impatience.

"That letter of yours will be akin to a laxative for Rani Shayla." Latif sounds amused. "She'll not want any troops that stop midway."

"The best troops need rest, Latif ji."

"Not if they have access to tez," Latif says.

Tez? I look askance at Kali.

"A magical enhancer," she murmurs in my ear. "Like Dream Dust, but worse."

Oh.

"Tez intake was banned in battle years ago!" Amar exclaims. "Even my father frowned on it—he said the side effects were not worth the benefit of enhanced magical powers."

"Raja Amar, your father never stopped tez from being grown and sold for export," Latif points out. "Now we have a queen in power who doesn't care a whit about tez's side effects. Several cartloads of it have arrived from Meghapur for the army's consumption during the war. Harkha found out when she went to check in on Cavas yesterday."

My heart kicks a beat faster: *Cavas is still alive.*

"Tez's effects aren't permanent, though," Councilor Maya says. "And its side effects are deadlier. In the years before it was banned, non-magi were forced to ingest it daily to work longer and harder hours. Nearly seven hundred people died before Raja Lohar decided it wasn't worth another rebellion."

"Yes, but my plan was to attack them when they didn't expect it," Amar says, frowning. "Our armies aren't trained to withstand a full battalion! My only other option would be to send out the letters *after* we have some reinforcements from Jwala and Samudra." Amar releases a breath. "And goddess only knows when those will arrive."

"What about the Pashu army?" one of the councilors asks, turning to Subodh. "Can't they help us?"

"Rani Sarayu has already offered us her birds for messages," Subodh says. "She suffered serious injuries while helping us. In good conscience, I don't feel right demanding more from her than I already have."

"I wouldn't feel right about it, either," Amar agrees. "The Pashu have gone above and beyond to help us in this war. That you are fighting for us, Raja Subodh, is more than anything I could ask for."

"Also, our army isn't as bad as you might think," Falak speaks out. "I am quite confident that we can hold them off for a day or two. Fight them until the effects of the tez wear off."

"But that might take days!" Kali points out.

"Not if they travel all night," Councilor Rayomand says thoughtfully. "Councilor Maya knows best, though. What do you say, Maya? Am I right?"

Councilor Maya scowls but gives her assent. "Possibly. Traveling at that speed will definitely exhaust their horses."

"And if we hold them off for the day, we could attack them at night," I say, thinking hard. "Living specters can touch things and people, right? Could they get into the enemy campsite and destroy their supply of food and water? What do you think, Latif?"

There's a lull in the conversation at my suggestion as we wait for Latif's response.

"Hmm. It's an idea," Latif says, almost as if he were considering it.

"You approve of this plan, Latif ji?" Amar prods. "I've never heard of living specters working this way before. Do you think they'll all cooperate?"

"I actually do approve of this plan." Latif sounds amused. "Organization isn't our greatest strength—every specter has a slightly different tether binding them to the living world—but I do think my spectral friends will cooperate if I ask them to. Many of the younger specters have been a little bored lately and would enjoy some mischief. Naturally, you all will need to fight the Sky Warriors first and tire them out."

Amar, however, still looks doubtful. "How would the living specters destroy their food supplies?"

"Firebombs," Latif answers again, with a readiness that makes me wonder if he already had the idea in mind. "Mix in a bit of eucalyptus and wild grass. The tiniest sliver of firestone dipped in magus spit. Or blood, if you prefer. Roll it up in some cow dung, and it'll explode on contact."

There's a brief silence.

"Is that . . . is that what you used to blow up the palace garden years ago?" Amar asks finally.

"I might have," Latif says, noncommittal.

More silence.

"Why don't we take a day to mull things over?" Sarpanch Parvez says. "We can meet here early tomorrow morning and vote on it. Agreed?"

"Agreed," Amar says, and the rest of us nod.

"What do you think?" I ask Kali as we step out of the temple. "Are we ready to fight?"

"I don't know," she says honestly. "But then, none of us Sisters thought *you* were ready to take on a tyrant. And here you are."

"Was that a compliment or an insult?"

"I reserve my compliments for the girls I plan to bed."

"You mean like Sami?" I tease.

Kali pauses next to a stone pillar, gesturing me to the side. We wait until the remaining council members pass by before she speaks again:

"Sami asked me to bind with her last night."

"What in Svapnalok—Kali! What did you say?" I demand.

"I said I would think about it. You know I've never committed to a girl, Gul. I've never felt safe doing so. But Sami is the only person I've met whose truth reflects on her face. I don't have to touch her to know what she's thinking. More than that . . . I *want* to be with her." Kali exhales sharply. "I'm not used to this kind of happiness."

"But isn't happiness exactly what we're fighting for?" I ask. "Why resist it?"

Kali bites her lip. "What would you do—if it were you and Cavas?"

I feel my breath catch. I haven't allowed myself to think about a future with Cavas beyond finding him alive and rescuing him. Anything other than that only brings forth expectations that are bound to crush me if left unfulfilled.

"I don't know," I admit. "I guess I see why you're so scared."

Kali shrugs. "Come. Let's go train with the others. For some reason, fighting always makes me feel better."

It makes me feel better, too.

Soon, I'm following along as Kali and Falak lead us through a series of moves.

"Forward!" Falak shouts.

The group charges—women from the Legion and non-magi swinging their lathis in perfect unison. While Kali and Falak correct postures and the placement of various arms and feet, I study the expressions on the soldiers' faces: the set jaws, eyes focused on an enemy only they can see. My heart swells with an emotion I've experienced so rarely that it takes me a while to identify it.

Pride.

"Halt!" Kali shouts.

The soldiers stop almost instantly, lathis raised high in the air, not moving a muscle until Falak calls for them to be at ease again.

"Well done," Falak says. "I am especially impressed by our new soldiers who have caught on so well—and much faster than anyone could have anticipated. It is my honor to induct you into the Legion of the Star Warrior today. You are a part of the family." A quick grin. "Tattoos, of course, are optional."

Tired faces break into smiles. Cheers ring out, followed by a ringing chant:

The sky has fallen, a star will rise!
The sky has fallen, a star will rise!

Falak turns to me, looking worried all of a sudden. "I'm sorry. I know I should have consulted you about inducting them into the Legion," she says in an undertone. "I thought—"

"You thought right," I interrupt.

"You're crying, Gul."

"I know."

It's odd: crying and smiling at once, feeling honored beyond measure and completely unworthy of the same. I wipe the tears from my eyes and try to encompass my thoughts into words. But maybe she understands, because Falak gives me a fierce hug.

"We'll fight for you with our last breaths," she whispers.

"And I for you," I say, meaning it.

38

GUL

The next day, everyone unanimously votes to send out the letters.

"There will be an attack," Amar says simply. "It won't take them long to trace the parchment I used to this area."

I nod. This is what I've wanted, what we've been training toward for months now, but a pit of dread still opens in my belly. Memories of the attacks in Tavan and Raj Mahal flash in my mind. I shake them off before they hook claws into my skin.

During a quiet moment that day, I meditate, looking for Cavas in the darkened temple of my mind. But I see no one. Not even the sky goddess or Sant Javer.

Emerging from my trance, I clutch my aching head, my throat swelling with fear.

"What am I going to do?" I whisper.

The trouble is that there *is* nothing I can do right now that can effectively get Cavas out of Ambar Fort—not without a full army backing me up. With the exception of my brief trip to Javeribad a couple of months ago, I have never felt this helpless nor this alone.

What's worse? Cavas's getting captured again isn't our only problem.

"The kabzedar rani has sent her soldiers to attack the tenements," Falak tells everyone later that afternoon. "They will arrive in a day or two."

Bodies stiffen; a few gasps dissipate in the air. But apart from that, the newly anointed Legion remains deathly still.

"If you do not wish to fight, I will give you one last chance to leave," Falak says. "This isn't practice anymore. No one will blame you or accuse you of cowardice."

There's a pause. "Why make us part of the Legion, then?" someone asks—a non-magus woman I don't know.

"I don't want you to feel you are being pressured to fight," Falak says. "This is war, and death is very much a possibility here."

"Death is an inevitability, Commander Falak." An older non-magus man speaks now, his soft voice carrying in the silence. "Especially for some of us. I would like some choice in my death. Preferably with a lathi in my hand."

"So would I," someone else shouts.

"So would I!"

"So would I!"

The words echo until they form a chorus that vibrates the very earth. Before I know what I'm doing, I step forward.

"So would I," I say. "I do prefer these to lathis, though."

Laughter erupts as I unsheathe my seaglass daggers, feel the heat of their green glow.

"I also have a small request." I pause for the noise to dim down. "When I am being attacked, I don't want any of you to step in to save me."

I pretend to ignore the murmurs that break out, the confused looks on various faces.

"Gul," Kali's whisper is harsh in my ear. "Gul, I don't think you should—"

"One moment, Kali Didi," I say. "Let me explain."

Perhaps it's the shock of my calling her my elder sister for the first time. Or perhaps it's the sudden silence my words evoke again, the crowd hushing to the point of breathlessness. Kali hardens her jaw and gives me a curt nod. *Go on.*

"I lost my parents when I was thirteen. They were murdered by the Sky Warriors, who hunted me for this." I hold up my right arm, the billowing sleeve of my tunic falling to my shoulder, revealing my birthmark for everyone to see. "This star that I was marked with. This star that led to the kidnappings and deaths of thousands of girls and women for the past two decades.

"I was lucky. I escaped. Not only that, I was rescued by a group of women who had sworn to protect the unprotected. A sisterhood formed from ashes, built on bonds stronger than blood. I tried to be one of them many times. But I wasn't ready then, and it's only now that I truly understand why."

After Juhi, Amira, and Cavas got captured. After Tavan and the deaths of thirty brave women. After Agni.

"Sisterhood is about samarpan. About putting others above yourself. So I'm saying it again. Protect yourself, Legion. Protect your fellow soldiers. But don't you dare attempt to protect me," I say firmly. "Quite frankly, what's the point of calling me the most powerful magus in Ambar if I can't fight for myself?"

A few laughs greet this last comment. In the distance, I see a pair of shining golden eyes, a thick brown mane. Subodh gives me an approving nod. Next to him, Kali's eyes are shining as well with unshed tears.

"The true king waits!" I shout, raising my arm into the air.

"The true king waits!" The Legion thumps their hands over their hearts in response.

That evening, moments before I step into the tent, I feel the cool touch of a hand on my arm.

"You meant what you said." Roda's voice sounds puzzled instead of mocking. "You don't want them shielding you."

"I don't," I say truthfully. "I never wanted you or Esther Didi to die. And I don't want anyone else to die protecting me again."

There's a long silence. "I will stop tormenting you," Roda says. "For now."

Warmth rushes through my limbs. When I lift the tent flap, I know the specter will be gone. She won't see the tears running down my cheeks nor feel the relief blooming in my heart. But that's okay. For now, I'll take refuge in hope and small victories.

39

GUL

The Sky Warriors arrive the next day in a cloud of dust and thundering hooves, their red spells fanning, hammering the barrier so hard that even a full foot within its boundary, I feel my teeth chatter.

Amar nods at us and taps his spear on the ground twice. Ten soldiers wearing blue tunics and dhotis march in from behind a building with spears in their hands, their eyes glassy, their faces a sickly greenish-yellow.

"Queen's curses," Kali breathes. "Are those . . . ?"

"Conjured? Yes," Amar says. "When the enemy has about ten times more soldiers than you do and more magic on its side, a few tricks are necessary. Don't look at me like that, Kali ji. I promise that none of these are real bodies. I used some old chicken bones and my own blood to conjure them last night."

Though Amar speaks lightly, I can see that the magic has taken its toll: His eyes are shadowed, his shoulders stooped like those of a much older man.

"How many did you make?" I ask, trying to tamp down my anxiety. "You didn't overexert yourself, did you?"

Amar leans on his spear as if curbing a tremor in his limbs. "I made enough. The conjuring isn't perfect," he goes on, evading my next question. "Yukta Didi tried to teach me many times when I was at Ambar Fort, but I could never get the complexion right. But for the sake of this battle, maybe these false soldiers will work."

And maybe they do. As the enemy soldiers move closer, ten false soldiers step outside the barrier and are instantly hit by atashbans.

I raise my daggers and nod at Subodh. *It's time.*

We race out, along with a small group of real soldiers from the Legion, their lathis raised high, followed by more of the false soldiers that Amar sends as backup.

Protect, I think, my teeth chattering from the impact of five atashbans, my shield glowing red from the reflected light of the spells.

A few feet away, Subodh swings his golden mace in a circle over his head. Every horse racing toward him slows down and blinks drowsily, eventually refusing to move, despite their riders' shouts and whips.

"Come and fight me, Sky Warriors," Subodh purrs, mocking them. "You aren't that afraid of an old rajsingha, are you?"

"Kill the mangy, old cat!" a Sky Warrior at the head of the pack shouts before leaping off his unmoving steed. His men follow, atashbans in hand, some shooting spells at Subodh, which he swats away with his mace like flies. I scan the cavalry for General Alizeh, spot her white horse somewhere in the distance, at the very back. It surprises me that she isn't front and center the way she was last time, but I don't have much time to think about why.

Carefully, I shoot a spell between the legs of several horses, spooking them enough to dodge the green light. Some unseat their riders, who are attacked by a group of Legion soldiers, lathis swinging, enemy spells dodged with clever ducks and magically amplified shields. Amar's false soldiers, to my surprise, can fight a little, too—they must be imbued with a complex magic that I'm sure I'll never understand.

I continue unseating more soldiers from their horses, until one breaks free and comes charging, forcing me to spin out of the way.

The Sky Warrior who targets me is younger than most, probably in her early twenties. She remains seated despite the spells I shoot at her horse, dancing out of the way with an ease that makes me reluctantly admire her moves.

Push her off, I whisper to her horse. *Unseat her.*

The horse swerves, confused, forcing the Sky Warrior to climb off and face me, rage shining in her dark eyes.

"Come on, Whisperer," she says. "Let's fight face-to-face."

If I thought it would be easier to fight her on the ground, I was wrong. She's taller and stronger than me. Within moments, I find myself panting.

"Soldiers!" I shout—a signal to Amar to send in more decoys.

They pour out, as if appearing from thin air. *Attack*, I think, taking advantage of the Sky Warrior's distraction, the spell from my daggers turning into arrows that sink into her shoulders and her thighs, forcing her to the ground with a cry of pain and making her drop the atashban.

Magic burns in my right arm and in the pit of my belly: an urge to kill that I've come to understand and despise.

No, another smaller voice protests in my head. *You are no murderer.*

Still struggling with this, I barely notice that the Sky Warrior has risen to her feet again, two daggers raised in the air. Her torso erupts with blood. She glances down at the spear jutting from her abdomen, before falling to the ground, surprise permanently plastered on her face.

"We're at war, Gul." Falak's voice feels like a bucket of ice pebbling down over my head. My commander pulls out the spear with a sickening squelch. "She would have killed you. Now isn't the time to be noble."

I told Falak and the Legion not to protect me. But, in this moment, I'm grateful she didn't listen. My hesitation to kill the Sky Warrior would have cost me—and everyone else.

Now, more soldiers are charging at us, an infantry of red-and-brown armor—and once more I turn to deflecting spells and sending some of my own. Though outwardly I'm calm, inwardly a storm rages. A part of me continues to hesitate, to fear the violence of the power growing in my body, as I shoot spell after spell.

In the distance, Subodh is swinging his mace at a Sky Warrior, who holds not one, but two atashbans in his hands. The fighters are well matched, Subodh's brute strength clashing with the Sky Warrior's inhuman speed and dexterity. It's only when the Sky Warrior turns that I see his face, recognize the reddened eyes, the vile, vicious smile.

Shall I make him light up again, General?

It's the man who tortured Cavas a few days earlier in my vision. He shoots a spell that catches Subodh in the arm, setting his fur ablaze. I watch, heart in throat, expecting Subodh to roll on the ground, to put out the flame somehow. But he sways as if exhausted and then crumples to the ground, the flames taking over his side.

I react on instinct. Eyes wide open, I go deep into the recesses of my mind, the world around me slowing. The power I was so afraid to use a few moments earlier rushes from my birthmark and through my veins, tempered by an icy calm. I raise my arms, shooting twin chakras from my daggers. They spin toward the Sky Warrior in a tornado of green and red light, slicing off the arms that hold the atashbans, my blood thrilling at the sound of the agony I inflicted on the man who hurt Subodh and Cavas.

I follow this up with a dozen green arrows and watch them sink viciously into the Sky Warrior's chest.

As he falls, I race toward Subodh, the familiar odor of copper filling my nostrils. I wipe the blood from my nose and aim my daggers at the sand surrounding the Pashu king, drawing on every memory that I have of warmth and safety and my parents tucking me in bed at night, the rough textures of my favorite woolen blanket protecting me against the cold. The sand rises in a sheet, falling over Subodh's unconscious body, dousing the flames.

"Get him back!" I shout at a pair of women from the Legion who hover behind me, petrified with fear. "We need to get him back!"

Easier said than done. It takes the three of us to lift and carry Subodh back toward the barrier, our bodies straining with effort. Amar's false soldiers form an additional layer of protection, taking the spells and hits meant for us.

I breathe a sigh of relief when the air from the barrier brushes my cheeks and a pair of strong hands draw me back inside. Sami.

"It's all right," she says. "We'll take care of Raja Subodh."

"That Sky Warrior was fighting like a demon from hell."

"He was on tez. He had the signs. The red eyes, the foaming mouth. Some of the guards in Tavan used it as well before draining the girls of their magic."

Rage builds inside my body, rising like a hawk on air currents.

"I'm going back," I say.

"Gul, you're shaking! Maybe you should rest a bit. Let us send in the reserve army next."

I push away Sami's hands. *Kill*, a voice within me purrs as I slip past the barrier. *Kill them.*

I allow it to pour through me, targeting heads instead of arms, hearts instead of legs. Magic burns my right arm, pounds steadily at my temples and under my diaphragm. I'm faintly aware of soldiers from our reserve army screaming, plunging the sharpened points of their lathis into any part of a scarlet uniform or a blue-and-silver one. The enemy forgets to laugh. They strike back, furious, forming a wayward web of scarlet light that kills not only our soldiers but also many of their own.

Amar takes advantage of the chaos, bringing out a few more decoy soldiers. These wear red uniforms similar to those of the Ambari cavalry.

"They're fakes!" a Sky Warrior shouts, seeing through their disguise. "Not real soldiers! Cut off their heads!"

Spells hack through the false soldiers, shredding them with alarming ease.

I'm thinking of a way to combat this new development when spectral voices begin ululating above us. A song rises in the air:

> The sky has fallen, a star will rise
> Ambar changed by a king's demise
> A girl with a mark, a boy with her soul
> Their fates intertwined, two halves of a whole
> Usurpers have come, usurpers will go
> The true king waits for justice to flow.

Rocks tumble over the heads of enemy soldiers and our own, forcing me to aim a shield toward the sky.

"Legion! To me!" I shout. We huddle under the shield while the living specters target the Sky Warriors and Ambari troops with small missiles, forcing them to put up shields of their own, impeding the attacks.

A war horn blows in the distance.

"Halt!" General Alizeh's voice, amplified in volume with magic, freezes her soldiers in their tracks. The Legion pauses as well, perhaps shocked by the sudden respite, each head craning to catch a glimpse of the figure in white, still standing behind the protection of four reserve armies.

"People of the southern tenements, I speak to you now," General Alizeh says. "Surrender. Give up the false king and the so-called Star Warrior. I promise that Rani Shayla will spare you and reward you handsomely for your efforts."

Deathly silence falls over the battlefield.

"Think about it," Alizeh says, her voice ringing with the confidence of a general who hasn't entered the battle once today—a sign of how sure she is about our losing. "You have the whole of tonight. Troops, retreat!"

Kicking aside bodies of Legion soldiers lying dead on the ground, the cavalry begins its retreat. I don't realize that I'm following them until two pairs of hands clamp my arms—Kali and Falak drag me backward, shouting in my ears, their words reduced to fragments my mind can no longer process:

"Stop . . ."

"You can't . . ."

"Control yourself . . ."

Savak-putri Gulnaz.

The last voice is the only one that gives me pause, finally allowing the two women to pull me through the barrier without a fight.

I'm alive, Subodh whispers through our bond. *Come back, child.*

Wails ring in my ears; it takes me a moment to realize they're mine. I don't know if I'm grieving for the women and men who died for us, or for myself—the part that died when Subodh's body burned or perhaps earlier, when Cavas was imprisoned for the second time.

Through the tears blurring my vision, I see Kali's and Falak's worried faces.

"Subodh," I manage to say. "Where is he?"

"I don't know if you should see him right now—"

"In the sick bay," Councilor Maya interrupts. "Don't worry, Kali ji. He will be glad to see her."

A hand takes hold of mine. I start when I see that it's Amar, with bruises over his cheeks and under his eyes, making it look like he was punched repeatedly in the face.

"What happened to you?" I ask, shocked.

"Conjuring and operating over a hundred decoy soldiers extracts its own price." Amar tries to inject lightness in his voice—and fails.

In silence, he leads me through the tenements, past the temple, to a building I've never seen before, its door marked with a snake-wrapped pestle and mortar.

"Here's the sick bay," Amar says.

Subodh lies on the ground outside the building, a man and woman tending to his wounds. "He was too big to fit any of our beds," the man tells us, looking worried.

A thick orange paste has been applied to one side of Subodh's bruised face and the upper part of his body, the smell rising from it nearly making me retch.

Subodh's mouth moves, a low rumble emerging. "There you are. I was waiting for you. Tell me. What happened?"

I tell him everything. From the way I sliced off that Sky Warrior's arms to the soldiers I killed later. Over and over, my anger a river pouring from me.

"I wanted to go back there," I admit, my voice raw. "I wanted to smear their blood across my face."

"As many warriors do," Subodh says without sounding the least bit angry or disgusted. "What do you think they would have done to you if you hadn't killed them?"

A shudder goes through me. "I hate this part of myself. The part that longs to kill."

"You're not alone," Amar says wearily.

"Every soldier pays a price in war," Subodh tells us. "People talk about the rush of battle, the glory that war brings. No one tells you about the smell of pus and poisoned flesh, how you will collapse at the sight of your own blood, or how flies and vultures will ultimately scavenge your friends' corpses on the battlefield."

We watch silently as more bodies are brought in on stretchers, blood coating their groaning faces and battered limbs.

And yet our war isn't over.

I feel Latif's cold presence in the air, moments before I hear him speak.

"Raja Amar," he says, no mockery in his voice this time. "There has been word from Jwala. Harkha dropped this off." A scroll appears suspended in the air; Amar snatches it up and unrolls it, a frown growing deeper as he reads.

"The Jwaliyan queen refuses to sign my agreement," Amar says flatly. "She says she doesn't wish to be bound to a side that might lose a war."

My heart sinks. "We still have Samudra, don't we?" I ask.

Amar gives me a wavering smile. "I heard back from her earlier this morning. Despite pledging troops to our cause, the queen of Samudra refuses to sign a binding magical contract. She was angry. She said that we either trust her or we don't. The only thing she has promised is accepting me as Ambarnaresh—if I win the war."

If. I close my eyes. *If.*

How can we win a war when we're struggling to win a single battle?

"The battle isn't lost yet," Subodh says, and I know he has heard my thoughts. "We have a whole night ahead of us. And I have an idea. You still have the Samudra queen's letter, don't you?" he asks Amar.

"Yes." Amar frowns. "Pointless garbage by now, but I still have it. Why?"

A gleam appears in Subodh's great yellow eyes. "Wars aren't always won on the battlefield. They're won by penetrating the enemy's mind."

40

GUL

The enemy camp lies several miles to the west of the tenements, plumes of smoke rising against a half moon from between shadowy tents.

"Don't they see us?" Sami whispers. "I feel so naked walking out like this in the open."

"It's the tez," Falak says, her face grim. "It lets you fight like a god, but once it wears off, there's always a demon to pay back. That's part of the reason the general retreated so early. She knew her soldiers needed to sleep off its effects."

Under the torchlight, Falak's gray hair is bright blue—thanks to a plant-based dye mixed with aloe that Latif said would fade the next time she washed it. My hair is striped with the same dye, and so is Sami's, Kali's, and the hair of every person in the crowd that walks with us—the surviving soldiers of the Legion, and several hundred non-magi from the tenements, their sickles and torches held close.

On any other day, our pretext as a Samudra army would be laughable—the attempt of desperate people at the end of their wits. We may share similar skin tones and facial features, but Samudravasis—especially soldiers—are taller than Ambaris, and there is no dye or magic that can truly replicate the black of Samudravasi eyes or the blue of their hair, so vivid that it appears to glow in the dimmest light. On any other day, I would have outright rejected Subodh's outrageous plan to disguise ourselves.

But things appear different in the dark if you are coming down off tez. And we *are* at the end of our wits.

Right now, the Pashu king crouches behind a copse of bushes ahead of us, his gaze flitting overhead. Watching for living specters.

"It's done," he says, once we reach him. "Latif delivered General Alizeh the letter—dropped it right onto her dinner plate. The last thing he saw was her calling for someone who could read Jalraag. We should get a reaction any moment now."

Soon enough, shouts rise from within the camp. The tent before us explodes into a cloud of flames, the boom so loud that it hurts my ears. The specters begin keening overhead, releasing more missiles—the firebombs that we made in the garden, using Latif's old recipe.

"If Latif were still alive, he could have had an alternative career in making explosives," I tell Subodh now. "It's really quite scary."

"Necessity makes inventors of everyone," Subodh says.

The Pashu king is the only one not wearing the blue hair dye. His left arm is in bandages, the strong scent of herbs still unable to mask the rotting smell underneath. But in his right hand, Subodh carries his spiked mace. He refused to listen when we asked him to stay behind tonight. "I have suffered worse," he simply said.

Now, we watch as the first few Ambari soldiers race out of the campsite and start howling at the sight of us under the torchlight.

"*Now!*" Subodh roars.

We run. Torches raised. Weapons high.

Tez-addled as they are, the soldiers still have the sense to scatter in various directions. But my aim is truer, sharper, finding targets in every retreating back. We move into their camp, toward the source of the commotion, raising our shields as a web of spells and weapons get thrown our way.

I focus on the soldiers who have taken up arms again, many in partial stages of undress, using my daggers to turn death magic into showers of arrows that almost always find their mark. The voice inside me no longer needs to chant for a kill. I'm killing and killing, laying bodies across the ground, soaking the earth red with their blood.

A scream rings through the air. Sami, I notice, has been hit in the torso by an atashban. Without hesitation, I ram myself between her and the burly Sky Warrior she was fighting.

Attack, I think, the word a roar in my brain. The light from my seaglass daggers splits, finding a way around the shield the Sky Warrior puts up, sinking into his calf and arm and eyes. He staggers, the feathery ends of green arrows sticking out from him like pins from a cushion, then disappearing when he collapses, leaving behind only several wounds, blood pouring from them.

I'm barely aware of the horrified way Sami looks at me. *Me*, not a man who would have killed her. But I don't have time to ponder that. The air around me reeks of smoke, blood, and burning flesh. Seconds later, I find myself ducking another spell only to look right at the woman I've been searching for.

General Alizeh, her gray eyes unclouded, her mouth forming words that promise Queen Shayla my head.

Arrows dissipate when I send them her way; daggers turn to dust.

"Don't be fooled!" she shouts at her soldiers from behind her glowing shield. "These aren't Samudravasi soldiers! These are merely Ambari dirt lickers, led by a wounded army, a foolish conjurer, and a teenage girl!"

The men around her blink hard, as if her words are registering, but not quite.

"Shouldn't have fed them so much tez, General!" I say, throwing up a shield to deflect the red spikes she sends my way.

Unlike her soldiers, Alizeh's brain isn't addled. She throws up a wall—no, a circle of fire—that loops around me, locking me in place. No spell I send penetrates it. Soon enough smoke pricks the back of my throat, makes my eyes water, begins stanching the air from my very lungs.

You have magic in you, daughter. My mother's voice hums within my consciousness, and on pure adrenaline, I spin, shooting the earth around me, forcing lumps of it over the flames. It doesn't work as well on hardened earth as it did with sand. Finally, a sliver of a passage opens up in the flaming ring, enough for me to slip through, singeing my hair and clothes, but leaving the rest of me unharmed.

The camp is in chaos. Tents topple, many burned to the ground. The specters' eerie laughs still ring through the air, but there's no sign of Alizeh or her Sky Warriors. I scan the sea of bodies—in uniform and not, black hair blending with dyed blue—and find an exhausted Kali sitting on the ground, finger-shaped bruises forming on her face and neck.

"She's gone!" Kali says in a hoarse voice. "General Alizeh. I tried to stop her, but someone caught me from the back and tried choking me to death. They would've succeeded if not for Falak Didi."

I take Kali by the arm, leading her away from the carnage, the fumes everywhere now sinking into my skin, along with the memories of what I've done.

I killed so many people.

Outside the camp, cheers rise in the air:

"Justice for the true king!" someone shouts.

"Long live Raja Amar!"

Amar, too, has a wide smile on his face, but up close, I see his yellow eyes are weary, his complexion paler than normal.

"He vomited after his first kill," Kali tells me in a low voice. "Falak had to take him away from the battle, make sure he recovered."

Yet, if Amar still feels the aftereffects of a weak stomach, he doesn't show it to the crowd, facing the sea of torches and raising his hands in the air.

"The Sky Warriors have retreated. The living specters destroyed their food supplies and drained their drinking water. We were successful today, thanks to them—and thanks to you, the people of the southern tenements, who put your lives on the line though many of you didn't train as soldiers."

More cheering.

"Yet, though this battle is ours, the war is yet to be won. I am going to need you more than ever as we march to Ambarvadi to challenge the kabzedar rani."

The crowd roars its approval, buoyed by this victory, though only earlier this evening they were terrified, their hands trembling as they striped their hair with blue.

Sami wraps an arm around Kali's waist. "His battle skills may be lacking, but the boy sure knows how to give a crowd hope," Sami comments.

"Maybe hope is what we need right now," I say.

Maybe that's all it will take to win this war.

41

CAVAS

"Samudravasi soldiers? Here in Ambar?" the guard says outside my cell, his loud voice ringing in my ears.

"Of course not!" his companion scoffs. "They were only dirt lickers with dyed blue hair. Our own armies were so high on tez that they couldn't tell the difference. You'd think the guards at the border would have known if a whole army from Samudra suddenly made its way up north."

"Rani Shayla must have been furious!"

"She was!" The second man sounds gleeful. "I heard her shouting at the general, blaming her for incompetence."

It explains why General Alizeh hasn't been in to torture me for the past couple of days. Come to think of it, neither has anyone else. It has given me more time than normal to recover from the consecutives, allowing Vaid Roshan's healing magic to properly take effect. In the cell next to mine, I pick out the sound of crackling—like fire in a hearth, but not quite. I'm about to slide closer to the wall and ask Juhi if she's okay when another voice emerges from the passageway.

"Nothing to heal here, Vaid ji," one of the guards says in a sneering voice. But he does nothing to stop Vaid Roshan from entering my cell. A healer's presence in prison usually means torture is bound to follow. I instinctively long to grow smaller.

"Don't worry," the healer tells me. "I only came to check on you today. No special orders."

I sag against the wall. Vaid Roshan hangs up his fanas and crouches to check my fingers, toes, and ribs.

"The bones are healing nicely," he says. His fingers lightly brush the wound on my forehead. "The scarring will fade with time. But you'll always have that mark on your forehead. Atashban wounds can be difficult to cure."

"Will it drive away the girls?"

A brief smile illuminates Vaid Roshan's face, making him appear younger, boyish even.

"Not with that sense of humor, it won't," he says, rising to his feet. "Though I believe *one* girl might mind if you started considering others."

We hear the guards speaking again, this time cursing the old soldier in his cell.

"Ayye, you! Get up!" the first guard calls out.

"Forget it. The old bastard can't hear you," the second guard comments.

"Let's kick his ears back in his head then."

"I'll see you," Vaid Roshan says, frowning in the direction of the guards. "Be well. Now let me see if I can stop those idiots."

The conversation reminds me of words Papa had spoken long ago, though I no longer remember the circumstances surrounding them: *People who hate often see little except for their own hatred.* There are people like these guards. But there are those like Vaid Roshan as well. Even Govind, who, despite what happened between us in the past, still seems to be on my side.

Once the vaid is gone, I press the green swarna to my mouth and whisper for my mother again. "Ma, can you hear me?" I think I feel the swarna heat up a little, but perhaps that's only wishful thinking.

Vaid Roshan must have succeeded in distracting the guards, because the conversation between them now shifts to the letter Amar sent out.

"Do you think we should switch sides if the rani loses?" A smack follows, making the guard shout. "Ayye! What was that for?"

"Not so loud, fool! And not here!"

Their voices turn to inaudible whispers, but the words make my brain work faster, hope rising in my chest. *Could it be?* Men like these guards are mercenary by nature—not exactly the kind of allies we need. But if they're considering defection, it's possible that success may be closer than we think.

The crackling inside Juhi's cell pricks my ears again. A *boom* follows, sending tremors through the ground under my shackled legs.

"What in Svapnalok—what are you *doing*, old woman?" the first guard snarls.

A horrible sound rises from the cell next to mine—Juhi, crying out in a language I don't understand, but one that makes me think of the sea.

"By Zaal, she's broken the shackles around her ankles! How did she—"

"How would *I* know? I'm as new at this job as you are! Get them back on her before someone sees! She's as mad as a blood bat!"

They enter Juhi's cell amid sounds of screeching metal doors and wails, their shouts cutting off with an abrupt *thud*. After all this time in the kalkothri, I can now tell what it sounds like when a human body falls to the floor.

Moments later, a ragged, blue-haired figure stands before my cell, keys hanging from a ring on the littlest finger of her still-shackled left hand.

"H-how?" I stutter.

"Basic Yudhnatam split kick," Juhi says, her voice hoarse. "Knocks them out every time. Oh, my shackles, you mean? I used this."

Something glistens in her hands—a green piece of glass shaped like a dagger blade.

"They never should have left seaglass embedded in my palm—even if they *were* using it to mangle my tattoo." A tremor enters her voice, her black eyes hardening as she reveals the injured hand. The tattoo she's talking about—the golden lotus of the Sisterhood—is no longer visible among the mass of barely healed scars.

She points the shard at her wrists, the seaglass crackling against the glowing blue of the shackles, followed by a small explosion of light and the booming sound I heard before. Carefully tucking the shard in the pocket of her ragged tunic, Juhi unlocks my cell, struggling with the stack of keys in her hands. Smoke begins rising around her—from the agnijal in the channels dividing our cells from the passage.

"Let's hope I can get us out before this kalkothri gets consumed by fire," Juhi says. "Can you stand? I need to get close enough to remove your shackles."

The smoke has grown thick by the time the door slides open. I've managed to get to my knees, but my legs are trembling now, from nerves and lack of use. Juhi kneels, taking my hands in her glowing ones, and the blue shackles crack open, falling off my wrists. She then does the same for my ankles before helping me stand.

"Amira's cell is at the end. Are you okay?" she asks when I begin coughing.

"Yes," I lie.

I have to be.

A clanging sound begins overhead, interspersed by terrible screeching and fires erupting everywhere.

"The doors," Juhi says. "Run!"

I can't. I can't. I can't.

But I do run, as fast as possible, my breath a pained knot in my side. Ahead, Juhi begins coughing as well, her hands glowing over us.

Air. Blessed air.

Stale and cool, blocked by the shield Juhi has thrown up, urging me forward with her voice.

"The shield won't hold forever!" Juhi's voice tightens. "Come on, Cavas! A little farther!"

A few steps.

Some more.

What feels like a hundred steps later, we pause before a cell already thick with smoke. Shooting a few spells, Juhi disperses it, revealing a figure hunched in the corner: Amira.

"Amira!" I hear Juhi's voice through a fog. "Amira!"

Slowly, painfully, Amira raises her head. Her cheeks are sunken, her body almost skeletal from starvation, atashban burns patching her arms and bare legs.

"I'm getting you out of here!" Juhi shouts. "I'm getting us all out!"

This time, things go much faster, with the keys, with the magic breaking Amira's shackles. Amira is worse off than I am; Juhi and I have to help her to her feet.

"Wait." Amira's voice is hoarse, barely above a whisper, but it makes us both pause. "The brigadier . . . in the cell next to me. We need to get him out."

"Amira, you can't be serious." If Juhi had energy, I'm sure she would have shouted the words. "I can't save everyone in this prison!"

"There *isn't* anyone else except for him. And the shadowlynx that ate his arm."

As if summoned by her words, caterwauling erupts from somewhere nearby. I spin around to see a fire-lined creature rolling on itself, howling in pain, its spiraling horns eerily reminiscent of the daggers Gul uses. I feel myself lurch forward—to do what, I'm not sure—when a strong hand grips my shoulder.

"We can't save it," Juhi says sharply. "Agnijal is designed to burn through any living creature. It is ten times stronger than fire, a substance that Lohar himself used in the design of his atashban. And we can't save that soldier, either, Amira!"

"Not even if he can help us in the war?" the other woman challenges.

Her dark eyes flash, and for a moment, I'm reminded of something Gul once told me. *Juhi may be head of the Sisterhood, but Amira is tougher than anyone else—the only one capable of wielding an atashban.*

"What do you mean?"

"No time to explain." Amira coughs. "We need to get him out. Now!"

There *is* no time. The part of the prison from where Juhi and I came from is now completely engulfed in flames.

"Brigadier Moolchand, can you hear me?" Amira shakes the unconscious man none too gently. "By Zaal, do you think he's dead?"

"Hang on," Juhi says, bending over. She presses a glowing hand to his mouth and murmurs a few words. Seconds later, the man blinks, his brown eyes foggy, unfocused.

"Can you hear us?" Amira shouts as Juhi simultaneously unshackles him with startling speed. "We need to get out of here!"

The man winces, as if the idea of having to save his own life feels too exhausting at the moment. Then, with an effort that can only be due to years of training as a soldier, he rises to his feet.

I scan the passage ahead. Smoke still rises from the channels, but the agnijal isn't yet fully active.

"This way," I tell the women and the still-drowsy man. "The side leading to Raj Mahal had a patch of Prithvi Stone blocking the exit," I say, suddenly remembering the awful, drowsy feeling. "Do you think there might be something similar here?"

"Probably something worse," Juhi says grimly. She turns to Amira. "Grab a weapon."

Amira holds up a piece of metal—the distinctive top of a guard's spear tipped white with sangemarmar and red with dried blood. "Already did."

I'm breathing fumes by now, the air so thick with smoke that it's impossible to avoid despite Juhi's shielding us from the worst of it. The soldier Amira insisted on taking with us finds it difficult to move more than a few steps at a time, and his right arm ends in a bandaged stump.

"Moolchand ji!" Amira calls to him. "Moolchand ji, you've got to keep moving!"

We're reaching the end of the corridor, a few feet away from a door barred with iron. Juhi and Amira raise their hands in unison. Red light blasts the door, making it erupt in vivid green flames. Screams echo around us, the kind that don't seem entirely human.

The man next to me swears. "There's a protection spell embedded in the door!"

"What does that mean?" I ask.

I get my answer seconds later from the fire itself: forming serpents, shadowlynxes, dustwolves, and a terrifying simurgh that looks nothing like Queen Sarayu.

"Move!" Amira shouts, her haggard face gray in the fire's reflected light.

We start inching backward, away from the spreading green flames—only to meet more smoke pouring in from behind us.

Death by smoke inhalation, or death by fire demons.

I'm contemplating which is worse when a rumbling sound to the left catches my attention.

"Stand back," Juhi says, pushing us behind her.

The smooth stone making up the passage walls crumbles, the bricks spinning sideways to form the arch to a darkened doorway, a shadowy figure emerging from within.

"Don't just stand there!" Queen Amba glares at our shocked faces. "Get in before the flames consume us all!"

42

CAVAS

iery green heads poke through the doorway and sever with a hiss as the bricks re-form, sealing once more into a smooth stone wall. Queen Amba's face glows under a lightorb, her yellow eyes as hard as the firestones she wears around her neck and in the part of her hair.

"Rani Amba." Juhi is the first of us to find her voice. "It's been long."

Amba raises one perfectly shaped eyebrow. "Don't bother with formalities, princess of Samudra. I saved you for the singular purpose of helping my son in this war."

Juhi smiles. "*Always a princess, never a queen.* Isn't that what you told me the day I first came here? But I was not meant to be a princess, either, Amba. I never competed with you for power or for Lohar's affection—if he had any to give."

Amba does not acknowledge the comment except with a narrowed gaze. "We are safe here for now. This passage—or the Way of Blood, as my ancestors called it—remains protected from the agnijal's fire. Only a descendent of the Chand gharana can access it; it requires our blood as sacrifice." Amba holds up a hand, revealing a gleaming red cut. "The passage will lead you out into the Walled City."

Juhi stares at the wound on the queen's hand. "Why don't you come with us, Amba?"

"I don't run from my troubles, Balram-putri Juhi. Ambar Fort is still my home. I did not leave when the man my family bound me with turned out cruel instead of kind. I certainly will not leave it in the hands of a false queen," Amba says. "Go now. The agnijal will soon burn away the protective spells that my ancestors placed to disguise the passage entrance. It will not take the Sky Warriors long to blast through the rock."

"What about Rajkumari Malti?" I ask. "Is she all right?"

The queen's cold yellow eyes soften. "Malti is safe. She misses her brother. She will be happy once you return him to her."

The pointed statement makes me bite back a smile, and Amira openly rolls her eyes.

"Your son will return to you himself, Amba," Juhi says. "And he will return wiser. Stronger. With the sky goddess's blessings, he will bring back the Ambar where everyone is treated with honor and respect, regardless of the magic in their blood."

"Amar is no warrior," Queen Amba says, her voice raw. "He never has been."

"He doesn't need to be—with Gul by his side," Amira says. "I should know. I've trained her myself."

Only days earlier, the comment would have sent my mind on a twisted, poisonous track. Now, I'm grateful that Gul is still out there. Alive and fighting.

"We will fight for the true king, as well." The soldier who had been quiet thus far, finally speaks. "Brigadier Moolchand," he says, pressing his hand to his heart, when Rani Amba turns to face him. "I was posted at the Amirgarh cantonment. I know my soldiers are still loyal to me and Raja Amar, regardless of the puppet brigadier the kabzedar rani has put in my place."

"Told you he was important," Amira murmurs.

"Moolchand," Juhi repeats with a frown. "Why is that name familiar? Like I've heard it before."

"You have heard it before," Amira says. "Dukal had a zamindar of the same name, remember? We found Gul in his stables two years ago."

"He was also my brother," Brigadier Moolchand says quietly. "Rani Shayla had him executed earlier this year for protesting the new land tithes."

No one speaks for a moment.

"The true king waits," I say, breaking the silence.

"The true king waits," everyone echoes.

"Now listen," Queen Amba says. "Once you're in the Walled City, make your way to the yellow district, to the smallest house at the base of the stairs. My loyal servant Yukta lives there. She will help you—provided you don't get caught. Ever since Amar sent out his letter, the Sky Warriors have grown more vicious about cracking down on anyone suspicious."

She turns to me. "Call for your mother once you get out of the tunnel. The kalkothri and this tunnel are protected with spells that the living specters can't penetrate for long periods of time. She told me that once you emerge from the tunnel, she can offer some protection in the form of invisibility."

"You spoke to my mother?" I ask, relief rushing through my limbs.

"Who else do you think told me the prison was on fire?" Amba asks wryly. "Your mother heard you when you called for her with that green swarna. Don't lose it. It was difficult for Govind and Vaid Roshan to smuggle you a new one."

With that final note of warning, she presses her hand against the wall. We watch it glow for a brief moment before seeing her melt through it—a spectral feat that I'm sure would have impressed Latif.

"Come on," Juhi says. "We don't want to lose our head start. Cavas, keep communicating with your mother through the swarna. It might help her keep track of us."

I nod, removing the green coin from my pocket, and whisper to Ma from time to time as we follow Juhi and her lightorb through the run-down passage, its broken tiles interspersed with muddy pits seething with bloodworms. I ignore the stings on my bare feet and calves, pull a bloodworm off my ear, and throw it against the mossy wall. Blood-sucking insects are the least of my troubles at the moment. Farther up, the passage narrows, forcing us into a single file.

"Hold on to each other," Juhi instructs. "The ground ahead is uneven."

Amira grips Juhi's arm, while I clasp the brigadier's shoulder. Unsteady on our feet though we are, we keep moving. The smell of sewage seeps into the air, thick as humidity, fouler than the waste pits near the tenements. And soon enough, we see the evidence in the dark puddles on the ground.

"Zaal's beard, this is disgusting!" Amira exclaims.

I force my eyes straight ahead, focusing on Juhi's blue hair instead of what my bare feet are sinking into. Ahead of me, Brigadier Moolchand's breaths turn into wheezes, while Amira lets out a string of curses that would blister the hardiest of ears. I'm so nauseated by the stench that I barely notice Juhi coming to a standstill.

"I think this is it," she says.

The lightorb dissipates, revealing thin shafts of light entering through a circular grille, its latticed bars encrusted with dirt and saints know what else. Sounds seep in as well: the hum of voices and loaded carts rumbling overhead, carrying supplies to Ambar Fort.

I hold the green swarna close. "Ma?" I whisper. "Are you there?"

"I'm outside, son," my mother says. I squint, making out a shadowy figure beyond the grille.

"Ask her if anyone is around," Amira says.

"I can hear you, you know," Ma says, sounding amused. "And no. No one is here. But that may change soon."

After some hunting, we locate a rusty latch at the top. Amira aims the spear at the latch, loosening it with a spiraling gold beam. The grille opens with a creak, and a few heartbeats later, we step out into the sunlight, blinking against its sharp sting. I turn to face my relieved mother, who wraps me in a chilly, yet comforting embrace.

"I stink," I mumble.

"You tolerate my chill; I tolerate your smell," she replies.

The others watch me with odd expressions. It must look a little strange to see someone hugging an invisible person.

The brigadier appears nonplussed. "I . . . I've never met a living specter before," he stammers.

"That's all right," Ma says, the smile on her face showing up in her voice. "I am not as terrifying as legend claims."

"Rani Amba said you can make us invisible," I say. It's something I should have guessed myself, having seen the specters protecting the boundary in Tavan. "But do you think you can do it for us when we're moving?"

"I can, but it will be very difficult. You will need to walk together, slowly enough for me to revolve around you. Also, invisibility will not mask other aspects, like muddy footprints or how you smell."

"I think your mother is politely reminding us that we came through a sewer," Juhi says with a brief smile. "Will we be able to see ourselves go invisible, Harkha ji?"

I start on hearing my mother's name, but then I recall how Juhi once said she knew Ma as well as Papa.

"Yes, you will, Juhi ji," Ma says. "You will also feel my presence. It will be a little . . . cold."

Juhi and I laugh. The others do not; they are likely not aware of the chill a spectral presence can cause to living bodies. After some discussion, it is decided that we walk as a cluster—Amira and the brigadier at the front, and Juhi and I at the back. My mother floats around us and it makes me dizzy to look at her.

We are, as Ma promised, invisible. The only way I know anyone walks ahead of me is by holding onto Brigadier Moolchand's shoulders and spying the faint brush of footprints in the red sand feathering the ground. The Walled City is built in tiers, its districts divided by houses and staircases of different colors. High-ranking servants, such as Govind and Yukta Didi, live in the yellow district, which lies exactly opposite to where we are now, beyond the main square.

At one point, the crowd's collective voice rises, freezing us in place.

"Keep moving," my mother commands from overhead. "No one is looking at you."

She's right. Everyone's attention is drawn to a circle of over a dozen men and women raising their arms in the air, spinning a lightorb made of blue flames. The man in the center of the circle leads the group in a chant: *The sky has fallen, a star will rise! The sky has fallen, a star will rise!*

"Move!" Juhi whispers. We shift to one side, narrowly dodging a Sky Warrior and a group of thanedars, who are now marching toward the demonstration, their lathis glowing purple at the tips.

"Get out!" the Sky Warrior shouts. "You are not permitted here!"

"Long live the Star Warrior!" the man inside the circle chants. "Long live the true king!"

A cold hand touches my shoulder, startling me.

"Come on," Ma urges. "Now is our chance."

We sneak past the guards, who are attempting to restrain the demonstrators with spells. Voices rise from the surrounding crowd—"Sitamgar! Sitamgar!"

The word is still echoing in my head as we reach the house at the base of the yellow staircase. My limbs begin to thaw, and I realize that we're visible again. Juhi is about to knock at the door when a woman in an orange palace-issued sari approaches the house, pausing a few feet away. My instinct is to immediately duck somewhere and hide, but it's too late—she's seen us.

"Don't worry," my mother whispers in my ear. "That's Yukta. I will see you again when it's time to leave."

I bite back a protest as my mother turns, disappearing into thin air. I turn to face the woman in orange again and soon enough, she confirms what Ma said.

"I'm Yukta," she tells us. "You may call me Didi, if you wish. Rani Amba sent me here on the pretext of an errand, and I came as quickly as I could."

Yukta Didi seems an appropriate way to address this stern-faced lady with her hammered silver hair and watchful green eyes. Her small house, painted a pale, sunny yellow on the outside and the inside, is completely spotless. A motif of latticed blue and gold moons hangs over the main wall, surrounded by hollow, triangular nooks. Oil lamps placed in the nooks sizzle to life the moment we enter the sitting area, releasing the odor of sandalwood and frankincense. Colorful rugs pattern the earthen floor, along with a plain but pristine white mattress for visitors to sit on.

I hesitate at the threshold, aware of how filthy I am.

"In the house, boy," Yukta Didi tells me. "Don't look so worried, and don't bother taking off your shoes. Dirt can be cleaned. There's a washing area out back. I'll find you some clean clothes."

"Juhi ji, you are the eldest, so you should go first," Brigadier Moolchand offers.

"Sau aabhaar, Moolchand ji," Juhi says with a twinkle in her eyes. "You are most kind."

"Why do Cavas and I draw the short straw on this?" Amira demands. "We are the youngest!"

"I don't mind," I say. As foul as I feel right now, it's still a relief to be inside a place where I'm not counting down the seconds to my next torture session.

"Don't take ages, Didi!" Amira calls out at Juhi's retreating back. Juhi is quick, returning freshly washed, in a clean brown sari and no longer walking with a limp. Brigadier Moolchand follows suit, and eventually, so does Amira. When it's my turn, Yukta Didi leads me to an outhouse in the back, where a steaming bucket waits for me, along with a change of clothes—a simple homespun tunic and dhoti.

"I kept these for Rajkumar—*Raja*—Amar, when he was younger," she says. "The clothes are a bit small for you, but they might still fit."

"Sau aabhaar," I say, meaning it. I *am* grateful—a hundred times and over—for any kind of help in this moment.

The water smells like lemons and sluices through the dirt much faster than I expect it to, much faster than water ordinarily would. The very feel of it seems to revitalize me, ridding me of exhaustion. *Magic?* I wonder. But in this instant, I don't mind. After cleaning myself up and dressing in Amar's old clothes—which barely fit, as Yukta Didi said—I enter the sitting room again, where the others are eating bowls of cumin rice and hot yellow daal.

Yukta Didi gives me a bowl as well. "Take a seat anywhere you like. I was telling the others that I took the liberty of mixing some sphurtijal with your bathwater. It's a magical potion that infuses the body with vitality," she explains when she sees my confused expression. "It won't last very long, but you'll be able to eat your meal without collapsing in exhaustion."

It's strange being inside a magus home, being treated like a guest instead of a servant. I forget my awkwardness, though, the moment a morsel of lentil-softened rice hits my mouth, the taste so good that it's an effort not to simply attack my food.

"Go slowly," Yukta Didi cautions us. "You don't want to throw up."

There does come a point when Yukta Didi snaps her fingers, and I freeze, wondering if she, too, shares the same views as many other Ambaris about half magi. My tense body uncoils, though, when she gestures to my bowl: Her finger snapping magically refilled it with fresh rice.

As I eat, my body slowly awakens, and I grow aware of the faint but distinct buzzing of a sound barrier in the walls.

"Now that you're here, let me update you a little on what's happening," Yukta Didi says. "There was an attack on the southern tenements, where Raja Amar was recently hidden."

"We heard about that in prison," Juhi says. "So it's true, then. They disguised themselves as Samudravasi soldiers and fooled the Sky Warriors."

"It was a terrible idea, in my opinion," Yukta Didi says, frowning. "Considering how well-trained the Samudravasi soldiers are. Had it not been for the tez-addled cavalry and the Samudra rani's letter to Raja Amar, the whole plan would have been a flop."

"Wait. Rani Yashodhara sent Amar a letter?" Juhi asks sharply.

"Yes." Yukta eyes Juhi warily. "She promised an alliance, troops if we needed them. However, when called upon to bind herself with a magical contract, she refused. Even when Raja Amar gave his word to free you from prison."

For a moment, Juhi's black eyes look furious. Then she releases a slow breath. "My sister and I were close as children, but never enough to get between Yashodhara's love for her kingdom. It's a trait of hers I've both admired and despised."

There's a long silence as Juhi's words sink in. Growing up, I never thought once that I'd pity a magus—especially a royal. Now, though, after hearing Juhi's story, I find myself grateful for Papa. Poor as we were, I never once doubted his love for me.

"I will always fight for you, Didi," Amira says firmly, placing a hand on Juhi's. "So will Kali and the Sisters. You gave us a home when we didn't have one."

"Gul will fight for you, too, Juhi ji," I add. "She never stopped thinking about you and Amira when we were in Tavan."

Juhi blinks several times, and I notice that her eyes are moist with tears. "I am not going to cry now after so many years," she says, making us laugh. "I'm glad that Amar and his army saved themselves. But I don't blame Yashodhara, either, for refusing to sign a contract. She *is* queen of Samudra, after all, and Amar is Lohar's son. *Blood follows blood*, as the old saying goes. Not that I always agree with it," she adds when Yukta Didi opens her mouth to protest. "Either way, now there is no place for Amar to hide."

"Raja Amar believes it's time to come out of hiding anyway," Yukta Didi says. "He and the Legion will likely be marching toward Ambarvadi as we speak. It's where I'm planning to send you four—to a safe house—until they get there. Raja Amar has supporters in the capital—indeed, many more supporters than we first realized."

"He *will* need a bigger army than what he has now," Brigadier Moolchand says, looking thoughtful. "Rani Shayla is not likely to repeat her mistake with the tez."

"We might still have some women in Javeribad," Amira says. "The Sisterhood—"

"Javeribad was razed by the Sky Warriors a few months ago," Yukta Didi interrupts. There's a compassionate look on her face. "People left it in droves. It's little more than a ghost town now."

"That was my fault." I feel the guilt of it eating away my insides. "I sent the Sky Warriors there. I put them on the Sisterhood's trail to get out of the kalkothri."

"You did *what?*" Amira shouts. "How could you?"

"Shhhh, Amira! He had no choice," Juhi says, glancing at me.

"Why? Because they tortured him? *We* didn't give up anything and we were in that hellhole longer than he was!"

"It was my idea!" Juhi says sharply. "*I* told Cavas to feed the Sky Warriors information about Gul and engineer a way to get out of the kalkothri. If you want to blame anyone, blame me!"

Amira's face crumples. She buries it in her arms, shaking off Juhi's consoling hand.

"I'm sorry, Amira," I whisper, my shoulders caving. No one responds.

Yukta Didi breaks the silence. "Life makes fools of us, at times, forcing us to betray others in ways we never would otherwise. I wasn't much older than you, Amira, when I was betrayed by my own—an illiterate aunt who loved me dearly but unwittingly sold me off to an Ambarvadi merchant to pay off a debt. In those days, the flesh market in the capital was much the same as Havanpur. No rules or regulations. A free-for-all, if you wish."

Amira slowly raises her head, her reddened eyes focusing on Yukta Didi.

"Years passed before I could forget the horror on her face—or forgive her for what she had done," the older woman continues. "You are young, Amira. As an old woman, I can only advise you to forgive Juhi and Cavas. Not for their sake, but for your own. Grief is a heavy enough burden to bear without the added weight of a grudge."

Amira's hard face softens momentarily. She still does not look at me, but somehow, I feel the hostility in the air ease, a lull settling over the room.

"You said that soldiers from the Amirgarh cantonment were willing to mutiny at your command," Juhi says to Brigadier Moolchand. "Do you think they will fight for you, if they know you're still alive?"

"I can't be certain," the brigadier says. "I had people loyal to me, of course, but I also had my enemies."

"You and the kabzedar rani are alike in that sense," Yukta Didi says. "Luckily, she has more enemies than all of you put together. By this time tomorrow, goddess willing, you will be at the safe house in Ambarvadi, talking to some of them."

We slip out of the yellow house at dawn, my mother casting an invisible shield around us. A few steps in, Amira nudges me in the back.

"I'm taking Yukta Didi's advice for now," she whispers brusquely. "But if you hurt Gul, you'll be on the receiving end of my spear. Understood?"

I bite back a smile. "Understood."

43

GUL

The road to Ambarvadi lies plagued with bounty hunters—men and women who have an uncanny way of tracking our campsites despite Amar's best precautions. A trip that should technically take us four days on foot is delayed by nearly two weeks of fighting and staving off people trying to capture or kill me. Amar, who is in more danger than I am, remains under constant guard, awake and asleep—also while going to relieve himself in the bushes behind our tents.

"An embarrassed king is better than a dead one," I tell Amar once, earning a glare from him in response.

Not a single Sky Warrior appears, which makes me wonder if they're stationed in the capital or at Ambar Fort. That we haven't been able to get in contact with Rani Amba or anyone else over there is also a problem. The only bit of good news that arrived through the specters was that Cavas, Juhi, Amira, and Brigadier Moolchand escaped from prison and are now at a safe house somewhere in Ambarvadi.

So why doesn't Cavas answer when I reach out to him? The thought nags at me, makes me want to pull out my hair after every meditation session.

"You'll go bald at this rate," Kali tells me, smacking my hand away from my head early one morning. "Be patient. He must have his reasons for not responding to you."

"It's been twelve days since they reached the safe house!"

"There may be enchantments protecting the safe house to make its occupants undetectable," Kali says reasonably. "Any magic coming in or going out gets nullified, which is great for secrecy, but it does make communication difficult for complements. Stop looking so sullen, my girl. At least you know he's safe."

Heat rises up my cheeks. I know she's right. I should be happy that Cavas is safe now and away from the kalkothri at Ambar Fort. I should also give him some time to recuperate his strength. Yet every day that I don't hear from him, I grow more anxious. Torture can deplete magic; couldn't it very well destroy the complementary bond that exists between us?

So? a voice in my head asks. *Why does that matter?*

I take a deep breath. Instead of meditating to communicate with Cavas, this time I simply do so to calm myself, to find sthirta in the seething ocean that is my mind. *Accept love, no matter how barbed it may look.* The words, spoken by the sky goddess months ago at Ambar Fort, appear in my mind now: sparks in a mass of darkly spiraling thoughts. Slowly, my heartbeats regulate and my body grows still. My mind, though still active, is no longer as turbulent.

Long moments later, I open my eyes. I never told Cavas that I loved him—not directly, anyway. But what else can define this strange thing I'm feeling now—a draw that goes beyond friendship, lust, or magic itself? Cavas, on the other hand, already told me he loved me. And he showed it time and time again—first by coming back for me to Ambar Fort, and later by enduring more than I can bear to think of. He could have changed his mind, truly turned loyal to the Scorpion. *I* certainly would have. But Cavas didn't. I might be the Star Warrior, but I've never had Cavas's resilience.

"I love you," I whisper into the silence. "And one day I will tell you this."

I'm rising to my feet again when Kali comes racing toward me, her face taut with anxiety.

"What happened?" I ask, my hands instantly reaching for my daggers. "More bounty hunters? Sky Warriors?"

She shakes her head. "It's . . . well, it's better shown than explained."

Curious about my friend's tone, which is tense but not fearful, I sheathe my daggers and follow her toward the center of the camp, where a group of people are gathered. I squint, trying to get a closer look . . . and realize they aren't human, the way I initially thought, but Pashu.

Gold-skinned and gold-eyed peri, their wings clipped by human slavers. Scaly green makara, still wearing the blue-and-white turbans of palace guards on their crocodile heads. They are gathered before Subodh, the peri watching as the makara open their jaws wide in an eerie croaking sound that raises goose bumps over my skin.

Subodh opens his mouth, lets out a similar croaking sound in response.

"It's been going on for a while now," Kali says quietly.

The peri are next to speak, their voices somewhere between human and bird, so chillingly beautiful that they make everyone stop and listen.

"It's said that peri can sing a human to sleep, can make their ears bleed with their voices if they wish," a voice speaks from behind us. Amar, who now watches the Pashu with awe. "It's why humans clip their wings. Clipping diminishes the deadly magic of their voices, makes them lose their will to live."

I say nothing, sickened by what I hear.

"It's a miracle that this lot survived," Amar continues. "The makara, on the other hand, went to my father willingly during the Great War, changing sides when they thought Raja Subodh was dead. I suppose you can call them survivors in their own way."

"Does Raja Subodh trust them?" Kali asks me.

After some hesitation, I reach out to Subodh through our bond. *Enemies or friends?*

After a moment, a response comes: *Neither at the moment. We will find out soon.*

"We don't know yet," I tell Kali.

"I'd drafted an order to free the captive Pashu in Ambar, you know," Amar says softly. "It was the day the Sky Warriors ambushed me. I never had a chance to sign it."

"Did you tell Raja Subodh this?" I ask.

"I did. He made Kali verify the truth of my statement." Amar gives me a wry smile. "Raja Subodh may say he's not a good king, but when it comes to the Pashu, he is as fierce as a parent protecting their young. If he didn't trust my intentions, I wouldn't be alive. Neither would the Pashu queen be ready to feed us during this war."

"I wonder how the peri escaped," I comment. "The man at the flesh market said that indenture contracts were magically binding."

"They must have killed their owners," Kali says quietly. "It's really the only way a contract can end before its time. That, or if the owners voluntarily let them go."

As she speaks, the sky overhead splits with a crack.

Heads crane up, daggers, lathis, and spears rising as a shadow emerges from the clouds. Sunlight glints off a pair of enormous wings, about six feet in length, with a wingspan twice that size. Silvery feathers shift color, hold a striking resemblance to the indradhanush mined in the Brimlands—amethyst, iolite, sapphire, emerald, citrine, spessartite, and ruby—every jeweled hue of the rainbow contained in their depths. From between the wings, gold limbs unfurl—a woman with long black hair and a bone-tipped spear in her hands. She hovers overhead, watching the crowd of peri, makara, and humans, shock and fury emanating from every inch of her regal face.

"Peri Armaiti," Subodh calls out to her. "You honor us with your presence. Please, everyone, make room for her to descend."

A small space opens up among the gathering and the peri lands, her wide gold eyes unblinking.

"I had heard rumors of some peri escaping captivity in Ambar. I was flying overhead, looking for them, when I heard voices. Singing our lament." Like Rani Sarayu, the peri's voice has a strange musicality to it while speaking the Common Tongue, birdlike and not, human and not. She pauses, watching Subodh. "I see that *you're* still here. Among *humans*."

No one misses the derision in her voice or the way she watches us— like we're vermin.

"Peri Armaiti—" Subodh begins.

"I told Rani Sarayu over and over that you weren't coming back to rule Aman," the peri cuts in. "That once more, you would use her and our people to fight a futile human war."

"You are mistaken, Peri Armaiti," Subodh says calmly. "I am not going to rule Aman again. I cannot—for I am not good at it. And never again will I pressure anyone to fight in a war of my choosing. I made that mistake more than two decades ago, and I paid the price tenfold. My rajsingha siblings were slaughtered to near extinction during the Great War; peri were captured and clipped; simurgh were nearly wiped out, with the exception of Rani Sarayu and a few others."

"You call the dead rajsingha your siblings, but none were *truly* your family, were they, Pashuraj?" the peri accuses. "None of them were related to you by blood. I, on the other hand, lost nearly all my loved ones. My brothers, Bahman, Ardibehesht, and Sherevar, were shot down from the sky by foul human magic. My sisters, Khordad and Amardad, were clipped and brutalized by Sky Warriors before their heads were chopped off. Spenta and I are the only two siblings left—and Spenta refuses to speak of their experiences in this war."

My eyes prick, grow heavy with tears. As I wipe them away, I notice that everyone else is much the same; some non-magi openly sob—an effect, I realize, of the peri's voice.

Subodh is the only one who remains unmoved. "I sympathize with you, warrior of the skies. But Pashu must also accept that we lost the Great War because of our arrogance. We underestimated our human opposition and the power of their maha-atashbans. We paid the price for that arrogance."

"Are you here to rub salt in my burning wounds?" the peri demands.

"No, Peri Armaiti. I would like to give you and your people a gift instead. If you will accept it."

Subodh raises his head, facing the peri eye to eye. A sudden glow surrounds his face, one that makes Armaiti step back, her strong wings brushing a gust of air our way.

"Pashuraj . . . you can't—"

"Take it!" he roars.

"What's happening?" I ask Kali. "What is he doing?"

"I don't know," Kali says, her tear-streaked face looking as baffled as I feel.

The peri reaches forth, touching Subodh's whiskered cheek. From there, she plucks a glowing golden drop and then turns, gesturing one of her clipped brethren forward. Slowly, carefully, she places the gold drop on one of the scars marring the peri's back. At first, nothing seems to happen. Then the peri begins to cry out in pain and shock as feathers erupt from his back, bones and skin stretching, forming wings where there were none.

"What's happening to Raja Subodh?" Kali cries out.

Still processing the miracle happening in front of me, it takes me a while to register the change in the Pashu king's appearance—the faded sheen of his fur, the streaks of gray shooting through his mane, his trembling limbs.

"He's transferred some of his living force to them." Amar sounds furious. "He's paying the ultimate price."

But Subodh does not stop there. He sheds another glowing tear from his eyes, regrowing the wings of not one, but ten of the peri who had come to him for aid, each haggard face regaining vitality as it is leeched from the Pashu king.

"Enough!" Amar shouts suddenly. "Are you trying to kill him?"

A shocked Armaiti glances at him and steps back. "The human is right. I can no longer take any more of your life from you, Raja Subodh. You didn't have to prove yourself this way."

"Yes, I did, Peri Armaiti," Subodh says, his voice sounding older than I'd ever heard it before. His brown mane is now completely silver, his fur gray. Liver spots dot his wrinkled limbs and torso. Only his eyes retain their brightness, a vivid yellow that now gleams with triumph. "I have lived far too long anyway. Seen too many battles. Why does it matter if I live for half a millennium instead of one?"

Armaiti stares at him, her eyes brimming with tears. Then, to my shock, she kneels, her head bowed, her spear held before Subodh. Peri behind her do the same, yet their new wings are not as still, blowing cool gusts our way, pushing the hair back from our faces.

"Pashuraj Subodh," Armaiti says. "For your sacrifice of life, I will fight for you and your human king as long as this war lasts and no longer."

"So will I," the ten peri behind her assert, a perfect chorus of voices.

"I accept your aid with gratitude," Subodh says.

He turns to the makara, who have been watching the proceedings with slitted orange eyes.

"I will speak to Rani Sarayu on your behalf, warriors of water and earth," he says in the Common Tongue—more for our benefit than for theirs. "You do not deserve punishment for your choice to survive the Great War. Neither do you need to fight for us now. You may leave in peace."

Three of the five makara who stood before him quietly slither away—a pardon was all they were seeking. Visible tremors go through Subodh's limbs as he thanks the two who remain, expressing gratitude for their loyalty.

"Well, Raja Amar," he says finally, turning to the future king. "Will these troops suffice?"

Human bounty hunters are no match for peri.

The very sight of the flying Pashu, led by a vicious Peri Armaiti, makes many of them turn tail and run. A few stay behind, shooting at the peri with flaming red arrows—which the latter simply pluck out of the air and blow against, dousing the flames like candles. The peri's flapping wings create a gust so strong that the bounty hunters struggle to remain on their horses. When they attempt to run, the peri chase after them, pluck them off the ground and hang them upside down by their ankles, uncaring of their screams.

I wince when I see a skull crash against the rocks below, as if it's nothing more than a coconut offered at a temple.

It's a war, Gul.

It's a war—and the peri have been holding on to nearly a quarter century of rage. The makara do not hold back, either. They slither after the bounty hunters at terrifying speeds, hissing, biting, their jaws crunching through skulls and bones.

I turn away from the carnage, my insides squirming. Warriors should not be squeamish, but somehow, despite killing so many people, I still am.

Later that night, long after everyone has fallen asleep, the peri's screams continue to ring in my ears—jubilation and triumph, underscored by anger.

We will reach the capital in two days, I remind myself. *Everything will be resolved there.*

For better or for worse.

44

SHAYLA

I learned as a young girl, even during the best of times, to remain watchful. To find patterns in an enemy's movements and then disrupt them without mercy. As queen, though, I often can't tell who my real enemy is. Or, when surrounded by enemies, I often have to decide which one deserves most priority. Like the man before me, kneeling on the floor, his head bowed, his nape vulnerable to my atashban.

The infamous Brimmish Butcher is surprisingly mild-mannered. Soft-spoken in a way that reminds me of a saint.

"Rise, Surya of the Brim." I use the title the leader of the mercenaries prefers, give him a polished, practiced smile. The Butcher smiles back, his brown eyes colder than mine.

"I hope you find our arrangements for your soldiers satisfactory," I tell him.

"Most satisfactory, Ambar Sikandar. Perhaps . . ." his voice trails off.

I wait in silence, not prodding him in the slightest. Two can play at this game.

"Perhaps we can amend the terms of the bounty," the Butcher says after a pause. "Should you win this war, my army and I will receive a small portion of Ambar for ourselves—the northern patch closest to the border of the Brim and Prithvi, stopping short of Meghapur."

A patch of land rich in tez and roopbadal—two crops the Butcher's minions consume the most of.

"*If* we win," I say pointedly, "I will consider this."

"Oh, my young rani, mere consideration isn't enough. I will not risk the lives of my army without a blood pact."

With a dagger hidden inside the sleeve of his tunic, the Butcher opens a gleaming line of scarlet in his palm.

On another day, I would have his head for his insolence. Would relish chopping it off myself. But today I'm held back by the knowledge of my makara guards deserting their posts, by the reminder of my kingdom's most secure prison now reduced to ash, its most dangerous prisoners— my greatest leverage against the Star Warrior—gone.

It didn't take long to discover the damned tunnel through which they escaped or link it to the only person who had access to it in this god-forsaken fort. Alizeh was her most brutal yet: She reduced Amba's fingers to stubs. It did little to satisfy me.

"Don't execute Amba now," Acharya Damak advised. "You can still use her as leverage. Spare a snake's life and—"

"Oh, spare me the proverbs!" I snarled back. "Had the shadowlynx not perished in the fire, I would have fed her to it, snakeskin and every-thing!"

But, as patronizing as he could be, I knew Damak was right. With new rumors about peri now joining the conjurer's army, I can't take any chances.

Using the point of my atashban to cut my own hand, I clasp the Brim-mish Butcher's in a punishing grip. His face loses some of its humor.

"I vow to give you a piece of Ambari land, Surya of the Brim," I say. "*Provided* you win this war."

The magic between us mingles, burns my palm for what feels like an eternity before I release him.

"You are dismissed," I say.

I don't miss the flash of hatred in the Butcher's eyes or the cold finality of his smile. He trusts me as little as I trust him. But, for now, there is the promise of food and shelter, of men and women to be taken for play by his soldiers, of loot to be gathered after the war.

He bows low. "Ambar Sikandar," he says before backing out of the room.

A moment later: "That was a mistake, Rani Shayla."

I turn to face the speaker—Acharya Damak, whom I asked to witness my conversation with the mercenary leader.

"I did not specify the sliver of land in question, Acharya ji," I say. "I said *a* piece of Ambari land. Which could very well mean this."

I point to a glass jar on my desk, filled with red sand.

"The mercenaries will not forgive you for cheating them," the high priest warns.

"It's good that I do not seek their forgiveness, then, isn't it, Acharya? Now, moving to the matter at hand. The conjurer and his army approach. Our bounty hunters haven't been able to stop them. According to General Alizeh's reports, the enemy are about a day's march away."

I pause. "I want a suryagrahan."

"The next solar eclipse is during the Month of—"

"Not an *actual* solar eclipse," I cut in. "A magical one. You and your priests are capable of that much, aren't you?"

"My queen, eclipses lie within the realm of the sky goddess. We priests can create an eclipse with magic, yes. But doing so will force us to go against nature, will unleash magic that goes beyond our control. The Holy Scroll warns against such abominations. It's too dangerous!"

"You have two choices right now, Acharya Damak. A magically created suryagrahan or the head of every priest in Ambar Fort on a pike—including yourself." I examine the cut on my hand, now bleeding onto the study's expensive paisley carpet, and look up at the high priest again. "What do you think is more dangerous?"

"But, Ambar Sikandar!" The acharya's sweat sours the study's perfumed air. "The sky goddess—"

"Enough of your quibbling! Do you think me a fool? Your sky goddess and other gods are nothing except a clever construct by priests such as yourself to wield power—to hold the naive and gullible at bay. The gods never have existed and they never will."

My words ring in the silence. There's an ominous quality to them, much like my nightmare about the Tree of Sins. I shake off the feeling and focus once more on the scandalized high priest. "Don't stand here gawking. Go prepare yourself for the ceremony."

I ignore the acharya's mutterings as he leaves the room; the old fool is likely worried about being reborn as a dung beetle in another life. Instead, I call for General Alizeh and Major Emil.

"Have you been readying for battle?" I ask them.

"Yes, Ambar Sikandar," Alizeh says at once, the eagerness in her voice far too evident. "I've realigned our battle plans here."

A scroll unfurls before me, revealing the order of battle, positioning me, Alizeh, and the Sky Warriors at the command center, and various troops ahead in columns: infantry from Dhanbad, Amirgarh, Havanpur, and Rajgarh.

I tap the marking for the Amirgarh infantry, watch it fade from black to gray. "Replace the advance troops here with Surya of the Brim and his soldiers. Emil, you have been in talks with the Butcher. You will now work in coordination with him to attack the first round of skirmishers."

"Wait—are you talking about the Brimmish Butcher?" Alizeh asks sharply. "Since when did . . . ?" Her voice trails off as realization sinks in. I tamp down the guilt I feel when she turns to face me. "You trust those tez-addled mercenaries over your own army? Shayla, have you truly lost it?"

"General Alizeh—" Major Emil begins, sending a nervous glance my way.

"What is she going to do? Kill me?" Alizeh snaps. "Shayla, I'm your general. I need to speak my mind here. The mercenaries fight for their own agenda. You are mad if you think you can control them!"

"I think I still have a better hope of controlling them than controlling possible mutineers from within my own army," I say coldly. "Isn't it so, Alizeh?"

Alizeh frowns. "Shayla, I have been loyal to you from the very beginning—"

"Then prove your loyalty, General. Fight alongside our mercenary allies."

There's a long silence. Alizeh says nothing, but I can feel her hostility from here.

"Rani Shayla," Major Emil says finally, a worried look on his face. "Perhaps we should consider what General Alizeh said. Surya of the Brim and his mercenaries can be a little . . . unpredictable. Would it not be wise to use them later, when our options are exhausted? The new brigadier you appointed in Moolchand's place says he has the army well under control by now."

I can feel them watching me, hear the words they don't speak out loud:

How close is she to shattering?

I release a breath. Perhaps Emil is right. Perhaps the mutineers are under control by now.

Yet when I speak again, my voice is brittle. "My order stands, Major Emil. There is no room for argument."

I tap on the scroll, replacing the Amirgarh infantry with mercenaries under the title *Advance Troops*.

"Prepare the maha-atashbans." More drawings appear as I speak—illustrations of two enormous atashbans next to the command center, under *Elite Troops*. Twenty feet long and nearly as wide, maha-atashbans were used by Lohar against the Pashu and Tavani rebels during the Battle of the Desert. Each maha-atashban needed an elephant to move it anywhere and at least ten Sky Warriors to power it. Though mobility is a pain as far as maha-atashbans are concerned, the weapons were the only reason Pashu forces—including peri—were nearly exterminated or captured. Tavan itself would have been wiped off the map if not for the Pashu king and those blasted living specters.

"Announce a curfew tomorrow, starting from dawn," I continue. "Civilians must bar themselves indoors until the curfew ends. If they are caught outside, it will be at their own peril."

"Yes, Ambar Sikandar," Major Emil says.

"Did you hear me, Alizeh?" I ask, when my general continues to remain silent.

"Yes, Ambar Sikandar," she says. "Is there anything else?"

I ignore the sly voice in my head that twists her words around—turning *sikandar* to *sitamgar*—a voice that has haunted me every night ever since I've taken over the throne.

"Yes," I say, my mouth turning dry. "Prepare the forces to fight in the dark. There is going to be an eclipse."

45

CAVAS

After weeks inside a torture cell, it's strange getting accustomed to life in the safe house. Thirteen days have passed, but I'm still liable to startle awake, chest heaving, my fingers aching as if they've been broken and reset in quick succession.

They can't get to you here, I tell myself each time. *This house is shielded from external magical attacks. You are safe. For now.*

Ramnik, the owner of the safe house and a high-ranking official at the Ministry of Truth, put up the house's magical barrier himself. Not only does the barrier prevent magic from coming in, but it also stops magic going out. This, in effect, has reduced my meditation sessions to mere breathing exercises. The first time I found out that I couldn't communicate with Gul, my anxiety spiked so high that they had to give me a calming draft. It smelled like lavender and honeyweed, its bitter aftertaste lingering long after I woke.

"Gul is fine," my mother told me soothingly. "I saw her myself."

Unlike the crowded center of the capital, Ramnik's three-story haveli is on one of the quieter back roads, the trunk of a thick neem breaking ground in front of his doorway, shielding it from prying eyes.

Moments after we crossed the threshold, two sobbing women threw themselves at Juhi and Amira. Today I look down from the house's open rooftop and spot them sitting in the courtyard—a younger woman from the Sisterhood named Prerna, and an older woman, whom everyone calls Cook, though she hasn't entered the kitchen once in the time she has been here.

"None of the other Sisters survived the Javeribad attack," Prerna told us—a fact that made me feel so guilty I could barely eat that day despite my hunger. Amira hasn't spoken to or looked at me once since learning the news, though she has been quieter in general, plagued with more nightmares and panic attacks than the rest of us.

Now, as the women talk to Juhi, Amira stands off to the side, contemplating the sky goddess's small shrine in the yard. The only people she talks to are Juhi and the brigadier, and their conversations seem to revolve only around Amar's attack plans.

I take a deep breath. I hardly expected Amar to include me in those very plans, but for some reason he has. Last week, Ambar's future king sent me a letter through my mother:

> *Dear Cavas,*
>
> *As you are aware, the war has begun. It would be my honor if you would lead the living specters and non-magi from the northern tenements in any future battles. I do not wish to impose on you, of course. But you and Gul are the two pillars on whom Ambar's hopes rest. Without you, I certainly cannot hope to become king. Please let me know your reply at the earliest.*
>
> *Yours sincerely,*
> *Amar*

"You don't need to answer right away. When you make a decision, call for me by speaking into your green swarna," Ma told me after I sat stunned on my bed for several moments. "You can let Latif or any of the other specters know, too. That green swarna is so powerful that you can contact all the specters in Ambar at once, if you wished. Get into the practice of being commander," she joked gently.

I smiled only weakly then. Now, on the roof of the safe house, my head still continues to spin. *Me? A commander?* I shudder. I still don't know what to tell Amar. And time is running out.

"Are you all right over there?" a voice asks.

I turn to find Brigadier Moolchand watching me curiously. In new clothing, with food in his belly, and our daily meetings about the upcoming rebellion, the brigadier nearly glows with health. I barely notice his missing sword arm.

"I'm fine," I say. A little cold, perhaps, but that's only because of the pair of living specters that linger beside me, day and night, at my mother's insistence.

"Shubhsaver," the brigadier cheerfully addresses the empty air around me. He does this every morning, without fail, hoping to strike a conversation with the specters, though they have yet to take him up on his offer.

"They're up there." I point at the floating pair over my head—a man and his son, who barely speak, even when they are alone with me. The brigadier looks up, repeating himself. Surprisingly, I hear the specters echo the greeting back.

Moolchand gives me a crooked smile when he catches me staring. "My mother used to say that kind words opened more doors than swords ever could."

"That's odd, coming from a man in your profession."

"Isn't it? My mother wouldn't have approved of my choices anyway. She died when I was a boy." He pauses. "Now that I can't wield a sword anymore, it doesn't matter, does it?"

"Not to the soldiers from Amirgarh," I tell him.

Over a week ago, someone showed up at Ramnik's house from the Amirgarh cantonment—an army lieutenant, who, upon seeing Moolchand alive, sobbed nearly as much as the Sisters did for Juhi and Amira. The lieutenant went as far as to promise to serve Moolchand on behalf of the entire army when the time came for a war—a vow that Ramnik's mate, a truth seeker, affirmed.

"Truths can change as human minds do," Brigadier Moolchand tells me now with a shrug. "I cannot vouch for every soldier in the Amirgarh infantry, even if they did want to mutiny before I was imprisoned."

"Well, you're still better off than me. Those soldiers trust you," I say, my stomach a pit of seething nerves. "I have no experience in leading an army. Juhi or Amira would have been better choices. I don't know what Raja Amar is thinking."

"Juhi and Amira can't see living specters," the brigadier reminds me. "Neither do they have any influence over non-magi."

"And I do?"

Over the past two weeks, whenever I've attended meetings with the sarpanch and Councilor Cama, the latter still glares at me in a way that could eviscerate, though he says nothing about Bahar or my mother.

"They listen to you, Cavas," Moolchand tells me. "Whenever magi leaders propose a plan, it's you non-magi look toward. Don't discount your heritage. People may call you a half magus, but that's a misnomer, isn't it? You are *both* magus and non-magus, and that gives you a unique advantage over everyone else."

I say nothing, surprised for a moment. "Have you been talking to my mother?"

Moolchand smiles. "No, but she sounds like a smart woman. I knew a man once who was both magus and non-magus. He was my squire at Amirgarh's fort. For the longest time, he hid his heritage from me, pretending to simply possess no magic. It's only when we became friends that he told me his secret."

355

There's an expression on Moolchand's face that piques my curiosity—a sense that I had when Subodh talked about Rani Amba. "What happened to him? Is he still . . ." My voice trails off as the brigadier turns away, showing me his back. "I'm sorry," I say. "I shouldn't have . . . It was none of my business."

The brigadier takes a deep breath, still not looking at me. "Things were different twenty years ago for magi and non-magi. Perhaps, with Raja Amar in power, things will be different again."

King Amar, who has promised magi, non-magi, and in-betweeners like myself equal status after the war, signing a magical contract to effect the same.

"Do you really believe they will?" I ask Moolchand. "I mean . . . don't you think it's a bit idealistic to believe everyone will simply change under Raja Amar's rule?"

I see hints of dissent even now. While Ramnik is cordial with me, I don't miss the way his mate quietly snaps her fingers in my presence, or how she ushers her four-year-old son out whenever I enter a room. It will take a lot more than new leadership to change magi prejudice or for non-magi to forget the wounds inflicted by magi in recent history.

"By believing in the impossible, idealists can change their own fortunes. Sometimes they can also change the world," Moolchand says, confidence reentering his voice. "But you are right, of course. Not every war is won in a short while."

Beyond the high wall of the courtyard, my attention is drawn to a pair of thanedars hammering their lathis against doors. They pause before Ramnik's house, staring at it in a way that makes me take a few steps back and disappear from view, though the enchantments are supposed to render anyone on the roof invisible to outsiders.

"Wonder what they're up to," Moolchand says, his voice low. "Perhaps Ramnik will know once he returns from work today."

Later that evening, Ramnik escorts us and Juhi and Amira to an underground chamber in the haveli. There, seated cross-legged on cushions across the floor, are a group of magi wearing colorful turbans. *Merchants*, I guess, by the elaborate style of the wraps, the turbans' pleated edges fanning out from the top left. Sarpanch Alok and Councilor Cama are there as well, the latter studiously ignoring my presence. As Juhi and Amira settle down, I note that the only empty seat is next to Bahar's father.

I force myself to take it, aware of everyone's curious gazes. The merchants must have been there for some time already. The small table in front of me is clustered with a fruit bowl piled with mango skins, and a paring knife, its blade still sticky with juices. Copper dishes lie heaped in one corner, dangerously close to tipping over. From another corner, a polished silver kettle rises into the air, filling four small, steaming cups of chai, a blade of green lemongrass jutting from its spout. Ramnik snaps a finger, and, to my surprise, one of the cups floats quietly toward me, hovering in the air until I take it. I've never seen anyone perform levitation magic before, and I'm tempted to ask Ramnik to repeat the performance.

Conversation starts the moment Ramnik closes the door.

"I've been hearing things at the Ministry of Trade," says a merchant wearing a red turban. "Rumors that Raja Amar and his armies are close. Might reach here as early as tomorrow. Thanedars have been marching through the streets, announcing that a curfew will begin at dawn."

"What about weapons?" the sarpanch asks. "Are there enough to equip everyone?"

"Not everyone, but enough to equip many," another merchant says. "My contact at the armory diverted a couple of cartloads off their regular track. They should reach the northern tenements by midnight."

My spine tingles. I am not sure if the chill comes from the continued presence of the specters or the plans that have been laid in place, plans that have been burgeoning for who knows how long.

"We will need weapons, as well," Juhi adds. "Spears, lathis, an atashban would be useful, too."

"Is there anyone among you capable of firing an atashban?" asks one of the merchants, his eyebrows raised.

"I am," Amira says.

The men stare at her and laugh. "An atashban isn't a toy, young lady," the merchant in the red turban says. "It requires power. More than any of us in this room possess."

"Like this, you mean?"

Amira retrieves the sticky paring knife off the table. Shouts rise from the merchants as red fire spreads over the wood. Red Turban spills his tea over his clothes, while the others press against the wall, terror blanching their faces. Amira flips the paring knife. Sand pours from the knife in a jet of white light, diffusing the flames, leaving behind a heap of smoking ashes and molten silver.

"An atashban, then?" Juhi asks Red Turban, her voice bland.

"Gods, woman!" he sputters at Amira. "You could have killed us!"

"Oho. So now I'm 'woman' instead of 'young lady'?" Amira mocks. "What did I do to deserve such an honor?"

"Come now, friend," Brigadier Moolchand interjects before the furious merchant can respond. "You challenged Amira Behen and she showed you what she could do with only a paring knife. My most seasoned soldiers are incapable of doing such magic—especially after being subjected to torture and imprisonment."

"Also, if I did want to kill you, you wouldn't be standing here before me," Amira adds, her hard voice belying the visible tremors going through her limbs.

"We believe you!" Ramnik says, hastily raising his hands in supplication. "Please, Amira Behen. That was my grandfather's antique tea table and our second-best tea set. My mate will not be pleased if we ruin any more items in this room."

Amira lowers the knife, looking somewhat abashed. "My apologies, Ramnik ji."

"Accepted." Ramnik turns to frown at the merchant. "And, Faramroz Bhai. You should know better than to challenge the Sisters of the Golden Lotus. Surely you've heard the stories about them!"

"I'm sorry." Red Turban certainly looks it—though I'm not sure if it's because he doubted Amira or because of his ruined silk tunic. "We'll make sure Amira Behen gets an atashban."

"Sau aabhaar, Faramroz Bhai," Juhi says. "We must remember that we are fighting for the same cause, which is to put Ambar in the hands of a good ruler. We cannot discount our warriors based on gender or age or magical capability. That's what Lohar did with Shayla and what Shayla did with non-magi during the battle near the southern tenements."

Heads nod around the room, along with exclamations of "Hear! Hear!" from the non-magi councilors.

"The enemy has its weaknesses, of course, as do we," Juhi continues. "Our strength lies in unity. To fight as one against those who sow seeds of discord, who have done this in many ways since before the Great War. We fight for Ambar. For a monarch who will unite us—hopefully for good, this time."

"For Ambar!" Ramnik cries out.

"For Ambar!" we echo.

Overhead, knocks rap the front door, rattling it in its frame. Silence falls over the room as Ramnik goes upstairs, no one daring to speak. He soon returns, a grim expression on his face.

"That was a thanedar warning us about the curfew tomorrow," he says. "You should get home as soon as you can."

"Be well, boy." Councilor Cama gives me a sharp nod; it's the only act of civility he will offer and I take it, pressing my hand to my heart in thanks.

The brigadier and I leave the women to sleep in the basement and head upstairs to our tiny room that smells perpetually of stale cooking oil. Soon enough Moolchand falls asleep, his snores filling the space. I lie awake for much longer, recalling everything that has happened over the past couple of days, my body still thrumming from the energy in the basement, hope a steady flame in my chest.

Slowly, I pull the green swarna from my pocket and place it close to my lips.

"Ma?" I whisper. "Tell Raja Amar that I'll do it. I will lead the specters and non-magi during the war."

Dawn rises with the sound of thanedars rattling their lathis against barred storefronts and locked doors. Overhead, a faint drumming penetrates the air, vibrating in my bones.

"Is that the army?" Prerna asks.

"No," Juhi says, frowning. "The army is summoned by war horns. This is something else altogether."

Something that makes Juhi withdraw the bag of cowrie shells Ramnik procured for her and start arranging them in a circle on the floor. Amira holds Juhi upright through the scrying session and then long after the latter emerges from her trance.

"It's her magic," Amira whispers to me. "It takes a toll on her."

"Darkness," Juhi says, sweat beading her dark-brown skin. Her expression is troubled. "I see only darkness."

Soon, everyone else wakes as well. Despite their sunken eyes, the Sisters look calm. Juhi sits in a corner, a belt with two sheathed swords next to her, while Amira examines the tip of her atashban. The weapons, I learn, arrived a few hours before daybreak, hidden in the milkman's cart.

Brigadier Moolchand wears a tunic reminiscent of his old army uniform, trimmed with shades of scarlet and brown, and a bright indigo turban that Ramnik carefully ties around his head.

A moment later, a knock sounds on the back door.

It's a non-magus delegate from the northern tenements, a burly man, who removes the blanket covering his body to reveal a sickle in one hand and a shield strapped to his chest.

"Son of Harkha and Xerxes," he says, addressing me directly. "Your non-magus army waits for orders outside. There aren't many of us—only a hundred or so—but we're eager and willing. It's an honor to fight under your command."

I know I should say something in response. But my words have choked in my throat and I simply bow deep to show him my respect. My fingers tighten around the shaft of my spear, one I'm no longer certain I can use. I close my eyes, trying to remember everything Subodh taught me in Tavan. However, all I can see is Gul going through the motions I failed at—Gul, whom I abandoned to chase after General Alizeh.

My breath emerges, rattling and shaky. *I can't be foolish this time. I can't get caught.*

"You won't get caught," Ma whispers quietly, reading my thoughts.

"We won't let you," two voices say in unison. It's the father and the son who have accompanied me in the safe house, their gray faces reassuring.

"I'm not the only one who needs protection. The non-magus army will need it, too," I say. "I want you to help them as much as you can. Make them invisible if you need to."

"We will," Ma promises. "Don't you worry about that."

"I don't know why Amar asked me to be a leader," I say for possibly the hundredth time that week.

"You underestimate yourself, Cavas of the northern tenements," the older male specter says. "You have survived more than any of us during torture; you have shown grit and guile when everything appeared hopeless. Among non-magi and the living specters, you are regarded as a great warrior."

"This is true," the non-magus delegate agrees.

"I'm not!" I protest. "Gul is a better fighter than I ever will be."

"Oh, don't bother with him," another voice says scornfully. I glance up, see Roda *pop* into visibility before floating down to take a seat beside the older male specter. "He's too far gone over her. She's the same over him. So annoying."

"You mean you can't hold on to your resentment anymore," Ma says, an undercurrent of iron in her pleasant voice.

Roda's scowling face straightens. "Apologies, Harkha Bai," she says, sounding strangely meek.

My urge to laugh fades as the sound of conches penetrates the air from south of the city, answered by war horns from the north, where Ambar Fort lies.

"The armies are here," Juhi says. "Get ready, everyone."

Swallowing my fear, I turn to the non-magus delegate first. "Follow Juhi ji and the merchant army. Listen to Juhi ji's instructions and shield yourself as much as possible from any magical attacks."

"Understood." The burly man nods his assent.

I turn to the specters.

"I want you to go ahead," I say, curbing the tremor in my voice. "Scout the area. See what's happening. I want reports every few minutes or whenever I call you through this." I hold up the green swarna, which now glows bright, hums in a way it never has before—with the sound of hundreds of specters. "At some point, I will ask you to distract the enemy—to play a little hide-and-seek, if you will—by making our soldiers intermittently visible and invisible. Is that clear?"

I expect smirks or arguments. But there are none.

"Clear, Cavas ji." The specters' high voices chorus in perfect unison. They fly out the open door, seconds before I register that someone had added—for the first time—an honorific after my name.

DRUMS IN THE DARK

19th day of the Month of Birds
7 months into Queen Shayla's reign

46

GUL

The sun rises by the time we enter Ambarvadi, beaming hot on our heads, across shuttered storefronts and padlocked doors. It glints on the spikes of Subodh's reptilian tail as he walks ahead. The two makara follow closely, their scales gleaming like polished jade. I walk with Kali and fifty warriors from the Legion, spears and shields held close to their sides. Armaiti and the peri fly overhead, keeping watch, the deeper we go in.

Subodh insisted Amar stay at the command center with Falak, Sami, and the remaining troops.

"If you wish to be Ambarnaresh, you cannot be rash with your own life," he reminded when Amar argued. "If we lose, you take the remaining troops and go back into hiding. As long as you're alive, Ambar still has hope."

Sami wasn't happy about being left behind, either.

"You need to survive this," Kali told her sharply. "For the both of us."

The argument led to a frosty silence between the two, lasting an entire day. But at night, as I was falling asleep, I heard Sami creep back into our tent. When I woke this morning, I found her and Kali tangled together, holding on as if they would never let go.

Now, among the winding, eerily empty streets of the capital, I'm glad that neither Sami nor Amar is here. Something feels distinctly *off* today about Ambarvadi. Strange drumming penetrates the air, hammering the inside of my skull.

"Did the Scorpion decide to use magical war drums to make our ears bleed?" I ask Kali.

"I wouldn't put it past her," Kali replies, frowning. She reaches out a hand, waves it ahead of her face as if testing an invisible pattern. "But these aren't drums. Not quite."

"What do you mean?"

"It's . . . they sound more like *voices*. Like chants thrumming the air."

I frown, her words making me uneasier than before. Now that she's mentioned this, I pick out patterns in the air that could be words, the most distinct of which sounds like *andhiyara*, the Vani word for darkness.

"Their advance troops are coming," Subodh growls, his voice loud in the silence. "Peri Armaiti can see them from above. Around three hundred men."

An entire battalion of trained soldiers against seventy-five men and women armed with spears and shields.

And the peri, who can swipe out probably ten of those men with a beat of their wings, I remind myself. *And Subodh. And Kali.*

And you, a voice says in my head. *They have you, too, Gul.*

A strange feeling goes through me as I turn around, nodding at the women who follow me, watching the strain on their tattooed faces ease. Shadowy figures crest the incline ahead of us and pause there. Amar's strategy, choosing to invade Ambarvadi, seems to have paid off in one way—we will not fight soldiers on horseback today. It's difficult for an armed cavalry to navigate the city's many narrow alleys and roads, let alone fight in them. If they do fight on horseback, they will be limited to the wide thoroughfares that cut Ambarvadi into quarters or be forced off horseback eventually.

Yet . . . as I squint against the haze in the air, I realize something isn't quite right. It might be magic, or perhaps the heat itself that is blurring my vision. But the troops that stand before us don't appear Ambari, aren't dressed in the infantry's brown-and-red uniform. Instead, they wear identical sand-colored turbans, tunics, and trousers, their sun-darkened faces obscured by wide silver blades. Heading them is a man in black, his face shadowed by a mask.

"Looks like the rumors about the Brimmish mercenaries were right," Kali comments, her words grim. "Rani Shayla has sold her kingdom to the highest bidder."

The drumming in the air grows louder, turns into a chant in high Vani that I can't understand, except for that single word: andhiyara.

"Lightorbs!" Subodh hollers at Kali. "As many as you can!"

Kali shoots sparks into the air, molding to form one, then two, then four lightorbs that spin over our heads, their too-bright glow competing with the sun, hurting my head and my eyes.

The light, I think. *It's far too much.*

Someone must have been listening to my stupid thought, because for one moment the sun still hangs in the sky.

And then, it doesn't.

Our lightorbs fizzle out, leaving behind a darkness so absolute that I think I've lost my vision.

But then the drumming starts again. Voices chanting: "Andhiyara. Andhiyara." Old Vani for utter, impenetrable darkness—the kind caused by a solar eclipse.

Overhead, I hear Armaiti shouting for control among the peri until her voice gets cut off by an awful scream. The ground before us shakes as a body falls from the air, spraying our faces with gravel and drops of mud. Or what I think is mud until I smell it.

Blood. Peri blood, I guess, by the feather I pull from my hair.

"Armaiti says she can't do anything without vision," Subodh says urgently over the war cries of the mercenaries. "We need lightorbs! Or another magical light source. Non-magical fires will not be visible during a suryagrahan."

"I'm trying!" Kali cries out. "But my magic keeps dying out for some reason! Gul, you try!"

But I have never been able to create lightorbs, and this doesn't miraculously change now. "It's not working!" I exclaim. "What kind of suryagrahan is this?"

"An abomination of the worst kind," Subodh says, his voice grim. "Be careful. Your magic may not work the way it normally does."

It's the last bit of advice he can give before his voice gets drowned out by thundering feet. I aim my seaglass daggers in the distance, from where I think the enemy approaches, and shoot a spell. Something crumbles ahead—the side of a building? An abandoned fruit stall? I'm not sure. I can feel the heat of my weapons, but I don't see them glow. I can't tell if the spells I aim are any good.

Something stings the side of my ear, forcing me to duck to the ground. Blood trickles down my burning lobe as screams rise around me, juxtaposing with guttural laughs. Red spots swirl before my eyes as someone kicks me in the face. I slash out, forcing myself to move despite the burning pain in my nostrils, hearing the satisfying sound of a man cursing me in another tongue before someone else kicks me in the stomach.

They can see us, I realize. *Even though we can't see them.*

I shoot a spell upward, where I think a chin should be, and feel a retaliating kick to my spine. The pain from this hit is so crushing that I lose my grip on my daggers.

Use me, the death magic inside me demands. *Kill them.*

Yet how do I use my magic in darkness like this, when I could very well hit a friend instead of a foe?

The enemy senses my hesitation, and soon enough, I find myself wrestled to the ground, daggerless, thick hands gripping my wrists and ankles, pulling hard on my arms and legs.

"Let's see what you can do now, little witch," someone snarls in my ear in the Common Tongue. My body seizes, frozen, as a rough hand moves up my left calf and then my thigh, leaving bruises in its wake.

Do something, Gul!

As thick fingers grip hold of the waistband of my trousers, another scream pierces the air.

No. You will not touch Kali!

I turn sideways and lean, biting the nearest bit of flesh I can find. Tasting blood.

The man's curse fades before my newly freed hands, heat coursing down my right arm, explode in a burst of vivid orange light that lets me see their terrified faces, shouting at one another, raising their wide talwars to bring them over my head.

Protect.

The steel hits my shield and melts, forcing the mercenaries back a couple of steps. I make out a few figures garbed in sandy brown, their eyes glowing green—probably with magic that allows them to see in the eclipse. It should be difficult to do two spells at the same time. But Subodh was right when he said my magic wouldn't work the way it normally does. It grows stronger, more sensitive to my brain's commands, the dagger in my right hand expelling a steady orange flame—both light and shield—remaining completely independent of my left hand, which slashes the air, a pair of bright-green chakras erupting from the blade, splitting the skulls, throats, and very centers of the two mercenaries who assaulted me.

Sounds grow warbled in my ears. Movements slow, everything shifting in a way that it hadn't since Tavan. Since Cavas got captured. It's odd, this sthirta, allowing me to be brutally efficient about dispatching the other soldiers who throw themselves at me. I leave behind a slew of bodies to reach Kali, my shield glowing to reveal her pale face and bloody daggers, the severed head of her tormentor lying on the ground beside her. Kali's gaze finds mine, her mouth and body trembling.

But before I can ask if she's all right, my attention gets drawn to another sound—Subodh's familiar roar as he battles the masked man in black, the latter's movements quick, almost airy in contrast with the rest of his soldiers, who continue moving at a sluggish pace.

Realization strikes a moment later: *Of course. He's meditating.*

The leader of the mercenaries emits the same sort of glow from his body as Subodh and I do, his eye sockets completely white. Yet while the man in black looks like he's just getting started, Subodh is already panting, his fur like hammered silver in this light.

The mercenary leader leaps in the air, like Juhi demonstrating her deadliest Yudhnatam stances, and brings down his arm. I've begun shouting seconds before Subodh closes his brilliant eyes, seconds before the mercenary severs his head, and the rest of us watch it roll across the ground. It pauses at the foot of another mercenary, who skewers it with his sword, lifting it high in the air.

"No!" My throat is raw from screaming. "NO!"

On any other day, my cries would have broken my meditative trance. But today, for whatever reason, they do not, adding to my horror as I watch everything unfold in slow motion.

Subodh isn't dead, my heart insists. *He can't be! This is just a horrible dream.*

But even my worst dreams rarely feature this sort of detail: the smell of acrid spellfire and burning flesh, the pressure building in my gut at the sight of blood dripping from the Pashu king's severed head.

Overhead, the peri sing their despair, a sound that cuts deeper than what I just saw. My limbs tremble. This pain will eat me whole if I let it. And I can't. Not now.

"Where are you, sky goddess?" I call out, allowing rage to push aside my grief. "Help us!"

"I am right with you, daughter."

The sky goddess materializes before me—trident in hand, her hair and eyes as black as the eclipse itself. Her body remains a strange vivid blue, the shade of the sky beyond the dark. Around us, people and objects grow still. A falling soldier freezes a few feet from the ground, his body diagonal, his eyes glassy, drops of blood suspended around him like rubies.

"Then why don't you help us?" I demand. "Why don't you get rid of the eclipse?"

"I cannot," she says dispassionately. "The gods are not allowed to meddle in human wars. We can *influence* them, yes. We can make prophecies; we can send our own children into the mortal world to serve a specific purpose. But we can do no more. The eclipse stands as is at the moment."

"This is *not* a real eclipse. They're meddling with nature! With *your* realm! It's an abomination!"

"Yes, it is. Humans often indulge in abominations, and the gods let them. But nature has its own ways of correcting abominations. While this suryagrahan has been detrimental to you, the magic it has unleashed will also favor you in ways that your enemies do not expect."

"Is that supposed to make me feel better? Subodh is dead!" I cry out, tears pouring down my face. "He's dead now, and the Legion will die as well if you don't do something!"

I point toward the people around me: a mercenary ready to plunge his talwar into a Legion soldier lying prone on the ground; Kali fighting not one but two Brimlanders at once, her left leg raised in the air, paused midspin.

"Subodh lived a long life, child. He was ready to die, whether you like it or not. If not today, then he would have died by the end of this month after transferring so much of his living energy to the peri."

370

I want to insist that she's lying. That Subodh could have survived. But even as the argument rises in my head, I realize how wrong it sounds.

"Remember," the goddess says. "*You must be a leader when all hope is lost. Subodh gave you hope, Gul. If you lose confidence in yourself, your Legion will, too. Use the powers you've been given to save them. You have enough within you—both of you—for that.*"

Both of you.

"Cavas," I whisper. "I need to find Cavas."

The sky goddess smiles. "I wish you luck, my daughter."

It's the last thing I hear before the goddess disappears and I'm plunged again into chaos.

A cold hand grips me by the arm. I react on instinct but only slice through air instead of flesh.

"It's me, girl." Latif's voice registers as I realize no one is standing next to me. "I've made you invisible for now. You need to get out of here. All of you do. It's too dangerous to fight in these conditions!"

"No!" I say. "If we retreat now, they will chase us outside, killing our other troops as well!" I may not be a seasoned soldier, but this much is obvious to me. "I need to find Cavas!"

I won't be able to fight this army on my own. But with Cavas's powers, we may be able to buy everyone more time.

"Send a message to Raja Amar that we need reinforcements," I tell Latif. "On no account must Amar enter the fight himself. You will stop him if he tries."

"But, Gul—"

"Hurry!" I snap.

I'm not sure if he listens to me. But I can't waste any more time. I sneak away from the fighting, into an empty alley, where I close my eyes and go inward, deeper and deeper into the recesses of my mind, until I find myself in the quiet sanctuary of a shadowy temple.

"Cavas!" I call out. "Cavas, where are you?"

I'm almost sure I can see his features begin to take shape, when my skull vibrates, pain blurring my eyes. Overhead, a man wearing black removes the mask from his face. His features swim into one another, white teeth flashing what might be a smile. I'm supposed to do something. To move. To fight. To push off the foot crushing my ribs, pinning me to the ground. But the mercenary's blade glows red and a hundred knives are now sinking into my skin, drawing screams that turn my throat raw.

My right arm pulses with heat, the magic within slowing. Fading.

Then, the shadowy figure spews a curse in the Common Tongue—something about living specters and killing the dead again if he could.

The world around me glows brilliantly blue. And then it turns black.

47

CAVAS

avas, where are you?

Gul's voice makes me spin in the dark, nearly crashing into the person walking behind me—Juhi, whose shield sends a shock up my arms.

"By the goddess!" she says. "Do you want me to kill you by accident?"

"It's Gul. She's in trouble." Panic festers like a wound in my gut. "She also feels . . . close. The last time I heard her voice so clearly, we were in Tavan, battling Sky Warriors."

Juhi says something under her breath and waves a hand, instructing me to step back. As I do, an orange shield erupts from her talwar, cutting through the dark of this strange solar eclipse in a way lightorbs and lanterns do not. A shield spell was the first bit of magic Juhi performed when the sky fell dark, explaining how soldiers from Samudra also used a magical eclipse to try to win against Ambar during the Three-Year War. "A big mistake," Juhi told us, without elaborating further.

Now, she frowns at me in the light of the shield, ignoring the questions rising from the army behind her. In the dim light, I see a few specters floating overhead, my mother among them, watching me with bemused looks on their faces.

"I need to meditate," I say.

"Here? Now?" Juhi demands.

"Gul and I have trained together before and also communicated over long distances. If I meditate, I know I'll find her," I insist.

"Juhi Didi, maybe you should let him try," Amira says, her dark eyes meeting mine.

"Very well," Juhi says after a pause. "Go on, Cavas. Meditate."

I close my eyes and begin breathing the way Subodh taught me. In and out, slow and deep. Slower and slower, Sant Javer flickering in the corners of my mind. This time, however, instead of the saint, I hear another voice speak, a woman:

"Open your eyes, child."

I hesitate. Each time I've ever attempted opening my eyes during meditation, I've lost concentration, eventually losing the thread that always connects me to Gul.

"It won't happen," the voice says, her words reassuring. "I won't let it."

I open my eyes, and instead of the darkened temple in Tavan, I find myself somewhere on the main thoroughfare in Ambarvadi, darkened havelis casting long, rectangular shadows across its surface.

"What's happening?" I hear someone ask. Amira. "What's that glow around him?"

"Where are you?" I ask the voice, forcing myself to ignore the murmurs that break out behind me. "Are you nearby?"

"I'm always close, yet never close enough, Xerxes-putra Cavas. Today, however, by calling on this eclipse, your world's magic has strangely shifted in my favor."

As she speaks, a form takes shape: a woman dressed in a sari the color of newly minted swarnas, her long black braid wrapped like a rope around her full hips. Silvery birthmarks patch over the luminous brown skin of her face and arms, the nebulous designs shifting with every movement like shadow and light. Though my heart belongs to Gul, it skips a beat now, heat flushing my cheeks. Aware of the effect she has on me, the woman smiles kindly, her quicksilver eyes gleaming.

"Follow me," she says. "You will never get lost."

Follow Sunheri and you will never get lost.

Papa's words echo in my head, and the question tumbles to the tip of my tongue.

"Are you—"

"Hurry, child. I feel her slipping away."

Without waiting for a response, the woman—the *moon goddess,* Sunheri—turns and begins gliding down the road.

"Follow me!" I call out to the others. "I think they're this way."

"Follow you *where?*" a man shouts from behind. "What exactly are we following? What's that light—" *Smack.* "Ayye! What was that for?"

"You can play detective, later, Faramroz Bhai!" I hear Amira snap. "There's magic at play here and it's dangerous."

She's right, of course. Despite the earthly manifestation of the moon goddess guiding us, I feel the air's malevolence, see spirits that I've come across only in my dreams. A snarling mass of light and shadow comes at us from the side, only to be stopped by Roda, who leaps into the air and kicks it to the curb, where it whimpers like a wounded dog.

"Unfulfilled desires are nasty things," the specter says, nodding grimly. "Don't worry. We'll protect you."

The specters do protect us, forming a barrier against the spirits as the goddess in gold leads us farther south, to where the battle is taking place. It's hard to not cringe on spotting a dead body or to avoid stepping on the blood-soaked ground.

"Not far now," Sunheri says, her silver eyes bright. Her skin, already luminous, begins to emit a strange glow—one that hurts my eyes if I look at it too long. She seems oblivious to the screams surrounding us, the corpses on the ground, or the circle of laughing men surrounding three women struggling to hold them off.

"Kali!" Amira shouts. "I'm going!" She streaks off, Roda following her close behind.

"You go and find Gul," Juhi tells me. Her eyes narrow, evaluating the scene before us. "We'll deal with the mercenaries. Soldiers, are you ready to dance?"

A roar rises behind me—the living and the dead combined—the sound drawing the attention of the fighters ahead.

"Charge!" Juhi cries out.

A specter detaches from the throng—my mother—following me and Sunheri away from the battle, to a side alley, where a body lies prone on the ground.

"Gul!" I shout, rushing to her side. Gul, bloodied and bruised, the skin on her arms and forehead clammy in a way that fills me with dread.

"She's still alive, child," another voice says. "The mercenary leader caught her by surprise and attempted to drain her magic. Luckily the specter Latif managed to distract the man and draw him back to the battlefield."

I look up, noticing for the first time that Gul isn't alone. A young woman sits next to her, wearing a sari the color of sapphires. She bears the same kind of birthmarks as Sunheri does, only her skin isn't brown, but the color of midnight, and she emits a radiant blue glow.

The moon goddess, Neel, I think. *It has to be.*

Unlike Sunheri, whose eyes are like liquid silver, Neel's eyes are the purest gold—so bright that it's difficult to look in them for too long. She gives me a gentle smile. "You recognize us."

"He does," Sunheri says. She places a hand on Neel's shoulder, instantly looking brighter, more beautiful than before. "Go on, child. Reach out to her."

"How? I don't . . ." I feel my voice break. "I don't know what to do."

"Take her hand," Neel tells me. "Let your heart guide you. Don't worry. You are under our protection right now. No one will be able to see or hurt you in this moment."

I clasp Gul's cold hand in mine, focusing on everything I remember about her—from our first meeting and kiss to the numerous times we argued and fought, the first time she made us both invisible to our sleepless, love-filled nights in Tavan. A web of silver light materializes before me, and at its center a beating golden heart.

I'm here, I tell Gul. *Let me in.*

Her heartbeats quicken, grow stronger, louder, syncing with my own. Blood rushes through my veins, hard and fast, with the force of a river during a storm. The magic throws me off balance and I wake to find myself lying on the ground, my mother's cold hands patting my hot cheeks.

"G-Gul," I stutter. "Is she . . ."

"She will wake soon," a gentle voice says. Sunheri. "You did well, child."

The two moon goddesses give me nearly identical smiles.

"I . . . I don't know how I can thank you."

"There is no need," Neel says. "In fact, we should thank *you*, Cavas. You and Gul. You see, earlier this year, during the moon festival in Ambarvadi, Sunheri and I took a chance. We saw a magus girl and a half magus boy kissing at the bazaar, and we decided unanimously to gift them with the power of being complements. We did not know if our magic would take hold. The gods may meddle as much as they wish when the world is in disarray—our godmother, the sky goddess, certainly does! But human will is equally, if not more, powerful. If either you or Gul chose to abandon the other, the magic we gifted you would have eventually withered, unused. It is our—and Ambar's—good fortune that you both chose to protect each other time and time again. And that makes your magic as complements more powerful."

Her gold eyes look into my stunned ones and, within them, I see other planets, other moons, other blue and gold complements, spinning so quick that they make me dizzy.

"We must go now," Sunheri says. "When we disappear, the eclipse will end and so will our protection. Do not look at the sun. Save yourselves from its wrath or you will be blinded."

Overhead, sunlight presses against black clouds, marbling them with gold. Neel takes Sunheri's hand, and they slowly disappear in the presence of the sun's growing yellow light.

Ma and I help Gul sit up, wait for her eyes to flicker open. They grow wide on taking me in. "C-Cavas? You're h-here?"

"I'm here," I whisper reassuringly. "No, stop—don't look directly at the sun! It will blind you otherwise."

She nods. To my surprise, a tear rolls down her cheek.

"Hey." I gently take her face in my hands and wipe away the tear with a thumb. "It's okay. I'm here now."

"Subodh is dead," she says, her voice raw. "The leader of the mercenaries killed him in battle."

I swear loudly, the bleak statement hitting me harder than I expect it to. "He . . . Raja Subodh was so *strong*."

"Even the strong can die," Ma says in her gentle voice. "Death does not discriminate in that way. Only luck does."

"Must be," Gul murmurs. Her eyes are still wet, but no tears spill forth. "Luck is the only reason I survived so far."

"Luck, Latif, and the moon goddesses," I say.

"What?" As expected, this captures her attention, drying her eyes completely.

Good, I think. *She needs to be strong right now.*

"No time to explain in detail, but Sunheri led me to you while Neel kept watch. It's a complement thing."

She stares at me for a moment. Then, without warning, her lips are on mine, her fingers woven tight through my hair. I hold on to her as fiercely, knowing—no, *sensing*, through the strange, spectacular bond we share—that this kiss is different. There is no flirtation here, no lust. Only a brief respite from the perpetual grief and trepidation that haunts us—that will continue to haunt us when we go back.

When we part, Gul's eyes blaze into mine. *In case I don't see you again*, I hear her think, the unspoken words ringing clear in my head.

"Come, you two," Ma says. "Gul, are your daggers still on you? Good. We must warn everyone not to look directly at the sun."

Gazes shielded by our hands, we cautiously make our way out of the alley and toward the main square, where a battle is still raging. An army wearing the colors of sand fights with men in red turbans and armor the color of midnight—Faramroz Bhai's merchant army—mixed in with non-magi and small groups of women and men wearing pale-blue tunics and trousers—Legion warriors.

"Who are they?" I whisper. "Those men in brown?"

"Mercenaries," Gul replies, looking around for someone. "They're being led by—oh goddess!"

A giant shadow plunges from the skies—a bird, no a *peri*, I realize, shocked. A fully grown peri with giant wings, grabbing hold of a mercenary and rising with him in the air, silencing his screams.

Wails rise from around us, the mercenaries making wild slashes at the air, clawing at their eyes. Already, I can tell from the way our side is moving that my mother's message about the sun has reached them—their gazes remain lowered, their spears aiming for torsos and feet rather than hearts. The only thing that draws our attention again is a fight at the doorstep to the temple.

Amira with her atashban, fighting a man dressed completely in black, unlike the other mercenaries, a man who moves like no other.

"That's him!" Gul says. "The mercenary leader!"

"Wait!" I grab hold of her arm, holding her back. "He's fighting Amira, remember?"

"That's *Amira*? Goddess, what have they . . ." Gul's voice trails off and for the first time I find myself seeing Amira the way Gul must see her—the too-sharp cheekbones, the shorn head, the still-healing burns on her bronze skin. Gul's gaze flickers over to the atashban burn on my forehead, her mouth hardening.

"Well," she says finally. "If anyone can beat that meditating bastard at his own game, it's Amira."

And it is. Only moments into the fight, I see that the mercenary leader is tiring. Amira leaps into the air, her atashban aimed right at his heart. Red light cracks through his burgeoning shield, the force of Amira's death magic throwing him several feet away, near a group of his own blinded soldiers.

His death has barely registered when a body falls from the sky, right on top of a dead mercenary. It's a peri with long black hair, lashes still fluttering over gold eyes.

"Peri Armaiti!" Gul cries out, rushing to her.

The peri's mouth gurgles black with blood. Instead of speaking, she grips hold of Gul's arm, her gold eyes turning startlingly white. Gul's face freezes, her eyes taking on a similar glow.

Then, with a final shudder, the peri closes her eyes, collapsing to death.

Gul quietly withdraws her hand, gently turning Armaiti's palm so that it faces the sky instead of the earth.

"What is it?" I ask urgently.

"She whispered to me that more troops are on the way." Gul licks her chapped lips. "Over a hundred—perhaps two hundred—Ambari infantry led by twenty or more Sky Warriors. Behind them, two elephants are pulling maha-atashbans to shoot down the peri from the sky. The peri can withstand the blinding magic of the eclipse, but the giant atashbans will kill them."

As she speaks, fresh war horns sound in the distance. Boots trample the paved ground, the sound akin to a thunderstorm brought to earth.

The Legion, spent from an entire morning of fighting mercenaries, look at us in despair. A pair of makara approach Armaiti's dead form, making sounds that crawl under my skin. Ducking balls of red fire, the remaining peri swoop down to earth, hunching their shoulders, their faces clearly terrified.

"Get ready to die, princess," someone behind us says. It's Amira, her dark eyes bleaker than I've ever seen them. "There's no hope for us now."

48

GUL

There's no hope for us now.

My bones are aching. My face and body burn with wounds. But what comes out of my mouth in response to Amira's pronouncement is pure habit, a retort based on years of trading insults and arguments with her:

"There is always hope, Amira."

The words fill my heart, envelop me in a warmth that only my parents once brought. I think of my father and his rumbling laugh, the press of his bearded cheek to mine. I remember my mother holding me in her arms when I cried, telling me everything would be all right. As bleak as everything appears at the moment, my instincts tell me that we haven't yet lost this battle.

I won't let us.

"Legion, to me!" I shout. "Arms at the ready!"

One by one, our soldiers unfreeze from their stupors and rush to join me, relief etched across their bruised faces.

"Stick together!" I call out. "Form the simurgh with me at the center!"

Almost instantly, the Legion falls into a haphazard V. I turn to the makara first, reaching out to them with my mind.

Do you still wish to fight for us, with Raja Subodh gone? I ask.

Coal-bright eyes blink at me. Then, a single word, a susurration more or less: *Yessss.*

You may join us then. One of you at each flank.

They break apart, doing exactly what I asked, adding bulk to each ragged wing of my battle formation. Next, I turn to the frightened peri and speak out loud in the Common Tongue, giving them the same choice that I did the makara.

"We will fight," a male peri says, turning to look at his companions. They nod. He pauses before adding, "We were sold at the same flesh market, you and I. You probably don't remember—"

"I do," I cut in, my insides tightening. "You sang the morning raag. Brought everyone to tears. I'm sorry, I don't know your name."

"Peri Mahiyar." The peri gives me a half smile. "Let's make them cry in other ways, shall we?"

"The maha-atashbans—" I begin.

"Are only effective when shot into the sky—or directly at a crowd of people on the ground. The elephants are still a ways off and we peri are capable of fighting in more ways than one."

Peri Mahiyar plucks out a pure white feather from one of his wings and gives it to me. "Tuck a feather into your waistband. It will protect you from our voices. Because when we sing this time, every unprotected ear is going to bleed."

He turns to the seven remaining peri, speaking to them in their bird-like language. Soon, everyone in the Legion is tucking feathers into their waistbelts or braiding them into their hair. Cavas gives instructions to a few soldiers I don't know—including a burly warrior who, apart from the blood streaking his face, appears unharmed.

I face a surprised Amira, who is watching me like she's never seen me before. "Will you take over if I fall? Make sure they keep fighting?"

She simply nods her assent.

"I'll get the non-magus army and living specters together as well," Cavas says. He cups his hands around his mouth and calls out: "Soldiers, are you with me?"

"We're with you!" a chorus of voices rises, pouring strength back into my tired limbs.

"We're with you, too, Star Warrior," another familiar voice says.

A smile flickers across my lips. "Thank you, Roda."

When I turn around, I spot a tall woman watching my every move, only recognizable by her long hair, now entirely blue, her cheekbones so much more pronounced than I've seen them before. My heart leaps to my throat. But now isn't the time for reunions—and I can tell Juhi knows this. She gives me a half smile.

"Whatever happens in battle today, Raja Amar survives," I say in a ringing voice. "If we are defeated, I want the survivors to run—to warn Raja Amar to take the remaining troops that we have and flee."

There may be little hope for us on the battlefield today. But there still will be hope for Ambar with the true king alive.

"Saavdhaan!" I shout. Spears and lathis and shields and daggers rise around me, waiting for the next signal.

Dust clouds the air as the enemy approaches: General Alizeh unmistakable at the head on her white horse. Next to her rides Captain Emil—the man who once reminded me of Papa—in blue and white, with the exception of his helmet, which is gold instead of silver.

No longer a captain, then, but a major.

The Sky Warriors wear strange metal plates over their helmets, angled at a way that keeps the sunlight from their eyes. Clearly, they're aware of the eclipse's effects. Behind them, wearing similar headgear, march Ambari foot soldiers, the tips of their long spears glowing red with death magic.

Without a word, Cavas and I turn to face each other.

"Stay close," I tell him, unable to suppress the hitch in my voice.

Cavas isn't fooled by my false bravado. Delicately, his callused hands cup my cheeks.

"You are my heart, the blood in my veins," he says softly, making my skin flush with warmth. "Nothing—not even death—will take me away from you."

The old Gul would have doubted his words. Doubted herself.

But I believe in the truth I see in Cavas's dark-brown eyes, trust the reassuring tendrils of his magic brushing at mine like his fingers. Waiting to be let in.

"I love you," I tell him.

There's a flash of surprise in his eyes, a wide smile breaking his face. I keep it in my mind as we pull apart to meditate, breathing in and out, our bodies reaching sthirta far quicker than they ever have before. Instead of looking glazed the way they once did, Cavas's eyes burn white—the way mine do.

"Charge!" My voice sounds hollow to my own ears, deeper than it is in real life. Every movement around me slows, allowing me to examine the enemy, to look for weaknesses in ways I wouldn't be able to otherwise.

Hidden in perches and alleys around the square, the peri begin singing, their voices drawing screams among the first line of soldiers who clutch at their ears, hands coming up red with blood. But the peri's tactic doesn't work for long. Alizeh and Emil shoot their atashbans into the air, filling it with the familiar buzz of a sound barrier.

"Specters!" Cavas holds a glowing green coin to his mouth, his voice vibrating through my veins. "Let's play a little hide-and-seek, shall we?"

Puzzled by the strange command, I watch as soldiers from the Legion begin appearing and disappearing, confusing the Ambari infantry enough to bring down a few of their own. Cavas himself is never too far from my side, reinforcing my magic whenever necessary, cautioning me against wayward enemy spells.

At one point in the battle, Cavas's voice rings in my head: *Amplify shield!*

I shoot him a surprised glance—and then notice a pair of Sky Warriors charging our way. Even in my meditative state, there is no time for me to move in front of Cavas and defend us both myself.

Gul! Cavas urges, his power tugging at mine. Drawing on it. *Hurry!*

I pour forth green fire from my daggers, watch the liquid gold of Cavas's magic merging with mine. A brilliant white shield rises before us, deflecting both of the Sky Warriors' spells.

Cavas and I grin at each other. It's the first time we've worked together this way—as a team, without fighting.

It's a good feeling, I think, merging my power with his again to block another spell coming our way.

As the battle progresses, rocks fall from the air onto the Ambari infantry—living specters acting on Cavas's command—several hitting their mark, many turning to ash before they hit the ground, thanks to Major Emil's intervention.

Furious, I aim a spell at his spurs while simultaneously whispering to his horse.

Buck him off.

Startled, the horse rears, the combined act of the saddle breaking forcing Emil off. Almost instantly, he finds himself facing the end of Amira and her furious atashban, a battle that I can tell will be far too well matched despite Amira's brutal skill.

"Brigadier Moolchand!" Cavas's voice draws my attention. *"No!"*

I spin around to find a pair of soldiers sparring in the distance, so similarly garbed that for a moment I wonder if the infantry have begun fighting among themselves. The only difference between the two is that one of the men has only one arm and, unlike the helmeted infantry commander, he wears a bright indigo turban.

So that's Zamindar Moolchand's brother, I think.

We have to stop them! Cavas tells me telepathically. *We can't lose the brigadier!*

As we fight our way through to get closer to the brigadier, something strange begins to happen. Four infantrymen break off from where they're feuding with a group of Legion soldiers and race toward the fighting pair. Instead of targeting Brigadier Moolchand the way I expect them to, they *shield* him, forming a barrier between him and the man he was fighting.

"What are you doing?" the latter says angrily. "Get out of my way!"

"No, sir," one of the soldiers says calmly. His voice isn't loud, but it carries to where we now stand, stunned. "We will not let you hurt Brigadier Moolchand."

"He's not your brigadier anymore, fools! I am!" The man lashes out with a sword—only to be impaled by a spear from one of his own men.

We aren't the only ones drawn to the scene. Soon enough, other Ambari soldiers are, too, more and more breaking away from their Sky Warrior commanders to protectively encircle the one-armed man.

"It's the Amirgarh soldiers," Cavas whispers in awe. "They're still loyal to Moolchand!"

So loyal that they refuse to move aside, even when shot at by the Sky Warriors.

So loyal that they turn on the men they were fighting with, joining forces instead with an astonished Kali, Juhi, and Amira.

So loyal that ultimately, out of sheer frustration, General Alizeh shouts a command that sounds like music to my tired ears:

"Infantry, retreat!"

49

SHAYLA

Retreat.

After a whole day of fighting and a near victory, forced to retreat thanks to mutinous defectors who should have been dealt with a long time ago.

But how do you deal with two hundred *of your own soldiers, Shayla? Do you round them up and imprison them? Do you order a mass execution?*

"Well?" I turn to General Alizeh, Major Emil, and Acharya Damak. Three people who *should* still be loyal to me. "Which of you is going to tell me how terribly flawed my plan was?"

"It wasn't as flawed as you think, Ambar Sikandar," Alizeh says. "The suryagrahan was a risk, but it worked. Their side lost more soldiers during the eclipse than we did. After the Brimmish Butcher fell, we would have won—if not for our own traitorous infantry."

I lock gazes with her and see no deception there. Only guilt. The kind that makes me want to throttle her.

"How do I keep a kingdom where my own soldiers won't fight for me?" My voice sounds bleak, even to me.

"Perhaps you don't need your armies to fight for you," Acharya Damak says after a pause. "The old kings and queens of Ambar often settled throne disputes with duels. You could challenge the conjurer Amar to one. The people feel they have a choice right now between the two of you. Take out their other choice and they will be forced to accept you as their queen."

The throne or the grave. I suppress an unexpected chill.

"Do you think the conjurer will agree to a duel?" I ask, raising an eyebrow.

"He will if his mother and sister are in danger," Acharya Damak says quietly.

There's a long silence.

"The spared snake proving useful at last," I say. "Well played, Acharya Damak. Well played. You may go now and attend to your normal duties."

The acharya bows before leaving the room.

I turn to Alizeh and Emil. "Watch him closely," I tell them. "He's the biggest snake of them all."

"Yes, Rani Shayla," they say.

I pull forth a sheaf of rolled parchment from my desk. "I think it's time to send a letter of my own."

The conjurer sends his answer that very night by return shvetpanchhi:

I accept your challenge.

The duel will take place tomorrow, in the maidaan—the empty land between Ambar Fort and Ambarvadi—*ensuring that no civilians accidentally enter the fray*, the conjurer insisted in his letter. It was a request I was glad to oblige.

The throne or the grave. Again, the chill, following me from the study to my bedroom, pervading my nightmares, where I find myself swimming inside a pool of my own blood.

My linens reek of sweat. I shed them, walk to the floor-to-ceiling windows, and stare out at the fog of pink magic floating over Ambarvadi in the distance. The curfew over the city ended at midnight. A few lights illuminate the streets or the windows of darkened—in some cases, newly abandoned—buildings. A city that never sleeps now strangely watchful in its silence. A knock on the door makes me spin, reach for the atashban at my bedside.

"Ambar Sikandar." The night guard is careful to keep her eyes averted from my disheveled form. "The general is here to see you."

"Alizeh?" I frown, lowering my weapon. "Send her in."

Alizeh enters, her gray eyes reflecting the moonlight from my windows. "You couldn't sleep, could you? Or you had a nightmare."

I will myself not to shiver. "How did you know?"

"You were like that at the academy, too. You never slept before an important battle. Or you would wake up, shaking from a bad dream, and come find me."

Tonight, she's the one who came. She walks to join me by the window, and for a few moments, we simply stand there side by side as we once did at the academy, a day before the final test, which qualified us as Sky Warriors.

"What if I lose, Alizeh?" I ask. "What if I lose everything?"

"You won't," she vows. "I swear on my life, you won't."

"You can't make such promises, Alizeh."

"I can, *Shayla*." There's a challenge in the way she says my name, daring me to correct her. "My life has always been intertwined with yours. No matter how many titles you throw between us. No matter how many lovers you've taken into your bed since me."

I turn and lock gazes with a woman I've known since my first day at the academy, a scrawny, gray-eyed thing who bit a boy so hard during a practice fight that she drew blood. My heart skips a beat.

"Alizeh . . . I . . ."

I made a mistake. I knew it that night and I feel it now, deep in my bones.

389

"I know it isn't the same for you. I've accepted this truth for a while now," Alizeh tells me with a shrug so casual that I almost believe her. "So let me do what I can. What I have always done. Let me protect you."

With a final, too-brief squeeze of my hand, she leaves me standing there staring after her, holding on to a grief I didn't realize I was capable of.

50

GUL

Silence shrouds Ambarvadi after our battle, a deathly quiet that makes the fine hairs on my arms rise, when the sun disappears and darkness sets in. Magic hovers in the air around the roof of the safe house, its dull, rose-tinted fog nearly obscuring the lone thanedar patrolling the street outside.

Cavas and I watch his lightorb pause before the door to the safe house and stare up at the roof. At us. They know we're here by now, of course. Along with Amar, Juhi, Kali, Amira, Falak, Sami, and others they would love to imprison. But a part of Amar's bargain asked that no arrests be made until the duel ends tomorrow. This includes Brigadier Moolchand and the defected Amirgarh forces, who have chosen to spend their night at inns and taverns across the city—those that haven't been abandoned by their owners, at any rate.

While it looks like Shayla is staying true to that promise, tonight is but a temporary reprieve. Breaking Queen Amba and Princess Malti out of Ambar Fort isn't an option—though I suggested it moments after Amar received the Scorpion's letter.

"You were lucky the first time," he told me sharply. "It won't be as easy to sneak in or out anymore."

He spoke little after that, only choosing to inform us that he accepted Shayla's challenge and that it would not involve any innocent civilians.

"A duel," I grumble again for what must be the hundredth time. "How could he have agreed to a duel with her?"

"His mother and sister are in danger, Gul."

"Don't look at me like that, Cavas. I don't mean we should leave them there. But let's face facts," I say, forcing myself to keep my voice low. "Amar is a brilliant conjurer. He has a sense of honor that can appease everyone, magi or not. But he cannot perform death magic. By the goddess, he can't produce an ordinary shield! We both know that!" If not for Cavas restraining my magic, *I* might have killed Amar months ago.

"Well, we can't do much," Cavas reminds me in his quiet voice. "Juhi said that the rules of dueling allow for no interference or replacements. Besides, Amira and Juhi both offered to coach him, didn't they?"

Full-scale chaos erupted downstairs once Amar agreed to the duel. Everyone wanted to offer their opinions and help. I knew that we needed to refrain from overwhelming our future king, but none of us could. Eventually, Ramnik stepped in, silencing us.

"Raja Amar needs his rest," Ramnik told us firmly before leading Amar away to his own bedroom for some privacy.

"Do you really think Shayla will not try to cheat?" I ask Cavas now. "Or that she cares about a code of honor written hundreds of years ago?"

"*Amar* does. He might abdicate the throne if it's won by dishonorable means."

I swear loud enough for the thanedar to grow still and raise his light-orb higher, beaming it barely a foot away from where we're standing. Though we're still rendered invisible by Ramnik's protection spells on the roof, on instinct, I slide down, out of sight, my back pressed against the short brick wall. Cavas follows, tilting his chin to the rose-tinted sky.

"Goddess save us from scrupulous would-be monarchs," I mutter.

"Honestly, I prefer Shayla to Amar right now. At least her tactics make sense."

Cavas laughs, the sound drawing the thanedar's beam exactly over our heads.

"Should we start chanting the prophecy for him?" I say, referring to the thanedar. "Make things more interesting?"

"Didn't think you cared about bored thanedars," Cavas quips. "We might regret it tomorrow."

The smiles fade from our faces. Joke though we might about our predicament, there is the very real possibility of the duel ending with Amar's death. Of a tyrant still ruling Ambar. Or worse: of the kingdom being thrown into a state of anarchy. Eventually, the thanedar's light moves away; perhaps he grew bored of us after all.

Now, in the darkness, in this terrible quiet, I hear the screams from the day's battle again, feel bruising hands spread my thighs apart. I see the mercenary spinning in the air, hacking off Subodh's head. I see Prerna and dozens of Legion soldiers lying bloodied on the ground, their limbs askew.

My breath catches in my throat and, before I know it, I'm heaving, my face twisted into a hot, wet mess of tears. Cavas's arms wind around me, but I barely feel them. In fact, it's only when I calm down, ages later, that I realize Cavas is sobbing as well. Ugly, heart-wrenching sobs that remind me how he hasn't had time to process the things that have happened to him at Ambar Fort, either.

"It's fine," I whisper. I'm on the verge of another bout of crying. "I won't let them hurt you."

It's how we spend the night, wrapped up in each other's arms on the roof under the fog, grieving and exhausted, pretending to sleep. We head back downstairs at dawn. Everyone else is awake as well, seated on the floor in Ramnik's kitchen, eating a quick breakfast of hot bajra rotis, leftover suji halwa, and steaming cups of chai. Or attempting to eat, as in Amar's case, shadows circling his eyes.

393

I sit down next to Kali and Sami, who appear equally grim, though they both acknowledge me with nods.

"He came out of the room late last night," Kali says quietly. "Asked me and Amira to train with him. It . . . did not go well."

Amira rises from her place next to Juhi and heads to the weapons I now see piled up in a corner on the floor.

"Why don't you tell them I was bad, Kali ji?" Amar says flatly, breaking the silence. "That I have no hope at defending myself against an unfriendly spell."

"Oh, stop acting so pitiful," Amira retorts. "The conjuring you do is ten times more complicated than a basic shield spell—and expends even more energy. Your biggest problem is that you keep reverting to it instead of trying something new. You are more useless than Gul, here, used to be."

My insides twitch—a reflex born more of habit than actual annoyance. Now, with Amira's anger directed at someone else, I finally begin to see the method behind her mad goading of a man who could very well make her life miserable if he survives this and becomes king.

Amar's yellow eyes harden. "What did you call me?" he asks, his voice so soft that it sends a chill down my spine.

"Useless," Amira repeats, her eyes narrowing in challenge. "Pitiful. Forlorn. Pathetic. Are you satisfied with these adjectives or should I go on?"

"Amira!" Juhi admonishes, shocked. "What in Svapnalok—apologize at once!"

Amira doesn't, of course. Neither does she break her deadlocked gaze with Amar. Spite etches a familiar look on her face—one that tells me that she has been pushed to her limit and that, true king or not, Amar *will* face the brunt of her anger.

I'm about to say something—anything to avoid a duel before the real one with Shayla—when Amar bursts out laughing. Loud and full-bellied, his sudden humor shocks us more than Amira's rudeness.

"You're right, Amira ji," he says. "I *am* being rather pitiful. Not a good look for Ambar's future king, is it?"

Amira blinks a few times. Amar's response seems to have deflated her anger somewhat. "I shouldn't have said that," she says finally. "I lost my temper."

"As my own mother would have—had she seen me now," Amar says, giving her a half smile. They're both still staring at each other when I clear my throat.

"Focus on a memory that makes you feel safe," I tell Amar, eyeing his flushed face. "That works for me."

Amar frowns. "Safe," he repeats, as if this is a new concept for him— odd, since I never imagined a prince of Ambar being anything but safe for most of his life. Then I recall Amar's strange life at Ambar Fort: his two brothers, who are better dead than alive, his ruthless father, who found amusement only by making others feel miserable.

"Or use this." Amira bends to pick up one of the shields lying in the pile of weapons. "Jwaliyan teak and sangemarmar chips. Nice and lightweight. Not as strong a combination as sangemarmar and yellow firestones, but it should hold up well against most attacks."

"I don't think I'd be able to lift a shield made entirely of white marble anyway," Amar says wryly. He takes a deep breath and rises to his feet, heading off toward Amira, who gives him the shield and also a light-weight sword and two daggers to belt around his calves.

"By Javer," Cavas whispers to me. "I thought they were going to kill each other."

"Oh, I doubt that killing was on either of their minds," Kali says.

"No," Sami says. A smirk flashes over her deceptively innocent face. "More like pouncing and . . ."

Sami makes a hand gesture that has Kali gasping "Samita!" before releasing a cackle.

Cavas covers his face with a groan. Juhi looks mildly amused. I hide my own grin behind my small tumbler of tea and take a fortifying sip.

It will be interesting to see Amira interacting with Queen Amba if this goes anywhere beyond . . . pouncing.

If Amar survives.

Mirth dissipating, I force myself to eat the last of my roti and drink my tea to its final dregs.

The duel allows each challenger to bring five witnesses, and so shortly afterward, Juhi, Amira, Kali, Cavas, and I join Amar and make our way through the city, which is still mostly quiet, barely moving despite curfew having ended. The sun is up, bright and hot in a cloudless blue sky, as we reach the maidaan, with the Walled City and Ambar Fort towering farther ahead.

Shayla and her Sky Warriors are already here. *Ten in total*, I count, frowning at the number, my anxiety climbing when I see the maha-atashban standing at the back, its enormous arrow directed right at us.

"There's a disparity in our numbers, Raja Amar," I hear Juhi say. "She's only supposed to bring five witnesses. And that maha-atashban shouldn't be allowed!"

"Well, we can't do much about that right now," Amar replies grimly. "Even if we send for help, it will take them much too long to get here. The duel might be over by then."

Cavas, however, is already whispering to someone—his mother, perhaps Latif.

General Alizeh claps her hands twice, the sound like firecrackers in the silence. In the space between the two groups, air bubbles, an invisibility spell lifting, revealing two bodies on the ground. A woman and a girl lie unconscious, entwined in a mess of long hair and silken nightclothes, their limbs bound with glowing blue shackles.

"Rani Ma, Malti!" Amar cries out, rushing toward them—only to be thrown back by a magical barrier that keeps him inches away from touching his mother and sister. "You said you wouldn't hurt them!"

"They *are* unhurt, boy," Shayla tells him with her cruel smile. "Well, except for your mother, who lost a few fingers for helping my prisoners abscond. They're sleeping for now. What happens to them later really depends on you."

Amar takes a deep breath. "Let's get this over with," he says, his voice clipped.

"Not so fast, conjurer—or have you forgotten the rules in your eagerness? Acharya Damak!" Shayla calls out.

A man I'd seen only once before in Ambar Fort appears. His white silk robes and perfectly coiffed hair do nothing to hide the high priest's ashen complexion or the visible tremor in his shoulders. Amar's hand tightens on the hilt of his sword, but his expression remains blank, as if he has seen nothing.

"We are here today, on the twentieth day of the Month of Birds, Year 1 of the reign of Rani Shayla, to settle a dispute over her claim to the throne," the high priest begins. "Her challenger is Amar, third son of the erstwhile raja, Lohar. The challenger will face Rani Shayla in a duel, which will go on without interference and will not end before the death of either. All weapons and forms of magic are allowed. There are to be no replacements for either of the challengers. As required by the Code of Asha, each combatant has brought in witnesses to ensure that the duel remains fair. In the name of the goddess of the air and the skies, may the true monarch win."

The acharya steps back after this short speech. He nods at Shayla.

The duel has officially begun.

They start by circling each other, Amar cautious and alert, Shayla appearing less so to anyone who doesn't note the cold clarity of her pale-brown eyes.

"What is it, boy?" she taunts. "Too scared to shoot a spell?"

As she speaks, a streak of red shoots right at Amar, which he blocks with the shield while simultaneously conjuring a flock of silver-tipped arrows out of thin air.

The arrows turn to dust within seconds of hitting Shayla's shield.

She laughs. "So predictable. You haven't fought a *real* battle, have you, conjurer?"

"It seems I haven't, kabzedar rani," Amar counters. "I only fought yesterday, when your own soldiers turned against you and joined my side."

"I wish he'd stop talking," Amira whispers.

I see a flash of anger enter Shayla's eyes at the comment—a small tremor in the hand that wields her black atashban. This time, when she shoots a spell, it nicks Amar's cheek, decimating his shield to chips of wood.

Wincing, Amar slashes his sword in the air, a movement that apparently does nothing except make the Sky Warriors laugh.

"We're not here to do talwar demonstrations, conjurer," someone shouts.

A smirk plays around Shayla's full lips until the sand around her feet begins to move, forming a creature that latches teeth into the flesh of her calves. Snarling, she chops off the conjured dustwolf's head, but another begins to take its place—this one an armored leopard, with milky eyes and a bleeding maw, distracting her long enough to allow Amar to aim another spell her way.

Shayla plunges the tip of her atashban through the leopard's neck, her shield deflecting Amar's other spell with such force that he flies back several feet. On the ground, he blinks repeatedly as if attempting to regain his vision. My heart balls in my throat. Next to me, Amira clenches and unclenches her fists. Neither of us can help him—the duel does not allow for this.

Yet Shayla isn't unaffected: Amar's conjured animals have left her bruised, shaking in a way I couldn't have predicted.

Shayla shoots a few more spells, which Amar evades by sheer luck, ducking under the atashban's beams that have by now set fire to the sleeves of his cotton tunic, forcing him to rip them off. Then Amar murmurs

an indecipherable chant before cupping his hands and clapping them together with a resounding *boom*.

A crack opens in the hazy air, spewing forth an undulating, buzzing
black mass.

Bees. A hundred, perhaps a thousand, stinging insects swarm around
Shayla, who barely holds them off.

Unlike the dustwolf and the armored leopard, Shayla cannot kill
the bees at once. They swirl and contort to form different shapes—a
sword, a dagger, an arrow that now presses hard against her shield, the
bees themselves only dying in increments, making her expend more and
more energy.

It shouldn't be a surprise. Despite being nicknamed after a poisonous
animal, it's clear from the strain on her face that Shayla cannot whisper to
any. I lean forward slightly, holding my breath.

Could it happen? Could Amar really win the duel?

As I'm thinking this, a white-uniformed body flies in front of Amar,
a snarl etched over her face. But before General Alizeh can do Amar any
damage, Juhi leaps forward and knocks him flat to the ground. She grabs
hold of Alizeh's hands and aims her atashban upward, its spell exploding
in the sky.

"Cheating bastards!" Amira's shout melds in with the drone of the
bees. "Come, Kali!" she says as they both begin running in the direction
of the two grappling women.

But Juhi doesn't need their help.

With a brutal efficiency I have only heard about but never seen, Juhi
catches hold of Alizeh's head and twists hard. I've barely registered the
crack and Alizeh's lifeless gray eyes when the Scorpion's mouth opens in
a howl that I can only describe as anguished. The bees pressing against
her shield glow gold for one instant: sparks from a flame turning to
smoke.

I think I see something else—the gleam of a tear on Shayla's cheek before her black atashban slashes forth, casting a spell that throws Juhi in the air, backlit by a dome of red.

Amira's and Kali's screams are still ringing in my head when Juhi's body hits the ground next to Alizeh, her eyes glassy, her scarred palm open to the skies, revealing flecks of a golden tattoo.

51

GUL

Subodh's death turned my insides hot, an anger within me unwilling to extinguish. Juhi's death turns everything cold, my fury tempered with a grief that makes the whole world still. Sthirta, I discover, comes much easier when the heart is numbed with pain, helping me pick out not only the magic glowing gold in my veins but also the bright particles that are Shayla's spell forming a spiked mace midair.

I don't bother with a shield this time. I sidestep the attack and send one in return, my seaglass daggers glowing without effort, carving a jagged red path toward Shayla's heart.

Four Sky Warriors leap before their queen, their orange shields exploding against my spell, the impact knifing my inner ears, throwing me back like a toy. I blink away the stars from my eyes, barely managing to roll away from the spell Major Emil sends my way.

"I thought you were one of the good ones!" I shout at him. "The only one of them with a conscience. I guess I thought wrong!"

As I hoped, my words make Emil hesitate—and give Amira an opening to shoot a spell at him in turn. It's not enough. Major Emil is well trained, far too experienced in battle to be caught off guard. Soon enough, he's joined by three other Sky Warriors who begin shooting a rapid series of spells—daggers, arrows, maces, and talwars that have Amira spinning and dodging, fighting for both breath and life.

Roars vibrate the soles of my feet: a bruised and bloodied Amar shaping sand and earth to form armored leopards, their iron-clad scales glistening in the sun as they launch themselves on Shayla and the four Sky Warriors that Kali is struggling to fend off alone.

For a single, startling moment, I realize that no one is targeting me.

Automatically, I look for Cavas, but he's nowhere in sight. Neither are Queen Amba and Princess Malti.

Calm, Gul. Deep breaths.

My mind stretches, reaching for my complement. *Where are you?*

Behind you, he replies almost at once.

I spin around—

—and still see nothing.

What in Svapnalok, I begin to swear, when I see them: footprints forming in the dirt, followed by indents made by something—two somethings—being dragged back, toward Ambarvadi, away from the maidaan.

Keep them distracted, Cavas urges. *Latif and I need to get the rani and rajkumari to safety. Don't worry about me. My mother will keep us invisible. Go now, Star Warrior. Protect the king!*

I don't need to be told twice.

I step alongside Amar and Kali, my daggers furiously carving spells into the air, drawing every Sky Warrior's attention to me.

That's right, I think. *I'm the one you need to fear.*

My heart pounds, death magic a song in my blood. I feel it rushing through my arms, ready to burst free, when my birthmark burns, the pain so terrible that I scream, blisters forming over my arms. My spell throws the Sky Warriors back, but it also breaks my state of sthirta, the familiar odor of my own blood filling my nostrils, everything returning once again to normal speed.

Amar beams a spell into the air, and a flock of shvetpanchhi burst from the skies in a storm of white feathers, their sharp beaks and talons attacking the Sky Warriors, drawing their attention away from my trembling form.

"Are you all right?" Amar's shadow hovers overhead, his yellow eyes full of fear. "Gul, what happened?"

"I . . ."

My magic failed me. The words rest on the tip of my tongue. But at the last moment, I hold them back. No, my magic didn't fail me. It was simply too strong. Too much to expend on my own. I can feel it again, hammering my ribs, fighting for release like a caged blood bat.

Use me, it urges, a promise both insidious and tempting. *Kill them.*

But I can't. If I do it on my own, I will kill myself.

"Cavas," I say. "I need . . ."

My voice trails off at the sound of a conch. Amar and I turn to see dust rising in the distance, spear tips gleaming in the sun. At the head, a woman wearing Legion blues rides a horse—Sami. Four other riders follow, including Brigadier Moolchand, holding the reins of his horse in his left hand.

"How . . . ?" Amar appears speechless for a second. "Who told them to come?"

"I did," Kali says, stepping next to us. Fresh cuts mar her face alongside still fading bruises. "I told Sami to bring the infantry after we'd had a head start out of the city."

As one, the Sky Warriors flock toward Shayla, gathering behind the maha-atashban.

"Surrender, conjurer!" Shayla shouts. "Abdicate your throne or I will shoot this thing and kill you all!"

I feel the blood drain from my face. The last time a maha-atashban was used, a city had nearly been decimated and would have turned to dust if not for the shield of an injured Pashu king and the strength of thousands of living specters protecting the survivors.

"She's bluffing," Amar whispers, his face ashen. "She has to be."

But she isn't. As our soldiers approach, I see that the atashban tip has been strategically placed to face them.

To face Ambarvadi.

"It's a choice between the throne or the grave, conjurer!" Shayla says in a ringing voice. "These soldiers are one thing, but do you really want the lives of more than two million innocents on your conscience?"

"It won't happen," I say loudly. "I won't let you!"

"Gul, no!" someone screams. Amira? Perhaps Kali. It doesn't matter.

"Gul, I'll abdicate!" Amar shouts. "I'll—"

"You will do no such thing."

My voice is both mine and not—the shape of it both familiar and strange in my mouth, emerging like a prayer, a song. It reaches the approaching army, making them stumble and pause a few feet away from us.

I step before Shayla, right in front of the maha-atashban, speaking in the same voice:

"Raja Amar will not give up a throne that is rightfully his. There will be no more bloodshed."

It's so simple, I realize. Maybe it always had been this way.

Inside me, magic snarls, rages. And bruised and blistered as I am, I no longer fear it.

Something flickers in the depths of Shayla's eyes.

"You're as mad as people say I am, girl," she tells me. "Too bad we've never been on the same side."

"Ambar Sikandar, we don't have to do this," a voice says urgently. Major Emil. "The devastation this will cause will be extreme. Raja Amar already said he will give up his throne!"

Shayla stiffens. Her hand gripping the sidebar of the maha-atashban trembles, slips to the side.

"*Raja* Amar?" she asks quietly.

A moment later, Major Emil drops to the ground, mouth open in surprise, the hilt of a small dagger poking from his throat.

When Shayla turns back to face me, I know that it no longer matters what Amar has promised her. She knows, deep inside, that even if she has Ambar's throne, she will never have its people.

"Maha-atashban at ready."

Shayla's voice trembles. But her hands positioning the giant weapon are sure. Dead steady. Terror blanches the faces of the Sky Warriors behind her. Yet, ultimately, they do not protest or argue with their queen. Their glowing hands join Shayla's, magic pulsing down the maha-atashban's thick gold barrel, blooming red at the tip of its black arrow. Hot swathes of air unfurl from the weapon, its acrid smell pricking the back of my throat.

"Fire!" Shayla commands.

Her face is the last thing I see before raising my daggers, drawing on every image and memory that ever made me feel safe:

My father reading a story to me from a scroll.

My mother catching me as I fall from a tree.

Amira and Kali, garbed like holy women, swaying in a pretend trance.

Juhi brandishing her split-whip like blue flame.

Cavas's brown eyes on a foggy pink rooftop.

Protect, I think, before the pain hits.

Before the blisters on my skin burst and bleed, my starry birthmark tearing open, releasing a colossal shield that's all sparks at first and then all shadow, gathering the maha-atashban's sunbright flame within its enormous black wings. This is magic unlike anything I've felt before, both light and dark, a power that I find myself reveling in, even as it promises to peel away my skin, my flesh, the last bits of my soul.

Consume me, the maha-atashban's magic says. *Free yourself.*

I embrace it, this magic that burns like fire, that fills my insides like a starry sky on a two-moon night. Then, with a final prayer to a goddess above, I throw my arms wide, my shadowy wings expelling the light from my body, sending the maha-atashban's spell back where it came from.

The world does not turn black in death.

It is bright and jarringly alive, its very light making my insides ache. *Why am I here?* I wonder, annoyed.

Here, weightless and afloat, among these heaving, keening, human bodies, their cries piercing me with inexplicable agony.

I fly over them, this army coated thick with ash, over a melted black maha-atashban, charred bodies clinging to the barrel. Farther ahead, splintered neem and palm trees line a curving road leading to a broken gate, a walled city thick with smoke and wails, and beyond that, a smoldering pink palace, its many windows punctured, some still exploding into fragments, the sound of the cracking glass accompanying the dirge-like atmosphere below.

I must go, I think. *I must leave this place.*

But, no matter how hard I try, something continues holding me back, nipping at my ankles like a dog, tugging my knees like a relentless, willful child.

It's an old memory, I realize. *One of my own.*

A recollection of slipping and falling to the ground, followed by a shadowy boy's unfettered laugh. Try as I might, I can't see the boy's face.

Curious, despite myself, I pause, taking hold of the hand he offers, allowing the memory to draw me once more to the living world. Past the damaged palace, the wailing city, and the broken trees. Past the ash-covered soldiers, the molten black mass of metal, and corpses.

I hover several feet above a crater in the ground, next to the maha-atashban. Tethered to the spot, I watch, fascinated by the hysteria of the bearded man and the three women kneeling by the hollow's rim—and more so by the strangely familiar girl lying inside, her face, wide arms, and matted hair smeared gray with ash, her bloody fingers curled around the hilts of two broken seaglass daggers.

52

CAVAS

Latif, Ma, and I have reached the threshold of the safe house when the explosion happens, tremors briefly shaking the ground, pain stabbing the inside of my skull.

"Cavas?" I can barely make out the scared voice calling my name. Ramnik. "Cavas, what's happening? Why did the earth move?"

Gul? I reach out to her despite my dizziness. *Gul, can you hear me?*

There is no answer. Nothing except a hollow where Gul's magic is supposed to be.

"Watch them," I gasp out as Ramnik and his wife stare at Queen Amba and Rajkumari Malti's prone bodies. "I have to get back!"

I have to get back. I have to get back.

Blood pumps through my veins, my numbed limbs prickling back to life, as I race through Ambarvadi's winding streets, which are slowly filling with people again.

"Cavas ji!" someone shouts, recognizing me. "What happened? Where is Raja Amar? Where is—"

"Move out of his way unless you want me to chop you up and cook you into a sabzi!" Latif roars, his voice so terrifying that the vegetable seller who asked the question falls back against his own overturned cart.

"Gul!" I shout, a stitch burning my side. "Gul!"

A black horse rears in front of me, blocking my path.

"G-Govind?" I stutter, stunned by the palace stable master's appearance. "W-what are you d-doing—*is that General Tahmasp's old horse?!*"

"Yukta Didi and I have been working to keep the rani and rajkumari safe for a long time. I followed you here from the battlefield. Hurry, boy! Hop on!"

The last time I'd ridden double at a gallop, it was with Gul on Agni, who could barely support our combined weight. But Raat is a warhorse, trained to carry more than a thin, middle-aged man and a teenage boy. He covers ground in a way I couldn't on my own, carving a path through air thick with flakes of ash, through the sea of infantry on the battlefield, and to a smoking gash in the ground, around which several burned bodies now lie scattered, a thick, meaty smell rising from them.

Choking on the stench, I slide off Raat and instinctively stumble toward the crater in front of a still-smoking maha-atashban, to the supine girl who lies within, drawn to the familiar haze of magic that still surrounds her. The three women and man who surround her look up at me now, tears streaking their ash-covered faces. Amira. Kali. Sami. Amar.

"She's . . . she's . . ." Kali tries to speak, unable to finish her sentence.

"She deflected the maha-atashban's spell," Amar says tightly. "She saved everyone."

I glance at the wrecked weapon, struggle to breathe against its gag-inducing smell. Corpses surround it as well, the one at the front still wearing a dented crown and black armor.

Ash forms a layer over Gul's face and eyelashes, dark blood running a trail over her torso. If I ignore that, and the bruises she received in yesterday's battle, I can almost pretend she's sleeping. Yet, when I hold a hand to her nose and graying mouth, I feel no breath. No whiff of anything remotely synonymous with life.

My knees meet the ground, dull pain rising up the bone.

"I'm sorry," I think I hear Amar say from a distance.

I say nothing. I don't even cry. I reach out to stroke Gul's right arm, careful to avoid fresh bruises, pausing at the gaping wound across the astral birthmark that started it all.

"Cavas," Amira says quietly. "Maybe you should—"

"No." My voice comes from somewhere deep and painful. A sound that makes them step back. "I won't leave her."

I will never leave her.

A faint pulse skitters under my fingertips. So light that I'm afraid to voice its presence.

Help me, moon goddesses. Help me, Sant Javer.

Their forms appear before my eyes as if summoned, though in this moment, they're gray and strangely spectral. Instinctively, I know that I'm the only one who can see and hear them.

"She's alive, child," Sant Javer says. "But only barely."

"Saving her could cost you more than before," Sunheri warns. "You must pour your magic—all your magic—into her. You will never be able to see living specters or your mother again."

I close my eyes for a brief moment. I think of my mother's portrait in our old house: her sad green eyes, her brown skin, her long black hair painted so lovingly by my father. The memory will fade with time, I know. So will Ma in her spectral form. But my love for Ma never will.

"I will do anything," I say.

There's a long pause before a gray hand reaches out to touch mine. It's only by the starry brightness of her eyes that I recognize her as Neel. The goddess of the blue moon smiles at me and says: "Go on, child. Follow your heart."

And so I do, once again, exactly the way I did during the eclipse. I reach out, mind, body, and soul, looking once more for the beating pulse of Gul's heart in a web of silver light—so small this time that I nearly miss it. Blood pounds in my ears, drowning out all other sound.

My heart throbs, harder than I've felt it before—so hard that I feel it's going to burst out of my chest. My body, however, remains calm, my eyes wide open, the sun—no, a star—filling my ribs with endless white light. A heart flutters against my palm, its beats scattered at first—like hesitant fingers on a drum—before growing steadier, stronger.

It throbs in my ears, a pulse that syncs with my own as the world around me goes black.

And burns bright.

53

CAVAS

A year later, they begin rewriting our history, calling our final battle with the Scorpion the War of the Maidaan. They describe the battle at first—from King Amar's duel with the usurper queen to the Scorpion's final demise, some scribes going into great detail about how the deflected spell melted her flesh and decimated her bones to ash.

Stories are also told about how I collapsed after pouring my magic into Gul, how she woke, coughing and gasping my name.

More pages, however, are devoted to what takes place the week after the battle—the week of King Amar's coronation in Ambarvadi. The ceremony is attended by the queens of Samudra and Jwala, the Pashu queen of Aman, and the king of the Brimlands, who openly sobs on seeing his daughters, queens Janavi and Farishta safe and restored to their original positions in Rani Mahal.

Murals are painted around the Walled City, detailing Amar's crowning in Ambarvadi's square, amid cheering crowds, unseparated by magical blood for the first time in decades.

The half magi versions also include living specters hovering above, most clearly, a bearded man in a turban floating over the new king. When I miss him, I sometimes look at that mural again, recalling the rapture on Latif's gray face as his body faded into nothing.

A greater miracle, one that people will talk about long into the future, happens a little over a year into King Amar's reign. During the Month of Tears, the river Aloksha began flowing again—thanks to an arch having formed magically in Prithvi's stone wall. The diplomatic feat will be attributed to the king's first ministers, Maya and Parvez, and to the queens Amba, Janavi, and Farishta, along with a council of magus and non-magus ministers.

Three years after Amar takes the throne, I walk into the walled yard of my little house, next to a cold presence I've not been able to see ever since I gave up my magic to save Gul. It had taken a long time for my mother to grow convinced that I would now be safe here in Ambar—"It's in a mother's nature to worry," she said simply, without further explanation. Perhaps it was selfish of me—I know my mother's soul needed to be at peace—but I was glad to have her stick around for a little longer.

Yet, over the past few months, as Amar grew stronger as a monarch, Ma's presence grew less solid. She is no longer able to touch me the way she used to. Today the only way I can sense her is by the faint chill in the breeze and the sound of her voice.

"I will always love you," my mother tells me, her words a balm over my aching heart. "Whether I'm here or not."

Gul and I plant rosebushes in her father's memory and tulsi to mark the spot where Ma fades: a sprig of pale green that takes root in the soil, eventually blooming into a dense bush sprayed intermittently with tiny purple flowers.

A GIRL AND A DOG

The village of Dukal
4th day of the Month of Moons
Year 12 of King Amar's reign

54

GUL

"Sitara!" I shout. "Arri O Sitara! Uff, where is that girl?"

"In the yard," Cavas says, walking into the house, a coil of rope around his shoulder. "With a stray dog."

"What in Svapnalok—why didn't you bring her in at once?" I demand.

"It isn't a shadowlynx, my chand. Also, she can be stubborn sometimes—like her mother," my mate says with a cheeky grin, a gray eyebrow raised. His hair and mustache have gone gray as well—long before they would have otherwise—a side effect of pouring his magic into me twelve years ago.

I toss my own silver braid behind me and roll my eyes, though secretly I want to smile. Accepting the kiss he presses to my lips, I step outside.

Long-nosed and long-limbed, the dog licks my five-year-old's round cheeks, wagging his tail while she scratches his ears. On instinct, my mind strains to form a connection with the animal—before remembering that I can't anymore. Cavas gave up his magic to save my life, but he couldn't save everything.

Over a decade has passed since the War of the Maidaan, since Amar was crowned Ambarnaresh and formed a new democratic council with magi and non-magi members at its helm. People say the council is the first of its kind in the continent, though Amar brushes this off, saying that the Code of Asha had described the concept a long time ago.

I'll take his word for it. The way I've been forced to take Vaid Roshan's word about not being able to do magic anymore, to always feel the side effects of that final shield spell—a sudden pain in the muscles, bouts of exhaustion that have me lying down for hours at a time, my scarred right arm aching, the pain so intense it continues to make me dizzy years later. On those days, Cavas sits by my side, and now my daughter does as well, stroking my hair and my face, telling me jokes that make me smile despite my pain.

But today I can't show that. Today, I must be a parent, and not simply a woman delighting in her child's presence. Both dog and small human cower as I approach, as if they're expecting me to shoot a spell at them.

"What are you doing?" I ask my daughter in a stern voice. "Whose dog is this?"

"He belongs to no one!" she declares, her voice loud, insistent. Cavas says she gets her stubborn streak from me, an assessment I agree with in the privacy of my mind.

"Sitara." My voice holds a warning. "Remember what Amira Masi told you about fibbing."

"I'm not fibbing, I swear!" Sitara widens her big brown eyes—an expression that melts the hardened Amira on occasion. "His name is Tarang! He told me!"

"Is that so?" I ask, feeling amused despite myself. *I'm going to have to have a talk with Kali and Sami later*, I think. *They have two young ones. They'll know what to do.*

"Yes! He also said the shopkeeper in the bazaar throws stones at him," she says seriously. "Many people do. That's so mean, Ma!"

I frown. Sitara hasn't yet been to the market. There is no way she could have known this information. Unless . . .

My skin prickles at the brightness in my daughter's eyes. "Tarang told you this. How, exactly?" I ask.

"I touched him and heard his voice in my head," she says. "I didn't know dogs had voices."

There's a long silence. When Sitara was born, she had no glow to her. Nothing that would mark her with any kind of magic, whatsoever. Not that it mattered to either me or Cavas. We were only grateful she was born healthy and whole. Untouched by the scars that marked us both.

"Ma?" My daughter bites her lip when I don't respond. One small hand curls around the tiny star-shaped birthmark over her right elbow. "Is it bad that I touched Tarang? That I talked to him?"

"No, Sitara." I gather her chubby little body in my arms and hold her tight. "Nothing about you is bad. Especially not your magic."

Glossary

Note: *You will find many of the terms below common to our world and the former empire of Svapnalok. However, there are a few words that differ slightly in meaning and/or are used specifically in the context of Svapnalok. These have been marked with an asterisk (*) wherever possible.*

acharya: A scholar and religious leader

almari: A cupboard

*Ambarnaresh: A title for the king of Ambar

*Ambar Sikandar: Ambar's Victor; a royal title claimed by Queen Shayla

*Anandpranam: The happiest of salutations

andhiyara: Darkness

angrakha: A long tunic that is tied at the left or right shoulder

*atashban: A powerful magical weapon resembling a crossbow

Bai: Lady; used to address an older woman, as a mark of respect

bajra roti: A flatbread made with pearl millet

behen: Sister; can also be used as a respectful way to address a stranger

ber: A sweet and tart tropical fruit, also known as the red date or Chinese jujube in our world

bhai: Brother; can also be used as a respectful way to address a stranger

chaas: A cold drink made of yogurt

chakra: A disc-shaped weapon with sharp edges

chameli: Jasmine

champak: An evergreen tree with fragrant orange flowers

*Chandni Raat: The night of the moon festival; native to Svapnalok

*chandrama: A sweet, circular pastry, garnished with edible foil and rose petals

choli: A short blouse; worn with a sari or *ghagra*

*Dev Kal: The era of the gods

dhoti: A garment wrapped around the lower half of the body, passed between the legs, and tucked into the waistband

*dhulvriksh: A desert tree with rootlike branches; native to the kingdom of Ambar and the Brimlands

didi: Elder sister

*drishti jal: A magical elixir used by *Pashu* to travel and communicate with each other; native to the kingdom of Aman

dupatta: A shawl-like scarf

ektara: A drone lute with a single string

fanas: Lantern

ghagra: A full-length skirt; worn by women with a *choli* and *dupatta*

ghat: A set of steps along a riverbank

ghee: Clarified butter

gulab: Rose

haveli: A mansion

howdah: A seat carried on the back of an elephant, sometimes with a canopy

*indradhanush: A rainbow-hued metal; native to the Brimlands

jambiya: A short, double-edged dagger

janata: Public

janata darbar: A public court held in the main square of the capital city by the old monarchs of Ambar

*jantar-mantar: An illusion; derogatory term for false magic tricks in Svapnalok

jatamansi: An herb used to darken hair

ji: An honorific, usually placed after a person's name; can also be used as respectful acknowledgment, in the place of "yes"

jootis: Flat shoes with pointed tips

kabzedar: Usurper

kaccha sari: A sari draped in a manner similar to a *dhoti*, for ease of movement; worn with a *choli*

kachori: A round, fried pastry stuffed with a sweet or savory filling

kadhi: A cream-colored gravy, made of yogurt, chickpea flour, spices, and vegetables

kaka: Paternal uncle

kaki: Paternal aunt

kali: A flower bud (pronounced "kuh-lee"); not to be confused with the Hindu goddess Kali (pronounced "kaa-lee")

kalkothri: An underground prison

karela: A bitter gourd

khichdi: A rice-and-lentil dish

khoba roti: A thick flatbread made with indents on the surface

lathi: A long wooden staff, used as a weapon

levta: A black mudfish

maang-teeka: A hair ornament; worn by women

madira: Alcohol

*makara: A *Pashu* who is part crocodile, part human

Masi: Mother's sister

mawa: A sweet paste made by simmering milk on the stove

methi bajra puri: A fried flatbread made with spinach and pearl millet

moong dal: Split green gram

***neela chand:** Refers to one's mate or soulmate in Svapnalok; literally translates to "blue moon"

pakoda: A vegetable fritter

pallu: The loose ends of a sari

paneer: A type of curd cheese

***Paras:** The language of the kingdom of Jwala

***Pashu:** A race of part-human, part-animal beings; native to the kingdom of Aman

peepul: A sacred fig tree

***peri:** A gold-skinned *Pashu* who is part human, part bird

prasad: Food used as a religious offering, normally consumed after worship

pulao: A rice dish made with spices and vegetables and/or meat

***putra:** Son; when used as a suffix, it means "son of"

***putri:** Daughter; when used as a suffix, it means "daughter of"

raag: A melodic framework used for improvisation and composition of Indian classical music

rabdi: A sweet, creamy dish made with condensed milk and nuts

raj darbar: The royal court

raja: King

rajkumar: Prince

rajkumari: Princess

rajnigandha: Tuberose

***rajsingha:** A *Pashu* who is part lion, part human

*rekha: A magical barrier

*roopbadal: Ambari plant that shifts flavors depending on how it's cooked

*rupee: A silver coin

Saavdhaan: Attention

sabzi: Cooked vegetables

sadhvi: A holy woman

samarpan: The act of dedication, submission, and sacrifice to a person or cause

sandhi: A symbiosis

sangemarmar: A white marble; native to the kingdom of Jwala

sant: Saint

*Sau aabhaar: A hundred thank-yous

Sena pranam: Command for an army salutation to a ruler

sev: Vermicelli

*Shubhdivas: Good day

*Shubhraat: Good night

*Shubhsaver: Good morning

*shvetpanchhi: A large, carnivorous bird with white and black feathers; native to Svapnalok

*simurgh: A *Pashu* who is part eagle and part peacock with a woman's face

sohan halwa: A sweet made of *ghee*, milk, flour, and sugar

*sphurtijal: Elixir mixed in bathwater for temporary boost of energy

*sthirta: A state of stillness or calm in meditation

suji halwa: A sweet semolina pudding

surma: A black cosmetic, used to line the eyes

suryagrahan: Solar eclipse

*swarna: A gold coin

talwar: A long sword with a curved blade

*tez: A fruit grown in the north of Ambar that can be ingested to enhance magical powers, but with hallucinatory side effects

thanedar: A police officer

thhor: A multistemmed, cactus-like succulent found in the desert

tulsi: Holy basil

*vaid: A magical healer

*Vani: The language of the kingdom of Ambar

*Yudhnatam: A martial art

yuvraj: Heir apparent

zamindar: An aristocratic landowner

Author's Note

Colonization and foreign rule are closely linked to Indian history. Even today, we see remnants of ideas or laws introduced to the subcontinent by its former British rulers. One of these laws included Section 377 of the Indian Penal Code, which criminalized homosexuality. In 2018, this law was finally declared unconstitutional by the Supreme Court of India.

Writing this series has not only been an excuse for imagination, but also an exercise in decolonization—in reconstructing what India might have looked like without the British at its helm.

Late medieval India offered an intriguing playfield. Back then, there were other foreign rulers—the Mughals, from Central Asia. Yet there have been periods in Mughal history when art and culture flourished, when men expressed love for men through poetry, when India's various faiths coexisted in harmony, without religious conflict. There were also women. Strong, bold, flawed, and fascinating, they captivated me the most during my research—from Mughal empresses and Rajput and Maratha queens to the Attingal Ranis of Kerala.

Homophobia and patriarchy aren't colonial constructs: They existed in the subcontinent long before the British arrived. Yet there were freedoms in the past—the freedom to speak freely and be one's true self—even for the marginalized.

The beauty of storytelling—and of fantasy—is that we're allowed room to imagine and to question present ideologies, to reconstruct worlds the way they may have been.

I hope my books will encourage more people to step out from behind the margins and bring forth their own narratives.

Acknowledgments

Sau aabhaar to:

The Canada Council for the Arts and the Ontario Arts Council—for funding this project.

Dad and Mom—I would take on tyrants for you.

My editors at FSG and Penguin Teen Canada, Janine O'Malley, Melissa Warten, and Peter Phillips—for loving this series and constantly challenging me to make it better.

My agent, Eleanor Jackson—for always giving me the best advice.

Beth Clark—for blowing me away with your cover designs each time.

Allyson Floridia, Tracy Koontz, Lindsay Wagner, Jessica Warren, Elizabeth Lee, Allegra Green, Katie Halata, Kelsey Marrujo, Gaby Salpeter, and everyone else at Macmillan Children's Publishing Group for your tireless work and support behind the scenes.

Kristen Ciccarelli and Erika David—for your words of wisdom and praise.

Lynne Missen, Sam Devotta, and Team Penguin Canada; Tarini Uppal and Team Penguin India—for championing this book in two countries I've always considered home.

My readers—for sticking with me through this series.

Dadar Ahura Mazda and Ardibehesht Ameshaspand—for granting me strength and courage when I most needed it.